MAGICAL INTELLIGENCE

MAGICAL INTELLIGENCE

M. K. WISEMAN

ISBN: 978-1-952458-01-9 (paperback)

ISBN: 978-1-952458-02-6 (ePub)

ISBN: 978-1-952458-03-3 (Mobi)

Library of Congress Control Number: 2020905011

This is a work of fiction. Any references to real people, places, or historical events are used fictitiously. Other names, characters, places, descriptions, and events are products of the author's imagination, and any resemblances to actual places or events or persons, living or dead, is entirely coincidental.

Edited by Tanya Gold and MeriLyn Oblad

Cover Illustration by Egle Zioma

Interior design created with Vellum

Published in the United States of America

1st edition: May 05, 2020

mkwisemanauthor.com

Chapter One

My name is James James, and I do not exist.

The words, written in an untidy scrawl, flashed across Myra's mind. Indigo on crème but deeply felt. The stark sentence faded as quickly as it had come. Hair tumbling from nerveless fingers, she sat on the edge of her bed and watched as the bedtime candles of half a dozen tittering girls swam back into focus.

Another of her "dreams"? Or was she merely suffering from an overactive imagination? Again.

Myra looked around, half-hoping, half-dreading that someone, anyone, had witnessed her falling into the vision. But no, the rest of the girls were too busy soaking up their last few moments of wakefulness with gossip, book reading, and braids.

She pondered what she had seen—albeit briefly. Rich ink on fancy paper, a sensitive yet masculine hand driving the pen. Anger had drawn the words haphazard.

She had felt it, radiating outward like heat from a fire. Anger and something else.

Desperation.

Were men-who-did-not-exist desperate? Myra wanted to know. She had to know. The emotional state of the writer, this insubstantial James James, had felt too clear inside Myra's heart. It had hurt to read the words, like watching a man pen his own suicide note. It had felt real.

But then, so had all of her previous daydreams. The ones that had gotten her into such trouble as to land her here, in an indifferent orphanage eight hundred miles from home.

Quickly picking up where her own bedtime braid had fallen to shambles, Myra worked her fingers through the thick tangle, setting the plait quickly, sloppily, before lying on her bed with eyes closed. She was now distinctly worried about this James James fellow. She must find him. She must.

Myra concentrated on not concentrating and calmed her breath.

A ship slipping from its mooring, her mind had little trouble drifting away into the stream of light that lived on the edge of Myra's subconscious. Subconscious. The term that doctor had used to describe her "problem." It was all the rage in certain circles. It was the sort of thing that set fourteen-year-old young women running halfway across the country to escape. The hospital—the asylum—was the next logical step under such a diagnosis.

Shuddering, Myra wondered what Doctor Subconscious would say about what she had seen just now, a vision that pointedly denied its own existence.

And with that she was thinking again. At this rate, she would never reach the light that lived at the edge of thought, a brightness it seemed only she could see. Perhaps that was why such visions so often came to her as dreams. In the waking world, she simply clamped down too hard on reality.

Reality? Myra was not the right person to judge what was real and what was not. Save for the orphanage bed. That was real. And soft. And a welcome change from empty railcars and barn floors. Most of the girls at the home were not happy to be there. But Myra? Myra felt safe. Safe from life. Safe from herself.

Safe from visions and the things she could do with her mind. Things that could get a girl in trouble. Things that could hurt those whom she loved.

Myra turned over to her side, curling into a ball.

And then her world exploded.

"Steve! Stephen Tomlinson!"

"Here! Aidan, I'm here—" I choked on smoke and bile, absently wondering which would kill me first. Probably neither, if the pain in my arm was any indication.

Rocking my weight left, then right, then left again, I struggled to upend the heavy wooden chair to which I was tied—a difficult enough maneuver without first having endured torture and poison. The added feature of the world being afire, well, that was just a bonus. Another perk of our line of work.

"Stephen!"

The cry came at my ears from further away. Frantic, I tested my bonds again. The ropes were unbreakable, the chair too heavy. Or perhaps I was simply too weak.

A new explosion rocked the building—probably another pile of munitions erupting into flame. I closed my eyes, trying to decide if the heat I could feel was coming from the inferno on the other end of the warehouse or from whatever Dr. Addair's agent had injected into my arm. I looked to the livid and bloody wound, itself a likely death sentence. I considered my final words. "Ai? Tell Laur—"

"Tell her yourself, I'm not a telegraph operator," a voice sounded close behind—female and therefore not Aidan's. I strained to get a glimpse of my rescuer, espying rouged lips and a shock of deep-red hair. Kady. She smiled crookedly, leaning close. "Gotcha. And . . . duck!"

I hunched down as best I could, wincing as a blast of magefire erupted over my head. Through the din of ash and flame, I could see a black-hooded enemy fall.

"Good shot. Didn't know any of them had stuck around." The words came out slurred. The room did a dizzy turn. My magic was gone. The light had been snuffed out. I was numb. I was dead. Dead and dying.

No. There was feeling. Kady cut the bonds pinioning my wrists, and with cruel and painful efficiency, blood rushed back into my fingers. Motion by my ankles informed me that my feet were, too, about to be freed. Not that I could do anything with them. I felt heavy as stone. For with returning circulation, the poison coursed through my veins, screaming its hateful song with every beat of my heart.

"Leave me."

"Not a chance." Kady's curt rejoinder came equally short of breath. The compact woman lifted and swung me heavily over her shoulder. The world turned upside down and began to bounce rhythmically in time with her lilting run. Regret settled back into my poisoned heart. If only we could have made it back to England. Aidan's team would have been good allies for M.I. A tad young, perhaps. Every one of them inexperienced and too quick to act. But then so was Benjamin. And James, he would have—

Everything blew sideways. Myself. Kady. The splintering wood and shattering brickwork of walls. Fragments of barrels and incendiary material—flotsam of the very stuff that had caused said explosion. Flames, blue and green, engulfed everything. Everything save for the pain. Twenty odd years of training abandoned me as I opened my mouth to scream.

Myra's screaming had woken her roommates. No less than eight pairs of anxious, glittering eyes stared down at her where she lay on the floor, entangled in her stifling quilt.

I did it again. Gulping back fear, the dream was slow to leave Myra. In the close-pressing darkness, the girls' silhouettes—loose, billowing nightgowns and coiffed-for-sleep hair—begged unfavorable comparisons to cloaked, hooded men with syringes full of burning poison.

With a shudder, Myra forced the thought away. Wakefulness pressed upon her, rendering the vision implausible, a nightmare and nothing more. Sheepishly, she climbed back into her bed, wondering what it was within her that drew such bleak pictures as she slept. What darkness did she carry within that demanded such violent release? Non-existant James' desperation could well be her own.

Excitement subsiding, the girls retreated one by one, leaving Myra to turn over in her bed, eager to escape their silent, prying questions and distant judgment. The bed shifted, and Myra felt gentle arms close about her. Emily.

Smiling into the dark, Myra leaned into the sisterly embrace, unsurprised to feel the familiar itch of tears tickling her cheeks. She closed her eyes and lost herself in memories of home as Emily, the closest thing she had to a friend these days, caressed her fevered cheek with a cool hand.

"Hush, dear. It's a ways off," Emily crooned.

"What is?" Eyes snapping open, Myra stared into the darkness, a cold sliver of fear slicing through her calm.

"Why, the warehouse fire out towards Chadron." Myra could feel Emily pull away, imagined her searching look. "Miss Rivera came by to check on us. Not everyone was asleep when it broke out and—"

"Where?" Myra tried to bite back the word, but it was too late. The half-strangled sentence betrayed her, and she felt Emily's tight camaraderie retreat under the frenetic urgency. Both girls sat up, Emily's arm dropping from around Myra's shoulder to point to the window at the far end of the long dormitory room.

"Right out towards Chadron. Said it's probably the munitions warehouse. We were all of us watching the glow when you screamed. Thought it the series of explosions that woke you—"

Myra was back out of the bed and halfway to the window before Emily's words had reached her ears. Even from here, she could see it—framed by the low hills, the distant fire a dull red stain on the clouds above. No, not clouds . . . smoke.

"Stephen?" Myra breathed the name, trying to calm herself, searching for the thread that would lead her out of the dark of her mind and back towards the light. She caught it faster than she had any right to expect. Or rather, she caught something.

Chapter Two

Myra stepped outside of herself.

Through the window and surrounding orphanage wall, she passed as might a ghost. And yet, within the unknown Something which pulled at her, Myra, for once, felt as though she was well and truly alive, not a shade or spirit. This last was confirmed by the searing heat and suffocating smoke that assaulted her senses but an instant later. A fire. An inferno. Hell itself come calling. Or rather, she to it.

Myra screamed, the reaction automatic in spite of its futile stupidity. The blaze took this opportunity to stuff Myra's lungs with smothering rags of smoke.

Wake up!—though she knew she would not, this being somehow more real than any fantastic vision. She did not ask how or why, insisting—*Myra, you fool! It's all in your silly, broken head!* The thought was no consolation with the bright flame-filled room going dark by inches and what little strength she had fallen to ash.

"I've got you," a masculine voice spoke within her ear, lightly accented and reedy, yet deep. An arm snaked about Myra's waist. Another arm slipped behind her shaking knees to hoist her up against the broad chest of he who had just uttered sweet words of rescue.

Rescue. Myra's soul breathed the word even as her head strove to clear itself. She was carried efficiently and without fuss out into the dark night and away from the conflagration.

"Stay here." The murmured command came half-hidden in the turn of his head. Myra's rescuer intended re-entry into the warehouse.

No, please. Myra could not understand her sudden reluctance to be left alone outside the circle of light and heat. She was safe. How dare she deny aid to those left inside? Still she protested, "Wait—"

A deep rumbling sounded from within the burning building. With this last defiant growl, the warehouse cowed to the rising flames, collapsing in on itself and sending out an exhalation of heat and ash.

The silhouette of her rescuer stood dark against the searing ball of flame rushing outward from the explosion. Myra threw herself at him, and together, they landed in an ungainly heap.

And just like that, he was swearing at her, writhing to gain the advantage. But it was the thrust of his emotion that had Myra darting sideways, seeking distance, equal footing under the sudden assault. Did he not realize she had just saved him?

Apparently he did not. Her opponent gained his feet and adopted an imposing glare all in one smooth motion. Or he would have been imposing were he not pointing a stick at Myra as though his life depended upon it.

His words were funny, too. All garbled and rushed.

Myra couldn't make out if any of it were English. Were it not for the distinct lack of fear in his eyes, she would have suspected shock. She moved to reassure him that she was as out of her depth as he and found she could not. Immobilized, as though she had been turned to stone.

With the sudden racing of her heart, Myra confirmed that not all of her was frozen in place. Just the important bits. Arms and legs and the like. Anger overrode terror—hadn't she experienced more than enough tonight to be past fear?—and she glowered her displeasure, happy to discover she still could.

The brief standoff afforded Myra her first leisurely inspection of the man who had just saved her life. His youth surprised her. He appeared to be two, perhaps three, years her senior. Dark unruly hair. Honest eyes. Forbidding mouth. This last somehow seemed displeased with its current task in frowning, and Myra instinctively knew that smiles were more commonly found there. His whole face, in fact, begged bright expression.

A stick? He pulls me from a burning building to threaten me with a stick? Her eyes wavered to her opponent's hand, skeptical. And yet Myra quailed. The flames flickered angry frescoes across the man's tense features. For all that he cut a strange figure, he seemed serious. Deadly serious.

Slowly, the man lowered his stick, crossing his arms and looking a bit pleased with himself. Pleased and puzzled. He circled his victim, saying nothing—though with the introduction he had given, she doubted she would have understood much of anything he had to say.

Myra continued her glare, daring him to make a move.

"Not one of them, then, are you?" Embarrassment replaced smug victory in the man's face. It rendered him unexpectedly handsome. The man drew his strange wooden weapon back out and waved it casually in the air.

Control returned to Myra, if not grace. She dropped like a stone to the hard-packed dirt. "Ouch! Watch it!"

A hand thrust itself into her vision, and she grasped it gratefully. With a lurch, the strange man had hauled Myra back to her feet. His free hand fluttered his hair with the butt end of his stick. His reddish mane stood on end, mussed and uneven. Somehow the gesture and its effect made him even more good-looking.

Frazzled as she was, Myra felt a heat build in her cheeks, and she looked away, as embarrassed as he. Her in soot-stained nightshift and slippers.

Hesitation. Confusion. Unbelievable sorrow. Newly freed, Myra's mind was caught in the emotions pouring off the stranger, and she struggled to stand her ground. Dream it may be, she was still fearful of what might happen if she were to fall unbidden into the consciousness of he who had rescued—then threatened—her. Manically she wondered if she oughtn't hunt about for a stick of her own. Just in case.

Muted, muttered conversation drifted lazily through the night, the drawling sort of calm that only Midwesterners seemed capable of when facing a crisis. Myra imagined she heard the soft crunch of dirt underfoot—impossible, of course, under the dull roar of the nearby fire. But she was aware of the men coming their way and was certain that the subsequent alarm was written all over her countenance.

The warning was mirrored in the face of her strange new acquaintance. "Come. We must go. Can you do it again, the trick what got you here?"

Myra shook her head, the gesture automatic in its honesty. *I'm not even sure I am here.*

But she was wise enough not to say as much. She had had her fill of people telling her she was crazy, thank you very much. No, the best course of action was to simply let this whole thing play out. She would make her escape to the real world as soon as she might.

"Nightgown or not, you're not dreaming, you know."

Again, Myra found herself transfixed by those bright eyes and so was barely conscious of his hand slipping into hers. A gentle tug drew her farther out of the inferno's reach. Together they hurried away, out of sight from the men who had arrived to address the problem of a munitions warehouse afire.

He reads minds? Turning her gaze inward, Myra pondered her new predicament. Too much. It was all too much. Striving to maintain her sanity, her subconscious gave a smirk. *Of course, if he does read minds, then he knows that you know simply for your having thought it, silly.*

And he would know that she found him handsome. *Oh, bother.*

Stumbling alongside, Myra calculated how long her thin slippers would last on the unforgiving hard stone and dust of the open plains. Various hurts now made themselves known, bruises and knocks that would trouble her before the night was through.

And with that, they stopped moving. Myra looked

up to find that the offensive stick was back out, a half-raised threat.

"You stopped me," came his accented complaint. The flat, simple reprimand belied the emotions beneath which it labored.

Again, Myra had to steel herself against the volley of anguish and despair. Inclining her chin, she challenged him right back. "You would have died in there like the rest."

Immediately she regretted her words. Her opponent crumpled, drowning Myra in a wave of sorrow. Defeated, dejected, and despairing, his broken gaze held hers. "Who are you?"

"Myra." A declaration. A defense. She used her own identity to maintain her independence of mind. "Who're you?"

He ignored Myra's question. "You're . . . you're a mage."

Frank disbelief mingled with surprise—*his or mine?*—sweetening the bouquet of emotion threading through Myra's consciousness. Suddenly the stick made sense.

A wand? He's as crazy as me.

"Are they dead?"

"I'm sorry, but I—"

"You were in the building. I can read the imprint of my friends upon your heart. ARE THEY DEAD?"

"I—" Memories of the vision that had woken her pressed upon Myra. She faced down the undeniable if absurd truth of the man's words. Stephen? Kady? They existed? The realization, tangible and strangely relieving in spite of the tragedy, stole what little strength she had left. Her confirmation came out a near whisper, "I think so."

Another sharp wave of despair swept through her and left Myra holding even more pain. Instinct took over, and she sent her heart to his, drawing off the man's sorrow and making it her own. She had first realized her ability to alter and absorb emotions at the age of eight. In the subsequent six years, she had become adept at it. For a time, it had gone far in helping her sidestep much of her parents' interest in fixing whatever was wrong with her. After all, they could not pursue what they, themselves, could not easily remember. It had also served to bring her ever closer to her younger sister. But that had all been before . . . *Before I ran away and left Alice on her own.*

Myra waded through despondency. The side effects of her strange power—in this case, a conversion of this Aidan's pain to one she could understand within herself —were something she was all too familiar with.

A new shuddering seized Myra. Aidan. Where had she gotten his name from? She wanted to think it the vision of Stephen's last moments. In fact, she could almost feel the shouted name, ripped hoarsely from Stephen's own throat. But a sickening drop in her stomach told Myra she had somehow stolen the knowledge of it right from Aidan's soul. Had he felt the incursion?

"Stop." Aidan's flashing gaze met Myra's, bright sparks of fire that burned her heart.

"I can't." Myra's shuddering became sobs. Aidan's soot-smudged features blurred into the surrounding darkness, and she shut her eyes to the tears. The realization that she was never to wake up from this nightmare finally sank in. She could not have explained why, but she knew that Aidan spoke the truth when he said she was not dreaming. And atop that, she had gotten people killed. Indirectly. But still, people had died.

No, not people. Mages. Myra caught this last and hung on for dear life. Another truth Aidan had spoken, nonsensical as it seemed. Still she asked, "What do you mean, saying I'm a mage?"

"Just that."

Myra opened her eyes to Aidan's puzzlement. He had managed to place her at arms' length, a cool and careful distance. It helped. His emotional turmoil no longer rioted her own.

"By all the powers above, you don't actually know how you're doing it, do you? How you came to be here, even?" This time it was a hand that rifled through his hair, a brief exhalation clearing the palette of pain and sorrow and leaving Myra room to breathe freely at last. Aidan's eyes would not leave her alone. It served as a stunning reminder of how beautiful he really was. Not that Myra needed one, especially as he now reached for her hands. "Out with it, Myra. Tell me about yourself."

Chapter Three

Aidan's accent had the delicious effect of warping Myra's name just so. Moira.

It had her wishing he would speak it again. Perhaps he might, provided her answers proved sufficient.

Because Aidan had incensed her curiosity. Because, for the first time since leaving home, Myra remembered what hope felt like. Mage, he had called her. If that—fantastical as it seemed—were possible, then perhaps she could learn to control that thing inside her which would not let her be.

Also there was the already-concluded unlikelihood of her shoddy footwear taking her away to safety.

"How do I know I can trust you?" Myra's past had taught her caution, and the words came automatically.

Aidan's smile grew lopsided, and Myra's heart flipped in her chest.

Oh, he most definitely knew the effect he had upon her. But for all his apparent rakishness, his undeniably strange demeanor, Myra could feel a trustworthiness that she simply knew to be right. For it came from the same place as her visions. It was a force all its own, a thing not to be denied. This man, too, had a power in him that set him apart. Myra wondered what it was, wondered if it were the same as her own.

"I'm from the orphanage up the valley." Myra indicated her flimsy shift and careworn slippers. "And when I was woken by the fire, I—" She hesitated, not entirely certain as to the "how" of her arrival in the midst of the flames. "I suppose I just leaped here from there. By . . . magic," she tested the word, half-fearing correction.

Aidan nodded, his gaze narrowing. He wanted to contradict her. She could feel it.

Don't worry, I find my story equally impossible. Myra quirked a smile.

"Was this the first . . . inexplicable happening . . . with which you've been involved, Moira?"

There it was. The trap. Myra thought quickly, arriving at a near-truth. "Yes and no. I mean, sure there have been things. It's how I ended up at the orphanage. But nothing of this magnitude. Normally, I just . . . feel what everyone around me feels."

She hadn't meant to have her words fall to ill-concealed melancholy. Emotions made her vulnerable.

"I must ask you"—Aidan's wand trained itself back on Myra, regret coloring his words—"have you heard of a Professor Silas Addair?"

Myra began to shake her head no, stopping short as she realized that, yes, she had heard the name. Recently.

"Doctor." She whispered the word and felt Aidan's anxious shift. She flinched and continued, "Not professor. Not as Stephen saw him, anyhow."

Now there was little chance of her hiding the truth

from Aidan, not as transparent as she felt. And why should she? *Because Aidan's wand is pointed at your heart, that's why, Myra. Truthful though he may be, you don't know he's not the enemy.*

The enemy. Had such a word ever entered Myra's mind before this evening? Was the thought, and the emotions attached, even hers?

The feeling of being in Stephen's mind pressed at Myra anew. A memory and nothing more; it could not hurt her, could not effect change. And yet . . . The sensation was novel and rather like walking around inside someone's head as though it were a room.

Myra cocked her head to the side, listening, probing, so engrossed that even Aidan's guarded lowering of his wand did not take her out of the moment. She narrated for his benefit, "Doctor Addair. Silas. He was not in the warehouse. Two—there were two—of his . . . wizards? And they poisoned m— They poisoned Stephen. Just before the explosion. But no Addair."

She shook her head in an attempt to clear her mind of the pain and the heat, terrified at the prospect of reliving Stephen's violent end. Returned to the present, Myra now saw that Aidan's gaze had removed itself from her and that his wand was now held in a shaking line back toward the infernal glow of the dying munitions warehouse, a divining wand of pure rage. She, once again, found herself lost in the labyrinth of emotion pouring off the man, leaving her little time to register relief over his clearly having not heard her slip-up with regards to her firsthand experience of the mage's torture.

"You have no direct memory of the Professor. No

connection that you can recall before the orphanage, before—"

"I don't know him!" Myra hadn't intended her protest to sound as sharply as it did. But there it was. Aidan would now know that he had hit upon a nerve. She could have listed every doctor she had ever been subject to—alphabetically, chronologically, by specialty . . .

Aidan interrupted further thought, "Then we must away to M.I."

"Em eye?"

"Stands for Magical Intelligence. Stephen's team of wizard spies. Offices are in London, England. Whereas mine are—were—" Aidan's voice wavered, threatening to crack under the pressure of emotion. His eyes . . . he still hadn't looked back to Myra. It was as if he was stuck, as though he had left something of himself behind in the fire and was seeking desperately to reconnect with it so that they could leave.

"England!" Myra whispered her surprise, fearful of disturbing Aidan but unable to contain herself. New dismay shook her. Leave America? Impossible. What with the expense and the time involved and her in naught but—

Magic, Myra. You're with a wizard, remember? Still, she had to ask. "How?"

This brought Aidan back to the present. His piercing gaze returned to Myra's face, setting her heart flip-flopping anew. Follow him halfway across the world? Perhaps. The hard grief in his face cracked, and he gifted her with a half-smile, undoing her completely. "TurnKey system. Fast. Private. Mages only, you know."

Myra knew better than to respond. Mage? Addair?

TurnKey? She wasn't going to repeat everything in one word bursts like a child. She could afford to wait for an explanation. It was not as though life was verdant with other options for her at present. And besides, him being a wizard meant, too, that he would likely be able to withstand the force of Myra's own terrifying ability.

In silence they picked their way through the low brush and shallow sandy rise and fall of the cold ground, distancing themselves from the disaster they had left behind them. It was in gingerly avoiding stubbed toes and jabbed heels that it took Myra several long minutes to realize their trajectory. Aidan was taking her straight back to the orphanage! Mind reader, indeed.

Myra slowed, testing the wizard's motives. Fear prickled her shoulders and arms, and she tensed, ready to run. Aidan slowed as well, endeavoring to stay alongside Myra. His sideways glance came tinged with empathy. "Almost there, love."

Myra's companion further curbed his pace, now shrugging his shoulders violently. In three short jerks, he had his jacket down around his elbows and in one smooth motion, he swept it off and up around Myra's quivering shoulders.

"Shoulda thought of that sooner," Aidan apologized, eyes back on the horizon. "I don't have a spell for the feet though, and train's probably going to be by pretty soon. Can you manage?"

"The train? I thought it was the Key Turning we were going to take?"

"TurnKey. Yes," Aidan confirmed with a curt nod of the head, now speeding the pace a touch. "But there are not a lot of Apex points around these parts. Closest one, I'm afraid, was that warehouse. And until we can get

M.I. to sort out your apparent kinesis abilities, we must take the train like other mortals. Least until we reach the nearest Apex."

"Kinesis?" There it was. She was parroting again.

"The gift of mages who can jump from place to place instantaneously. Such a wizard is known as a Kinetic."

"Oh, I'm no kinetic." Emboldened, Myra tried to dispel Aidan of his assumption. "Perhaps I simply fell through the TurnKey system by accident?"

Aidan chuckled, shaking his head.

"No, really. We are heading directly towards the orphanage." Myra realized, with a shock, that Aidan was looking straight at, straight through, her dissembling. She had let her guard down. Had he been waiting for her to confirm their destination? No, he was trustworthy. Something inside of her refused to believe otherwise.

This time, Aidan's responding laugh came freer, more indulgent. "No, no, Moira. If I say you've magic, then you have it. With my gift it is exceptionally rare for me to be wrong about such things. Particularly with what yours seems to do to it."

"Your gift?"

"I am—was—my agency's truth-teller."

There it was again, the past tense wording and sharp snap of Aidan's agony running up against Myra's own pain. This alongside the comforting hum of absolute truth. Suddenly, Myra found herself quite envious of Aidan's particular gift. It would make life so much easier to know the truth of things.

He continued, "By no means would we ever allow an orphanage to be placed over an Apex. Too dangerous. Can't have just any old ords getting in and mucking about."

"Ord?"

"Non-magic folk. Non-mages. Short for ordinary."

How rude. Myra took a moment to be indignant on behalf of her fellow man. But then she was a mage, wasn't she? "But you just said it's only for mage use. So how would any . . . ord . . . get in?"

"There are always exceptions." Aidan raised his hand for silence, stopping short his next footfall.

Exceptions. Despair began its creep upon Myra's heart, but a sudden jolt removed her from its path. She heard it before she saw it, a strange whirring sound she couldn't quite place. She turned.

"Down!" Aidan leapt between her and the streak of light that flew at them out of the darkness. A second, a third followed, blinding in their brilliance. Like shooting stars thrown sideways and from far too close, all reds and blues and greens. The wooden stick in Aidan's hand now proved its worth. It zipped sparks, countering the strange attack and offering fire of its own.

"Run, Myra!" He pointed.

Myra shook her head, too terrified to move. For once in her life, she was firmly locked within herself and her own emotions. The fear in her outshouted any feelings from others nearby. No, wait. There was Aidan's calm composure. His resolve, too. And then a sharp spike of angst.

Aidan went down on one knee, hissing. He held his wand arm tight against his side and complained through gritted teeth, "Stands to reason that if I could escape, so could they."

"Who?"

"Them."

Myra followed Aidan's gaze. She spotted two figures, their dark clothing rendering them nigh invisible against the nighttime landscape. Cloaked and hooded.

Memories chloroformed her mind. Memories of calloused and cruel fingers prodding her arm, inserting a needle in just the right place . . . Not Myra's memories, of course, but Stephen's.

Thus transfixed, Myra only distantly noted Aidan's free hand reaching into his vest and pulling out a pistol. Aiming, he pulled the trigger. An eerie red spark darted through the air and buried itself in one of the cloaked men. The other whipped one parting arc of fire at them before seeming to disappear into nothingness.

"Now, we go. Run." Aidan grabbed at Myra's hand.

"What was that?"

Aidan ignored her wide-eyed surprise, and together they took off at a sprint. Myra could feel the ugly tang of foreign anger touch her soul. It followed them, slowly falling behind and eventually fading into the soft breeze of the open fields.

Yet still, they ran.

"Hold tight," Aidan cautioned.

Together they hurried down the hill towards the approaching train.

"How are we——?"

Myra's question was answered before the words were fully out of her mouth. Leaping? Flying? Together she and Aidan gained sufficient speed and air to catch the steaming, swaying train as it rushed by. Through the open doors of a stock car—blessedly empty—and onto the floor, she and Aidan landed together in an untidy heap for the second time in the space of an evening.

Not exactly the way Myra had train-hopped in her exodus from home to orphanage. Then she had caught trains on their slow hastening from the station. This, this was madness. Or magic.

"Phew."

Myra glanced up to see Aidan wrinkle his nose in disgust. Apparently he had gotten the worse end of their ungraceful entrance.

A not entirely empty stock car, then. Sitting upright, Myra picked several sodden pieces of straw out of her hair. She concluded once more that the events of that evening were most definitely not a dream. Dreams didn't smell like a barnyard stall. A low chuckle rent the air, cutting the odor of cattle in twain with its brightness. For all that he had landed in stale cow dung, Aidan was taking the trip in good spirits.

"Moira, you gem. Look at what you've done to me." The mage lay on his back, fully spent, his chest rising in cadence with the laughter. "If I hadn't thought you one of ours before, I certainly do now."

He rolled over onto his side, growing stern. "Not hurt are you?"

Myra quickly shook her head. No, she was not hurt. Just . . . stunned. So far in her short acquaintance with Aidan, she had come to conclude that he used magic in the most unpleasant of ways. She remembered the way he'd hissed in pain and held his hand to his side and returned his question to him. "Are you?"

"Yes. But 'tis easily mended. Perils of the profession." Aidan grinned, showering Myra with a rush of relief. A part of her wondered if he was doing it deliberately, that he'd come to suspect that the collision of their emotional states went both ways for her. Still, Myra watched as Aidan flexed his hand gingerly but couldn't feel any evasion in his claim. And he was right. From what she had seen thus far, magic did appear to be a dangerous business. The sort of thing nice young ladies should stay far, far away from.

Her last conclusion, a gentle scolding in the back of Myra's mind, came at her in motherly tones, and she blanched. Myra, of all people, was not a nice young lady, now was she? She set aside her guilt and blurted, "England or Ireland?"

"Sorry?" This confounded him. Aidan sat up, attentive.

"Are you from England, like Stephen and his M.I. people? Or Ireland?" She had a right to know, and it certainly seemed a logical question. His accent was as Irish as Myra had ever heard, after all.

"Neither. New York. But my parents were from Donegal."

"Oh."

"Stephen was—" Here a sharp intake of breath, another reminder that Aidan was newly speaking of his friend in past tense. Myra lowered her gaze, feeling the man's grief anew. "Stephen had come to my team having given chase to a rumor."

Glad that she was not looking at Aidan, Myra found she had to press shut her eyes, lest they leak their threatening tears. What had she cost this man with her wayward, uncontrolled magic? His friends. Kady who'd tried to rescue Stephen, whom Myra had seen through her vision.

Or perhaps they were dead in any case. Perhaps Myra's incursion truly had saved Aidan from much the same fate as his team. And gave her answers she hardly dare hope for: a chance at knowing what was really wrong with her.

Magic. Not mania. Could she, might she, return home armed with this knowledge? Disturbed by the thought that she had benefited thus from Aidan's pain, Myra waited in silence for him to continue.

"You're doing it again, Moira."

"What?" Myra locked eyes with Aidan, surprised that he might have noted her soothing touch on his mind.

"I—" Aidan blanked his face. Careful. Clinical. His gaze searched hers. He seemed unsettled, hunting for the right words and finding nothing.

You and me both, wizard. I can't figure me out either. In fact, Myra would be astonished if anyone could. And with that bleak thought, their halting conversation died to silence. And, in the silence, Myra discovered that the sleep she had so far eluded, found her at last in the gentle rhythmic sway of the train car.

"Now, the TurnKey system of travel is, as I said, only available to mages."

Myra jumped. Amplified by proximity, Aidan's voice startled her out of a shallow slumber.

"The same spell that helped us aboard, I will use to aid us in disembarking." Aidan stood with his back to her, his eyes on the lightening sky. Apparently, he had no idea he had woken her. He turned to Myra, and she saw that the wand was back out, lying flat over the palms of his hands. "But first, we need to do something."

The crisp pre-dawn air cut through the stale cattle odor of the train car, and Myra rose, stretching stiff muscles as she did so. She eyed the wand in Aidan's hands, morbidly curious.

"Take it," he urged. "I want to test you."

Myra reached out shyly, then hesitated. "What do I—?"

"Oh!" Aidan's smile grew brilliant. "Just take it like this"—he held it as one might hold a knitting needle, relaxed yet firm—"but don't wave it about or anything."

The wand held thus for demonstration purposes, Myra's fingers brushed Aidan's as she reached for it, earning her a new blush. Moira. The heat of her reddening cheeks was quickly lost in a rush of something rather unusual. It was as though her soul had been freed, empowered. For the first time in her short life, she felt in control over the external forces that pressed upon her subconscious. She could hold true within herself and not fall prey to the emotional needs of others. And yet nothing had changed. Not visibly. Not internally. She was simply . . . whole. And without understanding why.

Aidan gently took back his wand. "How do you feel?"

"Horrible," Myra croaked, feeling empty, dizzy, lost yet again. She was back inside herself, trapped and broken. "I mean, that wand . . . It did something to me, didn't it?"

Smiling crookedly, Aidan turned from her, pocketing his wand. "Luckily, leaving the train is easier than getting onto it, as we will need quite a bit of magic at the Apex. Provided I am correct in my assumption that you have no knowledge of how to even call your power, yes?"

Myra hoped her blank look was answer enough. Was

wizardry going to be completely about her feeling dumb and out of place?

Aidan turned long enough to see that the non-response was meant to be a response to his query. "No matter. Provided nobody else has charged the system on us and no local municipality has been so stupid as to erect a telegraph line near the ley. And, if it doesn't work, we'll just pop out and walk from there."

Again, Myra had no answer. Was any of this supposed to make sense to her? He did know she knew nothing, right? Her mind still buzzed with how the wand had felt in her hand. The world shining so right, so true, and so suddenly. But now everything felt all wrong again.

"Kidding about the walking bit. Mostly." Aidan was now leaning from the car, precarious and nerve-wracking. In the dawning light, it rendered him even more attractive. The rake.

"You'll have to hold tight to me, regardless. And if you get lost for any reason, any at all, I will send Laurel looking for you—she is M.I.'s Ways-walker." He turned, his hand outstretched. "Do you trust me?"

"Yes." *I think so*. No amount of instinctive sureness could stop the tremor of anxiety that pulsed through Myra as she clasped hands with the mage. Perhaps that was proof enough of her sanity.

"Good. Good girl. Now hold tight, Moira. The Apex placement is . . . quite remarkable . . . when compared to the train's trajectory. And to save on my own tired magic, we're going to leap straight to the TurnKey from here. Don't let go." He turned to the door and then back again. "Oh, and hold your breath!"

Together they dropped like a stone. Right out of the

train and off the trestle to the waiting river below. Myra's heart squeezed, and she shut her eyes in horrid anticipation.

But the magic had them, and to Myra, it felt like falling into a well of butterflies.

Chapter Four

In spite of Aidan's warning, Myra gasped—she couldn't help it—and promptly filled her lungs with water that burned. Panicking, her eyes snapped open, stinging as water filled her vision.

Magic gone wrong? Betrayal by Aidan whom she had trusted? She was trapped. Lost inside a watery, frigid wasteland with no escape. It was pulling her apart. Myra could feel herself splitting in two . . .

No. It was Aidan's panic pulling Myra out of herself. Myra who now realized she was in danger of drowning and able to do little more than hold tight to Aidan's hand. The icy water dulled her struggles. A roaring sound filled her ears and stars burst before her vision, replacing the inky blackness. And then? Silence.

The world tilted around Myra, and she expelled smothering salt water with a violent heaving of her stomach. Gentle hands at her back rocked her forward and back. The motion aided her much-abused throat in vomiting the seawater. Torture. She felt like a broken well-pump. But then, to feel anything—to be most miraculously alive after her ordeal—was a gift she would not readily throw away.

"Out with it, love. You've swallowed half the Atlantic, and we must give the Earth back what is hers," Aidan's soothing purr sounded, and Myra could sense more than hear the trembling undercurrent to his tone. He confirmed it a moment later. "Truth to tell, you frightened me for a moment there. Thought I'd lost you through my mistake."

Myra ignored the latter part of Aidan's confession, her foggy mind instead fixating on the more puzzling portion of his words. Atlantic? As in . . . the ocean?

But speech was beyond the reach of her burning throat, and Myra did not ask for clarification. Stinging as they were—*with ocean water?*—she cast greedy eyes over the sodden grass and endless blue skies. She noted gently rolling hills that seemed to go on without end. No ocean in sight.

Aidan's coat steamed. Myra could feel it almost as well as she could see the faint clouds of moisture wicking away into the sunshine. Beneath it, her nightshift stuck to her wetly. If there had been any doubt that her previous evening's adventures had ruined the garment, it most certainly was now beyond reclamation. Standard orphanage fare, Myra did not lament its loss keenly but felt pangs of guilt all the same. She had been taught better than that, after all.

At the recollection, salt tears mingled with seawater, and she blinked them back. She must look forward. Not fall back into pain, into old ways. This man could help her. Him and his magic and his friends at M.I.

Myra turned back towards Aidan. She found that he had fared but little better than she. Dark circles beneath his eyes spoke to his own harrowing trip. Worry still lived therein and dulled their brightness. His hair was plastered wetly to the side of his head. A bloody gash across his left cheekbone trickled furious notes of crimson.

"Aidan . . ."

"Don't." He jerked away from her touch and turned to rise. "Come. We cannot stay long by the Apex Magnus."

"The what?"

"Apex Magnus in Cataibh. Sutherland. Main Apex of magic for the British Isles and, therefore, very dangerous to us while Addair's agents are about."

Aidan did not wait for Myra's response. Instead, with a quick furrowing of his brow, he bent and scooped her up, tucking strong arms behind her knees and back just as he had in the warehouse fire the night before.

Last night? The events since Myra's leaving the orphanage felt a lifetime away. In some ways they were, she supposed. Half a world away, at the least. A surprised squeak—well, more a squawk considering the raw state of her throat—escaped her lips, and Myra flung her arms about Aidan's neck to steady herself. Clinging as she was, she had the presence of mind to protest the manhandling. "Put me down. I'm not a baby to be carried about so."

"Hush. I'll not risk losing you in your weakened state," Aidan's response came brisk but kind. He shifted his stance, crushing Myra somewhat as he reached for the wand holster at his side. "This last leg of our journey will feel different this time, Moira, as we are to leap between two different systems of leys, two distinct magics. Far more violent, I'm afraid, than merely switching tacks at the North Atlantic Apex."

Myra watched, mesmerized and atremble, as Aidan lifted his wand aloft. Fire, liquid and blinding bright, snapped in halting spurts from the tip. Amber, violet, and pearl-white, the magic bubbled up like a fountain. It arced through the air in dips and whirls. Flames held aloft, light as smoke, the spell drifted on an invisible breeze.

The wand itself was engulfed in the bright conflagration. Yet the honey-colored wood remained unburnt. Aidan's hand trembled, the power flowing between him and the world via the wand terrifying and tangible.

Yes, Myra wanted this for herself. Wanted magic in spite of her fears, her self-doubts, her . . . disbelief.

The world about them wavered and then collapsed in on itself. Grass into sky into rock, soil, and sun; reality inverted as easily as one might turn out one's stockings.

And on the reverse?

This time, Myra had the sense not to scream. Instead she clung to her mute terror. Violence, Aidan had warned her against. But this? It was an unmaking, this magic. More than darkness.

And out of that darkness, a spark. One like they had encountered on the barren Nebraska plains. An enemy spell. An enemy hand. Couldn't Aidan see it? He did. A murmured word sounded close by Myra's ear, and an answering spell arced through the inky black. The hand recoiled, whirled away into the windswept nothing. Outrage boiled in its wake. She could see more pinpoints of light, fireflies dancing in the opaque stillness. But it was the emotion that had her. It warred—a singular anomaly that drew Myra forth from Aidan's protective arms.

"Oh, no you won't." Aidan clutched Myra tight and broke what spell the enemy mage had held over her psyche. And yet, safe within his grasp, her eyes still sought their pursuer, and she wondered at how far they might have to run to outstrip the enemy. Could they even? She and Aiden—they'd gone through magic, travelled to the other end of the world.

And then the journey was over, leaving them yet in darkness but one of a more concrete nature. Myra could feel stone walls pressing close, the stench of rot and stale air even closer. She gagged, salt-water bile rising anew to further choke her.

One, two, three sparks flashed in the blackness around them. Behind the gleaming wands, three faces glared.

"Bind her. Disarm him," one of the three mages spoke. His voice hovered on the edge of recognition in the back of Myra's mind.

"Myra . . ." The way in which Aidan spoke her name, slowly, carefully drawn out, removed the usual lilt from its pronunciation. "If you please, inform Stephen's team that it was I who sent the message to meet us here and that I am to be trusted."

Chapter Five

Terror choked her, robbing Myra of the ability to speak. Each of the wizards' wands sparked and crackled uneasily as the stalemate continued.

Her American friend was the first to lower his weapon. Its fire extinguished with the gesture. The darkness of the tomb took advantage and pressed ever closer. Aidan spoke, "My name is Aidan McIntyre. It was my department that Stephen was coming to meet. The others of my unit were Kady and Walter Moore. Moira, my credentials are in the left breast pocket of my jacket if you please."

With a start, Myra realized that this last was for her, and she reluctantly removed one arm from about Aidan's neck. She tested her voice. It came out cracked. "You can trust him. Stephen did."

Myra's heart did a backflip. Why had she said those words in particular? How had she known to? Nonetheless, three wands were held aloft. The enemy mages no longer directly threatened. Their magic stayed burning, however, lest they plunge themselves into total darkness with the ending of their spells.

Myra's questing fingers closed over the empty lining of Aidan's coat pocket, prompting another wave of cardiac acrobatics. It set her to shaking more than the cold damp of her garments had. Expectant faces pressed.

"Well?" Again that distantly familiar male voice. Impatience thrown like an assault. Myra instinctively felt that such a tone came often from the speaker, and so he meant nothing by it. She cringed all the same.

The words of apology scratched at Myra's already-raw throat. Aidan's credentials. Whatever they were, they were likely lost in the ocean or in the TurnKey system. She opened her mouth and croaked, "Gone."

"Then I have no choice."

Myra tensed at Aidan's words. She shrank into him and buried her face from the magic sure to come. Instead, his arms slipped from beneath her, gently lowering Myra to her own feet. A quick glance back over her shoulder witnessed the Irish-American surrendering his wand to the demands of M.I.'s leader.

"Moi—!"

Something hit Myra from behind. Strong arms pinioned her wrists, twisting her limbs upward behind her back. It wasn't painful, but she could see how it soon could be should she dare move.

"Don't struggle. Or by Stephen's honor I will end you." The woman who held Myra whispered the threat, lessening her grip slightly as she softly exclaimed, "My, you're wet all over, aren't you?"

"Dip in the Atlantic at the Apex," Aidan answered from over where the other two mages had him on his knees, wands pressed meaningfully to his throat. In the changed light, Myra could see them now. One appeared to be older than Aidan, yet not by much. The other seemed quite a bit older, and his wand's light wavered.

"A Maester of Triewes." The spokesperson for Stephen's team, the one whose voice Myra almost knew, eyed the surrendered wand. "But what of her?"

Aidan's eyes were fixed on Myra. A new apology lived there, and she wondered at it. Nodding to one another, the two men released Aidan and helped him back to his feet. The woman at Myra's back did not budge. A fact that Myra tested by attempting a shrug of her shoulders.

"Be kind to the girl, if you please." Aidan rolled his own shoulders, shaking off the effrontery of having been bested. He accepted his wand with much the same grace, giving a hard look to M.I.'s leader as he did so. Myra could feel his sharp ire mingle in with that of their captors'. He moved off to the side, arms crossed. "Dunno what she is, particularly, but she says she's not Addair's, and I believe her. What we do with her from this point is your prerogative."

"Please." Myra adopted her own tack. "You're hurting me."

"Oh, well, now she's lying." Aidan's eyes twinkled as he peered closer. "Well, near enough. She's uncomfortable—my fault on that. I dumped us in the drink while switching leys to find the Apex Magnus. Kindness? Please?"

Eyes darting to the woman at Myra's back, Aidan negotiated a lessening of Myra's imprisonment—not a release. Which did actually hurt. Just not in ways physical. Narrowing her gaze, Myra hit Aidan with all the

sorrow and betrayal she could summon. It wasn't hard.
She had followed him halfway around the world, nearly
dying in the process, only to have him give her up to
these . . . these sinister-faced strangers.

"What in the Ways?" The eldest of the three M.I.
wizards approached, wand at the ready but dimmed. He
wanted to see Myra, not threaten her. "I do not think
I've ever had someone use a gift in such a manner. Have
you, Laurel? Did Florence ever speak of such things?"

"No. Nothing like." The woman at Myra's back—
Laurel—shook her head.

"She exhibited kinetic abilities upon our first
meeting as well." Aidan's habit of mussing his hair
resurfaced. He drew his wand through the tousled locks,
leaving behind strange peaks and valleys. The familiar
and charming gesture had tears springing to Myra's
eyes. The freed anguish escaped her grasp to touch
those present.

"Ha!" Aidan abruptly ceased his idle actions,
springing forward, wand waving. "There! You feel that?
Says she doesn't know what it is."

"And as you believe her, Maester of Triewes, I
suppose we are to," M.I.'s leader said in a bored drawl.

"Don't you, James? Tell me you cannot feel what
she's doing with our emotions," Laurel spoke, her grip
on Myra lessening even further. "Though I'd say she
knows a fair bit more on the scope of her gift than she
lets on, even if she has no name to put to it."

Myra barely felt her newfound freedom. Recognition dawned at last. Though every ounce of her
screamed for silence, her lips failed to obey the plea. She
said, "James . . . You wrote a letter yesterday, did you
not?"

This was it. Her life was over. Wands were raised anew, Aidan's included.

Myra met her fate with a steady gaze held to James James' own.

The eldest of the M.I. team—the one whose name Myra did not know—broke first. He secreted his wand and put out a hand. "Come. Myra, was it? We'll see to it that you're warmed and fed. You've no plans to murder us in our beds or the like? Aidan?"

Myra shook her head, glancing back anxiously to James, to Aidan.

"She won't." Aidan snorted, his voice carefully mirthful, as if he found the whole thing a joke. His eyes, however, were wrathful, like an abused animal.

"Good, then. Let us repair to warmth, comfort, and hearty repast." The unknown gentleman had a voice that rolled like thunder. Deep, heavy, there was something reassuring to the tone. Myra decided she quite liked him. Especially as he offered his arm to her a moment later. The gallant gesture seemed fitting on the short, rotund, yet rather dapper man.

"We might have been followed." Aidan's warning brought them up short.

"You allowed yourself to be—?" James whirled back around and loosed his curtness onto the—what was it he'd called him? The Maester of Triewes? Myra quailed under the force of James' wrath. "So that's the kind of agent that gets his team killed then, is it?"

"James."

"Is it?" M.I.'s leader shook off Laurel's restraining hand. "That's what I lose Stephen to. Your incompetence. And then you bring it here with your—"

"I think it was me." Myra's boldness would see her

finished yet. The shock of her companions hit her like a blast of wintry air. She stood firm and explained herself, "That thing you can feel from me? Your emotions and mine all tumbled up together? They followed that. They — The enemy wizards . . . I felt their hatred and anger. I felt it connect with me, with my . . . magic. They followed my fear like a thread."

At her side, the older wizard patted Myra's hand. "Then do not fear, my child. Laurel?"

The woman had her eyes closed, and it seemed to Myra that her wand's light flickered. Two breaths later she spoke. "We're fine. The tail was lost in the Ways, and I've sent a bit of myself to distract them for a good long while."

Sent a bit of herself? Myra was only half successful in suppressing that shiver and turned to find that James had pushed opened one of the walls of the tomb. The site of their tense standoff turned out to be little more than a featureless mausoleum amidst a wooded grove, set within a very average cemetery.

She made a tentative step forward, following the rest towards the shifting kaleidoscope of pedestrian and vehicular traffic and far too many feelings for Myra to detangle. London in all its glorious chaos.

"Myra— Have we a last name, my dear?"

Myra lost herself in the comforting rumble of the eldest mage's tone. "Wetherby."

"Myra Wetherby. Robert Grafford. Pleased to make your acquaintance," Myra's gentlemanly escort leaned close—conspiratorially—to whisper hasty introductions. " 'Tis my home we're going to, as operations have become somewhat unofficial of late."

This last drew a sharp hiss from James. But it was

too late. The decision had been made. Myra was bundled into the coach with the rest. A mage amongst mages, safe from the prying eyes of ords but mired within the thick web of the emotions of the people around her. Aidan with his silent hate. James James with his confusing disapproval. Laurel's doubts. Robert's troubled optimism. And Myra's own trepidation, lost amongst the whole, a leaf in a gale.

Chapter Six

Myra could scarce look over the scenery that passed them by. Her mind was too busy with other matters.

Aidan would not meet her gaze. Seated between James and Laurel, he was more or less forced to face Myra where she sat alongside Robert. And yet his eyes continually trained elsewhere. Floor. Ceiling. Windows and doors. All seemed to have infinitely more pull for the man than his onetime companion in the TurnKey system.

Worry after the enemy mages who had pursued them in America? Guilt over their tumultuous escape, one that had led to Myra nearly drowning? Anxiety over their none-too-joyous meeting with Stephen's team? For once, Myra couldn't tell. But it wasn't simple sorrow. That sour note she could pick from any jumble, her heart having memorized its jagged contours long ago.

The carriage was too crowded—both with people and emotions. Though sizable, the conveyance was not meant for this many occupants. And thus beset from all sides, Myra could only hunch in misery in the midst of all the wizards and hope that the journey was a short one and that she could keep her feelings to herself.

"Here we are."

Myra's hopes were answered with the final stoppage of the carriage and Robert's rumbling pronouncement. Laurel and James exited quickly. The latter took his anger with him. The air of the coach cleared for Myra for the first time since their embarkation. It revealed to her something of Aidan's emotional state: rage. Pure and violent.

With a gasp, Myra shrank back involuntarily. She was now glad he hadn't made eye contact with her through the journey to M.I.'s headquarters. She could well have fallen into his psyche, involuntarily doing the strange sort of magic that had landed her in such trouble in the first place. She might yet.

Robert's steadying hand on her shoulder recalled Myra to herself. A rock, he anchored her soul for her, and she reached out clumsily with what powers she understood. She found that she could feel very little from him save for a blank sort of tranquility. *An unnatural calm.*

Myra glanced up into his face, wondering his story. Nothing all too remarkable lived within those eyes and behind that smile. Kindness, to be sure. He was a man who could be reasoned with, who did not live subject to the turbulent churning of emotion.

And yet . . . For all Robert's apparent merits, Myra could not help but think Aidan—terrifying, tempestuous Aidan—was still the most trustworthy of them all.

Truth-teller. 'Maester of Triewes.' What, exactly, is the extent of his magical skill? Myra wondered if she would soon find that out.

Imposing, like most old houses belonging to long-established, monied families, Grafford House seemed to sigh in resignation as it took on its two new refugees. Sitting on the fashionable side of Clarendon Place but not the largest on the block, it reminded Myra, uncomfortably, of home. Propriety; respectability. Those were the tenants here. Myra with her strange madness had no business being in such a place.

Pausing in the doorway, lest the mages' home swallow her whole, Myra debated her options. None came to mind. None save magic and answers and wizards.

"Wait here," Robert murmured distractedly, moving off behind closed doors and leaving Myra utterly bereft of further instruction. Madness, indeed. No servant, no doorman. Just a semi-dark, if opulent, foyer.

Aidan stood by himself. James and Laurel were nowhere in sight.

And a new fellow lounged at the end of the hall. His intense yet bright gaze informed Myra that he was there to keep an eye on the guests, should they attempt to do anything unexpected. Aidan still felt as though he wanted to, and Myra wondered if she oughtn't try her soothing trick on him.

"You're dripping." The unknown wizard gently shoved off from his wall, approaching them with feline dexterity. Myra stood stupidly, unable to think of what to say as the mage's approach brought him further into what little light there was. Younger than James or Laurel by a clear span of years, he was, perhaps, closer in age to Myra than even Aidan. And infinitely more good-looking, from what she could see of him. A sharp jaw and sparkling eyes complemented a shock of soft brown hair, carefully styled. More lynx than house cat, he rode easily within his tailored suit.

And in direct contrast, Myra dripped seawater onto the immaculate tile floor, clad in borrowed coat and nightshift. It was the first time she noted that she was wearing but one of the slippers with which she had left America.

Probably larking about the aether with Aidan's credentials. Myra cringed under the brief inspection.

"Myra." She made an attempt at politeness. No sense in being improper, even considering the circumstances.

"You need a towel, Myra." A quick flash of a smile revealed even, white teeth. The unknown gentleman stopped short, darting his gaze to Aidan. "Both of you."

"Thank you for the kind offer." Aidan narrowed his eyes.

Myra could almost imagine a growl rise in his throat. The two men were cut from the same cloth, rakish and cocksure. Like recognized like and did not quite enjoy what he saw. Had she not felt so out of sorts, Myra might have laughed aloud over the empty posturing.

A door banged open somewhere within the building. Footsteps sounded nearby. Robert reappeared, beckoning them to follow him. He had no towel, either. Myra wondered if Aidan might comment.

"Come."

They followed the one-word invitation, down several halls and through multiple doors into the bowels of the building. Myra had long since given up connecting her gaze to Aidan's and walked alongside Robert, steadfastly ignoring the man who had brought her into the clutches of the M.I. agents. She could feel the eyes of the nameless mage boring into her back as she walked.

One final turning brought them into a well-appointed and—most importantly—warm library. Myra longed to throw herself into the chair nearest the roaring fire and chase the chill from her heart. Perhaps she might just get that opportunity.

James stood in the center of the room with hands clasped behind his back. He gestured with a nod of his head. "The girl will sit there for questioning. You, Maester of Triewes, will perform the interrogation."

"Hospitality, man. Food, drink, dry clothing . . ." Aidan stepped forward, finally giving Myra some semblance of protection. Though hardly qualifying as a reassuring glance, it warmed her all the same to have Aidan step between her and the forbidding James.

"There'll be time for that later."

"We came to you for help. We came to you, having been pursued by Addair's men, and are treated like we're the enemy. Does not my gift make any difference to you?"

Myra did not listen to the rest of Aidan's protest. Instead, she began to shudder uncontrollably as the day took its final toll upon her. She took the indicated seat, suddenly unsure of her legs.

"Did not our Spells of Sedes Securus let you through the front door? Both of you, need I say? There are protocols. Or do the Americans operate however they see fit—?"

"And this is an official operation? Here at some house next to Hyde Park?" Aidan snorted. "Sedes Securus. You're even worse off than I would have imagined if that's what you're using to ward the place."

A cloak and blanket—both had been warmed by the roaring fire—were pressed into Myra's quaking hands. Without a word, the handsome mage whose name Myra did not yet know moved back off into the shadows at the far end of the room. It helped. A little. But the shuddering continued. Myra looked back to Aidan, who had stomped over to stand in front of her chair, arguing with James all the while.

M.I.'s leader remained impassive. "Your words I'll believe. As I must, considering your gift. But we need to know where she came from. Who sent her—"

"Fine." Aidan's lip curled. He hurled his first question at Myra, and she had to fight the instinct to duck. "Tell me, in detail, Miss Wetherby, how it was that you arrived in the midst of the burning warehouse."

"I told you, I—" Confused, Myra turned to address the rest, James, Laurel, and Robert having circled the sitting area to witness the questioning. Her eyes darted from one wizard to the next. "I just sort of appeared. One minute I—"

Robert moved to the side, settling heavily into one of the other arm chairs. "It's all right, Myra. Just speak directly to Aidan."

That's what I was afraid of. Myra tried to telegraph her discomfort to the older mage. Aidan stood before her, unhappy but compliant. Intense. He nodded in agreement with Robert. He said, "Explain just how you did . . . as you experienced events."

Myra gulped, overwhelmed and utterly terrified at the prospect of full confession. She knew, too, that they could feel it from her, her fear uncontainable in its ferocity. Emotional poison, Myra bled it into the air. Just as she had the night she'd left home for the last time. Just as she had when she decided to run so as to save herself and others.

Tell all? The doctors of her youth had taken her away for less than that. Odd dreams and out of place memories. These were nothing compared to the glaring impossibility of instantaneous transport. And here with no allies, no mother's love to stand firm against the darkness of better judgment; no father offering excuses to the proctors of practical, sanitary sanity. Physicians, she knew, came in every shape, size, creed, and color. Was this, perhaps, a trap? Was House Grafford the cage she had long feared? It could be that she was too late. Mages and magic. Perhaps she had already fallen into madness, into an unwakeable dream.

Myra looked to Aidan and found strength and truth amongst the wrath.

'You're not dreaming, you know.'

She clung to the memory of his words and found her voice. "I had one of my visions. One moment, I was in the dormitory and the next— I could only guess that, somehow, my desire to be in the munitions house pulled me there . . ."

"Visions. What are they?" James interrupted.

Myra glanced nervously back to James. Emboldened by the fact that it had been he who had begun it all, she addressed the Englishman, "It's like the letter you wrote. I . . . I could see you writing it. You were really quite unhappy, and I think that's what got me there."

"And this trick of yours, it only happens with mages."

"I—I guess so." The thought had occurred to Myra, even with her first knowledge of wizards being less than twenty-four hours old. It made a certain sense, she supposed. "I . . . I've come to think it's very intense emotion—fear, anger—that pulls me in, as if I'm inside someone else's head."

"Tell them how many years, Moira." Aidan's pleasant maltreatment of her name was back.

Myra lowered her eyes to avoid the heat that she could feel creeping into her cheeks. "I've had it happening since I was eight."

"Well past the point of Emergere—"

"But that's impossible, what with the sickness—"

"—Perhaps she has been stealing elixir?"

"Enough. She has already expressed to me her surprise at finding she has magic." Aidan waved his hands for silence. The discordant accusations died around Myra, and she emerged from her instinctive cringe in time to see the American agent's pointed look at the M.I. agents. He turned back to her. "Emergere is the point at which a young wizard's magic shows itself, Myra. Usually around the age of five or six. And with electricity's long-term effects upon our gifts, we require a remedy in order to keep said Dampening from—"

"Hsst—!"

Aidan waved off James' sharp warning. "There is absolutely nothing calamitous she can do with such knowledge, is there Mr. James? Unless you would rather question her yourself and determine for yourself the truth of her words? No? Then we go on.

"Your visions, Myra?"

"They've always been strong. Vibrant. The sort of thing that has folks looking askance at you. They've always been real to me, my fits. But this time it was different." Myra closed her eyes and steeled herself. "This time I felt firsthand what happened to Kady and

Stephen. I knew their thoughts. I experienced their pain."

Her whispered words fell loudly amongst the carpeted quiet of the library. For a long moment, nobody moved nor spoke, reminded anew of their fallen companions and Myra's dubious connection to it all.

When Aidan spoke again, his voice had an edge to it: pain barely mastered and justifiable anger. "But it's not just following, not passive. You can manipulate as well. We've all felt it. I could feel that you know what you were about, even if your control of it was . . . incomplete."

"Oh, yes. Feelings. That I can do with near anyone. Anyone I've gotten close to, that is. But, again, with mages it's somehow easier. I can feel your emotions—big or small. And can, subsequently, nudge my own against them. But I would never do anything to hurt someone," Myra was quick to address the accusation she could sense but not directly see. Tears threw a hasty veil between her and Grafford library. She sniffled. "I—I thought I was helping. I had no idea it might be danger-ous . . . or even if it was all that real. It felt . . . like a game I'd made up for myself. A good power to match . . . to match the bad. Something for myself. I thought I was helping."

Aidan changed tack. "Stealing powers. What of that?"

"No! Never!"

Aidan whirled on her, voice darkened by intense, unreadable emotion. "When we met I said you were a Kinetic. You denied that. I believed you. But there was something. Something else. You were less surprised than I would have expected."

"Right! I told you—"

"Kady Moore was a Kinetic."

Comprehension dawned, and Myra sat back in her chair, stunned.

"I read your guilt, Moira. Small, confused even. But guilt all the same. Over something you'd done to get yourself involved, get yourself into that warehouse."

Had her arrival at the warehouse prevented Kady's escape? More tears stung Myra's eyes. "I—I wanted to follow what I was sensing. I could see the smoke, the flame on the horizon and thought I'd dreamt it. I never meant to hurt anyone. I never meant to steal anything."

"Secrets then." James rose to pace the floor. "In my head. In Stephen's. In Aidan's. What would you expect us to do with a girl who has secrets, secrets of the Crown and—"

"What do you suggest? Is there any answer she can give that would satisfy?" Aidan redirected his pain, finding an easy target.

From his corner, the unnamed mage cleared his throat. Or it might have been a snort. Either way it was a purposefully rude noise. The man turned and left, leaving Myra to wonder at how much authority this James really had. Was it power or posturing?

Myra found her tongue. "I'm not sure I want magic. I mean, I want to know about it, about myself. Know about why I am the way that I am, now that I've found I'm not the only one who is . . . with certain powers. It is a relief, knowing I am not mad after all. But people died, good people—I could feel that. And while you all scare me quite a lot"—she gave a pointed look to James—"I can tell you, too, are good people. And that makes me want to learn more, to see if I can help and if I have a place in helping bring to justice those who killed your friends."

"Oh, I like her," Robert rumbled from his chair. From the way he was slumped, Myra would have thought he had fallen asleep many minutes prior. "Come, James. We know you do too, even if you have to make all this fuss and show. She confirms Steve's theory —painful as it is to us all to have such a reminder of his passing."

"We have to teach her, James. If she truly is Empathic, she must learn of her powers for her own sake." Laurel had approached. The mage gently lifted the cloak out of Myra's clenched fingers. She draped it about Myra's shoulders and then sank onto the arm of the opposite chair. It was the first time Myra had the opportunity to look the woman over. Elegant and exceptionally beautiful, the wizard turned her soft eyes to James, her pronouncement something between a suggestion and a command.

She controls James, then? Myra turned her attention back to James, who had affected a complete transformation under Laurel's mild upbraid. Though still imposing, the kindness that Robert had claimed from James could now be seen. It was guarded, tucked safely away from where the hard world could get at it and use such against him and his own, but the core of it was within him.

"She has the makings of one of us." James offered his hand.

"American. She's mine. Technically." Aidan flashed his lopsided smile. He hadn't recovered yet, his emotional state a dark, uneasy sea.

James ignored him. "Myra, we can train you.

Educate you about your powers. It's sort of what we do, in addition to our other responsibilities—"

"You mean used to." Robert roused himself, gaining his feet heavily and giving vent to an exaggerated stretch. He turned to Myra, elaborating, "M.I. stands for 'Magical Intelligence.' It was the inaugural branch of British Intelligence Services. Wizard spies. We were fired last week."

"Last week? But Stephen said that he was in America . . ." Aidan trailed off, deep in thought.

Robert chuckled. "He must have told you some careful truths then. We're ousted. Holing up here until we figure out our next move. And Addair's. It was James' resignation letter to which you were voyeur, Myra."

"Letter of complaint," James inserted quietly. He rose and left their small party.

Though a man could not go all his life shouting and threatening darkly, it surprised Myra to hear that James could so easily be a soft-spoken man.

Iron control. That, she wanted to learn.

James returned with a tea tray, M.I.'s mystery mage in tow.

"Tea." James arced his right foot to drag the small Pembroke table closer to where Myra still sat cocooned within her blanket and cloak. "Benjamin, Myra. Myra, Benjamin."

"We met." Myra quirked an eyebrow to Benjamin, who returned her cheeky statement with a silent, laughing grin of his own. He had in his hand a large bundle of cloth but had not yet moved to divest himself of his burden.

"Come. She won't bite. We've the truth-teller's word for it," said Laurel.

"A change of dry clothes." Tearing his eyes from Myra, Benjamin passed the unwieldy bundle into Aidan's arms, then turned to leave.

"Today's news," Robert called out, not moving from his warm spot by the fire.

"Thanks." Benjamin swiped up the pile of newspapers as he exited the library without a backward glance.

Hunger overtook all other preoccupations for Myra as the sweet smell of warmed scones and acerbic notes of tea wafted up from the table. Thus occupied, she hardly noticed Aidan laying her change of clothes on the arm of her chair and exiting the room with his own. It prompted a thought, however, which she gave voice to through bites of buttered pastry. "What is a Maester of Triewes?"

Chapter Seven

"Aidan's gift is that of truth telling, Myra." Laurel gestured that James sit by her. "But I think you need more than that in order to understand the depth of your own question. James?"

The mage nodded, leaning forward. Quiet intelligence radiated at Myra, and had she not been witness to the change in his demeanor, she would have thought there were two Jameses about. He began, "In 1853, Britain became involved in a conflict that later developed into the war between us and several allies and Russia. The theatre for the conflict was such that gathering intelligence was both difficult and dangerous. Perfect impetus for officers eager to distinguish themselves, but quietly."

"And thus the Department of Topography and Statistics was born," Robert broke into the conversation. "Formed by myself and two others—another mage and a natural philosopher."

"Professor Silas Addair." James raised his teacup in mock salute.

"Scientist for the team, Doctor Addair added a veneer of respectability to an otherwise ungentlemanly pursuit. Information gathering by questionable means was frowned upon by those in the military who found the rules of honorable combat to be entirely too strict to allow for such. Yes, he was one of ours," Robert elaborated, taking Myra's shock in stride. "And the only ord of the original three. But smart and brave as they came. Good man. Once."

Uncomfortable silence descended upon the small group.

"Time passed, and our little endeavor gained the necessary respect from those higher up to not only continue, but to grow. The DTS became M.I. and its numbers grew from three to five to half a dozen, myself and Stephen coming on at the time of the Afghan war and Laurel joining shortly after," James continued. "By then, Doctor Addair had married Florence, and their infant son was just about walking—"

"But you're forgetting Violectric Dampening," Laurel inserted.

"Yes. Well, I feel that's Robert's story to tell."

"It's yours as well. Go on, James." Robert closed his eyes and slumped deeper into his chair.

"Electricity sickness or, as we call it, Violectric Dampening, is a problem that we became keenly aware of through a treatment Robert received while recovering from a grievous injury. The electrotherapy, while it restored motion to the affected limbs, had the unfortunate side effect of negating his magic abilities."

"It was Addair who made the connection. Electricity and magic, oil and water. Worse than. For it wasn't a fair fight. It was poison, and it was everywhere."

Myra glanced around the library's dark depths, recalling something Aidan had said the night before. Something about telegraphs and the TurnKey ley lines. She said, "Aidan made brief mention of it when we were to travel via the TurnKey. That it disrupts how it works."

"Only the wizard who uses it." James shook his head. "Earth magic is unaffected. No, Dampening is an epidemic amongst mages, generally avoided by staying out of close contact with electricity."

"In my case, the damage to my gift was permanent." Robert roused himself, reaching for a scone. "Silas began an obsessive search for the cure, angered that that which had saved my life had also, in many ways, killed what gave my life meaning. The sickness was in science. And too, he believed, science held the cure. There was no telling the world to stop adding lines for telegraphs and trains. We were on our own, ghosts within the government, only as safeguarded and legitimate as they deigned. Our days as wizards were numbered."

"And the problem of the Dampening extended beyond us original members," James continued. "M.I.'s expansion had been more or less halted by the electrifying of the world around us. What wizards there were were often suppressed before they reached the age of Emergere, before they realized their powers. Those born with the gift were . . . lesser. You see, for us full mages, electricity is merely a temporary hobbling, a weakness from which we might recover. But for the lesser mages? Electricity is a permanent drain on their abilities. Laurie and Benjamin, your American friend, Aidan, they all are but shades of what a wizard truly could be, having one, perhaps two gifts amongst the many. Silas' own son—"

"And unlike full mages," Laurel broke in, "we cannot take or leave the gifts as we please. It is a twisting of the natural talent, nature's way to compensating, we believe. And all the while, Doctor Addair worked to secure a remedy, a formal curing of the Dampening which he had managed to temporarily ward off for us lesser mages through his elixir."

"Which brings us to you," James turned his focus back to Myra.

"To me?" Myra wilted under the sudden scrutiny.

"Addair's elixir. I do not need it. Stephen does—did —not. Nor Robert. Each of us having the full complement of magic. But for the lesser mages, without regular dosing of the Doctor's compound, the Violectric Dampening becomes permanent. You appear to not need it, unless there's something rather strange in your past that you've managed to gloss over even under the truth-teller's questioning." James' forbidding aspect had returned.

"Not me, no. I've had doctors aplenty to look at me for my madness, but nobody's stayed long enough to effect a cure." Myra stopped short, surprised. "Or whatever you would call it, now that it would appear I am not at all ill."

"No, my dear. You are perfect." Laurel reached forward, taking Myra's hands. "Oh, how Stephen would have loved to meet you—" Tears sparkled in the corners of the woman's eyes. Her sudden affection had Myra lowering her eyes, self-conscious.

"An Empathic. One who works the magic of emotion," Robert added in his own starry-eyed wonder, showing more animation than he had displayed in the short time Myra had known him.

"And with human magic being mostly inseparable

from emotion, you are not only able to join with someone else's gift, you can adopt it as well, provided they are using it and you are in close concert with them."

"For example, Aidan's gift is truth telling, a Maester of Triewes—to use the old term for the talent. Which means that he can tell when anyone about him is lying or, if he's very adept, concealing though technically truthful." James rose to pace the room. "Such a gift is practically inseparable from emotion, and when you are near him, you naturally acquire much of his talents for your own use."

"Aidan had suspected, if not quite understood, your gift," Laurel added. "Which, I would assume, is why he wanted you to tell us of his trustworthiness—believing your touch upon our emotions would also carry the force of truth."

At Myra's confused look, Robert continued, "The gift of Maester of Triewes is two-fold. When it is the natural talent of a lesser mage, well, he cannot lie, my dear."

"Such a gift is quite valuable in our line of work," James added. "I, having the full complement of powers for a mage, chose to specialize in combat and illusion."

"And I"—Robert pushed himself to the edge of his chair, puffing with the exertion—"I—" He paused, frowning in concentration, his right hand held out in front of him, palm down. The tick of a clock somewhere in the library's depths marked the long moments passing. Then, in the stillness beneath Robert's hand, there came a stirring in the air. It was followed by the emergence of a tiny cloud bank rolling in from nowhere. A flash of light and low rumble heralded a diminutive downpour of rain, the illusion made complete.

Robert shook his hand, spraying Myra with raindrops as he ended the spell. He slumped back into his chair, spent. "I, too, had the full complement of magic, though my chosen specialty was that of weather working. And on a good day, if I'm not so tired as this, I can work up enough of a squall to fill a space such as Grafford House itself. Far different from the days I could strand a cityscape in fog or parch a foreign land with unending sun."

"That . . . was wonderful!" Myra no longer cared that she gaped like a landed fish. Would she be able to learn that as well?

Laurel passed behind Robert's chair, giving the man a sympathetic squeeze on his shoulder. She addressed Myra, "And I am M.I.'s Ways-walker. It is my sole gift, the Dampening having affected my powers so that I am a lesser mage. But I was fortunate enough to have learned the proper use of my gift from Florence, one of M.I.'s founding members who, like Robert and James, had the use of all the powers. Through Ways-walking, a wizard can send her mind to other planes of existence, move herself and others where she wills it. The TurnKey system was devised by those skilled in the art of Ways-walking. It is, as some say, an older, higher form of Kinetics."

"And Kinetic I already know, based on what Aidan told me of Kady——" Myra stopped short her response as the door to the library opened.

"Look who I found in the hallway: a gentleman!" Benjamin called out the cheeky greeting, gesturing to Aidan who, Myra had to admit, cleaned up rather nicely. Reminded of her own disheveled state and the dry, clean clothes that awaited her, she hurried to finish the last of her tea and scone, feeling as though she had been caught gossiping.

Benjamin had taken up his position of lounging against the fireplace mantle, refusing, with a wave, Laurel's offer of a cup of tea. "Had one, thanks."

Aidan stood behind Myra's chair, making her nervous. Again.

"So the report from Stephen's activities abroad is brought by a representative of our American counterpart. Aidan?" James launched into the meeting with little warning.

Myra made to rise. "Should I be here?"

"You absolutely should be here, my dear," Robert answered, pouring her another cup of tea and gesturing that she sit back down. "You're one of us now. No secrets."

Aidan gave a curt nod to James and began, "My team, acting on behalf of our government with the understanding that this was a joint venture between us and the British Crown, met with Stephen as planned. The news that he had brought with him had put all teams—both magical and non—on high alert, having not heard anything about Addair's activities ourselves. Those up top considered it troubling that a mage of Silas' skill and reputation would have slipped past us undetected."

"I thought Addair was not a mage . . . ?" Myra whispered to Robert, puzzled.

"Things changed. 'Round about the time his wife was taken from him." Robert's voice was hard, and he did not look at Myra. Eyes to Aidan, he indicated that he should continue his report. He looked as phlegmatically dull as ever. His hands, however, gripped the arm of his chair with knuckles made white by tension.

"As a precaution, we made our rendezvous point the Heartland Apex, planning to travel onward to the warehouse that we had made use of for storing our supply of Silas' compound. Unfortunately, that pause, with its gathering of so many of our small force, was enough to tip off Addair's own men. They were waiting for us when we arrived.

"They captured us all too easily. Stephen they held separately. He—" At this it appeared Aidan might break down, the rest of his story never coming to completion. But he mastered himself quickly, finding a seat and passing a shaky hand over his eyes.

"It was as though the whole mission had been created for the sole purpose of destroying him. They didn't even bother to separate Kady, Walter, and I, throwing us into a cage like animals and walking away. It wasn't until it was too late that we realized our predicament: our prison negated our powers. We were helpless."

"A Faraday cage," Robert mused from his chair.

"Right." Aidan nodded. "Stephen, he . . . In addition to our supply of Silas' cure, the warehouse served as a munitions store. Stephen had done his homework. He managed, somehow, to start the fire that freed us."

"Somehow?" James interjected.

"Somehow. Because they . . . they tortured him. They took their time. What happened to Robert by accident, they did on purpose—" Aidan's voice broke again. "They— I could see them injecting him with something, and he went limp soon after."

"It felt like poison." Myra's addition to the conversation was out before she could stop herself. She clapped her hands over her mouth, feeling herself go red with embarrassment and no small amount of shame. Five interested pairs of eyes turned to her.

"Go on. You've knowledge we could not otherwise have, Myra." James sucked in his breath, a thin attempt at masking his anguish.

"It all happened so fast. And I didn't know it was real," Myra dissembled. "One of the hooded men— mages, I suppose—injected something into Stephen's arm, and he knew that it was stopping his powers. So he acted in the only way he could, which was to try to kill them all by setting the munitions afire. Trap them all there— Stop Addair's men from further evil—" Startled at the memory, at the clarity of Stephen's thoughts in her mind and what his hasty plan meant for Aidan sitting right in front of her, she mouthed the words "I'm sorry."

"It's all right, Moira. This is what we have chosen to do with our lives," Aidan reassured her, though he looked troubled.

She gulped. "Well, his plan worked. And it had the unexpected benefit of cutting power to the cage that held you. Stephen counted himself as lost, along with those whom he'd slain via the first explosion. But Kady, she refused to leave him."

Aidan picked up the story. "Her gift newly available to her, Kady leapt off into the blaze, searching for Stephen. I tended to Walter, but it was too late. He— He was gone." Now Aidan did break down in earnest. A strangled sob set his shoulders to quaking, and he passed his hand over his eyes. Whatever had struck down Walter, they were not to learn.

"And that's when Myra arrived, and you saved her," Robert rumbled from the comfort of his chair, drawing the attention of their small group off Aidan.

"And we're nowhere closer to finding Addair. And the last of the elixir is gone," Benjamin chimed in at last, stepping forward into the light. "Aidan made mention of it in the hallway. That warehouse held the last of the Americans' supply."

"And two bodies," Aidan intoned darkly, having mastered himself once more.

"Yes, he also made mention that he's mostly certain that two of Addair's men were killed in the blast but obviously not all, as Stephen had hoped."

Ice water ran in Myra's veins as she, again, recalled the quick fire fight as they had fled for the train. She locked eyes on Aidan, wondering if that merited inclusion in the official report. Or, perhaps, M.I. was in the habit of tallying kills, not enemies. She shuddered and allowed the Maester of Triewes to say nothing.

"Which brings me to today's news." Benjamin slapped his stack of newspapers onto the table in their midst. "None of it good. Either our informant is shirking his duties or there has been no whisper of Addair's activities since the events at the warehouse."

Chapter Eight

"So Addair is in the wind again." James' teacup clattered none too gently into its saucer.

"Or our informant is choosing to not inform. Remember, we are no longer tied to M.I.'s operations. They've other teams, other concerns. Chasing Silas was always more our problem than theirs; an old problem that they assume will be solved by the very technology which ousted us," Robert reminded him.

"Wait. How could there still be an M.I. if all the mages have been discharged?" Myra felt bad interjecting, but she simply had to know.

"They had a second and third team—100% ords— already in place when we found ourselves locked out of the offices, clutching the freshly penned letter that explained things to us wizards. Magical Intelligence has been renamed Military Intelligence. All memory of its beginnings have been wiped from the record. Officially speaking, we never existed. Addair never existed."

Aidan snorted, and James shot him a look.

Laurel separated them by inserting her own clarification. "What Robert says is not altogether true. The scientist they will cop to. But while we never served the Crown, set foot on official premises, worked with these people side by side for years, there has been one fellow willing to stick his neck out for us. The newly-minted MI2 continued looking into the affairs of one Doctor Silas Addair due to his apparent mismanagement of government files and scientific discoveries under his stead at DTS, and Julius has kept us informed of those proceedings as he did even before our unceremonious ousting. It's not much. But it's not nothing."

"Until it becomes nothing," Benjamin countered, tapping the piled newspapers in emphasis. "Nothing in any of these. Not even a whisper. With silence from the field, you're as good as locked in here with me."

Locked in here with me? Does he not go out? Myra darted her eyes to Benjamin and found him studiously avoiding her gaze. *Is nobody ever going to look directly at me?*

"Nonsense. Silence means neither MI2 nor Addair's agents are looking for those of us that got away from the attack stateside—Aidan and Myra. I, for one, see that as a victory," Robert said.

"Simply waiting for Julius to send another update would give us the leisure to bring Myra up to speed," Laurel added.

"And we're not going to check in with the director and tell him of Stephen's death?" James had found his feet. Myra could feel the sharp stab of his anger, and she flinched.

"They know, James," Laurel said. "They'll have heard of the attack on the elixir supply."

"Of course I know that. But I want to see, firsthand,

as they deny any involvement in the attack. I want to read their faces while they—"

"James!" This time, Laurel spoke as sharply as M.I.'s leader. "Stephen died believing in the Agency. It is not your place to cast doubts on their integrity over mere political differences. They're ords. They do not understand us."

"I'm with him on this," Aidan spoke up. "Addair was one of your own, once. Such betrayal could have happened again. What of this ord informant?"

"We're lamplighters," James spat. "Relics of a world that is passing away beneath us. Like the knights of old."

"I don't believe anyone who has seen our work, our methods, would compare us to such, James," Robert ponderously grumbled his way to his feet. Not for the first time, Myra watched the man in motion and wondered how he ever could have functioned as a spy. But then he had been out of the game for some time, to hear them tell it. And besides that, oughtn't a spy not look like a spy?

Myra looked around the group in alarm and noted that only Benjamin had not joined in the heated argument. Sometime during the opening volleys he had managed to slink back into the shadows, an observant ghost of a man. Him Myra could believe in the espionage capacity. He who never left the house.

Wands were drawn and voices raised further.

Frightened, Myra threw her mind into the midst of the bickering mages. While she had never tried to soothe more than one or two people at a time, she assumed the principles were much the same. And, them being wizards, she figured she would have an easier time of it.

It was that or hide and hope they did not destroy one another.

Myra absorbed the ire and distress. Blows such as would leave bruises on her psyche. She hit back with serenity and compassion. Level-headedness from the mad one in their midst, the girl who did not belong, still knowing nothing herself. Knowing nothing save for the fact that they needed to stop, lest they drag her emotional state into an inescapable pit.

The storm passed, with nary a comment or correction thrown her way. They had to have known what she'd done. And pointedly, purposefully, ignored it.

Robert was first to take a seat. "Sounds to me like we have a plan. Wait for word from Julius. Train Myra. Stop Addair."

"Fine." James sealed Myra's fate with that solitary word. "Wetherby, go get yourself cleaned up and meet me back here in . . . well, is a half-hour sufficient?"

Myra nodded mutely, unable to object in the wake of her emotional expenditure. It was all happening so fast. But then, who was she to argue, owing her rescue to these people and finding that they, clearly, needed the touch of her gift just to keep them from killing one another. *People who lost so much and yet promise me magic, promise me the world.*

For she had goals of her own. Things she had managed, quite by accident, to hide from even the Maester of Triewes. With control of her powers, Myra might stop running from her past. Might even—to use Aidan's parlance—"give the Earth back what is hers" and reset the balance sheet of fate in her favor. She could go back to Alice. She could go home.

And besides, Myra . . . she liked them. Odd as it

seemed and in spite of all, she really liked these folks, wanted to know more of them. Save them, if she could. Myra found her tongue at last. "Thank you. I'll be right back."

Clutching the bundle of second-hand clothes to her chest, she followed Laurel from the room, eager to impress upon everyone her willingness to learn, to contribute.

———————

Grafford House proved deceptively huge.

Myra was to have a whole room to herself—a whole wing, in fact—during her stay with M.I. Oddly enough, even wishing to return home, she actually hoped her stay amongst M.I.'s outcasts would be a long one. For she had discovered, for the first time in her short fourteen years of life, the sense of truly belonging.

They trust me? Myra tried on the unusual conclusion and found that it fit. She looked around the dim yet nicely arrayed lodgings. Tidy and neat. The only drab thing was herself. Well, that and the lack of proper lighting. A large four-poster bed, antique furnishings, it was as though she had stepped into Cinderella's life, trading misery for riches.

Myra unfurled the bundle of clothing. She laid its components out on the bed, placing the shoes by the door. The various pieces of the ensemble were in good repair and of recent style. So far she had seen nobody her age nor size in the house. Who on the team had worn these?

Setting aside that mystery by finding another, Myra was embarrassed to learn that she required every bit of the allotted thirty minutes to array herself tidily. For the provided dry change of clothing was as puzzling in construction as it was in origin.

Everything was loose and tight in turns. Myra was certain she had it all wrong as she applied first drawers then chemise to her still-shivering form. Slippery and fluid, the material for both seemed delicate as butterflies' wings, and she feared she would tear the ill-fitting garments in her haste. But, delicate as they appeared, there was something iron-hard about them as well. It was like donning the world's softest, lightest chainmail armor. She had never seen the like. Silk? Not cotton, certainly. And the warp and woof was all swirly. Impossibly made.

Alarmed and determined to think no more on it, Myra had turned to the next dilemma: the corset. Which, in the end, gave her no trouble at all. Snug and of a similar material to the rest of the underthings, the undergarment had none of the customary constriction one would expect, given its reputation and use.

In contrast, the irksome chemise bunched and sagged within its new confines, prompting Myra to twist and turn before the mirror in hopes of wrestling it back into obedience. It was in this way that she discovered the delightfully free range of movement this strange clothing allowed.

Myra decided it was time to attack the petticoats. Of which there was but one. And it was rather short.

Improper. Were they trying to embarrass her? Shocked into blushing, Myra tried to remember if Laurel's outfit had seemed similarly out of sorts. It had not, and she scolded her overly prim mind. *No, Myra. It simply has something to do with easy movement. Do not question such small miracles of fashion.*

Moving quickly to the dress that promised to cover all, she was pleased to discover that it was as proper as she had dared hope, though it, too, had its oddities. Puzzling over the line of diminutive loops that lay along the left-hand side of the bodice, she breathed a sigh of relief over the garment's suitably high neck, long sleeves, and hemline. What's more, the dress concealed with ease the sloppy bunching of the underthings, even considering the imperfect fit which demonstrated anew that the dress originally had a different owner.

Returning to the mirror, she attempted to smooth the clothing into submission, jumping as her pinky finger caught unexpectedly in the cloth of the skirt. *Pockets? Pockets! I have pockets!*

This discovery alone furthered Myra's peace with the strange garb.

By now the soft gum-soled slipper-shoes retained little power to surprise, and Myra donned them with efficient nonchalance.

Frustrated as she had been at every turn by the meddlesome clothing, Myra had little time left before her lesson for a quick dashing of water on the face and finger-combing of her loosened hair.

Not that she would have otherwise spent much time on this last. She wanted to get to it! Magic. Secrets and power. Self-control. As they had walked, Laurel had cautioned Myra. It had taken her three years of dedicated study to learn her gift. Such things did not come quickly nor easily, especially when one had bad habits to break.

Myra wondered if such natural talent, such apparent rarity of gift, could be considered a "bad habit."

But before she found that out, she first had to get back to the library.

Myra stepped out of her room and looked about her in dismay. They had come from the right and up the stairs. That much she remembered. Beyond that there were far too many turnings for her agitated mind to recall.

No matter, if she got turned about, she could always be put right. There was no sense fretting over looking silly. Not to people who had interrogated her while she wore the flimsy miscellany of her escape from America.

She struck off in the only direction she remembered, gaining confidence as she picked her way down towards the main floor. Distant muffled shouting caught her as she gained the final landing. Aidan and James, from the sound of it.

Guilt prickling her ears, Myra crept forward. Her slippered feet made nary a sound on the thick carpeting which lined the hallway. How could she not listen when they argued so?

She observed the grouping of M.I. mages through the crack in the open door and hid herself in the shadows just outside the room to watch.

"I'm just saying that it was an idiotic move to store the last of your supply of Addair's elixir—"

"Compound. We took it in pill form—"

"Compound, then. It was abysmally stupid of you to have placed it all at an Apex."

Benjamin moved across Myra's field of vision. Crossing between the two bickering mages, he took up a position at Laurel's side. Cool curiosity decorated his handsome features. It seemed to Myra that he looked straight at her, his eyes trained distantly on where she stood in the hallway. She told herself that he couldn't possibly see her. Could he?

Besides it was Aidan who had her worried. He had barely flinched under James' tirade. His only reaction had been his correction of term. It seemed he had turned to granite, stony resolve the only thing left in him.

"Silas. Is he English or American?" the rock spoke.

Now it was the rest of them who were frozen in place. None dared engage Aidan. Myra could feel the heat of his anger now. A burning almost physical, it seared her heart, spreading warmth with each beat until she was hot with his wrath. But she could not soothe him, lest she give herself away.

He continued, "Did we—myself, Kady, Walter—create your monster, his anarchistic offspring? Did we invite him to our continent, beg his cruel interference in our affairs?"

"Your government happily accepted his formula. You and your team benefited directly from his research—"

"Did we kill his wife and child?"

This last hit the M.I. team like a slap across the face. Benjamin, James, Laurel . . . Robert. Myra felt it: the guilt, the old pain of barely-scarred-over remorse laid bare. It had her staggering back against the wall. She gulped air, fighting a swoon and cursing anew her inconstant and inconvenient gift.

A dangerous exposure, theirs was the shame of complicity, and Myra could feel both apology and repudiation rise. Magic, wild and fierce as freshly birthed tears, rose in fingers and lips. Myra's spine tingled with it, and she fought to keep her autonomy, to not get swept out with the rushing tide.

"He is all of our problems, now." Robert was the first to let his fire die. "Silas, it would seem, is counting no differences between those who led and those what followed, brooking no excuse and marking no exception. And though it is rather too late to undo certain tragedies, it would be a disservice—a dishonor to those lost—to merely point fingers and lay blame, refusing to learn from recent events. Shouting at one another does not bring back Stephen, Kady, or her brother. It does not fix the problem of Addair's elixir."

James stirred, still angry but able to recognize Robert's simple sense. "The question, then, is: who else can we afford to lose?"

"Me." Benjamin was quick to dart into James' question, even as Laurel opened her mouth to speak. Shrugging, the young man affected a carefree smile. "Eventually we'll all go, save for you, James, of course. But I'd venture that we need a Ways-walker and Maester of Triewes sooner than we need a living, breathing encyclopedia. I can stop taking Silas' compound."

"And then me, provided we are left without a solution for any great length of time," Laurel put in her own offer, quick as she could. Her eyes darted to James, demanding he not question her judgment.

"Addair's mages appear not to have a Laurel or Benjamin amongst them, and so we expose nothing of ourselves with their intended sacrifice," Robert rumbled in once more. "Thank you. Both of you."

Through the exchange, James James had kept his

gaze on Aidan, ignoring even Laurel's silent plea. The message was clear. The truth-teller had better make certain he was worthy of the gift he was being given.

Benjamin's eyes were back on the doorway, back on where Myra stood just outside. Aidan's eyes darted to Ben. He then followed his gaze and frowned ever so slightly.

Time to go. Myra thrilled with the sudden fear of discovery. No secrets? Best not to test that just then. She moved onward, glad that she was a good twenty paces past the door when it opened but a moment later.

She turned to the sound and shielded her eyes against the light pouring out into the hallway, a dim rectangle set upon the dimmer canvas of the corridor. Aidan's gaze was on her. His piercing eyes radiated questions. "Hello, Myra. Feeling better, I hope?"

He's so cool about it. Myra marveled. She was sure that he had known she watched from beyond the doorway. And yet he said nothing.

"Much improved, thanks." Myra hesitated as she half-turned from him. She pointed in the direction of her hasty retreat. "The library?"

"Turned all about were ye, Moira?" Aidan walked toward her. His mouth twitched with familiar good humor. Yes, her secret was safe with him. He secured things further, asking, "Have you seen Benjamin? I'm to meet with him whilst you learn from Mr. James."

Have I seen Benjamin? So that's a game he likes to play. He is a tricky one, then. For all that it was a relief to know that she could trust Aidan, Myra could suddenly see a bit more what bothered James so. Such careful truths and with such practiced ease.

"Benjamin? No." She shook her head, wondering

what her lie felt like to the Maester of Triewes and knowing full well that she could find out if she really wanted. She didn't. Instead she found herself blurting, "I don't think he likes me."

"Young Ben?" This caught Aidan off step, and he stopped to regard her more closely.

"Young? From what I can tell he splits the difference between you and I by, what, a year? Two?" Myra snorted, her ire up without her quite understanding why. Perhaps it was his patent dismissiveness. "Might as well call me a baby, then."

"Nay, Moira. Most others with but a fortnight of years to their name wouldn't have handled recent events half as well as you."

"How did you know—?"

"If you learn to read people as I do, you get very good at grasping the essentials." He stopped to stare at her, fingers tapping his chin in mock concentration. Myra blushed under the scrutiny, for once thankful for the gaslight that illuminated Grafford House. "Fourteen —and just a wee bit more. Ye've been raised with manners—though a bit of you thinks you raised yourself. Simultaneously fearful and brave. Determined. Not the first of your family to be declared a beauty . . ."

"Hey!"

Aidan raised his hands in mock surrender. "The men who work the traveling shows hate me as well. Ah, here we are."

As much as his comments had caught her off guard, Myra had to admit that the brief walk had been nice. It was, quite possibly, the first time since meeting Aidan that she hadn't been burning, drowning, running, flying, or facing him as a potential enemy. It also helped that he had called her pretty.

The blush renewed itself.

"In you go, Moira. I'm off to go get myself an education of my own from M.I.'s walking, talking encyclopedia."

Ears burning, for Aidan's moniker for Ben was pointedly close to his own words—talk that Aidan knew she had overheard—Myra muttered her thanks and fixed her eyes on the doorway to the library.

Aidan McIntyre. Equal parts trustworthy and not. Were all the M.I. wizards like that? Did Myra even want to know?

Did she really have a choice?

Chapter Nine

Myra entered the library alone and discovered a much different space than earlier. The cozy armchairs and accompanying tea table had been removed. The entire floor had, in fact, been exposed. Myra could see the bundle of carpets in between two bookshelves, a soft hulking mass. A quick glance about the room confirmed Myra's suspicions: any furniture not of the bookshelf variety had been moved off to the corners, stacked and bundled so as to create an open space before the hearth.

"Don't worry, Myra, I won't demand too many acrobatics of you until I've a measure of your skills." James had entered the room behind her, silent on the newly barren floors. He was dressed much as she had seen him through the door jamb—all in black, impeccable, and dark as the shadows.

"Is it really James James . . . or just James?" Caught off-step, compliments of her nerves, Myra's curiosity got the best of her. She clapped her hands over her mouth, mortified.

"Ha!" Stepping fully into the room, James turned on

his heel so that he still faced her. "What a funny little thing you are, Myra."

Dropping to a crouch and jumping back up—clearly the suit he wore involved that same special tailoring which afforded such easy mobility—the mage drew his wand, moving about to stretch his limbs. Three long strides took him away so that he stood silhouetted in front of the still-roaring fire. "It's James James. My parents, the lovely Mr. and Mrs. James, had a sense of humor."

Watching, mesmerized, Myra started when James reached atop the mantle and turned back to her holding not one wand but two.

"For me?" Myra hadn't taken her eyes off the wand.

"Of course. It's not as fine as I'd like. But with your gift not following the rules generally understood by us, we had little chance of getting it right in any event. Even Ben's books had little for us to go on. The hope is that, with your Empathy it will grow to match you."

Delicate and polished, the wood had a reddish cast about it. And though it was not overly ornate, the simple coves and beads that ringed the grip distinguished it far above the practical simplicity of Aidan's. It was her wand. She could feel it in ways she could scarce describe.

But how? How could it possibly be hers, this price-less gift? She had only just gotten here, barely managed a change of clothes. And when could Benjamin have possibly found the leisure to check all those books, what with them moving the furniture about in the library?

"Thank you." She knew better than to resist such a gift. Time was of the essence here in M.I. Modest gestures of polite refusal had no place. But she had to know more. Especially as the wand was placed into her hand, the smooth wood warming to her touch in a manner she could only describe as unnatural. *Or magical.*

Myra gulped. Manners were manners. She said, "Your efforts and kindness are appreciated, and I can only hope that I am worthy—"

"Arm straight. Eyes up. Wand aloft," James ran over Myra's niceties, demonstrating with his own wand what he wanted of her. "And . . . that might do it."

At this last, he had backed himself away from her so that he approached the far end of the room. Standing with her arm held in the air and feeling excessively silly, Myra wondered what he was about. James had all but disappeared into the gloom some fifty feet away. She had her answers a moment later when she felt a tingling in her spine, like the rushing of a waterfall but faint.

"Whatever you do, don't lower your wand."

"Got it." Myra glanced upward to her wand. Her palms were sweating.

"Feel anything?" James' voice called from the darkness.

"I'm . . . I'm not sure. Maybe?" Myra peered into the dark. The whispering roar became crackling flame, became the shock of lightning.

"Yes. Definitely," she shouted back into the shadows.

"I'd suspected as much." James materialized at her side.

Myra shrieked her surprise.

James chuckled. "My apologies, but I wanted to test your sensitivity. Whether there was a limit on how far you could sense—and therefore take unto yourself— basic magics worked within your environs."

"And?" Myra cocked an eyebrow at James. Her arm was getting tired, her wrist cramping.

"See for yourself." He darted his eyes to her wand.

"Yeeeeek!"

Wand, fingertips—all were lost to the gloom of the room. No, not lost. Invisible. She withdrew her hand, dropping the wand with a clatter. Her fingers fine and whole and, most importantly, visible. She clutched them to herself, glaring at James. "I didn't even try. I didn't even know."

He smiled, bending to retrieve her wand.

"I thought there would be incantations and hand motions and . . ."

"Did we not say you've already been doing magic, Myra? Did I not say you've taken our secrets right from us?" He handed Myra back her wand, tapping his skull in illustration.

"Yeah, but . . ." Myra stared at the wand in her hand. "I thought it would be hard."

James shook his head, lifting his own wand. "Magic is actually rather easy. That's the trouble with it."

"So," Myra ventured, "what I'm going to be learning is how not to do magic."

"Let us just say it will be a—a mutual learning," James hunted for the words, studying Myra with the sort of detached curiosity she had come to associate with those of the medical profession. A shiver shook Myra's spine. An old saying of her mother's—something about frying pans and fires—rattled through her addled brain. Again the impulse to run almost had hold of her.

No! No more running! Myra stood firm, setting her chin. She would prevail. She would take charge of her destiny, do something good with her life when given the opportunity.

Through the muddied haze of her gift, she could sense James following her train of thought, sensing her struggle and waiting patiently through the storm. It was to his credit that he allowed her to make her own conclusions, come back to the lesson of her own accord. He was so very likable, in his own grouchy way. Stern and combative, he wanted the best for the people left in his care. Again, Myra felt Stephen's loss keenly, and she strove to move past her unconscious theft of James' emotional state.

"What do I need to do? Or, I suppose, not do?" She smiled, shy.

"Well, first—this is rather embarrassing—I need to warn Benjamin to stay as far from you as possible at present and to keep level-headed." James strode to the doorway, leaning outward into the dark hallway beyond. He turned back to Myra. "There are some powers you do not want, believe you me. I'll be right back."

Myra contented herself with studying her wand during James' brief absence. She knelt by the fireplace, marveling anew at the simple but elegant craftsmanship of the arcane artifact. It was hers. All hers. Oh, if Alice could only see her now. She would be green with envy.

And she would likely say 'I told you so.' Younger than Myra as she was—by nearly two full years—Alice had always been the more steadfast of the pairing, had always carried within her the confidence Myra had lacked. She alone Myra had believed when she said there was a cure in store for her sister, somewhere.

James returned.

"Now, when you feel me, let it happen. Don't fight it, and instead concentrate on how it feels within you."

"How it feels?"

"Sensation, emotion. Not mine, of course, but yours."

And with that, Myra felt a stirring within her. Similar to that which she had felt when Aidan first had handed her his wand but distinctly different. Her magic, not his. Fire and ice all at once. It was . . . It was like . . .

". . . Sticking my hands into a snowbank without gloves on," Myra observed. "But in here"—she tapped her chest—"instead of my fingers."

"Good, good," James encouraged. "Now, try to shut it down. Tamp it back into place. You are in control. You can see it, feel it, now. You know it for what it is, and you are its master."

Myra squinched her eyes shut, trying to do as James commanded. The fire within her flared and snarled, a terrifying, disobedient animal. She pushed harder, was rewarded by a dimming of the light, and gasped in dismay as it blazed back all the stronger.

"I can't," she choked, opening eyes to a veil of tears that had crept up on her unawares.

The bite of magic died abruptly.

James had ended his spell. His wand gently lowered, and he came to her, awkwardly placing a hand upon her shoulder. "Hush, now. I hadn't expected it could be done all in one day. As I said, doing magic is easy. It is the stopping that is hard."

James lifted his hand to escort Myra from the library. "And now I must apologize, for Benjamin has hit upon an idea that shall require use of this room, and as I said before, your powers and his are not necessarily compatible. And because we will be performing magic, I would ask that you stay in the furthest end of the house until called."

Cross as she was over having failed at her first lesson in magic, Myra was disappointed to think that she was being shuffled out of the way, a danger to herself and others.

Just as the doctors said. The thought snuck past Myra's weakened defenses, crushing her further. It was all a lie, this magic. The reality was that she was wrong in the head, weak, ill, something Other to be hidden away. And James hadn't the guts to tell it to her face. These lovely people would plan a secret meeting and find a way to—

"Ah, Aidan." James looked over Myra's shoulder. "Did young Ben tell you what books you would be needing to aid Myra in her studies?"

Myra's mercurial emotions reversed at the sight of Aidan in the doorway. Shame pricked at her ears. How quickly she had sold short the intentions of those who had taken her in. Had Aidan noticed? Just how good was he at reading folk?

The list of book titles swirled about Myra's head, a dizzying dance of words—both common and nonsensical—that left her reeling. Overwhelming, this magic. There was so much for her to learn. And she had but scratched the surface.

"She's a quick study," James' praiseful conclusion echoed distantly in Myra's ears.

Quick study? Had he not been in the same room as Myra for her rather limp attempt at controlling her gift? Dazed, she eyed the small stack of books James had gathered.

"A night of reading. That should be uneventful at long last, eh, Moira?" Aidan's smile lit the room, and Myra drew to it unconsciously.

Uneventful? Myra doubted it. No time spent in Aidan's company could be called such. She pictured Aidan, fierce and forbidding against the flashing brightness of the warehouse fire. She remembered the skillful ease with which he had defended them from Addair's men. The Maester of Triewes. Powerful and mysterious but altogether kind. Recalling their misadventures prompted a warm blush to creep back into her cheeks.

"Moira, what say you to discovering the Grafford House kitchens with me?"

Stomach rumbling in agreement with Aidan's sentiment, Myra recalled that her only sustenance since the previous evening had been a post-interrogation tea. And then she hadn't been all that hungry due to circumstances. That said, whoever was in charge of the estate's kitchens was sure to drive the two wizards out. One simply did not poke about in kitchens. Perhaps he meant the dining room.

She hurried to catch up to Aidan's long strides. The heat in Myra's cheeks spread, infecting her heart. Suddenly the idea of spending a quiet evening reading in the kitchens appeared an excellent idea. If allowed to stay, the kitchen provided easy chaperone. To be alone with Aidan for any length of time . . .

"Ah. This looks like the spot." Aidan banged through the hinged serving doors with a flat palm. One quick glance of the formal dining room was all Myra was afforded before she hurried into the kitchens close on Aidan's heels.

Flinching in apprehension, in memory of intolerant

kitchen matrons in a childhood long extinguished, Myra waited for the scolding that never came. The room was empty save for herself and the American mage.

No butler either, remember? Myra wondered once more at the curious people with whom she had fallen in. How did they survive?

Aidan had the answer. The mage breezed through the room, flicking his wand here and there, rousing stove and stoking fire. Cabinet doors opened to usher out bowls and cups. Silver sang into wakefulness with quiet whispering yawns. Eggs waddled out across the butcher's block to meet their hooded executioner in the form of frying pan and ladle.

Myra's knees betrayed her, and she sank into a chair near the door.

"I'm a dab hand at making egg messes and little else, I'm afraid." Aidan's voice became muffled as he stuck his head into the pantry, calling out, "There's some more bread if you want to make toast. It won't require any spells on your part."

Still Myra did not move. The kitchen, the very kitchen of Grafford House was magic.

Aidan had stopped his puttering to look at her. "Too much?"

Myra nodded, swallowing silly tears. Why, of all things, would this be what overwhelmed her? But overwhelm it did.

"Oh, oh Moira, dear." Aidan knelt swiftly at Myra's side. "There's no harm in it, love. No danger here. Just practical magics."

Myra was certain she could not put into words what really bothered her. Easy domesticity—something she hadn't realized she missed—should not be bereft of people as this was. "I knew that they don't keep any staff. And I know they've their reasons but for someone unused to magic . . ."

"You're not ord, Moira. You need to stop thinking, reacting, as one. Let the magic in. Don't stifle that gift else, in the end, it will injure you."

"What if I don't want—?"

"No. No lies, Moira." Aidan was so bold as to wipe a tear from Myra's cheek. "Your heart wants this. Your head is relieved to know it's true. And your soul . . ." He frowned. "Your soul will come 'round to having mourned what you've left behind. We all lose something when we gain this life."

Aidan stood, beckoning, "But first, let's get something in ye. None least because I'm starved."

He grinned, handsome again.

Myra would follow that man, yes. She let herself be led to the small table hid by the corner behind the fire. Leaning on the hearth-warmed wall, she sighed. "And then to study, I suppose."

"What? You think you haven't learned anything thus far?" Aidan shot her a quick look, testing her.

Myra weighed Aidan's words and actions, looking past scrambled eggs and toasted bread to where he had been confessing some of his own pain moments before. A wiped tear and talk of loss. And she hadn't felt even a glimmer from him, distracted as she had been by the rest of the magic. He had used Myra's surprise against her, employing the shock of the Grafford House spells to keep her safely within herself.

In looking at Aidan now, Myra could feel his pain, could feel its pull.

"We might be seeing a fair bit of one another in the

upcoming days," Aidan said. "For you see, your natural empathy is strong due to your Empathy. And the honesty of my gift extends to my emotions."

"We're a bad mix," Myra concluded.

Aidan grinned. He leaned back in his chair to stare at the ceiling, tousling his hair. "Yes. Perfectly terrible, which, I believe, is what James is hoping for. With me around, you've less chance of falling into the gifts of others."

"And I suppose you've more tricks up your sleeve with regards to magical distraction." Myra indicated the hastily summoned supper.

"I could come up with something here and there, yes." Aidan winked, putting out a hand. One of the borrowed books shot into it from across the room, and Myra braced herself, half expecting one to be launched at her.

He tossed the book onto the table and flipped it open to the index, dragging a finger down along the line of text that filled the page. Myra decided then that Aidan made an even more attractive scholar than combatant, and she was glad for her having already flushed her cheeks with the warmth of the fire at her back. He would think her naught but a blushing, stammering ninny if she kept this up for much longer.

You can only lay blame for your reactions upon your shock and surprise for so long, Myra. She scolded herself, feeling her heart leap and waver like a candle flame with every look, every gesture from Aidan. Inwardly, she cursed James for having found the truth-teller an apt catalyst to Myra's studies. Far from needing to learn to master her magic for her own sanity, she might well learn if only to protect the honesty of her heart from the Maester of Triewes.

"By the by, Myra, where is my coat?" Aidan did not bother looking up from the book at hand.

Myra half rose from her seat. "I forgot it in my rooms. It is drying by the fire; thank you for lending it me."

"Excellent thought. After its exciting journey hither and yon, I would guess that it needed a good airing before any further attempts at laundering can be undertaken." Aidan waved her seated. "I can grab it at evening's end. Think no more upon it."

Clasping her hands beneath the table so as to contain her growing excitement, Myra slid back into her chair and waited as Aidan beckoned three more books to his side. At length, he spoke. "None of these will do."

Flipping shut the cover on the book in front of him and letting the other three drift floor-ward, Aidan fixed his gaze back on Myra. "What is it you wish to know first?"

Another shock, and well timed, for Myra had begun to feel not only Aidan's magic, but power elsewhere within the grand home. It itched.

Myra needed no second bidding. "What was the trick with the wand?"

"I'm sorry, which?"

For a moment, Myra feared she had angered Aidan. His face darkened momentarily before clearing into pure puzzlement, a thought summoned then dismissed. Nevertheless, she pursued, "When you tested me. With your wand."

"Ah. The *Test Magicae*." Aidan was all smiles. "That

is one of the methods by which a mage tests the gift of another—the polite way."

"The less polite being what we encountered in the cemetery?"

The bitter look that crossed Aidan's face confirmed her suspicions. More or less. His smile turned wry, and he volunteered, "Would you believe that what I used on you and James used on me were essentially the same test?"

Oh. Myra hadn't expected that.

"The wand of a mage is a personal object. They—" He hunted for his words. "Very quickly they grow to us and become accustomed only to their master's use. That's not to say you could not use mine and I yours—though, again, with our particular gifts, that would be unwise.

"My claims to the team of who I was and how we had gotten there were readily verifiable to whomever performed the Test upon my wand. Carrying the imprint of my magic, James was able to tell that I spoke truth, as is the way of my gift. It wouldn't work quite the same with others. People are too good at deception most times."

"That's clever."

Aidan blinked. "I . . . I suppose it was."

He grinned, as though through the lens of Myra's compliment he was seeing the affront by James in a new light. "I've just gotten used to how things are around me."

See, that's how I feel, Myra wanted to add. Such would have likely been unnecessary. The Maester of Triewes already knew so much about her that to give voice to the complaint would have merely been grousing for grousing's sake. And, besides, he was talking to her and making her comfortable about magic, could she not at least meet him halfway?

The magical clamor elsewhere in the large house again rose to flutter in Myra's chest. Her vision lightened and darkened in turns, prelude to a faint. Focusing on her breath, she tried to see what was calling to her.

"Hey. Hey!" Aidan reached out, and snapping his fingers in front of Myra's face, called her back to him. "None of that now. We'll not spy on our own."

For once, Myra's reddening of her cheeks had nothing to do with what she thought of the Maester of Triewes.

He softened. "Tell me about yourself Moira. I know we talked before but . . . What know you of your background? You mentioned, in passing, experiences with your gift prior to last night. How came you to that orphanage, and how did you manage your magic in their company?"

Myra opened her mouth to tell her well-rehearsed story only to realize she daren't—couldn't—lie to him. In its place, the ugly truth tumbled out of her. "I ran away from a hospital. An institution."

Her voice sunk on the last word, and she bit back hot tears of shame.

Aidan shifted as if to speak, and Myra rushed past his compassion. "Where you found me? That was a good nine hundred miles from where I started out. Three different trains. And I stole proper clothes along the way so that they wouldn't press me too hard when I got to— When I arrived at the— Once I felt safe."

Again Myra's last word whispered out of her. And now she did dissolve into tears. Ugly sobs for a forced confession to Mr. Aidan McIntyre and his stupid truthfulness. He knelt by Myra's quaking knees and waited for acknowledgment. It helped that he did not force his kindness upon her aching heart.

"Sorry." She wiped her tears with a sleeve. "You're the only one I've told."

Wordlessly he nodded and then stood sharply as the tumult from farther away in Grafford House reached their door at long last. Moving to stand between Myra and the incursion, he brandished his wand.

Laurel stepped through the door. Tight-lipped and closed-faced, she crossed the room to the hearth where she curtly tut-tutted. With a whisk of her own wand she set the spell straight and then turned to leave. At the doorway she paused and directed her gaze to Aidan. "Don't mess with that."

Aidan's nervous readiness snapped in the air around Myra. "Is everything all right?"

"It is now." Laurel's saccharine smile did not quite reach her eyes. She left the kitchen as quickly as she'd come.

Myra had decided that the quiet room needed a long case clock by the time either she or Aidan moved to speak again. Unnerving silence, it deserved to be broken. She cast her eyes to the fire and realized that there actually was something of magic she'd hoped to have answered.

"The Spells of Sedes Securus. What are they?"

Myra surprised herself by remembering the name. Aidan, too, seemed impressed.

"Basic security. Spells to cover any small physical access to a place—good for doors and windows and such. Useless against anyone coming from other planes but that's a whole other thing." Aidan waved off the host of unspoken concerns he'd inadvertently introduced. "And things are a touch irregular around here."

As if I hadn't noticed. Myra smirked, happy to have returned to safer ground at long last.

"Back in New York, we'd an office—a bolthole, really. And just the three of us. Walter, Kady, and I. But it was an official government sanctioned holding, none-theless. Proper protections. Not just hexes and jinxes. And certainly not a private residence." Aidan sniffed, looking around as Myra had. With judgmental eyes. "I would guess that's why our Mr. Grafford maintains no servants."

Myra's brain caught on an inconsistency. "But there's the coachman."

"Yes. Benjamin mentioned that when he was explaining to me how we were pretty much in charge of ourselves here. Robert got that one past James by explaining that the man doesn't live here, never steps foot inside to see . . . well, to see the sorts of things that us mages find handy to have around. I believe that Robert simply cannot give up the luxury of having a carriage ready to hand. Keeps the gossipers at bay, too."

Gossips. Myra knew all too well about such things. Thinking of what she had used to think wizards were like, she wondered if she had merely changed out one grave misunderstanding from . . . ords . . . for another. She asked, "What about the rumors? Broomsticks and familiars—"

"And pointy hats and magic wands?" Aiden lifted his own in illustration. "Much of it, I daresay, is true. The window dressings, anyhow, if not the lore itself. The New York office had the Knowing Cat."

"The knowing cat?"

"A feline oracle. Our answer to not having a Benjamin," Aidan clarified without clarifying at all. Myra was beginning to think he was purposely leading her from question to question. She opened her mouth to ask about Benjamin only to find Aidan speaking again, this time mostly to himself. "I wonder where it ended up going when we did not come back. Likely a happier beast now, wandering the streets, its own master at long last. Was too smart for its own good, you know, like most of its kind. Even the ones that aren't bewitched."

From the tone of his words and the almost gleeful look on his face, Myra suspected that Aidan disliked cats and was glad to be rid of the creature.

An education in itself, the small talk carried them through the evening, and heart lightened by Aidan's mere nearness, Myra found herself slipping into a state of security she hadn't known in ages. With it came the drooping of eyelids.

At length, Aidan noted Myra's sleepy nods and whisked the dishes to the sink where, thankfully, spells were in place to take care of the scrubbing and drying for them. That the shock of it all had just about worn off for Myra indicated to her how truly exhausted she was.

But she remembered Aidan's coat when she opened the door to her room. Hurrying to the still crackling fire —*with a flue protected by Spells of Sedes Securus?*—she fetched the now-dry article for the mage, again thanking him for his kind gesture. With a tight smile, Aidan acknowledged her words and fished about the pockets, ending his search with an "ah-ha!" of triumph.

"Thought as much." Aidan eyed the coin in his hand briefly before palming it.

"What is it?"

Myra regretted the question immediately as Aidan worked his jaw, clearly frustrated that he could not dissemble. For a moment, she wondered if, perhaps, hers was not the worst gift one could have.

Decision made, Aidan fished for another coin, giving both to Myra to examine. Two five cent pieces, with the familiar "Unites States of America" and stars ringing the denomination stamped into the middle, she could not tell what made one worthy of comment over the other.

Aidan explained, "I did not keep a coin in the pocket of my coat. My money was in my vest pocket. This coin was placed later, presumably by our hosts while you were wearing it."

Myra recoiled, instinctively alarmed, yet puzzled.

Aidan touched his wand to the offending five cent piece. "This one is a hollow coin and a trick used by those in our line of work. They often contain a bit of spell component, or sometimes even poison, and are meant to eventually work on they who carry it without suspecting."

Here Myra's instincts crowed their triumph over her waning curiosity. A chill trembled through her spine. *Poison!*

Aidan was quick to reassure. "It likely only tracks the carrier—that is a common use for such. I would gather that they slipped it into your pocket soon as they accosted us, opportunity and insurance in the event you bolted back to your friend, and our enemy, Doctor Silas Addair."

For all of his casual dismissal of the trick, Myra was heartsick. Aidan saw it.

"Don't take such actions personally, Moira. I might have done the same if I were them. And, besides, suspicion often has its roots in untruth. I knew the magic was there soon as they'd slipped it in your pocket. I'd let no harm come to you. Now sleep."

Chapter Ten

Myra managed, somehow, to sleep after Aidan's crushing revelation of the false coin in the pocket of his coat. Between heartache and utter exhaustion, her body simply shut down at last, giving in to soft pillows and warm bed. But morning came quickly.

Having forgotten that England was half a world away from her home, Myra found herself rubbing sleep-sore eyes as morning dawned upon Grafford House. She could feel tiny prickles at the edge of what she now understood to be her empathic gift.

The fire that crackled low in the hearth of her bedroom: it was of magical origin!

She sat up, fully awake. Had someone come into her room while she'd slept? Unlikely. As she had learned but yesterday, such spells were easily done from afar. Why have magic for such things if the wizard must still get himself dirty with soot and ash?

"After all, even the kitchen is magic to save anyone any real work." Myra eyed the glowing coals with sleep-deprived peevishness. The bite of the previous night's having had to scrounge for food was slow to leave her. Aidan had appeared not to notice, taking the oversight in stride. The juxtaposition of the grand house with its inelegant, improper occupants astonished Myra anew.

"Mother would be appalled. Still, at least I'm not crazy." Myra eyed her wand. She had left it by her bedside the night before, and it had been the last thing she had set her eyes upon as she had gone to sleep. Promise. Challenge. Pledge.

She wondered if she might be allowed to spend time with Aidan again today. Heartened, Myra climbed out of bed and quickly dressed so as to cheat the morning chill. Cold and damp, the outside air pressed upon the windows in the form of a gray, depressing fog. It rendered the already gloomy interior of the house even more shadowy.

She hurried from the room, swiping her wand from the nightstand in one quick motion. Best to be ready. Just in case.

"Goodness, I'm already thinking like one of them." Myra dove into the hallway.

"Like one of who?" Benjamin stood outside the door. Or rather, he leaned, idling against the dreary wallpaper as though he hadn't a care in the world and nowhere that he particularly had to be. The latter was probably closer to the truth, if what she had heard about the mage was true.

"Thinking like one of us, I suppose." He peeled himself up off the wall, adding, "Talking to yourself is very . . . us."

He grinned. "Think fast, Thales."

Instincts quicker than her brain, Myra grabbed the hastily lobbed object out of the air. It was a rock. A pebble, really. Smooth and white, it rode well in the palm of her hand. "Thales? What is that?"

Benjamin chuckled and indicated she follow him down the hall. "Thales lived over 2,400 years ago; Greek. In the distant past, the word for philosopher and mage were one and the same. Thales was one of the greatest. One of the Seven Sages, his work forms the basis of much of our magic theory today. Many attribute the aphorism 'know thyself' to him. I thought such an observation applicable to your situation."

'*Know thyself.*' Myra turned the phrase over in her head. Benjamin had but yesterday called himself a "living encyclopedia." Had his font of endlessly prosaic knowledge something to do with his particular gift? And if so, what was so terrible about her being exposed to it? Come to think of it, Myra couldn't feel anything from him, or the house, or the other mages within it. The distant tingling that she had gotten used to had stopped.

"The pebble is a ward. Hold it, and it will help you stay within yourself." Benjamin had not forgotten Myra's other question.

"Thank you."

"Thank me? Thank Miss Frampton—Laurel. It means we can actually hold a civilized conversation. She and I worked it up last night while you were off reading with the truth-teller. 'Tis Laurie's magic that made it possible. She quite likes you, you know. She's all our mothers—including Robert's."

Myra laughed. *Likes me? Then what was all that about Laurel's frowning, snapping temper in the kitchens?* With a thrill of fear she realized that, perhaps, things were less well off in Grafford House than even she had guessed. And the M.I. mages did not want Myra to know.

Benjamin's disarming grin reappeared then disappeared as quickly as it had come. He leaned close, whispering, "Don't tell your American friend. The recipe comes from some of the mad Doctor's old notes. Something I read a number of years back."

"Don't tell Aidan? Won't he just find it out with his truth telling?"

"Didn't you know? I'm much smarter than him."

Myra looked quickly to Ben's face to find the tease and found none. Instead, she found something else altogether. An intensity, a boldness almost frightening. She looked away lest she fall into this new emotion, wardstone or not.

Seeking escape and eyes catching on an open door, Myra felt a pull of a different sort. Curiosity. Unaware that she had slowed her steps until Ben stopped alongside her, she tried to guess at the room's purpose and failed.

"That would be the laboratorium." Ben leaned close to offer explanation. The same thrill that had shaken Myra but moments before seized her once again. "Want to see?"

"May I?" Myra's eyes widened, noting some of the wondrous items within. Arcane objects, some of them seemed to glow with a light all their own. Others, still, appeared to be wrapped in darkness.

Magic and mystery. Much like Benjamin, who had impertinently taken hold of Myra's hands to draw her in through the open door. She did not protest, lost in awe as she was.

A small table stood toward one side of the room. Prominent but not the focal point. On its faded and cracked surface sat a device unlike any Myra had ever seen. Glowing globes balanced upon thin rods, connected tenuously and clearly reliant upon the whole to stay in concert with one another. The whole contraption gave a lazy turn as Myra watched, and it set her to wondering if the rickety lectern was up to the task of supporting its charge.

"Kosmogramme. Map of the worlds from a wizard's point of view." Benjamin dropped Myra's hands and gave the contraption a gentle push. The arc of the spheres changed directions, dipping and whirling as they crossed paths, menacing one another with their apparently careless careening but never colliding. The table itself rocked but did not give. The whole thing made Myra nervous. She approached, now noting hieroglyphs scored into the orbs and guessing them to be composed of some sort of crystal.

"It's beautiful. Is it magic?"

"It's a map."

Benjamin's shrugged dismissal of such a marvel bothered Myra as might a gnat at a picnic. She persevered, leaning ever closer and saw that there was no possible way for the orbs to be made of something so ponderous as crystal. They seemed the stuff of air, of aether; the metal rods connecting them seemed as anchors set with preventing a flying off into space.

A map. How . . . understated.

Folding her hands behind her back so as not to inadvertently disturb the floating globes, Myra turned her eyes to the other articles within the laboratorium. Shelves along the walls held further secrets and riddles: A hat cloaked in ever-present mist. A brass disc containing a double ring of symbols and letters. A box containing a collection of small lumps of metal sat next to a jar of coins.

At this last, Myra suppressed a shudder and moved her hands to the pockets of her dress, ascertaining that they were still empty. No coins to spy, poison, or otherwise bother her hidden within. Brushing past her discomfort—her distrust—Myra tried to concentrate on what Benjamin was saying.

He had followed her gaze and now had the brass disc in hand. He turned its rings as he spoke. "This is a simple rune cipher. We used to have a better one but—"

Again he shrugged.

"But what?"

"It was lost. To the OtherLands. Simple error in delivery of a message. Someone thought they could cheat time by reading a message in the Ways," Ben explained, then stopped, noting Myra's blank stare. "The more advanced cipher discs—the wholly magical ones—utilize the added component of celestial time."

Myra simply stared. How? How was it that ords could find magic no longer useful in, well, anything at all!

He placed the cipher back upon the shelf. "Come, let's to the dining room to break our fast before James comes in and finds his room disturbed."

They were the last to enter the dining room. Between the pebble, the coin, the laboratorium, Aidan, and Benjamin's hot-cold interactions, Myra had much to occupy her mind as she breakfasted.

"Myra? Laurel will have you in the library after breakfast," James interrupted Myra's introspection at the closing of the meal.

Relieving as it was to know she would not have to

suffer any further discomfort at the hands of M.I.'s master mage, Myra was disappointed to be deprived of the opportunity to demonstrate what she had learned since the previous day's lesson. But it would afford her the opportunity to thank Laurel for the wardstone. Hastily rising, Myra made to leave the room. Benjamin's pointed clearing of his throat stopped her.

Ears burning with embarrassment, Myra crossed back over to her place at the table and collected her dishes, following Benjamin who had waited for her. "I'm sorry, I forgot—"

"Lessons with Laurel today." Though he had been the one to point it out, Benjamin pretended not to notice Myra's blunder.

She nodded.

"Don't let her try any of her Ways-walker's nonsense on you."

Again, Myra's head shot up, and she searched Ben's smile for the ruse. There was none that she could see. She was powerless to stop the scowl that crossed her face, to prevent her hands from none too gently plopping her breakfast dishes down by the sink. A sink that magically whisked the plates and cups into the air, sloshing them with soap and water and making them fit for use once more.

But they can't magic up a butler or a self-propelling tea cart? These people. A rottenness poked at Myra's insides, a sharp stick that would not leave her alone. She had woken up on the wrong side of the bed. No, the wrong side of the world. Briefly, she wondered what would happen to her if she attempted to leave. Deliciously dark images assailed her. Would Aidan try to stop her? Would Benjamin? Or might they simply stand by, glowering and posturing at one another while James cut her down with naught but a simple gesture from his wand? In her ire, she nearly forgot to question whether it was even her own anger that gripped her. The thought caught her up short.

These people were dangerous, no doubt. But, then again, that was exactly what Myra had been looking for, was, in all likelihood, destined for.

So the real question was that of sides: were these people "all right"? Caught up in the magic, Myra had taken up with the first pretty face she had chanced upon. And while the ousted M.I. team had proven generous—and, in some ways, even kind—she had to keep in mind that this was only after they had threatened her, called every act of hers into question.

But Aidan's gift . . . There was the truth-teller to consider. Him she had to believe.

"Myra?"

Myra refocused her eyes back on the present. She hadn't realized she still stared unseeing at the dish-washing process. Ben stood patiently by, a studied nonchalance coloring his features. He cared without meaning to. And he was certainly not going to let her know of it.

Aidan's near. Realizing again what her own gift was doing, Myra turned towards the open kitchen door. Thus she evaded Benjamin only to run directly into the American spy.

"Ah, good morning, Moira. Laurel told me to—"

"In the library. Yes, I know." Myra hurried past, not bothering to address Aidan's stunned expression, a particular blend of astonishment and hurt. It mattered little to her that she was being rude. Escape. She needed to get out of here. There would be time for apologies later. After all, that seemed to be the way of it in Grafford House.

The library was empty. Though not as much as upon the previous day. The furnishings had returned to what Myra guessed were their usual positions. The fire in the hearth burned low and fitful. Fighting the shiver that stroked her spine, Myra arched her neck to peer into the dark without actually entering the room. It was so quiet it seemed dead.

What made me think that? Myra clasped her hands to her elbows, hugging herself in apprehension. Small comfort. She stepped forward into the reaching shadows cast by the bookshelves in what dim light there was.

Over by the window, Myra.

"Oh!" Myra broke the muffled silence, hearing her exclamation of surprise drop like a stone. The air was thick, carpeted as the floor beneath her feet. She clutched Benjamin's ward and felt the magic of Laurel's voice flee from her head.

Curiosity outstripped fear. Myra approached the far wall, seeking the light. Laurel sat on the ground before the window, her face to the white rectangle behind gauzy curtains. She looked like a ghost. Pale. Unmoving.

Please be seated. Laurel's voice invaded Myra's head once more.

Myra hesitated. Miss Frampton was seated directly on the floor, her face towards the curtained window. Her eyes were closed.

I will return to you in a moment, my dear.

Please. Find yourself a seat. One that does not block my light, if you please. The last correction froze Myra in the act of sitting herself in the window seat opposite the wizard. Laurel had not opened her eyes, nor had her lips moved when she spoke within Myra's mind.

Sorry. In giving her apology, Myra's Empathy borrowed from Laurel's gift.

"Excellently done, Myra." This time, when Laurel spoke, it was from her own voice and it landed upon Myra's ears in the natural way. The mage opened her eyes and smiled. "Your gift is strong and your instinct more so."

Myra reddened under the compliment, feeling as though the praise were unmerited and watched as Laurel systematically bent one wrist, then the other, hugging her knees to her chest and flexing her feet within their small, elegant slippers.

"Well now. That was an interesting lesson," Laurel said, standing up and offering a hand to Myra.

"But I didn't learn anything at all!"

"Ah, but I did. You've proven singularly adept at Mind Speech, which is my most useful contribution to the team."

"I said one word."

"Come. Over near the hearth, dear," Laurel beckoned. "One word from you is all it took. The Mind Speech is a part of my gift. Your being able to take it for yourself was all the lesson I intended for today. Arms up."

Arms up? Myra was nonplussed as she saw a tape-measure appear in Laurel's hand.

"We need to get you some gear that actually fits

you," Laurel explained, reaching forward to invade Myra's personal space with her measure-taking.

Myra bore the mild discomfiture by casting her eyes elsewhere in the room. The fire had shrunk lower into its grate, impossibly staying lit in spite of its grave neglect. A clock ticked nearby, out of sight. The soft sigh of the middle-aged building around them gave mild clues to the activities of its various inhabitants.

"Were you in the Ways then?"

"In a manner of speaking, yes." Laurel's invasive yet polite touchings continued as she performed her work with simple efficiency. Bust. Underbust. Waist, hips, and inseam. Rise, shoulders, and arms. The gentle manhandling progressed from boring to downright silly.

"Is that where my visions take me?"

Laurel stood back and looked Myra up and down, clicking her tongue.

"Crouch."

The command shook Myra from her careful detachment, and she looked at Laurel stupidly. *Crouch? Why? That's not part of the script.*

Myra almost said as much, too, before her legs made the better decision for her, obeying the wizard's request out of resignation. Her limbs, it would seem, were tired of ill-fitting clothing. Not that she could blame them. Especially if she were to be called to the sort of casual flexibility she had seen from both James and Laurel. And come to think of it, even Aidan.

"Your visions take you into other people, into their magic. Whereas my gift takes me to other places," Laurel addressed Myra's question at last.

"But you spoke within my mind."

"Via the Ways, yes. And your gift allowed you to borrow mine."

"But how does it—?"

"Raise your arms again, please." Laurel's mouth creased into a tiny downturned bow of concentration. "So that fits you relatively well, yes?"

Myra nodded. "Yes, thank you."

"Good. For I don't think we can commission something new as quickly as I would like considering our current position within the government." Laurel's frown changed tack as her emotions shifted from mere thoughtfulness to full regret. The fact that the mage still refused to separate the team from the government completely was not lost on Myra.

Laurel sighed. "I'm a lesser mage, Myra. My gift is but one of the many. And even then, it took me several years of dedicated study under Florence Addair to learn anything past the InBetween. The worlds are layered, Myra. Onion skins nesting one within the other."

Myra's head spun. She'd asked for a lesson. She was getting one. Her eyes darted 'round her to Benjamin's books. Maybe later she could ask him to explain things to her. In the laboratorium. After all, it had a map didn't it?

"What colors do you prefer?"

"Sorry, what?"

"Colors. Trim. Have you any particular preferences? Any specific dislikes?"

Myra had lost track of Laurel's tape measure and now trained surprised eyes on the pen and diminutive pad of paper in the woman's hands. A series of measurements and other notes, neat and tidy, filled the topmost page.

Laurel had beautiful handwriting.

"Blues. I like any shade of blue. And I hate lace," Myra managed, somehow more thrown by the practical, normal question than all that had preceded it.

"And greens? Are you fine with, perhaps, emerald?"

A keen eye assessed Myra's appearance. An expert eye. Ben's words rose in her mind. *'She's all our mothers— including Robert's.'*

Myra nodded again, willing herself to speak so that Laurel would not think her soft in the head. But no words came, just acquiescence.

"Excellent." Laurel stepped back from Myra for one final once-over. "Robert will have you next in the drawing room. He'll be expecting you, as I've already informed him that you will be heading his way."

Halfway through yet another nod, Myra blurted out, "Do you always sit like that when using your gift?"

Laurel cocked her head to the side, expressing surprise of her own. She smiled. "No, but it does help immensely, as do all such undertakings that benefit from the ease of non-distraction. The more stress that I am under, the more difficult it is for me to both perform my magics and use them in concert with others. Now, off you go. Robert's not a man to be kept waiting."

Chapter Eleven

As Myra entered the drawing room, a shadow detached itself from a wall, proving that the darkened space was not quite empty. With a startled yelp, she fumbled for her wand.

The lanky figure approached. His teeth flashed in a wide grin. Benjamin.

"Robert is late. As is his habit." The explanation was brief and, as usual, did not involve direct eye contact. Instead Ben walked straight past Myra to adjust the wall lamps near the doorway. She made no move to assist, judgment on his having clearly fiddled with the lighting solely for the effect it would have upon her.

With a gasp, Myra remembered to clutch her ward-stone lest she fall to . . . to whatever magic Benjamin possessed.

"Thymesis." Benjamin's bright gaze was back on Myra.

"Thy—what?"

"My gift." Benjamin leaned against a table and tapped his fingers idly along the edge. "My curse.

Thymesis is the magical ability to recall everything with perfect clarity. Every sight, every sound, smell, and action—burned into this brain forevermore. Every memory. Every thought."

"That doesn't sound too terrible . . ." Myra ventured shyly, approaching the mage. Not so terrible that it had warranted James' warning the day before.

"Depends on the memories." Ben did not elaborate further, instead fixing his eyes downward to where his right index finger industriously worked at loosening a splinter in the table.

"Ah, and here we are. My apologies for my tardiness. Flue in the library was acting up again," Robert rumbled into the room, not in the least appearing to be hurried. Close at his heels ambled Aidan.

Great. Double trouble. Myra sighed inwardly as Aidan and Ben fixed one another with an appraising glare. The latter actually managed to rouse himself to some semblance of proper posture under the scrutiny.

Both Benjamin and Aidan seemed to know what was coming next. Each moved to stand facing Robert, arms bent at the elbow, feet an easy distance apart, heads erect. Their palms would have been facing upwards toward the ceiling had their hands not been balled into lightly closed fists. Thus positioned, they appeared both relaxed and alert. They waited silently without fidget or complaint. Myra noted that they seemed to have lost their competitive edge.

Robert stood in much the same way, only turned so that he faced them. From the slight look of discomfort on his face, Myra assumed that he did not normally perform whatever exercise this was whilst facing others. She hurried to copy the men, finding that the stance provided an ease to the body that Myra hadn't before considered.

Newly grateful for the specialized clothing she had been given—and no longer as irked at the process involved in measuring her for new ones—Myra hastened to follow along as Robert breathed deep and lowered his arms, quietly uttering the simple command: "Begin."

A slow step to the side—sliding, like a sigh from the knees. Myra attempted to emulate the graceful motion. She had already fallen behind as this gesture morphed into a slow, controlled bounce, each of her companions raising his arms outward in front of him. In unison, they lifted their hands, draping their fingers and palms behind the motion of their outstretched arms, much as the hairs of a paintbrush linger on a canvas behind the painter's stroke.

Myra lagged further than that, blushing and trembling in turns. Had she missed important instructions somehow?

Now they were pressing their palms downward, as though pushing the air into the floor at their feet, their knees bending in concert so that they sank down, down, down . . . and back up, up.

Mobile or not in her specialized garb, Myra felt clumsy. And dull. The motions were simple, controlled, and slow. Even ponderous Robert could easily keep pace. They were a gentle wave and she a boulder careening down a hillside.

"You're doing just fine, Myra. You'll see that it repeats soon enough," Robert noted her lack of progress through half-closed eyes.

Aidan added his own observation, "The trick is to

feel your weight, your presence in this place, and then balance it against the world at large. It is the finding of a way, rather than the forcing of a path."

"What is it?" Less wavery now that she had something else to focus on, Myra tried to match the men and found herself closer than at first.

"*T'ai-chi ch'üan*," Ben chimed in without breaking form. He sounded half asleep and yet his motions—Myra noted with a strange sort of satisfaction—were as beautiful and fluid as the rest. It was tempting to simply stop and stare. He slid his eyes sideways to Myra, triggering a flush to her cheeks as he continued, "A Chinese martial art. We use it to discipline our bodies and ourselves; to gain a mastery over impulse and open our minds to our surroundings."

He cracked a smile. "I read about it when I was ten."

And it is a universal study? Myra shifted her attention to Aidan, eager to avoid direct confrontation with Benjamin's brash flirtation. The American clearly knew the routine as well as the rest.

In answer to Myra's unspoken question—likely he had simply read her face—Aidan worked a small shrug into his motions. "Like Silas Addair's compound to combat the effects of Violectric Dampening, we adopted some of our British brethren's practices for training and education. What with our singularly shorter history, the fledgling agency in the States was looking for an easy way to keep pace with the grandfather spies across the pond."

Myra and Benjamin snorted their laughter together.

Quite possibly the first and only thing I've managed to do in unison during the lesson.

"Less rabbiting, if you please," Robert's complaint rolled into the conversation, a quiet roadblock against further chatter. By the time the short program had concluded, Myra found herself bedewed with perspiration. A glance to her companions informed her that, in this, she was not alone.

Robert rescued her with an explanation at long last. "To be an agent of the Crown—" Aidan pointedly cleared his throat. Robert ignored the protest, continuing, "One must tend to body as well as mind. Magic is, in many ways, a physical art. Mobility, ease of movement in combat, strength, agility . . . these are not far removed from what one employs in use of the gifts. Quick thinking, right judgment—these skills do not necessarily come naturally and must be nurtured, cultivated until an agent mage can act with precision and moral surety."

Moving off to a side door leading to a small closet, Robert left the team to their own devices for a brief moment. It gave Myra a chance to collect herself and steady her breath.

And she needed it. Robert returned to the small group bearing long staves, and Myra felt her heart do a flip-flop, performing the anticipated gymnastics early.

Distributing the weapons amongst his pupils, Robert gave Aidan and Benjamin a long, hard look. Myra watched, mesmerized, as the two wizards took to the next portion of the lesson with relish. While each blocked and parried with practiced ease, she believed that each would love to land a blow upon the other.

Robert turned back to Myra. "Don't worry, my dear. I won't be asking you to guess at movements at this stage. And if this is too advanced, we can always just—"

"How goes the lesson?" James stood in the doorway to the drawing room. He had an eyebrow raised at Robert, a silent challenge to him for having almost softened the next drill for Myra's sake.

Myra solved the problem by grabbing a stave for herself and adopting the stance she had seen Benjamin strike before engaging Aidan. "It's going great. Honestly, it feels good to move about a bit."

And it did.

Robert made as if to toss his own stave to James, prompting more frantic leaps from Myra's heart. James was to be her sparring partner? James?

"No thanks. I'm not staying. 'Twould throw the numbers off." James held up a restraining hand. Robert kept his weapon and motioned for Myra to wait for him. The room rang with the crack of wood against wood, punctuated with the hard rush of heavy breathing. It served to mask most of Robert's hushed doorway conversation with James.

Still, Myra managed to catch a few fleeting bits. Something about Laurel and her inability to participate in the goings on in the drawing room. James' resulting anxiety. When Myra's eavesdropping concluded with Robert's asking, "Would you like my family's physician to see to Laurie?" she stopped up her ears altogether, feeling a tremor of fear quake through her. Laurel was ill? How much so? Was it the Dampening?

Gripping her sparring staff, Myra tried to mirror Aidan's motions as best she could from her position as spectator. She swiped ineffectively at the air and wondered if she looked as uncoordinated as she felt. Such forceful displays were unseemly for young women of her age. And yet, even with no combatant of her own, Myra felt a rush of exhilaration. The sensation of homecoming was stronger than ever; companionship and kinship—

I lay flat on my back in the cold, dark alleyway, gasping for breath as unforgiving hands clutched at my throat. Robbed of my ability to scream, I could only struggle ineffectively under the crushing weight of my attacker.

My wrist, the one which held my wooden stave, was bent at an odd angle. Broken. Useless and screaming with pain, the shattered bones let go the only weapon I had.

My assailant leaned close, burning me with eyes that glowed like coals within a hood of black. My lungs spasmed once, twice, as the fingers at my throat, thin and hard as bone, found greater purchase and squeezed.

A chuckle like a death rattle rose in the throat of he who murdered me. Recognition blossomed through the stars clouding my fading vision. My wand! I had a weapon still, one even the enemy could not escape, one I hardly dare use.

Instinct drove the words as I found my magic—

"Stop her. Don't let her speak!"

A gentle but restraining hand moved from Myra's arm to her mouth, stopping the garbled words from pouring from her lips. Greedily gulping in the oh-so-sweet air of the Grafford House drawing room, she lay on her back, willing herself into calm submission.

Another vision. Ill-timed and too horrible to think on.

Myra trembled as Aidan's hand moved from over

her mouth, freeing her as he helped her to a seated position. With shock, she noticed that her right wrist was not, in fact, broken, though her other hand had drawn her wand. The worried faces of Robert, James, and Aidan crowded around her, asking their questions without words.

"I'm fine," Myra croaked, arcing her neck to look for the conspicuously-absent Benjamin. Aghast, he sat far to the side.

As well he ought, considering the monster that I am. Myra let go the futile buoy holding her soul so that she might drown in her self-loathing. A doctor. Grafford House had its own doctor. *I'll have to run. Again.*

"Is she—?" Benjamin stirred, his face still a mask of fear and anguish.

"Out. Out with you." Robert turned to the other mage with a suddenness and fury belied by his usual taciturn state. "Now."

Benjamin fled without so much as a backwards glance.

"Damn it, Robert." Shaking his head, James stood and followed the other mage from the room.

Looking from Aidan to Robert, Myra tested how far out of their good graces she had actually fallen. "I'm sorry."

"Hush now." Aidan leaned in close once more, patting her hand awkwardly. "You tumbled flat out on us. Gave quite the scare. Not hurt are you?"

Myra shook her head.

"One of your Empathic fits, yes?" Robert's brow was still dark with anger. "I never ought to have let young Ben—"

Myra caught on at last. "Wait. It was Ben's gift that I . . . ?"

Good lord! With what sort of memories does he wrestle? A new chill struck Myra, and she began to tremble again.

"Come. Let us get you some tea, my dear." Robert helped Myra to stand and did not let go her hand as they exited the room. Warm and reassuring as was his wont, he escorted her to the library, Aidan walking ahead a few paces and fretting.

Chapter Twelve

Maybe it's magic tea. A mug of steaming comfort had been pressed into Myra's hands. Aidan and Robert sat in armchairs to either side of her. Honor guard. Insurance against another of her fits. Both men sipped in silence, each absorbing his version of events.

James had made it to the library before them, hauling in the promised tea service. How he had known was a mystery to Myra. Ben was notably absent, and James had immediately gestured to the small feast he had laid out before them. "Eat up, Myra. We've decided to have our main meal in the library today. Cosier. Good for rattled nerves."

Myra was unsure if the words were meant to carry mild reproof, but habit had the words ready on her lips, "I'm sorry."

The answer came in the form of a teacup, accompanying plate of victuals, and hard-to-read grunt. As such, Myra—and the rest—had not yet endeavored to move the conversation forward.

Uneasy embarrassment thickened the quiet air of the library.

Myra picked at her food, knowing she was being rude but fearful of what might happen if she attempted to force anything into her churning stomach.

"Like all wizards of his age, Benjamin is a lesser mage," James began the laborious process of cutting through the tension. "But, unlike Laurie, Aidan, and yourself, Myra, he has at least two major gifts."

Robert flicked his eyes towards James, daring him to continue.

Aidan looked positively furious. "You truly hadn't told her yet?"

"I had warned her. I had warned him. I thought it sufficient." James managed to sound as though he shouted back in spite of his having kept his voice even and low.

"He's a Necromancer." Myra blinked in surprise. She had pulled the information from Benjamin during her . . . Her what? Reliving of his memories?

James nodded. "Combine that with his Thymesis and—"

"And there's no way on this earth that you should ever have let Moira near him without the proper precautions!" Aidan jumped to his feet, reaching for Myra's hand. "Come. We're going."

"No. You're really not." Laurel stood blocking the doorway. Ben fretted in the darkness behind her.

"Sit down, Aidan," Myra breathed. It was all coming together in her dizzy head. She fixed distant eyes on M.I.'s Necromancer, grounding herself. "That's why you don't go outside. Too dangerous."

Aidan did not sit but moved off to the side, passive if

grumbling. That he had his wand at the ready, tucked up under one crossed arm, did not escape Myra's notice.

"Go on. Tell me of Benjamin." Already Myra could feel her heart swelling with empathy for her fellow mage. She again flicked her eyes to the hallway, a silent invitation, but already Laurel and Ben had vanished off into another part of the house.

"To say that our Mr. Egrett had a troubled youth would be to greatly dissemble the facts." Robert eased himself forward in his chair so that he could better address Myra. "Both his powers surfaced around the point of Emergere—a wizard's coming into his or her powers—"

"Five or six years of age. Give or take," James volunteered from his perch near the fireplace.

Robert frowned at the interruption. "As I was saying, he came into his own on both the Thymesis and Necromancy. We know this because he could remember it all with perfect clarity after we found him. Oh, damn, I just fixed that!"

This last was to the fireplace which had begun to smoke into the room. Robert heaved himself to his feet and began his unhurried shuffle towards the hearth.

"They don't even know where we are. Why don't we just let that one be, Robert?" James approached, waving thin tendrils of smoke with an offended hand.

"Safety is safety, my boy," Robert grunted as he knelt. "My house. My rules. You know as well as I that it's only a matter of time until the other side catches on and stops focusing on the web to watch the spider. And with silence from Julius, we've no promise that the Department is still looking out for us."

"Out of courtesy for your service to the Crown." Aidan curled his lip.

"Stephen's actions change nothing. He acted alone."

"He burned my team with his acting alone. And you can't believe that your Department doesn't know you've taken me in amongst your numbers."

"We're safe, Agent McIntyre."

"Safe." Aidan's eyes flicked to Myra. "Looks that way to me."

James dismissed the bickering, coming over to Myra to finish his lecture. He smiled at her, and for once, his voice was the softest in the room. "Where were we?"

"Benjamin's Emergere." Myra surprised herself at how easily the words rolled off her tongue.

James nodded, picking up Robert's dropped thread. "Normally, the abilities of a young mage flicker and die without the aid of Addair's cure for the Violectric Dampening. We can only oversee so much, and as the ords don't know of us, we often simply don't know of a wizard's emergence until it is too late to reverse the damage. In Ben's case, because of his specific gifts, we were able to find him in time to preserve his powers."

"I resurrected a man." Ben's voice startled Myra— and everyone else, it would seem—as he walked into the room unannounced. "And I was six."

"Needless to say, M.I. was quick to cover up the repercussions from the incident. And Benjamin stayed with me from then on," Robert finished. He shot Benjamin a glare as the young man moved further into the room to stand toe to toe with James.

"Laurie fixed it up good this time and suggested I refrain from sparring for the time being." Ben opened his hand to M.I.'s leader. From her vantage point, Myra could not see much of the bauble but could only tell that it glinted in the firelight like a gemstone. "There will be no more lapses, I can promise you."

James jerked his head, an indication that Benjamin's apologies were misdirected.

Myra sucked in her breath as Ben turned to face her, his eyes dulled by misery.

"Don't," she stopped his words with one of her own. "Please. Don't apologize for magic that you cannot help, for horrors lived that few can scarce imagine. Now I know what I know, and we know what we know. And with that, we can be more careful than simply avoiding things we don't understand and . . . and . . ."

Myra hadn't realized she was crying until a thickness in her throat stopped the rest of her words, and hot tears splashed down onto her splayed hands. "This magic. You could go mad from it, couldn't you?"

Benjamin smiled his winningest smile, though this time it came forced. "That you could. But only if we let it. The thing with magic is, for all the trouble it makes, it usually also presents a solution. So . . . Thales? Whether you want them or not . . . my apologies?"

Myra eyed the hand held out to her in friendship, wondering at what point in its lifetime that it had been broken. Thrusting the memory from her, she reached out a trusting hand of her own. The handshake sealed the pact. Aidan gave witness by rising to his feet and storming off to join James by the fireplace.

"Well, then," Robert provided his all-purpose and tension-breaking useless statement to the mix, rattling the tea tray as he reached for another scone.

The newfound peace, so much as Robert's actions, allowed Myra to realize at last how hungry she actually had become. The same heart that had cursed the magical machinations of the Grafford House kitchen now gave thanks for its bounty. Pastries and cold cuts disappeared from her plate within moments.

Newly freed from the double burdens of guilt and James' restrictions, Benjamin perched on the chair next to Myra—the seat that Aidan had abandoned in his huff. Insult to injury. The American agent buried his ire in conversation with Laurel, who had reappeared moments after Ben.

Myra reached for an egg, peeling it absently as she tried to absorb the events of the day, discoveries both exhilarating and frightening. *Never a dull moment with these people, I'm betting.*

Flake, flake, flake, bits of shell fell to Myra's plate like broken hailstones. Out of the corner of her eye, she saw Ben lunge forward towards her.

"Griggs delivered."

Two words and Ben had command of the entire M.I. team. Laurel's quick hands had a cloak winging its way to her waiting shoulders per the silent instructions of her wand. James was arming himself to the teeth. And Robert . . .

Even considering the earlier events of the day, Myra had never seen him move so quickly. The man was not only on his feet in an eye-blink, but had acquired hat and cane and was already halfway to the door before Benjamin could finish a curt nod of acknowledgment. And while the dim of the library may have been partly to blame for Myra's impression, it seemed to her that the memory of dark clouds hung about Robert Grafford's head, and his fingers glittered with the bright hope of lightning.

All this Myra noted as Benjamin snatched at, not the egg within Myra's hand, but the hand itself. Blushing, she could only sit and fight the ripples of illicit thrill bubbling up from her chest as Ben gently turned her entrapped fingers so that he could better view his discovery in the firelight.

"Looks like one of Brackenbury's new teams does know how to do their job. They've been on and off tracking two outliers—"

"Wizards? Ords?" Laurel broke in.

"Doesn't say. But they mean to close in. So we will have support regardless of who the enemy turns out to be." Benjamin eyed the strange charcoal-gray marks that marched around the upper crown of the boiled egg.

Myra couldn't make heads nor tails of it all and concluded the message must have been written in some sort of language of magic. No matter, for Benjamin could decipher it, and it was good to see that the Magical Intelligence Department of the British government had some of its spark back.

Save for he who had turned the tide.

Benjamin left Myra's side and, taking up Robert's newly vacated seat, opened upon his lap a book he had grabbed on his walk past one of the library shelves. The rest of the team might have been stone statues for all the attention he paid them after finishing his galvanizing announcement.

Ben might be resigned to his fate, but that didn't mean he had to necessarily witness it.

Aidan was slower than the rest. For his part, he was content to rouse himself from his fireside post and dart his measuring glance about the room. His eyes fell to Myra last. "You'll be fine staying here alone?"

Myra opened her mouth to remind Aidan she would not be alone—though it was painfully obvious that he already knew that—and was interrupted by Ben's snort.

"Three to two is good odds, Mr. McIntyre." James stood in the doorway with crossed arms. "You, yourself, are welcome to stay behind, if you would like."

Chapter Thirteen

In the end, Aidan went with Laurel, James, and Robert.

Which left Myra with Benjamin. Benjamin and a whole heap of books, actually.

"Come, Myra. I've the perfect reading nook for us."

Us? He thought it a good idea if they read together? Still, Myra forced back her trepidation. Things were fine between her and him. They had shaken on it. She had her wardstone. He had his caution. If Aiden thought her safe with Benjamin, then that was that.

And, besides, horrid memories he might have, but those were not necessarily Ben's fault, now were they? And the idea of spending time alone with the handsome wizard, side by side . . . Yes, that would do rather nicely after the day they had had.

The Art of War by Sun Tzu. Mandatory reading for spies the world over.

Everyone in Grafford House had read it. Read it multiple times. Well, all save for Benjamin, obviously. Director Henry Brackenbury had made all members of the newly formed MI2 study it. Their enemy, the mysterious and menacing Dr. Silas Addair, was an expert in its contents. And it was now Myra's turn to become well-versed.

They sat together in a cozy corner of the upper story of Grafford House, taking turns at reading sections, Benjamin occasionally stopping to clarify where the text's meaning fell short. His casual interruptions prompted Myra's face to flush in admiration. She wondered how many languages Ben had learned with his Thymesis. The text they had in hand was his own construction, worked from the 18th century French translation of the original.

"Skip this part. Too outmoded for our use," he said, reaching across to flip through to the next section. Smiling at Myra, he held his hand on the page, and for whatever reason, she found she could not look away from his sinewy fingers and wrist. And not for her having fallen into memories of its mangling just that morning. But because the nearness of Ben had startled her. It had taken away all ability to decipher the words on the page.

Stupidly, Myra stared at the open book. It wasn't a fit. Nor a memory. This was wholly new, and she found it frightfully exciting.

"Sun Tzu too much for you?" Benjamin sought her gaze.

Myra's blush deepened. "Yeah. Something like."

And just like that, she had killed the mood. Ben leaned back, removing his hand from the page. " '*Si votre armée et celle de l'ennemi sont à peu près en nombre égal et d'égale force, il faut que des dix parties des avantages du terrain vous en ayez neuf pour vous.* If your army and that of the enemy are about equal and of equal strength, you must have ten parts of the advantages of the land to—' "

A loud bang from somewhere downstairs had both Myra and Ben jumping to their feet.

"Shh." He raised an arm in front of Myra, cocking his head to listen.

"Ben! Benjamin! We need you. Quickly, please," Laurel's voice sounded, shrill and urgent.

More muffled banging could be heard. They both hurried to find the source of the discord, Benjamin turning to snuff the lamp with a wave of his wand before shutting the door behind them.

Myra and Ben spotted the rest of the M.I. team in the hallway outside the drawing room. Laurel led the way, still calling for Benjamin—Myra wondered why she simply hadn't used her Voice—while Aidan and James struggled to hold up Robert who slumped weakly between them.

"I'm here. Heavens, what happened?" Benjamin caught them up, leaving Myra to trail uselessly behind.

"Robert's been shot." There was no keeping the wobble from the words, though Laurel managed to keep her voice quiet.

Oh, no, Robert! Myra's hands flew to her mouth, and she felt the sharp sting of tears. She watched as James and Aidan gently helped Robert over to the couch. Remembering her wardstone, Myra sought its protection. Her hand slipped into her pocket, and she witnessed the proceedings from afar, not feeling she should stay and yet unable to bring herself to leave.

Benjamin knelt by Robert's side, speaking to him in low tones. Seeing Robert nod in response, even going so far as to crack a smile—broken by pain as it was—went far in securing relief for Myra.

Aidan came to stand close by. "He'll pull through, Myra. It's more the inconvenience than anything else at this point."

"But Benjamin . . . ?" She dare not look away from Benjamin's magic, having never seen the like from any of the team. Glittering sparks, somehow harboring a darkness within, surrounded his fingers and the blood-stain that marred Robert's waistcoat.

"Ben's the only one of us with magic right now." James joined Aidan and Myra to offer explanation and, more importantly, block her view of the proceedings. "Basic healing spells; Robert was not so far gone as . . ." He cleared his throat, continuing, "We'll recover, of course. The Dampening is but temporary now that we're away from the press of electricity."

"What can I do?" Myra blurted the words before giving the thought due consideration. *Help. Ha.* She hadn't the knowledge to do what needed doing.

Regardless, Laurel beamed at her. "Giving Benjamin some of your Empathy would help, dear."

Myra nodded and sent out all the soothing she could. To Robert, too. *Benjamin the only one of them with magic, James?* While she knew what he'd meant by his words, she wanted to show him. And so she sent out a radiant calming aura to them. James, Aidan, and Laurel all.

"So what exactly happened?" Benjamin rose to his feet and came to join Myra and the rest.

Robert, so far as Myra could tell, now slept. His face had lost some of its lines of pain, and his breathing was regular and deep. With the observation,

Myra herself now felt that she could breathe easy at last.

"Do we need to go . . . ?" James eyed the patient.

Benjamin shook his head. "I'd rather we stay here."

Laurel took up the briefing, speaking in hushed tones, "Brackenbury was none too happy to see us."

"But he was glad to have our help," James interjected.

"Yes." Laurel clarified, "They were wizards, the two that DMI were tracking. Hence the caution on moving in to take them. To make a long story short, we—the four of us—ended up in the service tunnels beneath Holborn after accosting the enemy at the now-derelict Station 57. Brackenbury's men? Nowhere in sight by then."

James stepped in. "They got what they wanted, the two unknown mages. Some bits from the old power station. It was in pursuing them through the tunnels that we discovered none of our gifts worked. Laurel's Mind Speech disappeared, and we were caught in a blaze of bullets."

"With no backup from those MI2 ords. We were stuck in the dark and fumbling for our pistols like a bunch of rookies." Robert sat up to add his own grumbling complaint.

"No magic," Ben mused. "Which means that someone is still using the electric lines, even if that station is no longer in operation."

"Which means," James broke in. "That we were likely set up to fail. Either by—"

"Don't say it," Laurel cautioned.

And with that, he did not have to. The silent implication hung more heavily in the air than if it had been said aloud. Myra's eyes found their way back to Robert during the long moment. He noted her worry and managed a smile. "Wizards take injury well, my dear."

"When we've magic at our behest, sure." James stomped away. "Take that away and we're as vulnerable as any ord. Remove the gift, and we bleed as fast as anyone else."

Chapter Fourteen

In the end, Myra was left to wonder how the team's informant next made contact. For a few days later a message from Griggs had the wizards of M.I. once again readying for action. This time with one marked change: Myra was to go with.

Aidan had, of course, raised his objections. Immunity to Violectric Dampening or not, she was a 14-year-old girl who should not be subject to the dangers posed by such a mission. James made the point that, unless Myra anticipated a lengthy imprisonment within Grafford house, then she had better make her magic useful to the team. Myra, herself, closed the issue by declaring—to her own surprise—that she was rather glad of the opportunity to come along.

Their task was a simple one. They were to determine whether the day's threat came from the same people who had escaped M.I.'s grasp earlier in the week. Observe and learn and then report back to Griggs. If all went as planned, the agents of MI2 would remain unaware of the wizards' presence as they followed through on their protection of England's monarch.

All piled close together in the Grafford House carriage. Myra found that she enjoyed the comforting buzz of her companions' tension within her Empathic gift. To feel as they did, all in accord. She had not realized the want of such belonging in her short life. Still, she stirred ripples into the pond by asking, "What is it they want with the Queen?"

"Her death." Robert turned phlegmatic eyes on Myra.

Stunned, she found she hadn't a response for such a chilling, simple statement.

"You're scaring her," James muttered. As if they couldn't feel Myra's apprehension radiating off her.

Aidan scowled. "And while you are technically speaking truth, Robert, that's not the whole of it. Is it? I second Myra's question. Why such an attack? What motives have they for such?"

"Perhaps it's for the affront of daring to wear a blue sash," Laurel intoned.

"Bah. Maclean's ravings never sounded like what James proclaimed. Not our James, of course." Robert leaned in, clarifying for Myra and Aidan's benefit. "Silas' son. The one our government eliminated 'for the good of man and mage alike.' "

"His gift, Myra, well, we never really figured out how it worked. He was a lesser mage, of course. But with his mother, Florence, having spent so much time in the OtherLands . . . Let's just say that his ability, best we could tell, was similar to that of an Observant's—the gift of reading the universe and seeing its patterns."

"He knew things. Impossible things. And paired with

a darker mind?" James shuddered. "Even death did not silence him. Or so Addair's agents would have us believe. They seem to live under the perpetual hope of a second coming, a rightful reincarnation denied when Benjamin would not use his gift to bring Silas' wife and son back to us."

"And hence the blue sash." Laurel gave a crooked smile. "The 1882 assassination attempt by Roderick Maclean was, in his words, guided by two symbols, the color blue and the number four, given him by a higher power. He was, in the end, deemed insane, but the events started within DMI a furious search for signs and portents. And if this attempt is being orchestrated by the two mages we met in Holborn, they are legitimizing Maclean's attack from ten years back and demonstrating that Addair's reach is deeper than the government will own to."

"And hence our secret involvement, lest we bias anyone against what information we gain," James concluded, looking out the window with an air of finality.

London rolled past, a moving picture framed and matted by the carriage window and trees of Hyde Park. A shortcut. One that presented less interference to their art. Which had Myra seditiously wondering if DMI wasn't better off without its reliance on wizardry. Shouldn't the public's safety not be subject to the whims of Violectric Dampening?

Nervously, Myra brushed her fingers against the hilt of her wand, cleverly hid within its bodice holster but easily accessible should the need arise.

"We're not likely to need the art today." Robert leaned close. "No matter what anyone may have told you. Observe. Report. Let the MI2 agents do their job."

"We're here," James spoke up, angrily brushing past Robert's caution.

The carriage rocked back and forth, the driver seeking a place for his occupants to disembark and finding none. Myra crooked her head to see out the window once more. Throngs of people, coaches, horses, and yet more people crowded the circle where the roads met. And suddenly the plan made sense to Myra. All of London turned out for a glimpse of the Queen and her entourage, if able. It was to be a very public game of cat and mouse, an opportunity both to draw out the criminal element and make an example of him in view of all.

Around Myra the tension grew pointed, hands strayed to wands and whispered words passed back and forth.

"Myra, we're to head up into the park," James cut through her thoughts, drawing back from the open carriage door. "Robert and Aidan will take up positions by the Wellington Arch, 'round the other way. Laurel is staying here. Easier for her to work when she's not in danger of being walked into or trodden upon."

"Best grab that wardstone now if you don't wish to have my voice in your head, Myra," Laurel cautioned with a wink.

Myra gulped, unsure she would be able to hear Laurel even if she screamed and shouted within her head, thrumming as her nerves were. She stepped from the carriage on wobbly feet, and suddenly felt the glow of a smile warm her insides, Aidan proving her wrong, as was his wont.

"It'll all go fine, Moira." His whispered words at her

back were such that Myra wondered if the mage had actually spoken them aloud.

Thanks. Uncertain she had actually been able to isolate Aidan from the rest for her Mind Speech, Myra hurried forward to join James, blushing furiously over her daring. She clutched the wardstone tight as they wove their way through the crowd.

Slowing as they reached the arch that marked the entrance to Green Park, Myra pondered James' silence. The hard-faced government spy was back—not exactly a huge shift from the demanding and often brusque mentor. Slipping the wardstone into a pocket so as to free her Empathy, Myra found the clarity she sought. James was indeed greatly unhappy.

James, she's circling your way. They're early, and I'm not sure if— Yes, I believe something has changed the plans and the men— ROBERT! BEARDED. BOWLER. BROWN CAPE.

Myra was barely able to process Laurel's urgent update and warning before the Queen's carriage crested Constitution Hill—just as planned, but apparently frightfully early. Timely or not, the monarch's presence gave rise to a hearty cheer from the crowd.

"There. A second one." James darted into motion, grabbing Myra's hand and jerking her along. The scene tumbled before her eyes as she sought to stay upright and running.

A woman's shrill scream cut through the excited din. Near, but not close. Myra whipped her head around in time to see a man fall to the ground, pinned by no less than three others. A gun clattered to the ground unspent, the weapon separated from its shooter. The bowler that Laurel had spoken of rolled to a stop some feet further on. Somehow, Myra found her eyes locked to Aidan's through the surging crowd.

And then two loud bangs and more screaming.

At Myra's side, James swore. Wand out, he had the other assailant in his sights, a man standing not thirty feet from the Queen's carriage, smoking pistol in hand.

Oh, no! Myra's heart tried to climb its way up her throat, hammering all the while. Frozen and useless with fear, she watched helplessly along with the rest of the onlookers as the attacker fired again, a puff of smoke and scattering of sparks erupting from the barrel of his weapon.

James has his wand out. Why doesn't he do something? Panicked, Myra reached for her own wand and felt a gentle hand on her arm. James. He turned to her, smiling—smiling!—and shook his head ever so slightly.

Myra looked back, seeing the man on the ground, lifeless. Or at least, none of the Queen's men seemed to feel called to do more than stare at the unmoving body.

"Let's go."

Myra shot another look to James. His wand concealed neatly back beneath his coat, he showed no more emotion than one might spare in cutting a loaf of bread. "It's done, my dear. Let the Crown's men handle this."

A ragged cheer—far less robust than the first—rose from the pressing crowd. Myra darted her eyes back to the carriage in time to see the Queen's waving hand retreat into the depths of the coach. Safe. Whole. They had not failed, then. Not utterly, at least.

And just like that, Myra's legs buckled beneath her.

"Got her?" James spoke over Myra's head to Aidan

who had, miraculously, made his way through the throng to catch her mid-swoon.

"He dead?"

Myra quickly found her strength, but leaned upon Aidan's arm as he inquired into the health of the second man.

Yes. Laurel spoke for them all. ***And, James, you'd better hurry. Brackenbury's men noted your actions and are likely to come calling.***

Myra, James, Aidan, and Robert redoubled their pace, hastening as they neared the Grafford coach. They were barely in with the door swung shut before Laurel hit them with the full force of her voice—speaking, not Mind, and therefore all the more chastising. "What part of care and caution did you not take with you? Three—three!—of Henry's men spotted you. And killing the attacker—?"

"The director can have his new ords look into it all he wants. They'll find naught but evidence of a squib." A strange smile tugged at the corner of James' mouth. "More proof that they're worse off relying upon such gadgetry." Playing with the window sash, he avoided Laurel's accusing glare.

"He was Addair's man, James James. Addair's."

"There's the other one. The one who never got a shot off."

"He was paid, I'll bet. A distraction so as to give the real threat actual chance." Laurel pressed, "We will need Benjamin's help, now. Your fault."

"So we need Ben's help, then. He's an agent, yes? That's what he's there for," James growled, shifting so that he matched hard glare for glare. "You contact Julius?"

"You know he hates it when I do that. But, yes, I did." Laurel extinguished her ire, forcing James into the position of lesser man. "He'll do his best to come at nightfall."

The conversation ended there, leaving behind uncomfortable silence and many questions in Myra's mind. Questions she would likely have to wait until evening for the answering. Asking James or Laurel was certainly out of the question. For once, Myra understood her companions' habit of not meeting her gaze. Perturbed, she fixed her eyes on the scenery rushing past the carriage window, a fast reprise of their tense journey played in reverse. Out of the corner of her eye, Aidan tried to catch her attention, something she pointedly ignored. The last thing she wanted to see in her mind's eye was Aidan's sympathetic face transposed over the memory of a man falling dead upon the ground.

Myra fled to the sanctity of her rooms upon arrival at Grafford House. Nobody stopped her. Perhaps they understood.

Understood, having killed men before. Myra forced down the heavy sickness rising in her chest. Fear. Or maybe it was guilt. She couldn't tell and that, in itself, was telling.

Emotional compass spinning erratically around its dial, Myra found her eyes similarly out of order as numb hands knocked blindly at her washstand. The shallow bowl tipped sideways, sloshing its contents over the table and down the front of her dress. The water pitcher was not far behind, its own wobble halted by its greater weight. It steadied her.

I saw a man die. Myra confronted her white-faced reflection in the age-frosted mirror. "I saw a man die," she repeated the thought aloud for the benefit of the empty room.

No matter that she had seen Stephen and Kady perish in the warehouse fire. Had even felt the flames, the incredible pain, firsthand. This was different. Somehow. And in ways she did not want to guess at.

Eyes back on the water swirling into the washstand bowl, poured by her shaking hands to replace that which had spilt, Myra wrestled with another unwelcome thought: Ben would understand. He could tease out the differences that her mind shied away from. But then again, Myra wasn't even certain she was thinking of Benjamin. It was Aidan's face that popped up in her mind's eye.

Magical Intelligence. Murderous Individuals.

It was no wonder that true gentlemen stayed far from such work.

A knock sounded on her door. Soft and all the more jarring for it.

Aidan.

Without quite realizing it, Myra discovered she could manipulate her gift with greater dexterity than ever before. As such, the newfound awareness washed over her with less surprise than she might otherwise have felt. Like the fleeting bouquet of fragrance spilt into the air by flowers, she could tell who of the mages was nearby by something that could only be described as the scent of their power. Even their changing emotions came tempered by individuality and harboring certain signs.

No storm ever came unannounced lacking the presence of worrisome clouds, just as no nighttime darkness fell without the sliding shift of eventide. And Myra was finding that she could read the sky.

Myra opened the door to Aidan, not bothering to wipe the effects of her hasty bird bath from hands and face. Far better to not have to explain the wide slash of wetness that still marred the front of her dress.

Leaving the door open behind her, Myra returned to her dressing table without a word, inwardly both seeking an excuse to draw Aidan out and hoping that he might simply note her state and leave her be. Perversely, she also hoped he might directly ask how she was so that she might lie to his face. This last wish was granted. Aidan worked his way to Myra's bed and sat, watching her all the while as she needlessly busied herself with her hair. He asked, "How are you feeling?"

"I saw a man die. Of course I feel horrible." Myra's heart skipped a beat. The lie had come too easily. Or, perhaps, it wasn't a lie at all. Like her emotions, the truth seemed to have gotten all twisted up with falsehood such that Myra could not separate one from the other. She only knew that she felt better than she ought.

Best let Aidan sort that for her.

"It's okay to feel comfortable with this work, Myra."

Myra froze, darting her eyes to Aidan's reflection in her table-side mirror. Myra, not Moira. He had been quite careful not to mar her name. So he had caught her lie?

She waited, something about his statement feeling but half-finished.

He rose, having said his piece and given Myra a long look.

It occurred to her in the moments after he left that

Aidan might have been seeking solace from her instead of the other way around.

"But if I do that for each of you, there'll be nothing left of me," she complained to no one in particular. She fiddled with her hair for another minute, staring down at the darkened patch of damp cloth on her dress slowly shrinking into nothingness. It would dry soon. She did not wish the rest of the household to see her clumsiness with the washstand and conclude that she was out of sorts. Under no circumstances did she wish anyone else to ask how she was feeling.

This time her lie was to nobody save for herself.

"Oh, blast." Myra's eyes again darted to the small indentation Aidan had left behind in her coverlet. She needed to clear the air with him. Perhaps together they could revel in the fact that nobody here ever told them anything, and they were little more than guests in Grafford House.

Exchanging empty dim room for empty dim hallway, Myra found, not Aidan McIntyre's retreating backside, but Mr. Benjamin Egrett. He leaned against the wall as was his wont. Arms folded, his face unreadable, he prompted, "They told me what happened. And that you handled yourself very well. Congratulations."

He's on his way. Laurel's Voice robbed Myra of the opportunity to respond.

Pushing indolently from his post, Benjamin flashed a wicked grin. "Come, Myra. Time for an interview with a dead man."

Chapter Fifteen

Hurry, if you please. It would not do to keep Julius waiting in the alley. The neighbors might become inclined to talk. Master of impatience, that Laurel. Myra kept her eyes on Benjamin as they walked downstairs to meet the rest. An interview with a dead man. Was he serious? He couldn't possibly be serious. Maybe he meant something else.

'I resurrected a man. And I was six.'

But . . . but there were laws of nature to contend with! Magic was nice and all, but surely, one could not simply bring a dead fellow back to life for interrogation purposes.

Aidan would be incensed.

Turning the corner, Myra's suspicions were confirmed. Aidan, James, and Robert stood in hushed conference by the door that led out back to the mews. She could feel Aidan's anger from ten paces distant.

Benjamin inclined his head. "James? Might you fetch the runegramme for me?"

"Is it in your laboratorium?"

Your laboratorium, Ben? Myra eyed the two men.

Seeing how Myra looked to him, Benjamin clarified, "A runegramme is another tool for decryption. Far better than a cipher disc, however, it can work as a translation device for languages in the OtherLands as it uses the runes of magic instead of symbols from this world alone."

"And fetch my pipe, too," Robert chimed in.

"What's that for?" Myra whispered, wide-eyed.

"My nerves."

A carriage stood in the alleyway out back of Graf-ford House. Black. Large. Obvious as to its purpose now that Myra knew what game was afoot. A man waited in its shadow, also conspicuous.

Not a spy then. Myra judged the man—Julius, appar-ently—as he strode forward to shake Laurel's hand and hold quiet conversation. Open, expressive face topped with a mop of tight black curls, the man had a jumpy demeanor, a quivery sort of smile. He looked like a person who was always thinking, always learning. He wore no ring on his ungloved hands, no hat upon his head. Pronounced jaw and wide cheeks, Julius might have been entering his twenties. And with his looks might well leave him still a bachelor. But he was not unpleasant to look at, his dramatic and overgrown features somehow coming together to make a whole.

Nothing about the man was subtle. Or forgettable. *Definitely not a spy, then. That or he's right awful at it.*

A gentle hand on her arm guided Myra backwards into the doorway. Robert. And helpful, as her legs shud-dered beneath her, threatening to give way as her eyes lit upon the carriage's cargo, now being brought into his home by Ben and Julius.

A body. They're bringing in a body. Myra gulped, focusing on getting air in and out of her lungs as she turned to go back inside. *Following a body.*

The door closed behind the small party with a quiet click. Acceptance. Confirmation.

Too late for turning back now.

"You will not have my gift for your use if you make her watch." Aidan stretched out a protective arm, a barrier between Myra and the rest of the mages.

"Frankly, I don't see that it is your call to make." James ignored Aidan, looking past him to Myra. "You can't pick or choose when it comes to magic, discarding or avoiding that which makes you squeamish."

Ben interjected, "I agree with Aidan. James, come on, man, you know that this—"

"He's right." Myra stepped past Aidan's restraining arm. "You cannot choose in magic. However, you can choose your actions. That person right there? You could have spared his life, turned those bullets into flowers, surrounded the Queen with shields and only kept our hands so dirty. We could have avoided use of Benjamin's most terrible power.

"But we did not. And those actions should be seen through. By all of us. It's part of it all—repugnant or otherwise—integral to what you do and what I've signed on for by allying myself with the team." Myra saw, in her mind's eye, the moment on the lawn with James, her hand straying towards her wand, ready to strike. She was complicit. She had lost the right to pick and choose, was not one to run away when things became scary.

"Bravo, Myra." Robert's words were nearly lost to the shadows, heard by none save for Myra herself and, perhaps, Aidan.

The rest acknowledged Myra's statement with nods of the head, small smiles. Only Ben did not meet her gaze. He fixed his eyes on the body beneath its coroner's sheet. "Let's go."

"Right!" Julius moved to step forward with the rest, hesitating as all eyes turned to him. "I can watch, right? I mean, nobody said I couldn't."

Ben ignored Julius, looking to Aidan. A challenge lay in wait, cousin to the usual competitive animosity between the two. "Can we rely upon you, then?"

"I, too, am—to borrow from Myra—complicit and cannot justify being elsewhere and doing elsethings."

"A simple 'yes' would suffice, truth-teller." Benjamin curled his lip and walked past, pushing the wheeled, cloth-draped cart down the hallway in dramatic fashion. High dudgeon followed him down the hall as he maneuvered the body to the waiting servants' lift. The team followed in his wake, a strange, disaffected funeral procession.

"Where are we going?" Myra's whisper to Robert rang loud in her ears. Irreverent, her mistimed curiosity.

"To the basement. Some magic does not belong to even the pale light of nighttime, the wholesome air of a home," Robert whispered back, the tenor equally harsh in the somber quiet. "We'll be taking the stairs, however. That dumbwaiter was not meant for heavy use and the corpse alone shall tax it greatly. Stay close and watch your step."

A door opened to a staircase both dim and dank. The full force of the stale must enveloped the wizards. Myra crinkled her nose, reaching gingerly for the handrail and thinking none too charitably that it smelled as though the Graffords had been diligently collecting the famous London fog for many generations.

And their careful collection of mildewed miasma is escaping. Myra gagged, descending into the darkness with the rest.

Wands aloft, M.I.'s mages called into being the same illumination that had confronted Myra and Aidan upon their first meeting with the team. Eerie against the weeping brickwork that pressed in upon the narrow stair, the pale white points of light bumped along with every step downward, downward, downward.

Myra suppressed a shiver, realizing that she ought to have raised her wand as well. But then, simple though it seemed, she did not know this spell. And nobody commented on her lack of participation, so that was that.

They reached the bottom of the cellar stairs. Benjamin awaited them. The body still lay upon its bier, covered in its protective sheet.

"Here." Aidan materialized out of the darkness to hand Myra a long match. "We all must participate, lest we not provide the spirit a hospitable atmosphere in which to return." He indicated a row of candles lining the mildewed baseboard.

"No spooking the spook, eh," Julius' voice rang harsh against the cellar walls. His joke clearly unwelcome in the somber, stale atmosphere, the ord shuffled dismally back into the shadows, cowed. His own match he clasped, forgotten, in his fingers.

Myra wasn't certain there was enough air down in the cellars to even light candles. Or maybe the squeezing of her lungs was due to her growing fears.

The light in the basement of Grafford House steadily grew as the M.I. mages went about their business. Myra followed Aidan to a section of unlit candles, accepting the wavering flame from his match to hers. Different than the illumination given off by the mages' wands, this light was less utilitarian and more symbolic. Warm and yellow, it softened the hard edges of the space, driving both the shadows and the stink of unused air from the gathering of wizards. And Julius, who now participated hurriedly, lest he be uninvited from the arcane proceedings.

"Myra, I would ask that you refrain from doing—or even intimating—magic for the time being," James kept his voice low as he spoke close in Myra's ear. His eyes swept the room, cautious.

With the magic Benjamin was about to undertake, it made sense that they all refrain from further use of their gifts. Around her, wands were being extinguished. Myra nodded sagely.

"M.I.'s director does not know of you, Myra. We'd like to keep it that way," James correctly interpreted her look. "Julius . . . Well, he's a smart man and can make his own conclusions. But anything an ord guesses at is likely to be wildly inaccurate. For your safety and his we're opting to keep him in the dark for now."

"I'll be careful." Myra slipped her hand into her pocket in illustration. She still kept Laurel's wardstone close.

"Good girl." James gave a small smile and left her to assist Ben more directly.

"Do you know what they're about here?"

Myra startled as Julius spoke to her. He stood close behind, a warm smile on his face. No menace, no jest.

Just polite conversation. Like they had met in a park and he was commenting on the weather.

She shook her head, nonplussed.

"Julius Griggs." He performed the tiniest of bows.

A gentleman, then.

Myra pulled back the offered hand of introduction, feeling stupid. "Um, Myra Wetherby."

"American. Yes?"

She searched his face, alarm pulling at her and stealing any answer she could have possibly given. He read her look wrong in any event, responding with an awkward, "I'm sorry for your loss."

Nonplussed, Myra spoke without thinking, "Oh, I'm not—! I mean, I'm not one of—"

She forced her flustered words to die lest she say something altogether foolish.

Ally or not, the man was an ord.

It seemed to her that her sudden leap to silence fit his idea of what grief looked like, for he looked away and fiddled with the edge of his cuff. "A lot of things have changed over here for us, too. And not merely from our loss of Stephen."

Something in the hardened way in which he said "changed" set a shiver through Myra's Empathy. Julius likely he had his own opinions on what had happened to DMI's original team. A true ally, then. *Why the caution, James?*

"They told you who I am, then. Yes? No?" Surprise rendered his squashed face handsome. Myra decided in that instant that she quite liked Julius. He took her smile as encouragement and continued, "I am . . . what is it your lot calls us? An ordinary. But an ordinary who makes extraordinary things out of the mundane."

He paused for effect, waiting indulgently for Myra's puzzled look. She obliged.

"I am an inventor. I make the gadgets that the agency relies upon. That the Queen herself relies upon. I dunno if you've been briefed on the events of today," he leaned close, a rapturous look enveloping his features, "but the Queen came under fire this afternoon—that's how this fellow got himself killed"—he jerked a thumb at the wizardly proceedings occurring near the sheeted figure—"and I got to see my latest and greatest in action."

Truly curious, for she had seen no invention, amazing or otherwise, nearer to the Queen than the carriage itself, Myra prompted, "And that would be?"

"A bullet-proofed—! A bullet-proofed parasol," Griggs finished his triumphant reveal in a whisper, guilty as a schoolboy in church. "Has two layers of silk with a fine mesh betwixt the two. Like chain mail."

Myra's face must have indicated her doubts, for Julius moved to insist on the point. He stopped himself as a low, droning murmur filled the cellar. They both focused their attention back on the wizards of M.I., rapt at what they were seeing.

The coroner's sheet had been pulled back so as to expose the face of the dead assailant. He lay still upon his platform. His face looked peaceful in spite of the scrapes and cuts which marred forehead and cheeks. Somewhere within that placid skull lay the piece of shrapnel that had killed him. Myra wondered if he would feel it upon waking.

At the dead man's side and holding his hand under the thin sheet, sat Benjamin, his head bowed.

James, Robert, and Laurel proved the source of the

droning. The words were those of magic, though Myra hadn't enough knowledge yet to understand them. Aidan stood by, unmoving and unmoved.

The sharp intake of breath at her side proved that Julius Griggs had quicker eyes than Myra. The droning increased in volume, grew frantic. Laurel shuddered and swayed. The motion drew a look of concern from James.

The white cloth twitched. Or was it a trick of the light? The candles, each and every flame, seemed to flicker in unison. Once. Twice.

"Aidan," Robert broke from the trio of chanters to call the attention of the American.

"It's no matter. He won't come," Benjamin whispered through gritted teeth. Beads of sweat stood out on his forehead. They glistened in the yellow light of the chamber, bright stars dotting a dark sky. For the mage seemed as far away, as inaccessible and unapproachable, as the heavens themselves.

"I'm finding his soul." Laurel sank to her knees, waving off James' concerns. Whether she meant Benjamin or the deceased was unclear.

A hand tightened on Myra's arm, forcing a scream up into her throat where it died before it could make entrance. Thankfully, for she did not wish to bookend the day with unwanted drama.

Julius clutched her arm, unaware that he did so. His eyes were glued to the scene before them, bright and intense.

The dead man sat up. Laurel slumped, spent. The chanting stopped, and James held Laurie in his arms, crooning comforting words. A temperamental shake of her head revealed she was not unduly hurt.

And good thing, too. For the reanimated corpse was now trying to stand, Aidan and Robert keeping him seated with much effort. The protective sheet had slid even further down, revealing a massive gash in the dead man's chest.

Myra did look away then, burying herself in Julius' sleeve before she had time to think of her actions. The goal was not to retch.

Griggs' comforting arm slid up and around Myra's quaking shoulders. A hissing sound, like air leaving a balloon, sounded from across the room. Myra didn't have the heart to look.

"I give you voice," Benjamin's command sounded deep and clear. He was back then, from wherever he had gone. Back and brought a dead man with him.

A handkerchief appeared before Myra's terror-stricken eyes. A second kindness from Julius. What she was to do with it exactly, she wasn't sure. But she was grateful for the gesture, nonetheless.

"I won't. I won't go," the dead man screamed at long last, still fighting Robert and Aidan for freedom.

"Do something, man," Robert yelled, his complaint mingling with that of the unruly, undead guest.

"I take your arms, I make them heavy. I take your legs," Ben bellowed. The thrashing of the prisoner ceased. Myra looked back on the scene, carefully keeping her eyes on the dead man's face.

His eyes rolling in his head, forced into near-paralysis, M.I.'s prisoner spat at Benjamin, "Take it all, magus. Take all and see if Our Great Master does not do the same to you tenfold."

"Did you act alone?" James rose to face Addair's man.

"As if I would tell you," the corpse turned his attentions to the questioner. " 'S not like I have anything to lose."

"We can put you in places you scarce conceive of in your nightmares." Laurel stood by James' side, strong once more.

"A Ways-walker. It was you who dragged me here, then. Not this broken man-child with power bigger than him."

"Shut it. Or we'll not bother saying 'pretty please' next time we've a question," James hissed. "Did you act alone?"

"Yes." The dead man offered up a spectral grin.

All eyes turned to Aidan.

Head cocked to the side as if listening to music only he could hear, M.I.'s Maester of Triewes appeared dumbfounded. Long moments passed. Myra found herself wishing for even the monotony of a longcase clock, if only to break the oppressive silence and drown out the painful drag of the dead man's lungs against the air.

"I . . . I cannot tell," Aidan stammered at last. He passed a shaky hand before his eyes, "It's as if— It's as if, in passing through the veil, he has lost that which separates truth from lie."

"What do you mean?"

Aidan bristled under James' challenge. "I mean that the dead don't follow our rules. They don't see things as we do, and so it all comes out—the truth, the lies—it all comes out blurry. Mixed up."

James answered with anger of his own, "Had we known that, you could have stayed upstairs and read like you'd wanted to."

"Had I ever questioned a dead man before today, I might have not bothered coming down here," Aidan shouted back. "My team didn't have a practitioner of forbidden magic within our ranks."

"Out with you, then." James pointed a finger, quivering with rage, towards the stairs. "If you're going to give him more than we get, then out with you this instant."

He needn't have bothered. Aidan had already stormed off into the corner, his lips pressed shut in mutinous animosity. The reaction automatic, Myra tried to soothe the angry American with her empathic magic, earning a nasty look herself from James.

I'd forgotten! She made her silent apologies, thrusting her hand into her pocket to grasp the wardstone. Aidan's grateful glance made James' ire worth it.

"Well, I'm not going to hold him here if we don't actually make use of the moment." Benjamin sweated through his words, still concentrating on holding up his end of the magic.

James whirled on Addair's man. "You acted alone today. There is none of the power on you. I cannot see what role you could possibly play—"

"Then you are blind!" he cried, arching his back so that the sheet once again fell away. There, low on the corpse's chest, was emblazoned a tattoo. From where she cowered alongside Julius, Myra could only tell that the symbol was complex, done completely in black ink, and had been greatly destroyed by the coroner's knife. "Addair isn't looking amongst the gifted for his glorious revolution. The answer is to be found in us, the greatly unworthy, who strive for answers. We seek the song of the universe and strike down all who do not raise their voices in chorus. Your Queen, she too will—"

The corpse grew rigid. Killed mid-sentence.

"We had our answer, yes?" Benjamin stood, speaking in his normal voice once again.

"Would have been easier to just lift the sheet from the first," Robert rumbled his complaint. "Come, let us repair upstairs. Griggs, the corpse is yours."

Chapter Sixteen

It was a somber team that returned upstairs to Robert's home. Dreary disappointment followed them up from the basement like the ghost of the man they had interrogated. And, like those superstitious few afraid of the spirits that inhabit the dark spaces, they left the candles burning until they had gained the top stair. Robert himself summoned enough of his art to turn and snuff the flickering lights with a wave of his wand.

"I'll take the Queen's watch, then." Laurel turned to leave. In the arguably slight better lighting of the upstairs, Myra thought she espied a sickly greenish cast about the woman's cheeks and lips.

Myra couldn't blame her, feeling rather nauseated herself.

"Let's just hope she's sleeping," James said, concern lighting his stern eyes.

"Let's just hope she's dreaming." Correcting the mage with a small smile, Laurel managed to gain a bit of her fire back before turning on her heel and escaping down the hall.

James hesitated. Torn. Clearly desirous of more words with Aidan, he paused mid-stride. But whatever he had to say to the Maester of Triewes would have to be voiced later. He followed Laurel down the hall.

"The Ways. That's where you go when you dream, Myra." Robert had noted Myra's curious glance. "It makes for excellent opportunities for our Walker."

The lift doors opened, whining and whirring their complaint at being put through their paces twice over the course of the evening. Benjamin wheeled out the cart and its re-dead occupant, huffing with effort. Griggs hurried to help.

"Myra?" Aidan turned concerned eyes on her, that same sharp gaze taking in the limp square of linen still clutched in Myra's quaking hands.

"Does that count as having killed him once or twice?" Myra's question surprised even her. Why was that the first place her mind went?

"Ords only die once, Myra," Robert's gruff but kindly answer commandeered the conversation. It drew her attention onto him and off Griggs' handkerchief.

Aidan snorted, his face hard. "So's much the pity."

Myra wondered at Robert's strange choice of words. Ordinary folk only died once. Did that mean wizards did not?

"Leave off," Benjamin came to the rescue, having left Griggs to escort the dead back to its hearse. "Myra, truly, you do not look like yourself. Come, let us go to the library and leave the completion of this task to Robert and Aidan."

Myra nodded dumbly. She felt . . . not herself. Numb. Cut off from her companions both magically and emotionally. Grateful to leave the whole mess with the corpse, forbidden magics, and even the fascinating Julius Griggs behind, Myra allowed Ben to lead her away.

Calm. Solid. And warm. Myra had all but forgot how comforting the heart of Grafford House could be. It had her thinking back on her tumultuous arrival and how they had brought her here, half-prisoner, half-ally—and half-dead with fright and exhaustion. Even then, the stalwart influence of the space had worked on her with a power all its own.

She looked about her as Benjamin dragged two high-backed chairs towards the roaring fire. Myra sat, belatedly remembering the loaned handkerchief still in her possession. The thrill of guilt quaked through her tired bones. She hadn't even said goodbye. Perhaps she might still—

"Myra." Benjamin inched closer to the edge of his chair until he sat nearly knee to knee with her. She did not realize she shrank from his presence, the memory of his magic, until a small frown creased his face. Shame.

"I'm sorry," Myra squeaked out, shame of her own for having judged so plainly. But his powers were fearsome. Aidan was right on that count. Surely Benjamin understood?

He understood. Understood all too well. He leaned back. He seemed disappointed.

What does he want from me? Myra cringed, this time at herself. They sat in silence. Each wandered his and her own thoughts, absorbing the events of the day in their own way. It was, in its own quiet way, relieving. Inwardly she thanked Ben for the kindness.

"He's gone, thank the gods." James entered the

library. He threw himself into one of the open chairs and flung an arm up over his eyes. "What a day, eh?"

Myra jumped, grateful for the distance she had put between herself and Benjamin. Aidan and Robert filed into the library a moment later.

"I forgot to say goodbye," Myra began her apologies. Guilt over Griggs' handkerchief burned a hole in the pocket in which she had secreted it. A blush crept unbidden into her cheeks.

What, is everyone in this house completely mad? Are you, Myra? Her mother's voice sounded in her head, reminding Myra of how many rules of etiquette she had broken today alone.

"Goodbyes? To the ord?" James peeked out at her from where he sprawled in his chair. Genuine surprise dotted his features. "Good riddance to him. Any longer and he might have been guessing at your purposes here. Or did you not notice him cozying up to you at every chance?"

Myra's fingers had quested their way into her pocket. She stopped short of Griggs' handkerchief, confused and hurt by James' insinuation. "Maybe he has a right to know. Julius is our informant. Look at what he did today for us. Surely that alone makes him trustworthy. Aidan?"

"Don't look at me." Aidan backed away from the challenge. He had had more than enough confrontation with James thus far today.

James snorted, replacing his arm over his eyes. He muttered disdainfully, "You know so little about ords."

"Until two days ago, I was one!"

"You've never been an ord, Myra. Whether or not

you knew." It was Benjamin who stepped in to calm her. "That marks a difference."

"I don't see how," Myra snapped back. And truly, she didn't. A week ago, magic wasn't real. A week ago, the gift she carried had been misdiagnosed as madness by every doctor up and down the Midwest corridor.

Aidan's sympathetic eyes were breaking her. *It's like he has my gift.*

He understood what she was trying to say. More importantly, he understood her thoughts just now, could read her like an open book. And yet he made sure to stay out of it. Myra had to fight her own battles.

"That tattoo, then." Robert claimed the last chair, forcing Aidan to remain standing. An outsider. Likely the gesture was unconscious. But James smirked his approval.

"Cut up as it was by the coroner's knife, it was still pretty plain from his tattoo that the Queen's assailant was of the Order of the Holy Flame." James sat up so as to more fully engage in the conversation. "Aidan, that's one of the local—"

"I know the Flameists; we have 'em, too," Aidan growled. "Mucking meddling lot, they occasionally get in the papers and make all manner of mischief for us proper practitioners of the art."

"Good cover for us, though," Ben interjected.

"Right on that count, yes," Aiden ceded the point.

"But do we believe him?" Myra inserted, earning the scrutiny of four pairs of surprised eyes.

"Of course we—"

"That, Myra, is an excellent question," Ben beamed at her. "Laurel believes that the other fellow was paid to distract from the real threat. Wrong positioning. Caught all too easily. But why should we trust an ord who, as he himself pointed out, had nothing we could hold over him?"

"That discounts our only lead," James pursued his objection.

"Or merely gives us the dose of caution that we need just now." Robert shook his head. "Steve's dead, lured by a tantalizing, all-too-easy rumor. The director, seduced into dropping us by his own misinformation. And Griggs—"

"Fine. What do you suggest, then?" James' accommodating tone slithered through the quiet room, dangerous as his temper.

"I suggest we—you—follow the lead. Attend the Flameists' next meeting. Quietly. With an eye to observe and nothing more." Ben sat back in his chair, unthreatened by James' glower. "You know, what we used to be good at."

"What will you need?" Robert sighed heavily, moving to rise.

"Pen and paper and a needle," Ben's response came crisp and businesslike. He winked, losing the starch. "And Myra? The handkerchief, if you please."

Myra gave up Julius' handkerchief with a furious blush. Embarrassed into silence, she couldn't summon the nerve to defend her still having had it in her possession. Instead she sat and watched Ben scribble down various notes and turn from his calculations to industriously poke holes in the cloth. Now acting as surety in the team's clandestine communications, Myra was certain the object would never be the same again.

The party then broke, each scattering to different parts of the house: James back to Laurel's side, Robert and Aidan off to parts unknown, Ben to his studies in cryptography. And Myra?

No one objected to Myra retiring to her rooms. Sleep took her before her confused emotional jumble could intervene.

Chapter Seventeen

"Alice. Look at me, Alice."

I blinked and tried to turn my head away from the stab of light which assaulted my face. I found that I could not. Something was holding me in place upon the lumpy bed and pillow. A man in a doctor's coat stood by my bedside, a square of pale yellow cloth in his hand. My heart strained within my chest, emitting frantic and erratic beats underneath a thin shift of a gown. Utter terror.

"You're out of humor. Your control of your power is incomplete. 'Tis my fault, really." The man moved to adjust something by my side. I could feel a strap tighten on my wrist, and I knew without hardly realizing it that my other arm was similarly pinioned. I opened my mouth to protest.

"No, no." The doctor's finger came to rest upon my lips. "We need you calm, lest we have another accident."

He turned away, speaking to someone else, someone I could not see. "Double this time, Hales. Anything less appears to be useless. I'll be watching her should anything go wrong. This is no longer inoculation. This is transformation."

He turned back to me, demanding, "State your name."

Alice. Was that it?

"Age?"

I don't remember.

"Do you know where you are? Do you know why you are here?"

At this, I shook my head as best I could, now feeling the strap held across my forehead and a tangle of wires that tumbled down past my neck and shoulder. My lack of actual responses prompted a frown from the man. He seemed to hesitate in his purpose. My frantically hammering heart found new cadences. The moment stretched for eternity.

I rolled my eyes around as best I could, seeing, at last, the other white-coated man, dingy tile walls, and a table full of large glass and metal jars with more wires sticking out. The doctor leaned in to place a gag in my mouth, some strange yet horridly familiar thing that tasted of leather and wood. My ears began to buzz, my skin prickle.

"On my mark. Now, Hales."

And then an explosion of pain. Lots and lots of pain.

Myra had the sense not to scream. But then, she had clamped shut her jaw so hard that her teeth hurt. Alone within her bedroom in Grafford House and with no recollection whatsoever of how or when she had gotten herself there. All Myra knew was that she was shaking with the memory of the most horrible dream she had ever had and that she was now safely back within her own mind.

"Dream or vision?" Myra whispered her question to the darkness and slid from the bed. She did not want to know. Just as she could not bear to stay lying down after what she had just experienced. "No, not me. Alice."

Breath catching, Myra had trouble saying her sister's name aloud.

But it hadn't been her Alice. It hadn't. Her sister simply felt different to Myra on some unnamable level. A coincidence then? Or confirmation that what Myra had just experienced while abed was nothing more than fears working their way through her psyche?

Sitting in a chair by the hearth, Myra tried to remember the man who had hurt her, the doctor, and found that part of the memory already fast fading from her mind. Strange. And more proof that whatever she had just thought she had seen was likely the product of an overactive imagination.

Yes. Yes it had to be. She remembered now the mark upon the doctor's hand, a strange reddish design of lines, like lightning but also reminiscent of the tattoo found upon the would-be-assassin they had questioned in Grafford House's cellars.

Every fear of hers had rolled together into one horrid nightmare. Relief swept through Myra at the conclusion. It prompted a new series of tremors, and she rose to look for her wardstone. No sense taking chances now. As she approached the bed, her ears buzzed and her skin prickled. Magic.

Some emotional outburst somewhere in the house.

Myra listened with her Empathy, sorting the threads.

Aidan and James. The former was likely getting his dressing down at last. She reached for her robe, tugging slippers onto toes that protested in the chilled late-night air. But curiosity was fast warming her soul. That and her steadfast ability to remain aloof from the sparks of anger that drifted through the house, tugging at her magic. That itself was a heartening discovery and one that merited further exploration.

Which is what she told herself as she padded to the door, pocketing her wand and ignoring the other voice in her mind. The one that warned her of the impudence of sneaking about at night like a burglar.

She paused, considering. Laurel. Laurel had not looked well. Myra's heart found its excuse. With James being most concerned with Laurie's health, it was only right that Myra check into the source of this most worrisome midnight outburst from him.

Again, Myra's dream rose to haunt her. So what if the woman whose pain she had experienced wasn't her Alice? She was somebody and deserving of their help, having connected with Myra's gift as she had. This woman, this Alice, must be a mage like them, yes?

If she was real. Of this Myra still could not be certain. And she lacked the details she would require in order to tell the team. Where was this happening? Was it even happening? Who was the man in the white coat? With such clear electrical power at his disposal, how could M.I. even attempt such a . . . Was it even a rescue?

Myra knew nothing. To tell them would be to confess her deepest fears. Truths of her soul she had managed to hide from even the likes of Aidan. To tell James would be to have him force her back into the connection. She had done it before. She could do it again. Especially as Myra had more control than ever over her gift.

"It was a dream and nothing more," Myra reassured herself through gritted teeth and continued onward. Real people simply did not do that to one another.

Clutching her wardstone tight, lest a stray wisp of her own anxiety give her away, Myra crept towards the disturbance she had felt from upstairs. Warded off as she was, she had to rely upon other clues. An easy task, considering the raised voices emanating from a study at the far end of the hall.

". . . Even if she's somehow his, she herself doesn't know," Aidan said.

"If that is the case, we can turn her. Use her ourselves. If there's anything to salvage, that is," James replied.

"You're not using her and then casting her off. Like she's some sort of soldier. She's not you, James. She has only the barest understanding of magic, her gift, the life we live."

"Barest understanding, bah. Talent she has and more control than she lets on; Myra is learning fast, and I'll not hear you covering it up with your careful truths," James scoffed. "You have read the truth of her, you who talks of whiffs of guilt in the bouquet of her emotion— or whatever flowery ways you like to put it, and it's up to me to determine what we do with that knowledge. An agent died—"

"Three agents. My team was there, too."

"—An agent of the Crown, on soil and in an op that was not under my control," James rolled over Aidan's interjection, incensed. "Nevertheless, I have to answer the fallout. Nevertheless, I have responsibilities. Before you insult me, truth-teller, you tell me how I really feel. Look into my eyes, and tell me to my face that I don't care what happens to her, to you."

If Aidan gave an audible response, Myra could hear not hear it.

"That's exactly right." The quiet intensity of James' rejoinder had the knell of finality about it, and fearing discovery, Myra clutched her little white stone to her chest and turned to flee from disconcerting truths and into deeper darkness.

She ran smack into a wizard. Benjamin. He smirked. "Gee, I take it that thing works?"

Stammering, Myra tried to work up an excuse that did not sound as guilt-ridden as the blush spreading its heat across her cheeks.

"You're a bit of a sneak, aren't you, Myra." Benjamin eyed her sorry state with more silent laughter, softening as he noted the tears which threatened to drown her eyes. "Come, Thales, you do realize that makes you more 'one of us' than ever, right? What is it you think we do here? Sneak. Spy. It's disreputable work and why mages were picked for such work in the first place. It's not respectable. It's not genteel. But it can be wonderful."

Myra studied her toes, imprisoned in their warm slippers.

"Come. Let us to the kitchens." Ben offered an arm. "Rule one of sneaking: have a good excuse ready for the moment you're caught. I, for one, am fond of a late night repast."

Grateful, Myra looked into Ben's eyes. She caved. "You do the cooking."

Her weak joke was rewarded with a grin.

Rakish, but still soft as the kindness by which he had rescued her from her faults just then. It was a strange sort of way to be a gentleman. Altogether too sure of himself, too bold. And simultaneously gentle. Myra hadn't known that such could be attractive in a man. With Benjamin's constant posturing to Aidan, it was hard to spot this side of him save for in the dark of night with the lamps turned down.

Myra's early judgment of him had been precipitous. Like the gaslight, Ben's spark was tempered differently than Aidan's. He was not hard like the rest. Not loud, not scary, not overly flirtatious, even. She was sure that he was aware of his handsomeness, of course. But it was to his credit that he did not wield it as a weapon, as Aidan was wont to. Benjamin was, in fact, borderline apologetic about it.

Alarm bells rang in Myra's head, herald to more blushing, stammering, and awkwardness. She felt Benjamin step back from her, allowing her the space needed to collect herself and meet him when ready. He truly did know a frightening amount of things.

The bravado was warranted. No mussing of the hair required.

She followed him down the hallway, stopping at his whispered, "A shortcut."

With that, Benjamin whipped out his wand and made a sign over the paneled wall. A person-sized, rectangular portion shifted to the side. Darkness yawned beyond.

He held out a hand, as if sensing Myra's apprehension. It was then that she realized she had stopped clutching the wardstone in her pocket. Her fingers clasped his, and he drew her forward into the hidden passage.

"You'll need better control over your magic if you're to use this shortcut on your own. It's not an advanced trick, but it is something," he explained, whisking the door shut behind them. Myra and Benjamin were left to inky blackness. "Now. I'd like you to take this next spell from my mind, Myra."

Benjamin's wand sparked a pinpoint of light, dulled so as to not task their eyes in the pressing dark.

"But I don't—"

Ben's finger pressed against Myra's lips. "None of that. It's my turn for a lesson now. Call it the price of snooping about and listening in on the conversations of the Misters James and McIntyre."

He moved off further down the narrow passage, and Myra hurried behind so as to stay within the edge of his wand light. And then the light vanished!

"Ben—" Myra hastily swallowed her exclamation, fumbling for the little white wardstone. For she could feel a rioting of emotion outside of herself. She had to block it off. She must hide.

The point of light reappeared several feet off. It illuminated a corner and Benjamin beckoned. Angrily, Myra caught him up.

"This isn't a game, Thales. You learn or you get hurt." Venting his own angry whisper, Benjamin bent close and pointed with his wand. A steep stairwell fell away from them not three feet off. "When I say to try to do something, you do it. That's how the team works."

"From what I can see, your team is hardly that!" Myra's whispered retort cut the close air.

"How dare you."

"How dare I? When I overhear James talking like I don't matter. Or Aidan who only tells the truth because he has no other choice. Or you who—" Myra had the sense to bite off her last accusation. They had arrived in the kitchens. She dutifully ducked to follow Benjamin out of a short door that he had opened via his magic.

"Or me who what, Myra?" Benjamin leaned back against the sink edge. "Me who uses my skills to keep the people I love alive and well? Me who would see everyone—even ords—safe from the likes of Addair and his men?"

"Alive . . ." That word Myra stuck on. She couldn't get past it, try as she might. And so her legs buckled.

"Shit." Benjamin leapt forward, throwing his arms about her waist so that Myra did not fall.

"Sorry," she croaked. Why was it so hot all of a sudden?

Benjamin managed to drag a stool over to Myra for her to sit.

"Okay. So you've made your point." Divested of his burden, he crossed his arms, frowning. "Now what to do with you."

"Do?" New fear shook her, and with it, Myra managed to meet his gaze, pleading.

"You're not cut out for this. Not fighting it at every turn. What we do, you have to come to in your own time. And not merely because you've no other choice." Benjamin knelt before her. "Listen to me, Myra. I won't ask you to repeat hearsay. But whatever James has said, he has said it with love. Aidan I cannot speak to. Him I trust because I have to. You are right on that count. But James? James I trust with my life."

"But—"

Benjamin rose, not bothering to hide his look of contempt. "For someone whose gift is empathy, you've a shocking lack of it, Myra."

That did it for her then. Angered, Myra put out her palm wherein rode the wardstone. "May I?"

He looked from the little white rock to her face and back to the rock, curious. She let the stone fall into her lap and then hit him with every emotional strand that she could grasp. She explained to him without words her fear, her utter terror, over the powers that M.I. commanded. She gave him her sorrow and her guilt. Lastly she gifted him with her hope, the feeling that she had come home at last. Her broken hope born of feeling that she belonged but might yet prove unwelcome in the end. Or abandoned. Left in some dark place, after they got what they wanted from her.

She said, "Nobody has ever fully understood how I feel. Understood and—"

"And remembered," he completed. Benjamin rose and frowned. "You're drowning. Drowning in your gift and don't know which rescue to trust, having been offered too many false promises."

Myra nodded. "Every step forward feels like the wrong one. You say that your James James acts out of love. Whereas my regard keeps me from making any move whatsoever lest I . . ." She waved a hand, indication as best she could of her invasion into the lives, the heads and hearts, of those around her.

Benjamin dragged over a second stool and perched upon it. After a long pause he ventured, "Yeah, well, at least use of your gift doesn't make corpses walk around."

Myra wasn't sure whether to laugh or cry for him.

The weak joke seemed, to her, to indicate both as perfectly acceptable reactions.

Benjamin slid his gaze sideways. "So why do you trust me?"

Myra opened her mouth to argue the point. But she had forced the truth of her emotional turmoil upon him. This knowing that he hadn't the ability to forget it, that his shared experience with her would remain as fresh and vibrant, as painful and poignant, even as time passed. She said, "Because, as you'd said, I need to try."

Benjamin considered her response before nodding and rising. "Come. I think we've pretended through our late-night excuse long enough to have sidestepped both James and Aidan on our return to our rooms. And, Myra? Thank you. For not avoiding me altogether."

By the time he had escorted her to her room, Myra had learned the trick of lighting her wand directly from Benjamin's massive store of memory and knowledge. A small beginning, but at least she had a light in the dark.

Chapter Eighteen

"Repeat after me: I do not glide through shadows, I become shadow. The wind masks not my steps, I am the wind," James coached.

Myra did as she was told, repeating the spell and feeling foolish. If she managed to flicker out of sight at all, it was for but a moment. Her magic fizzled and died.

"I do not glide——"

"Yes, yes, I know," Myra complained through gritted teeth. She tried again with only marginally better results.

James' accompanying smile disappeared just as quickly. "You're working too hard at it, Myra. Remember that you were able to imitate these magics without thought on the first day you were here."

Yes, James. She knew this. Did not need the reminder, thank you very much. Myra knew full well she was overthinking it. And trying hard not to perversely making it harder not to overthink it. She grumbled, "Why do we even need these words, then, if the spell clearly works without them? What is it I'm supposed to do with them?" Another thought surfaced, found a voice in her questions, "And why's it in English, anyhow? Shouldn't a spell be all arcane and chant-y?" A memory of Benjamin's dark magics arose, spectre-like in her mind.

James weathered Myra's many protests with uncustomary patience. After a pause—punctuated by raised eyebrows—to ensure she was finished, he spoke, "The words are for you and not for your magic. Order. Control. Like the *t'ai-chi* practice, they are meant to steady you and take you away from the hard concentration that tamps down your art. Which is why it is in English."

"It's distracting."

"I can give it you in another language if you'd rather."

"No." Myra shook her head. "That'd be worse."

"I assumed as much," James said. "But I also would demand of you that you master this form of casting. It would go a long way, I believe, in breaking you of some of the habits you've come to lean upon."

Myra stared at him blankly. Doing magic quick as thought, without all the extraneous, was a habit to be broken?

"Do not misunderstand me, Myra," James read her look. "You have a strong connection to your gift. But you've spent so much time, so much effort, in tamping it down that you've destroyed all purposeful access. Unlike most, when you actually add intent to your use of the art, you kill it stone dead, as is your habit."

Intent. The word rang within Myra, sending reverberations through her bones.

"I do not glide through shadows, I become shadow." Myra left the magic to its own devices, using the words to control her breath. A mantra. She had read about them with Benjamin. Her fingers and arms, what part of her torso and legs she could view—each faded to nothingness. Success.

Aidan. His spellwork wasn't in English.

Myra winked back into sight.

"Ah, you almost had it." James held a dramatic hand to his forehead.

Myra ignored him, still distracted by her errant thought. "Aidan. He does not do his magics in English."

James snorted. "I should think not. Gaelic for him."

"Oh."

"Again. I am the wind . . ."

An hour later, Myra had become both shadow and wind. Together, she and James had traipsed up and down the halls of Grafford House, unseen by all they encountered.

Until they found Aidan. The mage had taken over the training salon. Assorted weaponry lay scattered about the room. In its midst, Aidan sweated shirtless, breathing deeply as he cycled through a program of slowed-down combat.

Myra was doubly glad that her invisibility hid her gaped-mouth stare.

"I know you're there, you know," Aidan called out without glancing up from his careful exercise. "The illusion of invisibility is but another form of lying."

James' hand on her arm rescued Myra from herself, redirecting her shock and outrage so that she did not have to lose her grip on the magic. Training within training.

They slipped away quietly, Myra following the breath of James' power. She considered the sensation of having had an invisible hand touch her arm. In some ways, it was more haunting than that of seeing a dead man rise. She shivered, repulsed. *Show me something beautiful in the magic, James. Please.*

Returning to the library, James let drop his illusion, dismissing her by declaring. "I do believe you are ready, Myra, for something more advanced. We will continue after lunch."

She'd done it. Great. But what Myra wanted to know was why Aidan had not been fooled. A fact that James seemed rather content to ignore. That in itself was disconcerting.

And so, back to Aidan she marched.

"So you, on principle, could also see through a disguise, yes?" Myra threw her question at the unsuspecting truth-teller. Luckily, for both their sakes, he had put his shirt back on. Probably anticipated her coming. But only just. The room was still a mess, the mage's face still bedewed with perspiration, his hair damp and flyaway.

Aidan quirked a smile, clearly enjoying some sort of private joke. He reached for a nearby towel, bending at the waist to give his head and face a vigorous rub. "See through any disguise? Not quite."

"But invisibility—"

He straightened, his strange smile deepening. He raised his eyebrows in mock challenge.

"Wait . . . but you said . . . I thought you couldn't lie!"

"I did not lie, Moira."

"You said—"

"What did I say? What is it I actually said?"

Myra couldn't quite remember. Especially in the face of Aidan's flushed smugness and perfectly unruly hair.

"I said: I know you're there . . ."

"And 'Invisibility is but another form of lying.' "

"But I did not say one beget the other." That smile still.

"But you—"

"I let you conclude such." Aidan tossed the towel to the side, reaching for his vest.

"You implied!" Myra's temper got the best of her. None least because he was clearly playing her for a fool. "You're a . . . a dirty, rotten sneak."

Aidan's smile fled, his face crumpling as the game turned on him. "I've had a decade plus to practice at finding the edges of truth and lie. Said honing of my skills served my country well."

"But not your team." Myra's biting cruelty continued. Him with his tantalizing damp curls and smug face. "You may not lie, but you're certainly dishonest."

Aidan's face closed to her. He waited.

But Myra's apology stuck in her throat. She hadn't the heart to speak further after such thoughtless, angry words.

With a curt nod, as though arriving at a decision, Aidan turned and bent to pick up the various items discarded throughout the room from his solo training session. Myra's eyes followed his motions, noting the grace by which he moved, his arms filling with weapons for which she hadn't a name. She longed to break the silence she had built up between them.

Myra backed out of the open doorway, eyes on Aidan until the very last second. Still, he ignored her.

"You're not even going to ask?"

"Beg pardon?" Myra took half a step forward, her only concession.

"You're not going to ask how I knew?" Aidan shoved shut the door on the training materials, likely setting up an avalanche for the next person. He turned to Myra, expectant.

"So how did you know?" Myra ventured, ashamed in the face of his blameless, bland acknowledgment of their tangle just then.

"Your gift pulled at mine. I felt you," Aidan said simply. He moved to lean upon the back of the low couch that had been shoved haphazardly to the side in an effort to make the small room bigger. "That and you bumped the door. Thought you might appreciate the pointer. Invisibility is only skin deep."

Nodding quickly, her ears burning with embarrassment, Myra took her leave of the Maester of Triewes. She could keep from bumping into doors. That was mere practical advice, and she thanked him for it inwardly. But the revelation of how easily their gifts could pull each at the other? What was she to do about that?

Aidan had understood Myra's words, the heart of them rather than the syllables that combined to the hurtful, defensive nastiness of self-preservation. He knew how she felt, knew her better than she knew herself. Nothing was invisible to him. Which made him more dangerous to be around than Benjamin. Well, so far as Myra's aching heart was concerned.

Alone at last in her rooms, Myra could cry her honest tears unseen. It was a stupid grief. She had lost far more in the past and shed less tears. Atop that, she had come to gain more than what she could have hoped to find, here in Grafford House. But her heart—*my foolish emotionally immature heart*. It loved Aidan.

All because of her Empathy. That Myra knew without quite knowing why. Something in them had connected the night Aidan had taken her away to M.I., snatched her from the clutches of a burning building and utter terror.

But the Maester of Triewes did not feel the same. And could not lie to save her feelings.

Chapter Nineteen

London was never truly quiet. But as Myra and James gained the streets following luncheon, she wished that M.I.'s lead wizard had chosen a less conspicuous time to try out her invisibility in public.

"Very good, Myra," James muttered at her side, keeping his voice low. With the din of street traffic, he did not have to work hard to remain out of hearing by all save Myra. And considering the self-absorbed manner in which many of those around them rushed about their business, Myra wondered if she and James would have been rendered near invisible without aid of their magic.

"This way, Myra. Time for the promised adventures."

Staying close by James' side in the closed comfort of Grafford House had felt, to Myra, like a strange derivation of hide-and-seek. But out in the open, the game changed, becoming that of Blind Man's Buff— only with all participants blindfolded. And with this change, the wizard's reaching for her hand to draw her into a nearby alleyway became less of an out-of-body sensation and more akin to reaching for another's hand in a pitch-black room. Scary. Instinct driven. Fun.

"Come." James' whispered word pulled Myra back from the pressing traffic of the street. Here M.I.'s lead agent let drop his invisibility so that he might better instruct Myra in the next lesson. He motioned her back into the deeper dark of the alley, giving a glance upwards to ensure they were yet unobserved. They were quite alone.

"Pickpocketing." He let the word sink in with a wicked grin.

Myra gawped, the idea not doing much sinking. In response she could only manage a whispered, "No. That's . . . I can't."

The hesitation and mild protest earned her a thorny look from James. His searching gaze went unmet, and he gave vent to a heavy sigh. He held out a hand and said, "Wand please. And drop the spell."

What? "No, I hadn't meant— I don't want to—" Heart pounding, Myra shifted to cover, to protect, her wand. Invisible as the gesture was, the force of accompanying emotion likely made clear to James what he otherwise could not see. He did not move, a stern and uncompromising school teacher awaiting the asked-for contraband while the rest of the class tittered nastily.

Myra was certain her angry blush was first to reappear when then she dropped her invisibility. Still, she did not surrender her wand. Within her modified wizard's bodice, the thrumming of her pulse seemed to push up against her wand's holster, her troubled heart repeatedly assuring itself that the weapon still lay there.

"No." Timidity choked off terror, conveniently

providing Myra the middle ground required for her to turn her back on James and enter the flow of sidewalk traffic. Safe. Unless James did something desperate and expose them to comment.

Heaving lungs outstripped Myra's brisk pace, leaving her light-headed as she hurried back towards home. She dared not look around, fearful the gesture might somehow weaken her and empower him. The house of Robert Grafford waited, comfortably unperturbed by the drama just outside. The front step beckoned. Myra quickened her pace. James stepped out from the mews.

Jumping, Myra let out a startled yelp. James' aspect was as dark as his all-black attire. He began, "Myra. A word, please."

Breathless, her eyes smarting, she brushed past him, gaining the door and giving the handle a desperate and thoughtless push.

It, of course, did not yield, trapping her outside with James. "Myra, please."

She wasn't sure how but James managed to gentle himself. It was enough. Myra's hand fell to her side.

"Myra. You cannot start a task—in public, doing magic, others reliant upon you—and stop short. That's not how it works."

"Don't make me hurt people." Myra shook her head, angry at herself for her new harvest of tears.

James reached for the door, waving his hand in a curious looping fashion before grasping the handle. It opened to his magic. He ushered Myra inside, away from prying eyes, though there were few about on a street such as Clarendon.

James? Laurel's Mind Speech sounded in Myra's head, setting her bones to vibrating.

Still playing at gentle James, M.I.'s lead wizard gestured towards the left-hand room. The formal receiving room. Not the library or even the training salon. Treatment for outsiders. Or maybe it was chosen for its proximity, comfortable chairs, and the relative privacy the room afforded. Laurel entered through a side door, closing it behind her with a quiet click and sympathetic glance at Myra.

"She doesn't want to hurt people." Myra caught James' preamble before he began quiet conference with M.I.'s Ways-walker just out of earshot.

Myra shifted uncomfortably in the ornate parlor chair as first Laurel, then James, then Laurel again darted glances at her, scrutinizing and pitying.

Myra's imagination ran away from her in those long moments. She was going to end up like Ben. One of M.I.'s secrets. Locked in Grafford House for the safety of herself and others until she could figure out a way to be a functioning and useful member of their team.

And all because she, what, wouldn't pick some unsuspecting ord's pocket? James hadn't exactly said what they were to have taken. A harmless enough trick, considering the broad spectrum of things done by the agents of M.I. It was not as though James had demanded Myra pull her wand and assassinate someone.

What is it you think we do here, Myra? The "we" slowly threaded its way down through her chest, a stone dropped into water. Heavy. Damning. The violence? The stakes of it all? She had known it from the first. Her protestations were childish in light of all that.

Laurel approached, James straying behind her. His fingers fidgeted with his wand. His eyes stayed downcast.

James feels bad. Real bad. And without Laurel having had to yell at him.

In that moment, she quite liked him. He seemed ordinary, less wizardly.

Goodness, it's not as though us mages aren't people!

"Us" and "we." Yes, there was no getting out of her predicament. And, obviously, a part of her didn't want to. Myra shook the thought from her and tried to meet Laurel's gaze.

The woman dropped into a crouch, resting her hands upon the arm of Myra's chair. An intimate gesture, eye to eye, it made them equals. *'All our mothers . . .'*

"James tells me that you won't use your gift for ill," Laurel began.

Myra blinked her surprise. She hadn't thought to put it that way to him.

"Such principled thought is commendable," Laurel crooned. "And with you being, what, all of sixteen—?"

"Fourteen," Myra corrected, automatic.

"But, of course, with your background you would be mature for your age." Laurel nodded. "And, with that considered, we'd never demand from you such violence as our profession tends."

Laurie paused, considering her words. Myra afforded her the opportunity, using the time to glance at penitent James. Her hand strayed to its wardstone, and she resisted the urge. Myra could manage to stay within her own heart at present. She needed him to see that he had taught her that much at least.

"Childish tricks. Surely you played such at the orphanage?" Laurel continued, finding the tract she sought.

Myra shook her head, then changed her mind and nodded. No sense falsely taking the high road. Memories sprang from the fertile ground of fond recollection. Quick friendships and good-natured pranks of young people with lonely hearts and idle hands.

"There now." Laurel's smile lit the room.

"We're not saying it's the same thing, Myra," James joined in, coming to stand behind Laurel, his hand on her shoulder. "But then we're not the sort of lot that plays at checkers, hoops, and hair-braiding. We're—"

"Extra-ordinary," Myra completed with a small smile. She would have a hard time ridding herself of the mental image of James braiding Benjamin's hair.

"Precisely." Laurel stood. "Though that does not make it fair for us to force you into crossing any lines in your training that you deem cruel."

"I've seen war, Myra." James swiftly knelt, taking Laurel's recently vacated place. His eyes were earnest as he looked into hers. Hard, yes, but human. Myra was doubly glad she had avoided clasping Laurie's wardstone, for she could tell that James wanted her to feel as much as hear him.

"War on an international scale. True battles of soldier to soldier combat. Those were our training grounds. Robert, Laurel, and myself. We've tortured, maimed, and killed in the name of the Crown. Done so without scruple. Without hesitation. It . . . it alters your perception of cruelty," he confessed, faltering somewhat. "What you object to? For me it seems so harmless in the face of what I have done and am capable of doing when so ordered."

Myra nodded mutely, understanding that which James spoke of was beyond comprehension for her in

her innocence. Thus far she had had but hints: the darkness of Ben's memories, Robert shot in a fire fight, the
queen's attacker slain . . .

Myra tried to reorient herself around the jagged
truth of James' hard morality. She tested, "And Aidan,
he's killed people."

"Aidan, too," Laurel confirmed. "Both with his
magic and without its aid, I'm sure."

"Though it's not to say you've fallen in with
murderers."

Haven't I? The thought flashed swiftly. What she said
was, "Are all wizards like you? I mean, are there any not
in your line of work?"

This time it was Laurel and James' turn to blink
their surprise.

"Well, the Flameists, then," Myra pursued.

"The Order does not do real magic."

"How else could you expect to sneak in there under
cover of invisibility spells? If they were performing
actual magic, such would be impossible," Laurel
explained.

James scoffed, himself again. "Ords, the lot of
them."

"But then isn't it logical that ords should be dealing
with this? What about Griggs' people, the agents of
MI2?" Myra countered, cross over James' sweeping
dismissal of non-magic folk.

"The Flameists and other practitioners of such
beliefs are, more often than not, the type of citizens that
the authorities are willing to give a pass on." Laurel's
explanation prompted a deepening scowl from James
but no actual response.

Having opened herself up to James via her magic,

Myra could feel his perceived betrayal by the system he had served with heart and mind. With it, she could understand his principles, his precepts of right and wrong. She did not merely like James the human being. The core of Myra, her very Empathy, sounded to his call.

She would master invisibility—along with a host of other new tricks and talents. Myra would work to become an integral part of the team, of the mission itself. While the residents of Grafford House awaited the alignment of the moon, stars, and whatever else the Flameists needed to come into balance before their upcoming ceremony, she would prove her worth to James James.

Chapter Twenty

Nighttime London had far too many people for Myra's taste. Sucking in a breath and concentrating on not dropping her spells, she tried to keep an eye on her mark. He strode ahead, unmindful of the two invisible wizards furiously ducking and weaving amongst the other pedestrians in their attempts to keep up.

Damn you, James James. Swearing—to herself, luckily, though it still brought to mind her mother's scolding—Myra narrowly avoided a collision with a gentleman. She half skipped, half jumped over the man's cane. A clammy drizzle had set in and made the sidewalk slick. Still she did not fall.

Smiling, Myra decided to meet the game at last. Dashing ahead nimbly, she liberated an apple from a passing cart and chucked it at an umbrella—Robert's of all people. It had the effect she intended. Whipping around in surprise, M.I.'s weather-worker frowned up into the heavens then down to where the street urchins darted amongst the more genteel populace. Myra suppressed a giggle and slowed her artful dance. Somewhere ahead of her James was also frowning—though invisibly.

Serves them right, making me play tricks like that. She had her reward. Robert's slow smile spread over his wide face as he again swung his umbrella up over his head. He gave a curt nod to nobody in particular and turned to resume his ponderous pace.

And that's when it happened. Something or someone slammed into Myra's side. Careening under the impact, she clutched her sore shoulder and tried to spot the assailant, swallowing yet another stream of impolite language. Yet her invisibility stayed true. Unfortunately.

A moment later, the jolt she had received on the sidewalk was rendered a mere nothing. Myra turned and found herself face to face with a horse's flank. The hard side of a growler, black and boxy and terribly immutable, caught her in an instant. At least that's what she perceived to be the case.

Fractured details swam through Myra's mind as the world tipped sideways, and every bit of her screamed in pain. She then lost her grip on her spells, or so she assumed from the sudden grouping of onlookers gathered around. From where she lay flat upon her back in the filthy street, she could see no less than twenty pairs of shocked eyes. At her side—too close!—a spooked horse's hooves pranced and stomped. But she could not move. Everything hurt too much to do so.

Stars above, am I dead? Some distant part of Myra's mind managed to remove itself from her howling excruciation long enough for her to ponder such a possibility. She dismissed it. In no way could being dead hurt like she did.

With frantic, darting eyes, Myra watched as the horse was drawn off and quieted. Two gentlemen ushered over a policeman who, of course, decided it was more important to berate the cabby than see to Myra. And where was her voice in all of this? She tried it out and found that only a terrified, pained yelp could escape her.

"Yes, yes. We'll be getting someone by." Myra couldn't follow the disembodied voice. In fact, it all seemed rather blurry rather suddenly. Her injuries coalesced into something akin to meaning for her brain: shattered leg and bruised ribs. Maybe a broken arm, too. And something odd with her forehead, a hot trickle of . . . She refused to think of blood, no. That would lead to swooning. But perhaps it was too late for that caution. The fuzzy sensation had invaded her eyes, wrapping her vision in a cottony white. Almost like fog.

No, it was fog.

"I've a carriage at my club. I've sent a man to fetch it." That voice rang familiar. Robert hove into view above her. "I know the girl. Family acquaintance. Her father's father was friend to my own." He bent down. "It'll be all right, Mary."

Mary? Luckily, Myra's question did not reach her face. She was too lost to pain.

Robert reached over her for something. Myra's eyes followed his every movement, straining downward to watch as he spread a dark and shapeless something over her waist and legs. A blanket. Likely given to him by the hapless driver who'd hit her while she'd played at being invisible. With one last uneasy look that brushed past her face, he rose and turned, blowing his nose loudly in a massive white handkerchief. It served to half-cover his words. Myra thought the tremulous sentence contained a highly improper oath and the words "that's a lot of blood."

The strange, wispy fog continued to swirl about the scene, muting sound and sight. It was a blessing. With it, Myra found that she could distance herself from her own part in the drama—though, perhaps, it was mere shock removing her from the pain. A double blessing. For it gave an explanation, if a belated one, for how a growler might have collided with a young girl without the driver or anyone else first seeing the danger to her. People's memories were funny like that, looking for answer, for explanation, to the point of revising hard facts to make their minds comfortable.

The Grafford carriage arrived, and many gentle hands attempted to lift Myra into the conveyance. In moving, Myra could now see the frightful amount of blood that had caused comment from Robert. She also had the distinct impression of something slipping from her hand, and she clutched blankly at the air, feeling pain return to her in a rush. But she and Robert were both hid from sight within moments, the driver taking up a swift but careful rein to the horses.

James let his invisibility drop and retook her hand in his. Myra's injuries grew bearable once more. She figured it showed in her face for, with the easing of the pain, James' own hard features softened. She risked another glance to Robert.

Robert Grafford fared better than he had in the moments following the accident, but his mouth remained drawn in a tight line, and his eyes were still reddened with ill-concealed distress. He caught her looking at him and tried on a smile. It failed spectacularly and instead buried Myra in a rush of the man's fear, anger, and . . . what was that last? Affection. Were she in any position to blush, she might have.

"Your magic," she charged. What Myra had wanted to voice was apology, admission of her own role in the accident. Or assurance that she would be fine. Or something else equally useless and potentially untrue. Even a simple thanks would have sufficed.

That time Robert's smile reached his eyes. He spoke softly, "Yes, Myra. That is my fog through which we are travelling at present."

Turning, he reached out a hand to slap the carriage roof. Their ride slowed, then halted.

"I'm still sufficiently incensed to continue this fog, but James, you'll have to do the next bit as I haven't magic to spare," Robert muttered.

"I'm keeping Myra stable," James complained through gritted teeth. "We're not actually going to your Club then, I take it? You worried me for a moment there. Thought you upset enough to make the slip up."

Robert's cold disdain echoed through the carriage. "No, James. Unnerved as I am, I am still myself and know the right play. We're pausing outside this one long enough for you to whip up the proper illusion. That of me rushing young Myra inside. The tight lips of this particular establishment will provide an excellent stopping point in the event hostile eyes have followed our movements."

James sighed. "How much of a change do I need to effect on the carriage's appearance once we leave the adjacent alleyway, then?"

"Enough. We're not stopping for a doctor and

haven't the luxury for a roundabout path back to the House, no?"

James' minute shake of the head and pressed lips told the urgency of the situation. And with that tense exchange, Myra slipped further into the quiet calm of James and Robert's combined magics.

Clarendon Mews was ablaze with lanterns when the Grafford carriage rumbled in out of easy sight of passersby. Aidan, Laurel, and even Benjamin were waiting to help. But it was James who had the honor of carrying Myra in himself.

They did not even bother going all the way to the drawing room and, instead, stopped in the kitchens where a space had been cleared for tending their injured agent. Laid out upon the massive wooden table and watching the kaleidoscope of worried faces slide past, Myra tried to ask how they had known of the accident. Her question came out as a wordless whimper.

"Hush, Myra. And don't move." Benjamin leaned close and gently tried to coax Myra's fingers into letting go of James' hand. She would not. Nodding grimly to himself, he opted to work his magic around the small inconvenience.

In the end, Myra was left to wonder how exactly healing magic worked. She slipped into unconsciousness before she could learn that particular brand of spells.

Chapter Twenty-One

Myra woke to find that she lay in her own bed and own rooms within Grafford House. From the dim light of the coals on the hearth, she could see evidence of someone's abandoned vigil. A chair had been pulled up alongside where she slept, and the bedside table held an abandoned cup, plate, and book. She had not been forgotten.

But she was alone. Saddened, for she had thought that she might wake within the comfortable library, surrounded by the concerned and loving faces of her friends, Myra sat up without thinking.

Her stunned gasp came easily and without pain. Every bit of her seemed to be working properly. No scars. No wounds. It was as if the memory of yesterday's tragic events had been rendered a dream. Correction, a nightmare.

A gentle knock sounded on the door a second before it opened. Laurel slipped into the room, tapping the side of her head. "I felt you wake. How are you feeling?"

Myra wanted desperately to burst into tears. And

yet, none came to her. She felt . . . fine. Which was quite discomforting.

"What did you do to me?" Myra offered the flat question and pointedly set her gaze upon her hands. From the corner of her eye, she saw Laurie light the lamps with a wave of her wand. The wizard then came and claimed the vacated bedside chair.

"Benjamin healed your injuries. As he had previously done for Robert."

No cooing and fuss. No motherly, soothing sweep of Myra's loose hair from her forehead. No embellishment. Just words. And, oddly enough, it helped. It helped to know that Laurel seemed as unperturbed about the whole thing as Myra herself.

Myra took another deep and steadying breath. "How did you know?"

"That you were awake? When I eventually convinced James to give up his vigil, I stayed just outside, using my Ways-walking to keep an eye without having to stare at you."

"I meant last night. Outside." At this Myra finally felt an uncomfortable wavering in her limbs. But still no tears. It was as though she had finally run out of them, had run out of any sort of ability to express emotion.

Laurel reached for Myra's hands. The woman's fingers were chilled. She said, "James called out to me as you came close upon the house."

"Mind Speech."

"Just so." Laurel nodded and then shrugged, flashing a bright smile as she did so. "He's quite clumsy at it, but he does try. I could gauge the need but none of the particulars. It was rather a . . . rather a shock to discover that it was you, Myra, who had been so injured."

"I'm sorry."

"Whatever for, my dear?"

"I allowed someone to push me off the sidewalk and into—"

"Push you!"

Myra stammered, feeling a fool for the unintended implication. "No, no. Someone bumped me is all."

"Enough to put you directly into the path of a horse and cart." Laurel's eyes glinted and her voice grew hard. With it, Myra felt the thrill of self-doubt edge its way into her chest.

Laurel stood and turned her gaze to the doorway. "We need to brief everyone else on this new turn. Are you feeling up to that?"

"What time is it?"

"Just past seven."

Myra nodded and, with a shudder, realized she was clad in but a nightgown. Healed though she was, she did not want to contemplate the likely state of the previous day's dress.

As if reading her mind, Laurel rose and crossed the room to pat a soft and shapeless mound of material which lay over a chair. "And I'm the one who re-dressed you for sleep, Myra. Library in, say, a half an hour? I'll stay just outside. Call out if you need anything."

That morning was the first time Myra had seen Grafford House in sunshine. Sure, the cloud-wrapped morning she had spent with Laurel in the library had given way to muted brightness. But today the curtains could not hold back the light from out of doors. Heading with Laurel down the hallway, Myra found herself staring at her swishing skirts as her steps took her from shadow to sunlight to shadow back to sunlight.

An emerald green silk, Myra distantly wondered if the new dress was too bright for proper spy work. She certainly felt as though she would stand out from any crowd.

After yesterday's incident, that was fine by her.

The rest of the wizards had gathered in the library. Myra could feel their assembled anxieties before she reached the door. With a deep and steadying breath she entered, Laurel close at her back.

"Please don't fuss." Myra went on the offensive before any of them could say one word to her. "I'm fine. Really, I am."

Aidan made sure that he met Myra eye to eye, his blazing gaze boring into her from across the room. Unblinking, she met the silent test with measured calm. At length he answered, "I cannot say I am not glad to hear that, Myra."

A carefully worded response. Still, Aidan had not suggested an untruth within Myra's own claim, so she was satisfied. She took a seat and then turned back to Laurel, trying to gauge how she ought to proceed. Myra's silent question was met by bland encouragement from the wizard.

Facing James, Myra said, "Again, I am well. Truly. But I've something unpleasant to discuss. I told Laurel this already, but I was knocked into yesterday. That is how I ended up— Well—"

At this, Myra began to quake all over. She took a steadying breath and continued, "She and I were wondering if that accident was not an accident."

James James half rose to his feet. His eyes never left

Myra's face. He sat heavily and seemed to turn his thoughts inward before speaking. As such, Aidan was able to get in his questions first.

"Did you see who shoved you, Moira?"

"No."

"Were they, then, invisible as you and James?"

"I don't think so." Myra felt a heat rising into her cheeks, and she looked down so as to avoid the truth-teller's gaze. "I mean, I was just pushed. On my shoulder. It happened so fast that all I could think was how annoyed I was for having been jostled so roughly, and then there was the carriage and . . . It was an accident. I'm sure of it."

"But you aren't sure. And the fact is you were pushed, and hard enough to fall under the crushing hooves of a horse." Thus far, Robert had witnessed the proceedings through heavily-lidded eyes, fully his calm and unperturbable self once more.

"That was my worry," Laurel volunteered at last.

Peevishly, Myra wondered why Laurie didn't just take over the discussion then. From the corner of her eye, she saw Benjamin stir. He'd been leaning up against the mantle, but now he quietly moved to exit the library. Nobody made to stop or question him for his actions.

The annoyance that had been building in Myra over what felt like an impromptu interrogation now changed and became anger that she could so easily have fallen to an attack upon her person. That anger soon turned to hot rage, ire that there were even such enemies out there in the world, and a deep desire to meet them and beat them at their own game. Not that she relished the idea of throwing anyone under the wheels of a cart, per se.

"We can only indulge in base conjecture today,"

Robert said, heaving himself heavily to his feet. "I am glad you are well, Myra."

Laurel followed him out, leaving Myra with only Aidan and James, each of whom seemed more than content to challenge her with piercing looks.

"I would like to make the suggestion that Myra remain safe within the house until such time as we can determine whether or not yesterday's events were an accident," Aidan ventured, sliding his gaze to James.

"It was an accident, Aidan! Too many people on the sidewalk at once. I slipped up." The reasonable part of Myra's brain screamed at her to stop talking, the part of her which remembered yesterday's searing agony and pure terror. But the better part of herself, the bit which trusted her team and her magic and her own way within the world, that part wouldn't have her cowardice, continued, "And if it was not an accident, then it begs the question of how anyone knows I am here and would know to expect me working magic."

"And to have known your gift well enough to see through your invisibility last night," James offered his own logic at last.

"How sure are we about Julius Griggs?" Aidan asked.

"If I agree to keep Myra here, will that stop you from questioning my judgment at every turn?"

Am I even going to get a say in this? Myra had sense enough to keep her objection to herself. She watched as Aidan's jaw worked emptily.

"Fine." He strode out of the library, giving Myra's shoulder a light squeeze as he passed her chair. "Talk to me if you feel the need, Moira?" And then he was gone.

Which left Myra alone with James. James who

seemed to wilt in the scant seconds that followed the truth-teller's exodus from the room.

"It was an accident," Myra repeated stupidly. She hadn't any empathy—magic or otherwise—left to spare for him.

"There comes a point in this business where you simply do what you must, no matter the cost," James spoke without looking at her. "You wake up one day and find yourself numb to the risk. For honor. For duty. But the magic? It has its limits—and said limits increase with each passing day. Wizardry will fall to electricity."

Rising to his feet, James went to stand by the fire. Enraptured by the flames, he continued, "When magic fails, we die. Not because our lives depend upon it— though there are some gifts of the lesser mages that work along those lines. In some ways that is where the agents of MI2 are superior to us wizards. They cannot depend upon the tricks and cheats of sorcery to heal and save and so are smarter, sharper, and less inclined to getting themselves into serious peril. Even the peril of mere accident."

Myra had risen to stand by James. The fluttering of her Empathy showed her that she was not numb, not by far. Rather she was home. She was here and she belonged. Honor and duty? Those were words she now believed she understood. She had been tested and come out unscathed—quite literally.

"Stephen saved my life. Not once, twice, but count-less times. A give and take. Risk compounded upon risk. That was the way of it back then. Robert, Laurel, Silas . . . We all knew the dangers, of course." James gave a wry smile. "Ran headlong into all manner of trouble with Steve at my side. Why I didn't go with him this time—"

Rapt, Myra waited for James to continue. But he seemed stuck. Either on the memory or the words. It was a pity, for never before had he seemed so . . . human. She opened her mouth to speak.

James continued, "You've said that you had a vision of his death. Experienced it, in some form or another. Him and that Kinetic American, Kady. Tell me, Myra, did he—" Here the words fled from the wizard, momentarily leaving him to mouth silently, his chest heaving with emotion. "We all know it lurks out there, our very own death, waiting for us on some dark day. Our worst fear is not facing it. Did Stephen— Did he die well?"

Plunged back into the memory of fire, the pain and chaos, the smothering smoke and faint breath of hope, Myra relived the fear, the despair, the screams. And, closer still, James splintering in the calm safety of the library, breaking. He needed it so badly from her, this answer. And, as it was just him and her alone in the room, no Aidan around, Myra decided to be brave.

"Yes. He died well."

It felt good to lie.

Chapter Twenty-Two

"Hullo, Myra," Benjamin hailed her as he walked down the hallway. His waving hand held a small, rectangular, brown . . . something.

"And hello, Ben," Myra responded to the greeting with a shy smile of her own. In the two days following the carriage accident, things had returned to something akin to normal in Grafford House. Following Myra's pointed request that they not fuss over her, M.I.'s Necromancer had first lapsed into silent avoidance and then gone over into all smiles and affability. He was back to his old rakish, borderline flirtatious self once more.

Myra concluded that Ben was certainly a pleasant enough fellow. So long as you overlooked his ability to make the dead rise. And that he couldn't help now, could he?

The item in Ben's hands was thrust in her direction. The handsome wizard raised one eyebrow, quizzical and teasing at the same time. "Package for you, Myra."

"For me?" Myra hesitated. Holding back as though the small box in its brown paper wrapping might bite, she wondered: who even knew she was here? Who besides . . . ?

Ben's knowing smile deepened. The mage held back a laugh. Poorly.

Oh. Julius Griggs.

Myra made no attempt to hide the blush that heated her cheeks. Let Benjamin think of it what he would. After all, he had been the one who had sent the message. Why didn't he open the response?

"It's not polite to open another's mail." Ben shrugged his explanation and leaned against the wall with his hands up behind his head. Waiting.

So he draws the line at opening and not looking over one's shoulder. Myra cocked an eyebrow of her own, daring him to laugh again as she sliced through the paper's edge with a fingernail.

"Guess I'm impolite then," she said. She unfolded the enclosed letter and handed it straight back to Ben unread.

"Ha." He took the letter from her and cast his eyes over it quickly. "He sends his regards. And a token."

The last seemed to spark genuine surprise from Benjamin, and he arced his neck to see what else rode within the small box. Myra moved it out of his line of sight, tsk-ing at his presumption. "Now what was it about another's mail, Ben?"

"No fair."

Myra held up the box's contents for the wizard to see. Teasing or not, she couldn't keep Ben from it for long, she supposed. Julius' "token" was a small metal doodad on a chain—and not even all that pretty. She figured it was likely coded into Julius' response; some little toy for the team to do goodness-knew-what with. "It's just a pendant."

"That it is." Ben's attention was back on the message. Darting to and fro, his eyes crossed and recrossed the page. Myra could almost feel him thinking.

When he looked up at her again a moment later, he had a strange look on his face, one that he managed to put away as quickly as it made entrance. He said, "I'll tell the team what the message says. And that—," he eyed the pendant in Myra's hand, "—that really is for you. Something I'd suggest you tuck away for later, private, examination."

Myra opened her mouth and shut it. A secret? Why?

Benjamin smiled yet again. Calculating this time, the expression had lost its warmth. "Seems your kind returning of Julius' handkerchief has found a soft spot in the ord's heart."

And with that, he handed Myra her letter, then turned and sauntered down the hallway, leaving her to stare, gape-mouthed, at the back of his suit. No retort came easily to mind, and she let him have the last word.

In the end, Myra was thankful she had waited to read Griggs' letter until she was safely settled in her rooms. She had never been wooed before. Even if it were just for appearance's sake to any potential interceptors.

And while the contents of the communication were tame by most any standard—*and part of the game betwixt M.I. and their informant,* Myra reminded herself over and over—she could feel her face transition from warm, to hot, to fully on fire as she absorbed Julius' message.

Certainly hidden information was coded into the words. Benjamin had seemed satisfied, anyhow. Perhaps that was why Julius had chosen to be less than terse in his response? A longer message meant for more opportunities in which to hide his actual purposes.

Ben had been right to intercept and, subsequently, run interference on Myra's behalf. She could only guess at the response she would have had to endure had James, or even Aidan, learned the literal text of Griggs' message to the team through her.

First off, Julius seemed to think Myra, herself, was an ord!

"How dare he!" transitioned quickly to "I'm as bad as the rest." Considering how far past the age of Emergere she was, of course he would have assumed as much of her. Still, what else did Julius think she was doing in Grafford House in the company of a team of wizard spies?

James would be pleased.

And this presumption of his—along with a healthy dose of "kind regards"—had led to Julius sending her the pendant. Under closer examination, it was less ugly so much as . . . unique. Odd, even. The gleaming metal, the way the swooping shape caught the light and seemed to funnel it through the design, had a sort of pleasing aesthetic. It was certainly finely worked.

"Something he made himself, then," Myra concluded. She remembered the rapture with which Griggs had spoken of his other such workings. Yes, this was far better than a chainmail parasol. Opening the clasp, she slipped the gift around her neck. It suited her. "Strange for the strange."

A knock on the door startled her, and Myra quickly covered the pendant with one hand as she rose from the dressing table. "Who is it?"

"Me," Ben's voice came muffled through the door.

"Come in," Myra bade him enter, rising to greet him so that he might see, simultaneously, the pendant and her resultant blush. Far better to let him know all, concealing nothing. For he already knew the face value of the letter's contents as well as its hidden meaning.

"Lovely," Ben drew the word out, teasing her as he gave the curiosity a questioning look.

"I think it's supposed to do something. Giving it an excuse to sacrifice form for function."

"That it does." Ben grinned.

"Oh, shush. I think he made it himself, I mean. That said, there are few hints as to its purpose, but I think I have some ideas. Thank you."

He placed his hands over his ears, rolling his eyes. "Don't tell me. That way I can deny all when questioned." Reaching forward, Benjamin dropped the charade. "But, truly, Myra. I think some people deserve their secrets. You don't have to impart to me the Great Pendant Purpose. A simple reply for him would be nice."

"A reply? You mean from the team, right?"

"If that's the way you want to play it, certainly." Ben's eyes grew wicked. "It can be more fun that way."

Myra's blush renewed its lease. Awkward shyness descended on the room.

"Welcome to the game, Thales." He sat uninvited at her table, unearthing pen and stationary. He seemed to note, for the first time, Myra's abject misery. "Don't worry. My purpose here was to serve both ends. I'll help you pen a safe response, one that plants a false trail of our own next moves should anyone intercept this letter. Coded as the underlying message will be, Griggs will know that your response had to come through me and will therefore take that into account.

"We're not giving you away to the man, Myra. Merely providing a cover for our newfound easy communication. Goodness, you're an innocent." The reassuring words drew Myra back, a cautious cat. Arching his eyebrows, Benjamin got down to the business of encoding a reply—that is to say, torturing Myra with his teasing. "Now, how do you feel about romantic sentiments? Dear? Turtle? Chuckaboo?"

Chapter Twenty-Three

The very second Ben had gone, Myra dove into distraction via the strange little device sent her by Griggs.

Fiddling with the tiny clasps and hasps, she discovered that bits were easily pushed, locked, and changed by deft maneuverings. In short minutes Myra had reconfigured the item into a tidy mess. Despair shook her. *Oh, bother.*

In the entire scope of the pretend romance that she couldn't quite figure—nor, necessarily want—Myra had botched the one thing that had interested her. Her secret. Something for her that she could call her own.

Never mind the generosity of a roof over your head, wand, clothing . . . It's not exactly as though you've nothing to your name. Myra laid aside Griggs' trinket. She startled as Aidan's voice rang within her otherwise silent rooms.

Casting a wide-eyed glance to the door, Myra saw that Benjamin had shut it behind him. So where was it coming from? A soft, lilting verse, akin to a lullaby, she found it rather amusing that Aidan should even be singing such. But not in her room.

Hunting high and low, Myra eventually returned to her desk and the pendant that she had carelessly laid there. Something in her memory caught—Aidan's voice, low and clear yet lacking depth. Solid. The tone reminded her of . . . of . . . swimming with her sister on a hot summer's day, their voices curiously muted yet clear beneath the water. They had toyed with a similar discovery later, earning them a scolding for playing with doors. But, Mother, the sound had carried well!

Amplified. Like Aidan's singing.

Myra reached for Griggs' bauble, turning it on its side with the flick of a finger. Silence rushed back at her.

Oh, how curious.

She turned the pendant back over onto its face. Nothing. No, wait, there it was. Fainter, halting. Aidan had altered his inflection in his changing of the verse. Less pronounced, more under-his-breath, came the melody.

Myra leaned close. Putting her ear to the wider end of the device she found that she could hear more nuance from up close. She held her breath, willing her pounding heart to quiet so that she might better hear. Changing her mind, she moved the device from table to floor, bending so that her ear again came into contact with the smooth side. Her face lay almost flat along the wood flooring. This was far better. If terribly uncomfortable.

"Not the most clandestine of undertakings," she noted, flashing a wry grin. But then, perhaps Griggs, being an ord, was not well versed in subtle. He certainly hadn't appeared that way to her on their one meeting. Shifting, Myra's thumb knocked against one of the tiny knobs left sticking out from her clumsy manipulations.

The sound grew sharp, the audible equivalent of coming into focus.

Words and phrases from Julius' letter came together in her mind. "Listening." "Inclining one's ear to hear the sound of a beloved's voice." Messages within messages. A tricky fellow.

"And undoubtedly, in speaking of a beloved's voice he did not mean for me to listen in on Aidan." Myra laughed silently. Pretend though their courtship was; poor permanently-bachelored Julius.

It was a kind gift from one ord to another, with both surrounded as they were by wizards and spies. Even if one was not actually an ordinary. Still, the pendant was likely to provide some sort of practical application for Myra.

She was a bit of a sneak, after all.

A thought; a brilliant—and defensible—idea struck. Benjamin's reading nook above the library would be perfect for such an undertaking. Provided anyone was below. And provided, of course, that Ben had left the small collection of reading material there for her perusal.

He had.

Settling on the floor, book in hand, Myra tested her pendant. Eyes to the door and ears to the ground. Almost immediately she could hear footsteps in the room below, soft but not muffled.

"How's she doing?" James, commanding and distant once more.

"Frighteningly well. But then you knew that already." The feminine rejoinder came coy and slightly chastising. Laurel.

So James takes that tone with everyone, no exception. Myra fought to suppress the shiver that snaked up her spine. Something about the interaction between those two. She had never seen the like. Were they a couple? Old friends with liberties? Myra had no experience with women as free as Laurel.

Was it cultural? Were all women of England as headstrong and outspoken? Laurel certainly moved like a man—or, more correctly, rather like the agents in Grafford House. Confident. Graceful, if inelegant.

Myra hid from the thought and shifted her focus.

"James, you haven't the authority to make her an agent." Laurel again.

"I haven't the authority to tell her what she's having for breakfast tomorrow, but we have to do something. This is war."

"Not our war any more, James. We need to keep ourselves safe. Bringing her in only—"

"Bringing her in does just that, then. Give that as your reason if it helps you sleep at night. Her gift, her immunity to the Dampening, we must have it for ourselves. And she's ready. I can hear it in her voice when she speaks. You saw how she handled herself the morning after the Stratton Street incident."

A long pause. Myra wondered if the conversation had been interrupted by a new arrival. There had certainly been a fair bit of shuffling about—this learned from clumsy, excited manipulation of the diminutive controls on Julius' pendant. *Or, someone is climbing the stairs to take me to task.*

"I've spoken to Aidan," James' continuation called Myra out of her fretting. "He's taking care to make sure she comes around of her own accord. With his skills and rapport with her, I thought it best."

"You mean her having eyes for him."

"His concerns are genuine. I've no fear that he'll take unfair advantage of her infatuation. You know as well as I that he's in no position right now to act—"

"That's not what I meant." Laurel's playful tone vanished. "She could get hurt without him meaning her to."

"That's the truth-teller's problem, Laurie. Regardless. Or did you think one beget the other? Our using her—"

Myra sat up, shaking with rage. Tears spilled from her eyes, marking her arms and the cover of the book beneath. That James. Where were Benjamin's reassurances now?

And Aidan. They were to use him against her?

They know how I feel for him? This last realization shook Myra as fully as had the thought of the wizards planning a future for her unasked. If James and Laurel could tell, then Aidan certainly knew.

Granted, with his gift and hers, it made sense that Aidan would know. On occasion he had made it more than apparent that he understood the effect he had on her. Maester of Triewes. Truth-teller. Surely he would not deliberately mislead her, knowing how she felt for him. And, surely, in caring for her he could not be forced into acting against Myra's own interests. That would be but another form of lying, a line which, she was certain, he could not cross.

My defender . . .

They all were, though. In that, Benjamin was right. Ben, Robert, Laurel, and even James—perhaps most especially James. They cared what happened to Myra.

They wanted her to flourish. Were there ulterior motives? Of course. Such were everywhere.

Even within Myra. Arriving at Grafford House, she had not wished to learn magic, to use and control her gift, in order to serve some greater purpose. She simply wanted proof that she was not as mad as she had been deemed.

Myra laid back down onto the wooden floor, arms behind her head. Beams reached up into the darkness, a private cathedral of comfort. The attic of Grafford House, of her home. A family—albeit a strange one, accepting and caring. She could do much worse.

Myra shifted, lifting Julius' pendant so that it dangled on its chain, glinting in the half-light of the garret's one lamp.

M.I. had allies. They were not alone.

The mages of Grafford House were on the side of right, this Myra knew. Knew without the truth-teller's presence acting upon her gift and forcing her mind.

And yet—

Again, Griggs' pendant caught the light, performing a lazy counter-clockwise spin in midair, and she pictured his kindly, squashed face with her mind's eye. Aidan didn't know if they ought to trust Julius. But M.I. needed the ord. Didn't they?

Myra sat up, restless and unable to think any more upon it. She extinguished the lamp and pocketed the aural spyglass, descending the steep ladder that led back into the livable portions of the house.

She had a confession to make.

In the end Myra's cowardice almost carried her past Aidan's door. In fact, it might well have, had the door to his rooms not been open and the sought-after occupant inside noted her indecisive pause in the hallway. Guilt stopped her from avoiding his greeting, and breathless, she entered.

"Goodness, Moira, you run as if you've a possession of demons at your back." Aidan craned his neck so that he might see what else had accompanied Myra down the darkened hall.

"Nothing as such." Myra overcame her hesitation and entered. "I was merely hurried."

"Not in a hurry now, are you? Sit." Aidan gave a nod to an open chair. Clothing, books, and other arcanea covered the others in the room. Through the doorway leading into the next, Myra could tell that the bedroom was in much the same shape.

She sat.

"What troubles you, Moira?"

Myra took it in stride that Aidan knew instinctively that something was bothering her. She glanced towards the still-open door, flinching.

"Is it someone here?" Aidan's eyes darkened.

"No, nothing of the sort." Myra waved her hands, alarmed over having given so wrong an impression. "It's . . . me."

Aidan nodded slowly, his penetrating gaze turning to Myra. He waited. She glanced at the doorway again.

"Oh, bother." Aidan waved a hand. The door closed none too gently, and Myra jumped. He winced. "Sorry."

Myra stared at the closed door, bracing herself for the confession of her truth. Instead, something else entirely came out. "Aidan, I lied. To James."

"How so?"

Though Myra could tell that Aidan still trusted her, his hand strayed to where he kept his wand concealed within his vest. An unconscious gesture, she wasn't even sure he was aware of it.

"He wanted to know about Steve. About his . . . his death."

This time, instead of his face darkening, Aidan's eyes widened, opening to shatter Myra with bright compassion.

Myra continued, "I told him that he died well. I—I lied. And, what's worse, I wanted to."

"That's only natural, Moira. The sparing of a friend's—"

"That's not it! I . . . I had to, yes. But it also felt good. Just to lie, you see?" Hunching in misery, Myra slouched in her chair, not sure she was getting through at all.

"I see."

"Well I don't. For me, it's all a jumbled mess," Myra complained, biting her lip as she realized her tone was coming dangerously close to whining. This was not at all how she had wanted the conversation to go. "The truth. Lies. Magic and madness. You."

"Me?"

Myra blushed. "All of you."

Not entirely a lie.

Aidan leaned back, resting on the edge of his desk, his arms crossed. "Moira, what is it you want?"

From you?

"From your experiences here. To become an agent, fully one of us, replete with the choices and actions we must take? A mere escape from life as an orphan? Time to sort yourself?"

"Absolution."

Aidan shifted, alert once more. Trouble returned to

his eyes. "What is it you've done?"

"I steal memories. The magic of others. Secrets." Misery consumed Myra. "I'm . . . I'm not right, you know. Up here." She tapped her head in illustration. "I hardly understand myself, and I keep getting pulled into other people's problems. And it's nice and all because it's a good thing, I suppose, but then James has all these grand plans for me, and I just don't know. I want it. But I just don't know."

"What don't you know?"

"If I should be here; if I'm a good person . . ."

"And whether we are good people, are on the side of right, if such a thing exists," Aidan prompted, relaxing once more into empathy for Myra.

"Yes." *Which is stupid, really, because I'm telling you all this. You who are one of them.*

"Ah. But by questioning such you have some of your answers before you. Only those who desire to do what's right question whether they are doing so. And you, Moira, are a good person."

The words were said with emphasis, not that Myra needed it with Aidan's gift. She said, "I'm on the side of truth, at least."

"Truth. Truth's a tricky thing, Moira." Aidan's smile quirked, a hiccup of humor Myra could not quite read.

"Does the guilt ever leave you?" Myra found another angle. *And have you any yourself?* She made her second question in silence. Perhaps the truth-teller's perspective would provide for her the clearness of conscience she sought.

"Again, such questions should prove to you the sureness of your heart. But then, perhaps, that knowledge is something that comes through either the burden of years to your life or myriad experience. Neither would I wish rushed upon you, but I acknowledge that ours is a calling—through our gift—that oft forces such earlier than is anyone's wont."

"So, no." Myra scowled. It was tricks upon tricks with him.

"No," Aidan answered Myra's frown with a smile, reaching out to grasp her hands. "But if it would clarify things for you, I would, myself, confess something to you."

Myra's pulse quickened, and she briefly fled from the confrontation, internally running from Aidan even while her gaze sought his. Thus caught, she waited, frozen and fearful and hopeful.

"I blamed you for their deaths. I did." Aidan's pain radiated at Myra, rattling her with its honesty. "But that was me being stupid, wishing the impossible, tricking myself into believing that Kady and Stephen, on their own, could have gotten free of that trap.

"It is possible, you understand, for one with my gift to move beyond plain fact and reason into the realm of mere hope. Such is not easy and requires a fair bit of blindness on my part." He switched tack, bringing the lecture into line with Myra's question. "Perhaps that is why you find your answers so elusive. Even I, with my years and experience, find that my heart can, on occasion, override my head and fool my gift. And in such moments I question all, including myself. At such a juncture I am vulnerable to deception. Absurd, yes, considering the bounds of my magic. But therein lies the core of my convictions and trust. I am not my gift. I am far more."

"James, Robert, and Laurel?"

"They're good."

"And Silas Addair?"

"That man is as close to soulless as I believe possible, and for us, the need to stop him reaches beyond mere political allegiance and becomes moral obligation." Aidan had long let go Myra's hands while he had talked. She was glad now that he had done so, hard as his eyes became. Even separated, however, Myra found herself swept up in his passion and enmity.

Heart swelling with the unspoken vow, Myra found a semblance of a shaky peace within herself. Perhaps the only way she might identify her confederates was through anathema. She rose to leave, stopping short as she realized the deftness with which Aidan had side-stepped all that she had come to confront him over.

Frustrated, for Myra could feel the conversation had drawn to a close without her, she regained her seat, crossing her arms. Sitting in silence, she willed her uneasy sea of emotion back to calmness. Where to begin now that they had reached the end? Could she but say more? Should she just be out with it all and see what happened? It wasn't as though he didn't know her heart. The rest of them did.

Aidan interrupted Myra's tumbling thoughts, "There is, of course, much for you to learn about life itself before you can truly use your gift as it is meant."

"What's that supposed to mean?" Meant as only an internal snap at the wizard, Myra was stunned to find her temper getting away from her so easily. So much for calm and centered.

"Emotional maturity."

And what do you mean by that, Aidan McIntyre? Myra glared daggers, daring the mage to continue.

He fumbled, flustered under Myra's ire. A part of her reveled in his discomfort over having reopened the conversation, having forced him to come round to her point at last. He said, "Well, you're all of fourteen years old. Not exactly flush with life experience. I happen to know, for example, that Benjamin Egrett is penning your letters to Julius Griggs—"

"He has to!" Myra exploded. "It's his job."

"I'll grant that you make for a most excellent cover for our sudden uptick in communications with the ord inventor." Aidan's smile came cool and controlled. "I'll also grant you that his expertise in coded messages is unparalleled. But you, yourself, needn't be involved."

Myra lapsed into her sullen silence, her folded arms a barrier, a defense against further scolding. Didn't she know that it was a dangerous game to flirt with Julius Griggs when she would rather be—?

Aidan knew it. And he was telling her such in the dark flash of his eyes. He himself was discomfited by the whole thing. Not just the mess with MI2's ord but with himself.

And there Myra had the truth that she had come for. Aidan was jealous of the attention given Julius by Myra. Jealous and worried and angered all at once.

Aidan stole Myra's confession for himself, "There will be time for all that, Myra love."

Myra's answering smile was crooked, barely covering the ache in a heart crushed by Aidan's honesty. But it answered for her what she had come there to know: James had been right about Aidan being honorable towards Myra and her feelings, even if he hurt them in the process.

Without another word, she made her escape.

Chapter Twenty-Four

Myra could feel Ben's elation clear across Grafford House. Bright but fractured, like sunlight through a stained-glass window, the young M.I. agent's delighted surprise tingled in the crisp pre-dawn air.

"So I'm never to get another full night's rest in this house, is that it?" Tugging on slippers and hastily pulling her robe close about her, Myra quietly padded out of her room to see what the commotion was about. Ben's excitement was contagious. There was no chance of a meek and uninterested return to sleep now.

A strange disquiet tugged at Myra's eyes and mind as she walked the darkened hallways. That same strangeness, call it instinct, had her avoiding use of her wand. Instead, she ran to escape her unease.

A voice spoke close within her ear:

"Duchenne. Du Bois-Reymond, Moritz Meyer, and Robert Remak. Teilleux and Auzouy. We stand on the shoulders of so

many who've come before. We owe them the glory of our vision!
Hales, fetch me the original Leyden array. I think I might finally
have hit upon the right solution.

"It has been said 'We are moving from the Age of Steam to the
Age of Electricity.' But I shall take it further. We shall usher in the
Age of Magic."

Whipping around, Myra saw nothing. She hadn't
expected to. The voice had been unfamiliar to her. Like
James' letter, her vision that time had been a flash of
insight and little more. She was left not knowing who
had spoken nor why. But she retained the imprint of
fear on the part of whomever she had fallen into.

Hair charged with the electricity of gross anticipation; skin sticky with half-remembered perspiration;
mouth dry and sour; Myra wasn't sure she wanted to try
gathering enough control to follow that thread. And
besides, what could she learn from something so vague?
Then again, wasn't chasing down such visions something she was meant to do as part of the team?

Ben would know what to do. She could ask him.

The Necromancer had installed himself in the
library. He did not see her enter, his face eagerly pressed
into the topmost of a swaying stack of books. Myra
stood patiently, waiting for acknowledgement. She was
instead treated to a one-man-play on the topic of
broken joy. Oblivious to all outside of the book in hand,
Ben flipped back and forth between pages, stopping at
intervals to close his eyes and vent quiet exclamations.

Now Myra had stood there far too long. Should she
clear her throat and alert Ben to the fact that he had an

audience? Perhaps she ought to back silently away and enter again, taking care to make more noise. Or—

Or it was too late to do any such thing. Benjamin lifted his eyes to look directly at Myra. New surprise papered over the old, joy atop joy. It buried the uneasy loss that rode beneath the whole of his emotional state. He was on his feet in an instant, eagerly gesturing she approach even as he stepped forward, knocking over the stack of books in his haste.

"I've forgotten something," Benjamin explained.

"What?" Myra's question served several purposes. Surprise. Confusion. Ignorance. Luckily, it seemed this last was covered by the other implications of her outcry. That or Ben was too caught up in his discovery to point out how Myra had momentarily forgotten the extent of his second magical gift.

"My dreams." Ben gesticulated wildly, his careful but intense whisper a reminder that they were the only two yet awake. "I awoke and felt them fade from memory. A slate hastily and haphazardly wiped. I've been testing myself ever since. I had to know it to be true. And it is. Myra, I've gained the ability to forget."

"You stopped taking Addair's elixir."

He nodded. "Soon I'll be as ord as Griggs and the rest."

Ben's face, so filled with warring emotions and sparkling with tears born of newfound freedom, pressed close to Myra's. Too close. With the sudden closing of the distance came a heightening of electricity—and not the Dampening sort—between them.

Though fearful that Benjamin might well forget himself, mad with joy as he was, Myra did not shy away. A part of her actually wondered what it might feel like to be kissed. She figured it likely on par with the happiness now expressed in Ben's face.

And suddenly, Myra felt the terrible weight of her own gift. She had managed an uneasy truce with her powers, but here was something new again, something with which Myra found herself ill-equipped to deal. Benjamin's emotional state—normally so hidden away, so dark—shone brightly at her. He had become as mentally attractive as he was physically handsome. And Myra was unsure what, if anything, she was supposed to do with it. Could she even hope to separate out what he wanted versus what she did?

And did that even matter in light of how much Benjamin was hurting underneath his euphoria right in that moment? Unasked, Myra seized that thread of darkness and burned it away with her Empathic powers. *Forget the horror, Benjamin.*

She buried him in elation. She forced further gladness onto his soul. Let him be happy. For once, let him not live in dark memory, hiding from the present and minimizing all future experiences so as to protect himself. The curse had ended. Benjamin could remember or forget as he so chose.

Myra's magic showed the way, and she closed her eyes, innocent yet expectant. She felt Benjamin lean close. His breath brushed her cheeks, stirred her eyelashes. He paused, an eternity.

In the instant before their lips met, Myra felt herself go hot and cold all at once. And the moment they made contact? She was glad to have previously travelled the TurnKey network, for the sensation gave her a baseline for what she now felt. Focused, as though the world had collapsed in on itself leaving just Myra and Benjamin.

Ben's hand somehow found its way up the side of Myra's neck, the gentle touch prompting a new avalanche of thrill. The smell of him, a strange sweet bitterness. The co-mingling of their emotions . . . The sharp tang of guilt, a reminder that Myra, young and unchaperoned, was openly kissing a boy.

And then the kiss was over. It left Myra breathless and more than a little shocked that it had actually happened. Looking into Benjamin's eloquent eyes, so close to hers, she could tell he felt much the same way.

The gentle creak of a door somewhere in the upper reaches of Grafford House brought them back to their senses. Myra and Benjamin were no longer the only ones awake. And though M.I. ran an unconventional home, to risk discovery at this stage would be folly.

At this stage? Am I meant to continue on after this? New problems presented themselves for Myra's inspection. For all that she knew Ben admired her, and that, in return, she found him interesting, Aidan still lived in the back of her mind. How mortifying if he should find out.

"I'm sorry." Ben's hand was up over his mouth. Defense against Myra being forward a second time? A wiping away of the evidence?

No. Self control. A physical barrier to his own rash impulses.

"Don't be." Myra's own weak attempt at an apology came belated and without punch. "We both were feeling . . ."

"Enthused?" The hand removed itself. A crooked smile peeked out at her.

"Vulnerable."

Benjamin leaned in. He sought her gaze, not allowing Myra to look down and away. He seemed surprised by what he read there. "Was that . . . was that for me or for you?"

Stunned by Ben's insight, the realization that he could have sensed her carefully hidden jealousy, Myra sat back, removing herself from his mislaid compassion. She said nothing. She spoke volumes.

Hurt flitted briefly through Ben's eyes, a dimming of his fire. He, too, sat away from her now. "You don't need to be an empath to read people, Myra."

"Oh, but Empathy is so much more than that," Myra began, pausing to hunt for the right words. "I lose myself. It's a falling into someone else, an unasked-for invasion of the deepest, most intimate sort."

Intimate. The word hung in the air between them, pointing an accusatory finger.

"You'll learn to control it, Myra. And you will be all the better for it. You'll soon appreciate what wondrous things your gift can do."

That angered her. "If learning and control is the answer, then why couldn't you have—"

"You truly haven't figured out how vastly different our abilities are, have you? You with your head-hopping, seeing others from inside their magic and even borrowing bits of it. Are you truly that daft, or do you just pretend to it?" Ben's own temper met hers, roused by the same trigger.

Myra blinked. No, there would certainly not be a kiss to follow the first. The sweet, sensuous boy was gone. In his place sat a man as prickly as James and as temperamental. Poison darts.

Quick as it had flared, Benjamin's anger began a cautious retreat. Myra felt the riotous waters calm until she had no more access to his emotional state than the next person. He let her in anyhow. "What's the cruelest thing you can remember, Myra? What disappointments? Slights? Horrors? I have them all. Every word on the page, every syllable uttered in my hearing, yes, I retain those. The joys, yes. But the worst parts of my life . . . they live alongside me. Nightmares. I cannot shake them upon waking."

"I know that, and that's why I—"

"Threw a bit of happiness my way? As if thirty seconds of peace can erase a lifetime of pain. That's not what your gift is for, Myra."

Myra bowed under the weight of Ben's outburst. Yes, she knew. Yes, she understood how his particular blend of gifts could be—no, was—impossibly cruel. And yet, he continued on, bleeding out in front of her and with no way for Myra to hide from it, coward that she was.

"For a time, when it was first proposed that I memorize—ha! memorize—a good portion of M.I.'s files, the sum of their gathered intelligence, I threw myself into the work. I thought, erroneously, there was a capacity to my aching brain. And the sooner I met it, the sooner I could crowd out that which tortured me.

"Instead, it worsened. The noise! It helped to drown out the horrors in my past, but in exchange I was prey to the frightful sound of thousands of facts clamoring to be recalled for use, a chattering library that refused to be silenced. But there was no backing out. Not now that the team relied so heavily upon my knowledge. Forgetting was, as you know, impossible. I owed M.I. the use of my gift. For all that I suffered, lives were saved by it."

Ben took hold of Myra's hand. And suddenly, Myra could feel it, a frightful sensation within her head and

heart to rival that of her first kiss. Literary passages . . .
Dull facts about foreign lands, the movement of armies,
recited aloud . . . A mother's smile . . . James scolding
over an inept casting . . . The memory of Myra staring
back at herself through Ben's eyes and the feel of her
hand in his, warm, soft . . .

The scream and squall of non-forgetting overwhelmed the senses. It was a madness to which Myra
had never sunk. Even in her worst moments. Far from a
loss of control, it was a total lack thereof.

"I've learned to restrain most— Nay, I've adapted,"
Benjamin hastily corrected himself. "I do not leave Grafford House for the dangers it poses me, as you know. But
the dangers to myself are not all from Addair or his
mages. The witnessing of an accident can haunt me for
the rest of my days. Conversations, too many to count—
I retain them all, and with as much clarity as they were
overheard."

Well and truly hearing him at last, knowing she
could never hope to fully understand, Myra squeezed
Ben's hand. He allowed her to return to herself, her
blessedly quiet self. Why he had not abandoned his gift
until now, until his hand had been forced, lent her
greater understanding of him still.

Incredible what this man knew. His contribution to
his team, his country and queen, beyond value. Myra
imagined the years stretching out before them.
Benjamin was but two, three years her senior. What if
he were to live as long as James, as long as Robert,
under such an unrelenting blessing and curse?

"And that's just the part I'll let you see." Benjamin's
voice broke, a strangled crescendo that brought Myra

back close to his side, their shoulders and knees touching but lightly.

Recalled to Ben's memories of her, Myra valued the simplicity of the close companionship. Could she give him more than that one kiss? A part of her still wanted to. More than ever, in fact. It was as though she was seeing him for the first time, and the inversion of the proper steps to courtship had her blushing.

The day had continued to brighten, bleaching the gauzy library curtains to a translucent white. Through them, the left half of Ben's face was unevenly illuminated, the warmer yellows and oranges of the library lamps serving to create an uncomfortable dichotomy. Two faces. Two distinct halves of one person. Even now, how much did Myra know about Benjamin?

She turned her gaze to the window, setting her eyes to the narrow space where the curtains failed to meet. It had snowed during the night. London, renewed. A clean slate.

"Benjamin Egrett. Don't tell me you're getting in some extra cramming before your— Oh, Myra, you're in here, too."

Aidan!

Leaping to her feet, Myra affected innocence. She failed utterly. Or at least she was sure she did under the scrutiny of the Maester of Triewes. *And how's that for achieving a bit of emotional maturity?*

He was too polite to acknowledge the lapse of decorum, fixing his eyes on Benjamin and continuing, "I had stopped by your rooms at James' request. He seemed to think you and I would benefit from a tête-à-tête on the art, a shoring up of resources in light of circumstances."

That's it. He's mucking with his hair again just to set me on edge. Myra gritted her teeth, smiling through Aidan's preening. *And it's working splendidly, damn the man.*

Myra made her excuses and her escape from both mages. She figured that she would have ample time later to deal with each. Once she had, of course, figured things out for herself.

Chapter Twenty-Five

"Myra." The name assailed her as soon as she had gained the hallway.

Glancing about the dim walls in alarm, for she did not recognize the voice, Myra pulled her wand on the stranger lounging against the far wall. Heart hammering, she held her ground to the intruder. Her mind raced through several options. Scream and bring Aidan and Benjamin running? Hex the man herself?

"Hold, my dear. Hold." Quick fingers plucked the hat from the gentleman's head. Robert's familiar form replaced that of the stranger's. And Myra found herself gawping and smiling all at once.

"You've more of your gift back?" Guilt poked Myra's ribs, renewed thoughts of Benjamin's predicament and her reaction to his news.

"Not quite." Robert gave a slow shake of the head and indicated she follow him. " 'Tis but a trick of this hexed haberdashery."

A thin circle of misty fog ringed the crown of the hat, bumping up over the knuckles of Robert's hand where he clutched the brim and flowing down past his wrist only to dissipate. Myra had seen that hat before. She blurted out, "That's from the laboratorium!"

"Yes. Come, we're escaping to its solitude," Robert said.

"But won't I be in the way?" Two people in one small room didn't exactly offer solitude.

Robert did not address this and simply strode off down the hallway.

Left with the dilemma—she was likely being rude no matter which she chose—Myra abandoned considera- tion and followed curiosity. As they walked, she kept her eyes on the hat in the weather-worker's hand. The day was just begun. How could Robert possibly have a need for solitude at such an hour? And why the disguise within his own home?

"I'll apologize in advance," Robert began. "There was no plan to have a lesson for you in my laboratorium as of yet. But I felt it an appropriate addition to your education. Too many tricks around. Good to know of some of them."

Your laboratorium? It seemed to Myra that the room changed ownership daily. Perhaps her turn would come tomorrow. Burying her smirk, she entered the room of wonders.

It was as exotic as she remembered. The small rickety table was still diligently struggling under its Kosmogramme. Eerie light still filled the air. Closing her eyes, Myra breathed deep, wondering if she might sort out the various magics around her now that she had honed the use of the senses given her by her gift. The air, however, was carefully neutral. Or maybe there was simply too much going on. There were, at the least, a hundred—no, two hundred—such objects vying for her attention.

Robert replaced the foggy hat upon its shelf. Right where Myra had seen it on her first morning in Grafford House.

"And so, Myra, what does it do?"

Myra froze. Why did the question make her feel so guilty? *Because I didn't expect there should be a test, that's how.*

"Apologies. That was unfair of me." Robert settled himself into a wingback chair. "It's one of my own, you know. My design. My artifact."

Myra hunted about for a chair. The furniture in the room was near invisible, surrounded by arcanea as it was. The wingback's partner was but half-concealed by a low shelf. If she was careful, Myra could sit within the space, so long as she remembered to not bump her head upon standing. The laboratorium really did have a cozy air about it. Turning to Robert, she smiled her appreciation of his skills. "So that fog then . . ."

"Also mine, yes." The wizard's eyes grew misty, and he seemed to leave the room for a moment. And then he returned, full of thunder and spark once more. "The idea was to conceal a person's individuality as does the fog. Describe whom you thought you saw in the hallway outside the library, if you please."

"I . . . He . . . She . . . They . . ." Myra blushed. She couldn't remember.

"Height? Weight? What was the person wearing?" Robert pressed.

Humiliated, Myra shook her head. Each idea presenting itself to her mind rang false. The person had not had a build similar to Robert's. And yet, how had it been different? Had it been different? And, though clearly he had been wearing a hat, Myra couldn't imagine him—or her? them?—having had one.

Robert's chuckle rumbled comfortably through the room. "Again, I've been patently unfair."

"I felt that there was magic," Myra shot back at last, breathing easy as her mind caught on the one thing she could be sure of. And she knew she had gotten it right when the mage looked as though she had stolen his wind from him.

"Now that shouldn't be." Robert frowned, reflectively thumbing his chin. "Supposed to be an ord disguise."

"Oh, I'm certain of what I felt. And I cannot begin to tell you anything else. But that's what had me pulling my wand rather than acting proper and cautious."

"Good job, that." He nodded at last, brightening. "So you felt the magic of the artifact itself."

Myra shook her head. "Its workings. I can't feel it when it's over there on the shelf, jumbled amongst the rest and not being used. But when you had it on, you were all over power. Now that I know it for what it is, I can see that it functions as a cloak of sorts."

"I wonder . . ." Robert's contemplative fingers had resumed their prodding of his chin. But whatever it was he wondered, he did not make clear. He moved on. "What is it you want to know?"

"About?"

Robert waved to the room. "Any of it. The tricks and tools of the trade."

For this Myra had a ready question. "Why don't you use it all the time?"

"Ah, but we do."

"The hat. You've never used the hat before. Not around me anyway. And why use it this morning?"

"Such magics lose their glamour if overused," Robert began, settling into his chair. Hooded eyes lowered, and Myra wondered if she would have her answer before he dozed off on her.

"Finite use?"

"Not exactly. Yes, all things wear out—wizardry being no exception. But the effectiveness can be lost if it's all tricks all the time. You saw through it mighty fast."

"But my gift—"

"Bah. Everyone's gifted in their own way. Or did you think it was just us mages who were special? Look at your Julius Griggs. There's a man of talent. And not a spark within him."

Thinking of Julius, of how it led her back 'round to thoughts of Aidan and subsequently Benjamin, Myra tried to return their conversation to that of Robert and his hat. "This morning then. In your own house. Why?"

"I discovered what you did, that young Benjamin is losing his gift."

A thrill snuck up Myra's spine. She sat further back in her chair, quashing it as best she could.

"Not as you could, of course. No, I simply knew his time with his Thymesis and Necromancy was coming to a close based on how long he's been without Addair's elixir. The trick I played upon you just now? I thought it would be an interesting experiment. See if he could remember the un-remember-able as he once was able."

Robert's fog hat couldn't fool Benjamin either? That, Myra found interesting. And with her thoughts on Benjamin again, she could feel a blush beginning its burn in her cheeks. She turned the conversation, hitching her breath at her daring, "Tell me about Silas Addair."

"For that, Myra dear, I would need my pipe." Robert roused himself, hunting about his pockets for the needed implements. For a moment, Myra feared she had pressed too hard, misjudged his temperament and annoyed or, worse, hurt him. But a sharp snap of a match being struck and the acrid tang of burning Cavendish simply served as an interlude before the answer.

"Professor Silas Addair was a member of the Department of Topography and Statistics. Though, perhaps, by starting there, I am getting ahead of myself. Through family connections, and a good deal of patriotic curiosity, I and Miss Florence Trivett found ourselves serving in the burgeoning Crimean Conflict in the early 1850s. Both of us young—just a whisper above yourself in age, dear Myra—our fathers had been longtime friends who had gotten themselves involved in the affairs of that end of the world. Protecting Company interests in India, you know. On account of us both being mages—a family secret, I can assure you—we were allowed to accompany them there, to the edge of the action but no further.

"We could see to our own safety. And we did. That is not to say that we were not loved by our families. They did not wish to put us in undue danger. But you have to understand that, even then, wizardry was considered no good. Dirty. Neither Florence nor I had much to expect from life save to be safely married off to one another and left to retire on our small family fortunes. Swept under the rug of domestic respectability, as it were.

"But we wanted more. I thank my dear father for understanding that about me."

Myra stirred within her own chair, thinking of her family and how little they had understood her gift. But, to blame them was patently unfair. None of them had known what it was Myra faced when she fell into her fits. To them, magic would have been as unbelievable as it was un-thought-of.

Robert continued, "It happened quite by accident that Florence and I distinguished ourselves to her father's outfit. A mere gathering of information on the movement of Cossack troops—again, through mere curiosity and boredom—and suddenly we were important, distinguished. Still odd, of course. Still feared, even. But some fellow up top got it into his head that mages were the way to win from there on. A way to save lives. The Department of Topography and Statistics was born. Our family secrets were secrets no more. In certain circles, at least."

"But Addair was not a mage. Yet." Myra made use of the pause in Robert's narrative.

"No, not for a long time," Robert said, his pipe all but extinguished in his fingers and eyes still in the past. "Silas came along because we needed legitimacy, even then. The Department . . . Well, you can gather from its obtuse name that the intent was to appear as a mere surveying outfit. Practical and pragmatic. The very opposite of intrigue and underhanded military dealings. The opposite of everything thought of wizards and magic.

"Silas Addair became the public face of the Department. His research provided both cover and aid for my and Florence's clandestine information gathering. There were others, of course. Ords. But we were the core. We were the reason for it all. And then my childhood friend, lovely Florence, fell in love with Silas, as people that age are wont to do when put into difficult situations."

If Myra detected a note of bitterness in Robert's words, he hid it quickly under a rather showy relighting of his pipe. A rumbling clearing of his throat, and the M.I. agent had his story going once more. "Time passed; we won the war and slid into uneasy retirement, collecting more mages along the way as the world worked itself up to its next conflict. By the time the Second Afghan War rolled around, Florence and I were training our replacements in the form of Stephen and James. The Dampening was making itself fully known with the world's increasing enamorment of electricity, and Addair was throwing all his efforts into saving us—and his infant son—from its effects. Laurie came to us as our first lesser mage, having been raised on Silas' elixir in order to preserve what powers she had."

Silence filled the room, broken only by the crackle of Robert's burning tobacco and the quiet swing of the Kosmogramme's orbs along their paths.

Robert's story had answered much for Myra. But not all. She dared, "When did Silas become a mage?"

The mage's brow darkened at Myra's impertinence, but his aura did not fall into anger. It seemed that his pause was merely a gathering of fact and a choosing of words, as he was forthcoming with his answer but a moment later. "For that we return to young Benjamin. Eleven years ago, he came to us. A broken, frightened child, his gift was not as easily concealed as the rest of ours. His family was not a wizarding one, so we hadn't been keeping an eye on them for any instances of Emergere.

"The Department had for itself a fair amount of work concealing what had actually occurred with the child. And, even then, rumors persisted. Said rumors cost the life of Florence and her son.

"Poor Benjamin, new to his terrifying powers, either would not or could not bring Florence and little James back to life at Silas' demand. It was at that point that the Professor broke with us and with the government. He destroyed his records, sabotaged nearly half of what elixir remained for our use, and ran off to goodness knows where. As far as we understand things, Addair's research has since consisted of attempts to make his own mages, somehow becoming one himself—if a lesser mage."

"And what is his particular gift?" Myra said.

"He is a Mien-caster. Doctor Silas Addair, dangerous enough with his intelligence and animosity towards us, can change his face at will. But only his face, only the basic outward trappings of his appearance."

"Which is where Aidan comes into this, yes?"

"Stephen went to America seeking the truth in a rumor that Silas' methods and men had been spotted. We had hoped that, yes, allying with the gifts of our American counterparts, we might identify and eliminate the threat. No muss. No fuss." Robert roused himself, using the heel of his shoe to knock the dottle from his pipe onto the ground. With the flick of a wrist, he made the whole mess disappear. Myra wondered at it. Was there some OtherLand full of Robert's spent pipe tobacco?

Myra tore herself away from the distraction. "Would

Aidan be able to see through the disguise of your fog hat?"

"I suppose he might." Robert returned to his sanguine lounging in the wingback.

"But that's half our team that can see through it! How is any of this useful?" Myra gestured to the surrounding arcanea.

Robert's brow furrowed, sorrow rather than annoyance overtaking his features. "Stephen, God rest his soul, was the only mage I knew who ever took stock in the idea that your powers—the gift of Empathy—might exist. Your powers, Myra . . . they are impossible. Well, not impossible. Obviously.

"As for Benjamin, he cannot see through the disguise. He simply is able to remember the face one adopts with it due to the quirk of his perfect memory. Interesting, surely. But useless due to the fact that nobody else can see and recall the unremarkable as he is able. He would stand alone in his convictions, looking for a suspect only he could identify.

"And as for Aidan . . ." Robert shrugged. "I don't much care for what James says on his count. You'd best leave Aidan alone, young Myra. He's been through a lot. And he's too honest—" He broke off, gaze turned inward as he sought the best path forward. "As with everything, Aidan's too honest with his emotions. He has regard for you, and I think that hurts him."

"I'm aware of his fondness—"

"He carries such pain, Myra. Surely you've felt that in him? The loss of—of his team in America. He's not ready yet for what your presence offers him."

Offers him? How dare Robert insinuate such! Myra bristled, angry and embarrassed.

"You're both young and each subject to the limitations of your gifts." Aware of Myra's distress, Robert tried to blunt his warning, "You are aware that, at 18, he's the youngest to head up such a department? Even outstripping James, who took over for me once he and Stephen joined up with us in the Second War. But, the Dampening has limited the numbers so heavily and . . . Where was I?"

"Aidan being young. And I should leave him alone because my presence is a burden upon his life." This Myra said through clenched teeth.

Robert chuckled and leaned forward. "Now, now, my girl. I don't mean it so bleak or as cruel as that. But I think you know what game you're playing at with both the American and our Benjamin. And even Julius— Uh, uh, Myra." Robert stopped her interruption with a wag of his finger. "Even Julius. Because we all know it's Benjamin's cryptography upon which you're leaning. Which colors that false courtship in its own strange way. An empath should know and understand jealousy, too."

"What do you suggest I do?" Myra hunched in her chair miserably. Guiltily.

"I suggest learning a thing or two besides magic, my girl." Robert winked. "Such as, when to back off and hide yourself here in the laboratorium, away from all the drama."

Chapter Twenty-Six

Myra followed Robert's sage advice and found that, for a few days at least, she both advanced in the practice of her gift and avoided unnecessary drama. She found it maddening how right the man was. And refreshing. Though this she admitted only to herself. That said, at least someone in Grafford House was not altogether without decorum.

And then her peace ended as, under this new routine of calm certainty, Myra woke one morning to find new clothing arrayed and awaiting her. She mentally thanked the wardrobe fairies for yet another gift to match the other three ensembles previously accumulated under similar circumstances and moved to inspect the dress. She blanched.

A smart pinstripe. Cream. And edged with little red tassels. Hideously fashionable. Terribly impractical for M.I.'s line of work.

Was this a joke?

Myra looked to the cabinet to where her other outfits hung in state. Biting her lip, she affected deliberation but knew her decision had already been made for her. She fingered the cloth again and peered closer at the construction of the garment. It looked to be as uncomfortable as it was the latest fashion. Stiff. Constricting.

Ord clothes.

Myra dressed with reluctance, feeling the world retreat, separated as she was from it by her iron cage of corsetry and thick poplin. Her fingers pulled at the cloth, testing. No pockets. No place for her wand. At this last, she felt the hairs on her arm raise in brief alarm.

A knock sounded on her door, and Myra jumped.

"A moment," she called, dashing over to fetch her wand from her nightstand, gratefully noting that she, at least, still had her comfortable footwear. She opened the door and found herself face to face with Laurel, who beamed at her.

"Good morning, Myra. I see you've managed quite well on your own."

Myra took Laurel's surprise with a wry smile of her own, managing a clipped, "Yes, thank you."

Laurie saw right through it. Of course. She captured Myra's hands within her own, her eyes bright and mischievous as she maneuvered around the wand grasped therein. "Best leave that behind, dear. It mars the disguise."

Disguise? Oh! Myra gave a wobbly grin, feeling stupid and apprehensive at the same time. The only folk liable to spot the subtle differences between this and mage-modified attire were wizards themselves. Where could she possibly be going that required her to present herself so fully as an ord? *And why is it I am so quick to question these kind people over and again?*

Myra's wonder was interrupted as Benjamin appeared at the end of the hallway. She felt the blood drain from her face and instinctively knew, to her mortification, that it rendered the stylish outfit even more ill-fitting for her. She had no recourse. For two days she had studiously avoided Benjamin after their encounter in the library. And here he was walking straight towards her as though nothing had passed between them. Perhaps, in his eyes, nothing had. Myra wilted under the new worry, forcing color unevenly into her cheeks with a furious blush.

"Ah, Myra. I was coming to fetch you. Going out?" Ben's explanation faltered as Laurel caught his eye. A silent questioning ensued. He sauntered towards them, undeterred.

Myra cast quick eyes over both Laurel's and Ben's getups. Neither mage wore ord clothing. Subtle as the differences were, she had gotten used to noting them— through wearing such herself. Benjamin's reaction was confirmation that the observation went both ways. To his credit, he seemed hurt after their two days of non-interaction. But then it might have been merely because he, himself, never went anywhere.

Myra said, "I don't know—"

"Breakfast first," Laurel interrupted Myra's attempt at deflection, stepping between the two younger agents. The act gave motion to her brisk tone. They walked in silence, Myra and Benjamin's unsteady peace bent under Laurie's no-nonsense authority.

Agents. Not young friends. And certainly not paramours.

Myra's blush migrated down across her neck and up into her ears. She burned from the scrutiny that

Benjamin passed her way. Out of the corner of her eye —she dared not try to glance at him directly—she could see that judgment had been passed. But his look was unreadable. Not disapproval, thank the gods. But he wasn't exactly harboring some secret compliment, either.

The hallways yawned endlessly. For every step forward, Myra felt the carpeted expanse drag on, lengthening to prolong her torture. She looked to Laurel, begging interference, "Does this have to do with the Order of the Holy Flame?"

Laurel flicked her eyes to Myra, then Benjamin. Blessing on Myra's query and permission for him to answer.

"*Liberi Ignis*; Children of Fire." Benjamin's terse response provided Myra enough surprise that it shook her out of control of her gift. He was jealous. Deeply jealous.

So, his mood is not about the kiss then. Myra felt her insides warm to match her fading blush.

Ben elaborated, "Addair's mages are more commonly known as simply The Children. Therefore, I believe it a tenuous link to the Order that you all shall shortly be investigating." Again came the dig, the subtle reminder that he must stay behind, as always.

Myra bit back her apology. Likely he had heard enough of them in his lifetime as an agent. She settled for soothing him with her Empathy as best she could.

"James will provide the rest of the details as need-ed," Laurel continued for Benjamin. "But it was Ben who figured out the subtext of Julius' most recent message. The key meaning of it."

"Yes, he sent another one to you, Myra. But I didn't

bother delivering it this time." Ben sighed. "Which is why it is you who must go with James, I suppose."

"And why you, my dear, must present yourself as ordinary a person as possible." James' voice behind them made Myra jump. He strode forward, his usual black on black attire sharp and ready for all possibilities. The sight of him was, perhaps, the most reassuring thing Myra had encountered all morning after finding that she was to leave all magic behind her for the day.

Relieved her of charges, Laurel smiled thinly and gave James a passing peck on the cheek. "You'll remember Stephen's Sholes, James?"

"I'll remember, Laurie. Though I despise that contemptible machine." James returned the pale affection with a warm smile. A sad smile. Stephen's ghost still walked amongst them.

Myra looked away. And found herself accidentally engaging with Benjamin, who had lost his jealous edge. He beckoned her forward, away from the senior agents and towards the breakfast that gave a tantalizing call from the nearby dining room. The tinkle of cup and saucer and scrape of cutlery on plate informed her that others had already broken their fast. She followed Ben with a relieved heart, seeing approval spark his eyes at last as he cheekily looked her over once more, commenting, "Stripes. Never would have thought such on you, stick that you are."

"I hadn't enough advanced notice to change my body carriage to match the latest fashion," Myra sniffed, enjoying the game immensely. Her eyes began to drift towards Ben's mouth, and she corrected herself swiftly. She instead grasped at his rising mood. "You, Mr.

Egrett, tend to be up on haberdashery in spite of your reclusive nature. Any pointers?"

"Don't flirt with Julius."

Myra gawked, unable to separate tease from warning. Perhaps they were inseparable, coming from Ben. She nodded, not finding words to answer. Letting him have the victory, she allowed Benjamin to help her to her seat at the table and noted that his eyes sparkled merriment at her. Still an enigma, that man.

Robert looked up from his meal only just long enough to wave a "good morning" at the two newcomers. Whereas Aidan sat across from Myra, his eyes raking over her outfit and drawing his own conclusions. Conclusions he kept to himself.

Certain that both men had heard Benjamin's comment, Myra mused over the differing reactions. She found that Aidan's quiet judgment irked her, and at length again concluded that, for all his indecorous behavior, Benjamin was the better gentleman there. Excepting Robert, of course, who was proper in all possible ways.

Hiding amongst her spiced potatoes and sausage, Myra wished that the two rivals would leave her out of it for once. It was hard enough navigating Benjamin's verbal darts and Aidan's protective posturing without them also taking shots at one another at her expense.

It was, appropriately enough, James who rescued her. "Myra, when you're ready? No rush, of course."

He ducked his head in and out of the dining hall to deposit his statement to her in one smooth motion. Myra rose with alacrity, startling Robert, Benjamin, and Aidan to their feet. With a small smile, she gathered her dishes and swept into the kitchen to make her escape.

Men.

The Grafford House carriage had been pulled 'round the front.

Apparently, while Myra was to play ord, James had no need for such subtlety as disembarking from the mews. He helped her into the coach and then instructed the driver, "Carlisle, please."

They jolted into brisk motion. Myra gave vent to a small squeak of surprise. Subtle, no. Hurried, yes. She glanced to James. But he had returned to his usual impassive self. Silence made for an awkward third occupant during their journey up now-familiar Constitution Hill.

At length, James leaned forward, bringing gloved hands to his chin and resting them upon his cane. His lips barely moved as he said, "I've some business to attend to at headquarters. It was requested that I bring you with. A show, openly, of our mystery guest within Grafford House, as Mr. Griggs might have let slip your presence amongst our company to those with whom we used to work. Your story will be that your elder sister was Kady Moore, and your gift fell to the Dampening before anyone could preserve it via the elixir."

Myra blinked acknowledgement, aware now that James was attempting to mask their communication to anyone who might be attending. She tried mimicking his stoicism, keeping her voice low. "I'm an ord. Got it."

"Good girl." James leaned back, fixing his eyes out the window, every inch the bored gentleman. Myra followed suit. Her boredom, however, was genuine.

The carriage inched along, hemmed in by traffic. Eventually, James reached up and rapped the ceiling, swearing under his breath. He set his eyes on Myra, piercing her with his impatience. "Care if we walk it?"

Shaking her head, Myra prepared herself by looking out the window. She did not recognize anything. But then, buildings around town looked much the same to her. Squished together. Some better, some worse off. And it was crowded. Reminded of her constricting bodice and pinching corsetry as she shifted on the bench, Myra really did not relish the walk. Even if it proved to be but one block. She also had the sense to know that James' request was, in reality, an order.

The driver deposited them with a promise to return. And within moments, Myra found herself adrift with James in the surging whirlpool that was central London in mid-morning. He navigated them into the current of people, Myra catching her breath and managing a fresh glance around as they slowed to match the pace of those around them. She noted a sign: James Street. The insolence of that man!

Five long blocks had rendered Myra rosy-cheeked and footsore. Her slippers, while clever, were not meant for such abuse. She wondered if they would ever be the same again.

James Street had led them to Victoria and around to Wilton Road. And that was the end of Myra's usefulness on that front, having been all turned around by crooked roads, ill-tempered horses, and a multitude of strangers. But at least the traffic had thinned somewhat. Myra's initial fears of standing out in a crowd had been quelled by the simple fact that most folk seemed intent on their own pursuits—namely the nearby train station.

And so it was that she failed to be impressed by which building along the block she and James entered save for the plaque out front that declared in bold letters:

Whitte & Wight Imports Ltd.
Appointments Only.

Whisked inside by polite manners—ladies first—and her own simple desire to be somewhere quiet and dark, Myra barely had time to wonder if they had made such an appointment.

But there they were. Myra's eyes were slow to adjust.

Her ears caught on faster. The steady tick of a clock, the chaotic crepitation of paper being dropped by the sheaf-ful, and a man's cursing introduced Myra to DMI before she could separate the large wooden desk from the dark paneling that covered the walls of the narrow front hall.

Surprised that she could have missed such an elephant, piled high with all manner of administrative jumble, Myra soon understood why the issuer of said foul language had let fly his colorful statement of dismay within earshot of his company. He couldn't see her either.

At Myra's side, James cleared his throat.

Under the pointed admonition, a red-faced man peeked over a tottering stack of papers, his actions threatening to send this second after the first. He grew redder when he realized a lady had been privy to his ungentlemanly outburst. He half-rose, leaning as best he could over the massive desk and endless mounds of work that threatened total avalanche. "Beggin' your pardon, Miss—?"

"Moore," Myra smoothly inserted herself into the man's embarrassed pause. Mousy and thin in the face, he looked the sort that was easily alarmed, a nervous dog of a man. He also looked the sort that turned such energy into results. A dynamo who made up for his small stature with action, even his mop of dark hair seemed to quiver. His eyes gleamed eagerly, making them appear smaller, like glass beads in a china doll. His nose, however, was thoroughly out of joint. Myra concluded that it had been broken—perhaps more than once—in the past.

He leaned further to take her hand. Another pile of papers slid to the floor with a crash, unheeded by a custodian intent on more important business. Myra felt the knot inside her chest loosen. She had chosen right by her forward actions. Mage-like but not too far out of the ordinary. James stood by, arms crossed around his wand. Myra didn't have to look at him to feel the glow of his approval.

"Black," the desk-bound agent huffed, keeping introductions as understated as Myra had come to expect from her time in Grafford House. He turned to James. "Here about the last of yer effects, then?"

James peeled off from where he had been leaning against the wall. The corners of his mouth jerked, an expression that, on anyone save James, might have been a smile.

"And you can put that wand away, James. You look ridiculous." With a grunt, Mr. Black slid out from behind his desk. Papers crunched underfoot and forced another birthing of foul language hastily checked. Myra had to work hard to stifle a giggle. "Come along, then. And don't—don't touch anything."

With a start, Myra realized this last was not directed at herself but, rather, still to James. Did the ord-mage division run so rough as that? Curious, Myra picked her way past the desk, on the heels of James and Mr. Black.

The entrance faded behind them, the hall growing close and dingy as they continued onward into the bowels of the DMI headquarters. Their guide tried to make idle talk with each of them in turn. "Miss Moore. I hear tell that you're more'n like one of us than one o' them. Had a sister of the wand, though, did ya?"

Myra nodded, keeping her eyes downcast to help conceal the lie. She figured it worked in her favor. After all, hadn't Kady died in a firefight between mages only last month?

Mr. Black answered with a series of muttered condolences in a tone somehow reminiscent of his swearing and did not press her further. He moved on to James. "We've a bet going as to where you've hidden yourselves. Any chance of helping me out on that point?"

The former agent gave nothing.

Black tried again with a new angle: "And Laurie. How's she feeling? She'll be, what, fifteen? Sixteen weeks along?"

If anything James' jaw tightened, but he gave little more response than that. As for Myra, she only kept her shock hidden through every trick of emotional self-control she had learned. Laurel was pregnant? That explained so much.

But Black had moved on, seeing as he was going to get nothing from his two visitors. "Kept it untouched, as you'll note. Weren't sure at first if you'd all be a'comin' back, see?"

At the agent's wide gesture to their surroundings, Myra realized that the shabby decor was carefully intentional, like the gaslight that illuminated Grafford House. She glanced at James, seeing if the courtesy had made any impression on him.

"Granted, Griggs has made his improvements—not sure you can feel that. No? Well, then, tha's good, I suppose," Black continued, running roughshod over James' silence.

Julius Griggs. Even his name sent Myra's skin to prickling with anticipation.

"Myra."

Her anticipation reached a new pitch. She turned to the speaker, feeling as though she were underwater. Sluggish; simultaneously impatient and reluctant. M.I.'s carefully worded letters of false courtship fluttered up between them in Myra's mind, fanning her shyness. *'Welcome to the game, Thales.'*

Warm welcome, indeed.

"Julius Griggs." James robbed Myra of the chance to speak his name.

Chapter Twenty-Seven

Julius Griggs. In the flesh. Every inch of his crumpled suit and fly-away hair just as Myra remembered. He stepped towards them with a skip in his gait. His broad face beamed, welcoming and eager.

Mr. Black managed to frown and smile all at once. Myra could feel his pent up energy building further and sidestepped away, lest it find sudden vent in the close quarters.

Julius cut in smoothly, physically separating his quarry from DMI's agent but remembering to seal the maneuver with some level of propriety. He said, "Black, mind if I . . . ?"

"There was paperwork. They're here. I've other things." Mr. Black, flustered and sputtering, tried to continue onward with his task of shuttering M.I.'s offices once and for all. He returned to his first excuse, "The paperwork's been done, you see. And—"

"Bah. There's nothing there that can't be packed by you, right? Nothing so much that James and Myra here cannot carry it back with them themselves."

"Carriage," losing steam, Black managed the solitary word.

"Several blocks off and walked the rest, am I right?" Julius fixed bright eyes on Myra. He didn't wait for confirmation. "Come. I have much to show you. Won't be but a tick."

"But——"

"Black," Julius barked.

"It's fine. I trust you, old man. But, two boxes at most, if you please? Griggs was correct about the walk." James went so far as to give Black a reassuring squeeze on the shoulder before turning to follow Julius back towards the light. Myra hurried along at their heels, escaping from Mr. Black's gape-mouthed impotence.

They squeezed past the desk blocking their path, Myra hissing her anxiety as Julius carelessly brushed perilously close to its contents. She could feel Black's eyes boring into them, waiting for the misstep that would allow him to pull her and James from Griggs. A tug-of-war of allegiance.

They gained the steps, Julius jabbering away over . . . well, Myra couldn't make heads nor tails of it. Foreign words flew past her ears, scientific concepts and theories far beyond her ken. A beige hallway—so well-lit as to be agonizing—gave way to a cozy room which spoke volumes about Mr. Julius Griggs.

More study than office, the lighting was less harsh therein. Or perhaps the new electric illumination struggled to do its job effectively within the towers of shelving and their tightly-packed contents. Myra concluded that gaslight under such circumstances would likely be a hazard. Books. Spare parts for God-only-knew-what. Clothing—*blush*. Tools. It was astonishing to think there was any room left for Griggs in his office, never mind two visitors. And yet, while the behemoth desk one floor beneath their feet was stacked and piled with any manner of bureaucratic red tape, Julius' mess carried an air of usefulness.

How did the man ever find anything at all? No wonder he was perpetually hatless and gloveless!

Julius Griggs stood in the midst of his treasures and beamed at James and Myra. Beamed at her, really. Myra blushed under the mental correction and wished she had worn her pendant today. It would have been . . . kind.

"Apologies for the Dampening, James," Julius picked his way to a chair, gesturing that his two guests do the same. "Getting close to the right formula, you know. Close."

Looking around her and feeling her blush grow, Myra tried to sort out which in the room was sit-able and which was merely a well-disguised pile of munitions for Julius' oddball campaign. She sat, hoping that the brown accumulation of leather and stuffing was, indeed, a chair.

James looked equally uncomfortable, though Myra could tell that it was the electricity rather than eccentricity that was getting to him. He sat perched upon a stool, having boldly removed what appeared to be a rudimentary device for toasting bread and placing it onto the floor next to him. He grimaced. "If you plan on talking secrets, with the power present in this building there's little I can do to aid in that."

Griggs waved off the mild complaint. "Bah. Don't let Black get to you. Ever since they bumped him down to desk, he's had a chip. DMI has the new MI2, sure, but it doesn't mean we've forgotten our own."

"You mean, we're still potentials for elimination someday down the road, should we prove a liability to the security of . . ." James waved his hand to their surroundings, his face characteristically dark.

"Don't be an ass, James James," Myra surprised herself by speaking. Even more so by her words. It was something Laurie might have dared say to him, but not Myra. Julius' response was to throw back his head in laughter. James merely stared dumbfounded.

Griggs recovered first, wiping tears from the corners of his eyes. "I can see the mage in you, Myra, even if the Dampening quelled your gift before you ever made use of it. Fire and spirit. Unconventional and outspoken. You speak as well as you write, and I would be willing to bet that, in a few years, even your connection to the likes of James might not be so large a blot on your reputation that you could come work with us when we get MI3 going."

Myra feared her cheeks would never cool again, so furiously did she blush. She looked to James for rescue.

"Why, precisely, is it that you brought us in here?" James got right to it.

Julius stood abruptly, hands fluttering and eyes shining as he once more descended into technological nonsense. "In addition to that which the Department commissions, you know that I perform tasks for the Queen from time to time. Side projects. Unofficially tied to my performances under Brackenbury's stead."

"Grafford's carriage," Myra interjected. Her hand hovered over her breastbone unbidden, a reminder of Julius' pendant that she had foolishly chosen not to wear.

"Quite right. Helpful items utilizing that which the

Department grants for my use. Yet completely off the record," Julius' voice drifted up from where he'd dropped to rummage 'round on a low shelf. On hands and knees, he had his head practically out of sight behind a pile of bric-a-brac. With his back to James and Myra he proved himself completely oblivious as to proper decorum.

"Ah-hah!" The triumphant exclamation heralded his return. Turning, he seated himself directly on the floor and held up a copper-clad box for inspection.

Two blank faces blinked at Julius.

"Oh, come on then." Julius scrambled to his feet, giving his trousers a few smacks to clear them of dust.

"What's it for?" Myra let curiosity take her.

"That's right. You wouldn't feel it as James does," Julius said. "James?"

Still blank, James stared at the device. It was as though his mind and eyes were having a public falling-out, and Myra and Julius got to witness it. At length he said, "It creates fields. Electric fields."

"Not creates, James. Siphons," Julius corrected. "Pulls the electricity from the air. Channeling. Harvesting. Following Tesla's radiant energy theory, I decided on a more practical application. If we could suck the electricity out of the air—filter and capture it here—then, perhaps, we might find ourselves a ready solution to Violectric Dampening."

"But that's wonderful!" Myra exclaimed. "Isn't it James?"

James' shock had turned to horror. "Julius. You've made a weapon. Can't you see that? A weapon against us."

"No, no, no," Julius moved to reassure his friend.

"This is for good. It's like Addair's elixir. A magnet for the sort of power that hurts yours, see? Something that I could try to make embeddable into the places your kind frequent, provided I can solve the issue of insulation. Something wearable, even, given time to allow you free movement anywhere that electricity—"

"It. Is. A. Weapon." James' anger made his words staccato. "Watch." He pulled his wand, made a sign in the air. The resulting curse fizzed and popped, scattering sparks that seared the eyes and made Myra's nostrils smart.

"And that's something small, Julius." James put away his wand. "Gods help us if I tried something akin to Laurie's Ways-walking, or Kady's Kinetics, or even Robert's Weather. Dr. Silas Addair's work is never quite a complimentary comparison, Griggs."

Julius looked stricken. He swayed and reached, unseeing, for his chair. "I'm sorry, James. I hadn't—I hadn't thought—"

"Destroy it."

"Beg pardon?"

"Does anyone else have the plans? The wherewithal to make it?"

"No, but—"

"Destroy it."

"James!" Myra was on her feet, tears in her eyes as she looked from mage to ord.

"Myra. You don't understand. We have been ousted. Myself. Robert. Laurel. What's to stop this from being used the other way around? To make fields of fire that our gift cannot penetrate. Or torture us, as Addair's men did Stephen." James' anger filled the room, making the space small. He shot a glance to Julius. "Was that all, then?"

Julius slumped in his chair. "It is done. James, I'll kill it, yes. But remember. Remember that it is you who asked for such. I'll not be responsible later on when you find yourself needing it. Progress will happen. You've no call on that. Next year they plan on opening up the new electric train lines. You cannot stop the future, James James."

"Then damn the future. And damn you, Julius Griggs! I'll not be any less of myself for the sake of the progress of man." James made sure that he got the last word in. He collected Myra and marched her down the stairs and out into the street, claiming along the way the two boxes Mr. Black had managed to squeeze onto his desk.

Thoroughly shaken, Myra imagined she could still hear the echo of Griggs' warning as the two mages again found the flow of traffic and made their escape into the depths of London in search of the carriage that would take them home.

Chapter Twenty-Eight

Griggs never again contacted the team during the week following his heated argument with James. The spying upon the Flameists' ceremony that the M.I. mages were to undertake would happen without further help from their informant. He had imparted what he would.

Myra was annoyed at him as much as with James. Julius could have at least bothered to forward some sort of apology, coded within another missive for her. But nothing came. Not even a veiled wishing of luck, or good fortune, or whatever one said to agents embarking on a mission.

Such encouragement would have helped quell her jangling nerves as Myra sat in Grafford House's carriage on a Friday evening, working her invisibility spells and squished between thin air and nothing. Well, not nothing. James and Aidan sat on either side of her, performing the same spells, shoulder to cramped shoulder within the tight space. To feel pressed upon and yet have no evidence for one's eyes—it made Myra slightly queasy.

Equally off-putting? Robert's studied ignoring of his companions. With the windows open to passersby, Myra figured the illusion complete: Mr. Grafford, heading to his club, as was his habit of a weekend's eve. There he would disembark, contriving some delay in shutting the carriage door behind him, thus providing his invisible cohorts opportunity to slip out unobserved.

The only problem would be one of balance. Three people exiting a carriage in close, hurried succession without causing the coach to creak or list under the weight would be a trick. It being an M.I.—former M.I.—conveyance, they did have engineering on their side. Said Grafford House vehicle was equipped with the means to withstand the more gentle of disembarkations without signaling the shift in weight. Griggs' developments were to be thanked for this. Contributions from "the time before," to quote Robert.

But Myra wouldn't be thanking Julius just yet. Atop all her other worries, she simply didn't think she could be as light-footed and graceful as required when leaving the coach. They had practiced the maneuver in the mews with a tray of water perched atop the carriage. She had spilled it every time. If only she could use magic for something other than invisibility. A Kinetic's abilities were looking more and more desirous to her.

The carriage stopped. Myra looked out the window, laughing at how she did not have to move much to get the vantage point to see. *And good thing, too, cramped as we are.*

Another traffic snarl. Shouting and a horse's shrill whinny. A discordant group of expensive hats coming together and then dispersing. People being people. The carriage lurched onward.

I'm probably looking right through Aidan's skull. The thought was less entertaining than one might believe. Myra turned her eyes back to Robert, trying to quash the prickly feeling that rose in her chest.

The carriage stopped again. This time, anticipation colored the air for Myra's Empathic sensibilities. Robert harrumphed and shifted, inching forward on his bench. The door opened, and he stepped down a moment later, dropping his cane as he did so.

"I got it. I got it," he huffed at the attendant. Robert bent ponderously to claim the cane from where it had fallen against the step.

James. Aidan. Their presence cleared out in the space of a breath. She could almost imagine them half-stepping, half-leaping over Robert's outreached hand. The carriage barely moved as each disembarked, grace rendering their motions as invisible as they. And quick. Myra wished she could see them at work. But, no, that would invite comparison to her own clunky movements.

Myra sucked in her breath. Her turn. James and Aidan stood waiting. She could feel them close, ready to help her in the event that she faltered. Motions smooth, every limb in perfect harmony and balance, she used her training to exit without swaying the carriage . . . much. She glanced back in alarm, as the coach creaked its protest over her less-than-graceful exit. The man up top made a show of shifting about, resetting the reins and generally giving visible excuse for Myra's error.

"Well done," Aidan whispered at her side.

Well done, driver. Myra wanted to correct him. She didn't. No time. Already Robert had gained the steps of his club. Myra and her two cohorts needed to make themselves scarce before they were tripped over or bumped into.

The house where the Order was meeting was but an eighth of a mile away. The M.I. agents were, of course, not to take the main thoroughfares. Too many people, animals, and carriages to dodge.

It was alleyways and mews for them. The going slow. And icky. Here, just as in Myra's initial training in the early morning hours with James, the tracks of their passing could be marked in the mud and worse that caked the lesser-traveled paths. Theirs were just several footprints amongst many. And with the deepening gloom of evening coming on, the invisible trio passed through the unfashionable part of the fashionable side of town undetected.

The door to the home was open when they arrived. The butcher's boy they had paid off to make such an arrangement was nowhere in sight, leaving no clue as to how he had accomplished this feat. Myra was pretty sure she was better off not knowing. The kitchens were similarly vacated, save for a tabby sitting where he likely was not allowed, industriously washing one paw. It gave Myra the shivers that the feline looked right at the trio of invisible wizards, its piercing green gaze seeming to follow them as they picked their way towards the cellar door. It was enough to prompt her to double-check that her own spell was holding. It was.

Cats. Creepy. A sigh of relief snaked out of Myra's lungs as the cellar door swung shut behind them. Relief and anticipation. She was in it now.

The inconsistent chattering sounds of a social hour drifted up towards the three M.I. mages as they crept down into the cellar, rubber-soled shoes marking no evidence of their passing. Only Myra's hold on her gift informed her of her companions' presence ahead of and behind her on the narrow stair.

In contrast to Grafford House, this home had an oft-used cellar with clean stone walls and a wholesome air. Though, like Grafford House, the illumination was much the same. Gas light instead of electric. A lucky boon for the M.I. team.

A dozen or more gentlemen and ladies huddled together in small groups, chatting. Small glasses in gloved hands, the idle smell of pipe smoke, the Order's gathering had more of social hour than sorcery about it, more front parlor whispering than witchcraft.

James called Myra back with a gentle touch upon her arm. A tidy group of barrels sat in a darkened corner. The space behind gave the trio a cunning hiding spot. The cellar still functioned as a cellar, then. They ducked in, settling into their observations and letting slide their spells a touch so that, bereft of Laurel's expert Mind Speech, they might better communicate in silence.

Names and titles, whispered close in Myra's ear by James, flitted in and out of her head. It confirmed why MI2 did not wish to interfere with the operations of the Order of the Holy Flame. Men and women of import, lords, dames, magistrates, police, bankers and solicitors, even close relations to members of Parliament were affiliates of the Order and thus untouchable. And oh, how they talked! And of nothing!

Thus crouched between Aidan and James, Myra waited and watched as sociable knots of the Order's faithful tied and unwound, London's finest talking and drinking themselves into an unsteady quiet. She had begun to think that her legs might never again straighten properly, cramped as they had become, when a hush descended upon the room.

A middle-aged man entered. He had the look of a servant about him, all phlegmatic boredom and expertly reined judgment. He passed robes to the gathered Flameists and made himself scarce. His exit took him close by the hidden audience as he went back up the stairs leading to the kitchens. Myra thought she saw a slight smirk on his face and couldn't blame him.

Fine and fashionable clothing disappeared beneath shapeless robes of black. Coifed hair and impressive mustaches hid themselves beneath wide hoods. Ladies and gentlemen made indistinguishable from the caricature of a wizard. Such theatrics.

" 'Tis a good thing we managed to arrive before they covered up," Aidan murmured, drawing a nod from James.

Positions were taken up, a careful and tidy separating of persons into concentric circles. Staves were passed into reverent hands. And swords. And cups. Myra guessed that coins would be next and rolled her eyes. Someone—man or woman, within the robes it was hard to tell—moved to turn down the lamps. Shadows and darkness, what light there was caught on the arcane artifacts and gave good effect to the scene. Eyes glittered deep within their hoods.

James was right. The ords had no magic.

Why are we here, again? Myra glanced at her companions and then looked back to the assembled Flameists. A low hum began amongst the would-be wizards. The circles began to move. One clockwise, the other counter. The Flameists moved along their tangents, a curious, shuffling sort of step. The motions felt embarrassed, apologetic even, to Myra's eyes.

A basket was passed about. There was the coin, then. Donations. The jingle of various coinage mingled with the soft hiss of paper. Ah, the glory of having a well-off patronage. The basket filled in no time at all.

Somewhere out of sight a man's deep voice intoned to those assembled. Myra caught something about a gate and its subsequent opening and shutting, a flow without beginning or end. Bogus it might be but Myra found it mesmerizing.

The dance picked up its pace, growing in confidence. Wands, cups, swords, and coin were raised. The humming increased. Now the man in charge had to shout to be heard above the din. Something about the elect who were to be Called Up during the night's ceremony.

That's how Myra heard it. Called Up rather than called up. The emphasis was unmistakable. It drew her from her stupor. Myra exchanged a look with Aidan and James. *Called Up. What's that?*

Their faces were equally puzzled. *So nobody knows. Okay.*

Myra turned her attention back on the ceremony, surprised to note that a new leader had come into the center of the whirling circles. His robe was different from the rest, emblazoned on the edges with arcane symbols that flashed dully. Gold on black. He knelt, fiddling with some sort of apparatus on the floor. What he was doing, specifically, Myra could not tell. For the movement of those around him concealed much and seemed to make the whole scene waver in the gaslight.

The Flameists slowed to a halt, facing inward. At

Myra's side, James and Aidan's magic flickered and died. Her alarm was reflected in each of their eyes. Aidan gave vent to a soft curse.

"There." James seized Myra's arm. The unknown item that had accompanied the Order's priest into the center of the circles lay in state, whirring and crackling away. Barren, naked electricity danced over the device, illuminating its brass and rubber casing.

Before Myra and her companions could much ponder its purpose, the small machine was obscured from view by a scuffle. Two members of the Order were seized and bound, stripped of their robes and wrapped in what appeared to be burial shrouds.

The elect. The struggle appeared to be merely symbolic for one, he having ceased his resistance almost immediately. He lay as though dead, his arms crossed upon his chest, supine upon the ground. The other, too, had ceased her fighting with her brethren but continued to suffer from rather obvious fearful anticipation, most especially when the burial cloths reached her face. Together they lay, heads together on the ground, aligned with the hissing, spitting electrical machine. One calm, the other distressed, they waited.

For long moments, nobody moved—excepting the small movements of the one elect yet unresigned to her fate. The pause gave Myra opportunity to really wonder how it was they were to get out of there, what with James and Aidan's powers useless at present. What was the recharge time to their gift after such an encounter? Would the Flameists extinguish their machine soon enough for the M.I. agents to effect their planned escape before such time that someone thought to check the dark corner behind the barrels? And what was the machine for? Defense against the likes of James and Aidan? Or something to do with the Calling Up?

A door opened to the cellars, ushering in a thin stream of illumination from the upstairs living space. Like lightning, like God's own finger, it jabbed into the midst of the gathered Flameists. A man's stretched and wavering silhouette descended within that column of brightness. The stairs creaked his arrival, even as the door swung shut on ill-oiled hinges, snuffing out the light.

The newcomer wore no concealing robes, carried no arcane symbol of occultist's fancy. Bald but with the barest of mustaches to indicate that he had once sported blonde hair as a younger man, the gentleman was clad in a trim black suit. Remarkably similar to what James preferred, in fact. He had a kind face. Empathetic eyes. A statesman; a politician; a learned man.

Myra glanced to James and in doing so, caught him in the act of recognition. Fury. Blind hatred, as well as a generous helping of fear, crashed through his face, leaving a blasted destruction in their wake. Myra was perversely glad of his current disablement of gift, else she would have fallen straight into his emotional storm. She could feel it pulling at her even now and had to use every bit of her training to fight it.

"And in his own skin, too," Aidan murmured. Myra risked a look at the Maester of Triewes. He was managing far better than James, but a similar tumble of emotions was having its way with him.

"Silas," James hissed the name. For a moment, Myra feared that James would draw his wand and dart out into the midst of the assembly to wreak his vengeance. But no, he had no powers at present. And, with this many loyal dogs—many of them armed with their symbolic but deadly swords . . . No, such a demonstration would not get very far. Thankfully, James seemed to recognize this, hunching down to better conceal their presence. "Myra, you are our eyes and ears now . . ."

She nodded invisibly, checking her spells to make sure that such a claim was, indeed, true. They held. Myra stood up for a better look.

"You've heard my story. I know why you are here. They are one and the same, you understand," Dr. Silas Addair began. "You know why the fairies leave rings upon the forest floor and grassy meadow; you know how to follow the will-o'-the-wisp in and back out of the bog. But what you don't know—"

A puffball of light appeared in Addair's left hand, eerily purple and tearing at the eyes with its brightness. "What you cannot, yourselves, grasp . . . is magic itself."

He snuffed out the spell, rounding on his adoring worshipers, "But you can. You can, I tell you! These two. What makes them special? Nothing. Nothing whatsoever. What makes them my elect? Because I say it is so. After this night, they are to be numbered amongst the chosen, my Children."

He paused, kneeling beside one of the bound elect. The hand that had held the purple light now clasped a thin knife. Silvery-white, it seemed to glow with an illumination all its own. Addair asked, "Why do you suppose it is that God made man?"

Without waiting for answer, he plunged the weapon down into the burial cloths of the woman at whose side he knelt. Even from where she crouched, even in the half-light of the lowered gas lamps, Myra could see the red stain blossom over the white wrappings, and she had to press her hands to her mouth to stifle a scream.

James yanked Myra back down out of sight lest she lose her grip on her spell and expose them all. "I'm okay," she mouthed to him, moving to rise again. As eyes for the team and with Silas present, she dare not miss seeing something important.

"God made man . . . to pursue the Devil." Addair's knife flashed again. Another cut. Another red stain. The woman's attempts to quell her screams were further muffled by the burial cloths, rendering it all the more terrifying.

"And man made good that promise." Addair sat back on his heels, reaching for the knobs on the machine and prompting more sparks. He nodded to his robed master of ceremonies, the man moving forward. And subsequently into Myra's view. A moment later both men had moved to the other side to repeat their actions on the other of the elect. In their wake, wires ran from machine to shrouded woman. Addair and his man held close conference, manipulating settings on the machine and then stepping back.

Silas threw wide his arms. "Behold, God makes man."

The machine gave off one, two, three wild pulses, drawing similar trembles from the two Flameists attached to it. Burial cloths were shaken from limbs, scorched and burned. They pooled on the floor around the elect, mingling with the spilt blood, a birthing. Electricity crackled and arced, purple as the mage's power had been. Above it all leered Dr. Silas Addair. The room held its breath.

A snap, a flash of light—blinding bright and pure

white—and then they were gone. The elect. The purple electric arcing power. Addair. The machine alone whirred happily away in the center of the remaining Flameists.

Myra swore, surprising even herself.

But it was not the abrupt disappearance of M.I.'s infamous enemy—along with the evidence of his evildoings—that had Myra losing her grip on her spell of invisibility. Nor was it the two figures rising from a grate in the floor at the far end of the room. Nor was it even the terrible chaos into which the assembled fell as said two individuals opened fire with pistols, twin furies loosed upon the not-so-innocent.

No, it was the fact that one of the figures looked fully into Myra's eyes—a lucky happenstance rather than intended meeting. It was Stephen. Alive.

Chapter Twenty-Nine

James and Aidan were on their feet within seconds, eager to prevent further damage and disaster to this their only solid lead. Thus, Myra hadn't time to warn them before each found themselves staring at their former partners who wove and whirled like twin devils in the midst of the bloodbath that the Flameists' ceremony had suddenly become.

Bereft of a custodian and in the midst of an all-out battle, Addair's machine wheezed and coughed, sputtering to a halt. And with that its electricity died, and Kady was everywhere at once. Quite literally. Myra watched the Kinetic in action, unable to follow the woman's actions and mesmerized by that fact alone. Stephen proved more than capable with a pistol, especially when James joined the fracas at his side. Together they worked to stop those ceremonial swords being put to use. And Aidan, well, he was firing off spells quick as he could, but his face told Myra that he was fast falling into shock.

"We've got to run," Stephen called above the din, his

voice familiar to Myra's Empathic soul and therefore sending her into the same type of downward spiral which gripped Aidan.

"The machine, though," James protested, firing magic indiscriminately into the faces of the hooded Order members.

"Leave it." Stephen grabbed James bodily as he ran past. "In here. All of you. Quickly. Kady, the doors?"

Materializing by the floor grate, Kady yanked it open with a grunt. "Yes. Cellar is sealed. Come on, you."

Quick though she would like to be, Myra was slow to follow the rest, prompting Kady's annoyed urging. Aidan. James. Stephen. Each hopped straight down into the darkness without so much as a backward glance.

Myra, however, needed that last look around the room, if only to ascertain she was really seeing it all correctly. Bodies—some alive, most not—were strewn over the cellar floor. Black robes pooled in black blood. The machine glimmered in the midst of all, pristine. Myra hurried to find footing on the small ladder of the shaft beneath the opened grate, her eyes on Kady. The American spy was flitting between each of the gas wall sconces, extinguishing the flames. And turning up the gas. Myra could hear the hiss even across the long room.

The cellar darkened with the last of the gaslight's extinguishing, leaving Myra nothing to look at. James, Aidan, and Stephen waited below. She could see points of light from Aidan and James' wands. She jumped down the remaining few feet, falling ankle deep into odious muck. Above her, the grate clanged shut.

"What about Kady, she's—?" Myra began, still looking up into the dark.

"Right here." Kady tossed her hair with a grin, leaving a finger-streak of soot on her cheek. "Come on then. Time to run. Not sure how well my seal will hold against the lantern, and whatever is down here smells as flammable as what is above."

They ran, fleeing through the sewers of London like a mischief of rats, wands raised to light the way.

James quickly caught Myra up. "Can you feel the magic I am doing, Myra?"

She slowed, trying to catch her gift on his. "Yes."

The air freshened around them. Myra took in a grateful lungful, picking up the pace once more, noting how they had fallen behind when James had stopped to help her with his clever little trick. "Thank you."

"Save your breath. We're no longer meeting Robert back at his club," James said.

And with that, Mayra had no more breath to waste on pleasantries. Kady and Stephen led the way. It made a certain sort of sense, as they had apparently come to the Flameists' ceremony via this route in the first place. They slowed at last. Not a full stop, mind you, but their pace became less a full-out sprint and more a swift jog.

With each soggy footfall, Myra began to wonder if they were going to run the entire way back to Grafford House. Or perhaps Stephen and Kady had holed up at another locale.

"Doesn't this seem a little extreme to you?" Myra grumbled her discontent as her footing slipped on an uneven bit of paving hidden somewhere under the muck. It would not do to roll an ankle, or worse, take a tumble into the morass through which they slogged.

Nobody answered. They were probably all concentrating on their footing as well. Myra supposed a likelier cause: a spy didn't complain. Well, she was complaining. She would complain so long as they had ears to hear. *And noses to smell.*

Memories of Stephen and Kady's demise—*daring escape*—replayed in Myra's mind, mingling with what she had just witnessed at the Flameists' ceremony. "Can't Kady just—?"

"No. I can't," Kady herself spoke up, cutting off any further protest Myra might have made.

Myra slipped again, catching herself hard on Aidan's quick reflexes. She risked a look to his face. Kady was back. What did that mean for the team? For Aidan? Of course, in trying not to think of what she had felt pass between the two American agents, Myra could only think of such. She hoped that the smell of the sewer refuse would cover up her thoughts, mask them from Aidan's sharp senses.

The stink was certainly making breathing difficult. Myra's grip on her magic slipped as surely as her feet, and she gagged in the sudden influx of the stench around her. The air was poison. Her lungs burned. She grew afraid that she would lose strength before they had reached their destination.

This new complaint rose to her lips. Myra lacked the air to give it voice. Stars began to dance in her vision, lighting the tunnel as it swayed to and fro, to and—

The group slowed to a halt. Stephen had Myra's arm, steadying her. Instinct prompted her to reach for his art, anything to aid her faltering spell. She remembered all too late that he had none. Poor Stephen. The rest of the team breathed heavily, though none seemed as uneasy on their feet as Myra.

Stephen was looking at her strangely. "Who're you, then?"

"New recruit. Myra, Stephen. Stephen, Myra." James exhaled heavily, moving off to inspect the walls of the intersection in which they had found themselves.

"Breathe, Myra. Breathe, girl." Stephen's concern morphed into a bright smile. "You've got to get more running under ye. Builds the lungs."

Considering the noxious atmosphere, Myra was not all that certain she wanted her lungs "built."

Aidan came up to them, saying, "We've another few blocks to go. I can ask James if you'd rather walk it."

Stephen's questioning curious look found a new victim. Aidan obliged, "Steve, she's an Em—"

"Moving." James grabbed Aidan's forearm, bodily redirecting him before he could finish the word. Even in the dim tunnel, it was evident that he was glowering . . . as usual.

"That information can be exchanged"—James gave a meaningful look to the dark, slimy walls—"later."

Turning, they urged their legs into reluctant motion once more. Myra kept apace, refusing to slow the team. Not that she necessarily needed any more urging to not linger in such a space. But she still had questions, questions that persisted when they finally gained the surface via an out of way alleyway a few short minutes later. Rags from a nearby bin—Stephen's own foresight, Myra was assured—cleaned most of the sludge and worse from them. Magic took care of the rest.

Blinking in the cleansing fog that had built during their time below ground, Myra looked about for a landmark, any sign that they were in familiar territory. The idea of walking further weighed heavy upon her already tired legs. But Myra still wanted to know, "Won't the police find that massacre?"

"What massacre?" Kady flashed a grin and snapped her fingers. Myra felt the pull of power from the Kinetic, the tug of an invisible cord leading out into the darkness. A deep rumble sounded, and an orange glow ascended up into the foggy night air not quite a mile away. A fireball, it painted the underside of the clouds in lurid detail. The shock of sound came a moment later, the roar of fire and explosive lamentation.

"Time to go." For one who had nearly died in a similar blast, Kady was certainly glib about the whole thing. It took a gentle tug on Myra's arm from Aidan to remind her that they still had some ways to travel before returning to Grafford House. And it would not do to be caught in a gape-mouthed stare at the conflagration they had caused, should anyone make the connection between errant lantern, prematurely extinguished gaslights in a cellar, and a team of rogue wizards.

The light fog that had settled into the honeycomb of London's streets was enough to congeal the night's traffic and aid M.I.'s ragtag team of wizards in their hurried darting from alleyway to back street. Stephen, Myra quickly discovered, could not become invisible as they. Nor could she "lend" him the power to do so. To throw her gift at him was to toss a cupful of water into a dry riverbed. She could almost feel his barren, thirsty soul soaking it up, yet it made little difference.

Nobody of the team questioned Stephen as he led the way through the deepening shadows. At his back trailed four ghosts who swirled the fitful fog with their invisible passing. And no ords—constabulatory or otherwise—prevented the former mage's headlong dash into the slums of East London.

Myra was long past wondering where they were going. Instead memory replayed the events of the evening in garish color across her mind's eye. Cool introspection replaced horror. Curiosity substituted repugnance.

So, I'm already dulled to the work done here. Myra held a small funeral for the last of her innocence, enjoying the resultant wave of sorrow that swept through her at the thought of all those men and women who had died. Not wholly jaded, then. There was humanity within her, if allayed by the hard reality of what it was they must do as agents of right. Her stumbling steps informed her that a good deal of what she was not feeling was merely exhaustion tempered with shock. Stephen alive. Kady alive. And with that revelation, an answering revival in Aidan.

Myra's reconsideration of this last was stoppered as she nearly ran smack into a blank wall. It loomed suddenly at her from the darkness and forced her companions to a halt. Close around her, the rest of the wizards gathered, waiting as Stephen navigated the wood boards that blocked the entrance to his safe house. An intricate puzzle of sliding slats, the racket he made set Myra's teeth on edge and set her hunting for her wand in case their presence brought any ne'er-do-wells. A quick glance about confirmed that she was not the only mage to do so. James, Aidan, Kady . . . each of their wands flickered into sight around her as tiny points of reassuring illumination. Even so, they were still hard to see within the pressing darkness of the alleyway and growing fog. Wands at the ready, the group entered the dilapidated house at Stephen's heels, Kady taking up the rear guard so as to close the doorway in its proper configuration.

Two brilliant points of light met them in the interior blackness, wands trained at their hearts.

Chapter Thirty

"Steve!" One of the lights clattered to the ground, extinguishing as she who had held the wand rushed forward to embrace Stephen. Alternately crying and laughing, Laurel tried hugging and looking over M.I.'s long-lost agent all at once. "We thought you dead, you idiot."

Robert lifted his wand, altering the illumination so that it might better aid them in the close pressing darkness of the abandoned building. Myra lifted her wand as well, adding her own light as brief, hushed, explanations were made.

Laurel, it would seem, had monitored their movements from afar, sensing the violent rise and fall of Myra's emotional state via the threads of the Other-Lands. It was she who had led the charge to recollect Robert from his club—no indelicate task, considering the reputation of said establishment—and rushing to find the wayward agents via Myra's gift.

"And so, into the carriage we go," Robert rumbled the conclusion, giving Stephen a gruff pat on the back, eyes twinkling with well-suppressed emotion. "You're with me, old fellow."

"Yes. Sorry." Laurel turned back to the remaining group, thinking. "And James, you too. Unless, Kady?"

"I can take two." Kady's smile was lopsided. "Am used to doing it."

Laurel gave a curt nod. "Myra, you're with me."

Myra moved to join her gift to Laurel's, stopping as a gentle hand touched her arm. James. His eyes were on Laurel, hard and questioning.

"Oh, of course." Laurel shook her head, chastising herself for her oversight. "Myra, you have to go with Kady, as you know where it is we are going."

And with that, she and James disappeared from sight.

But . . . ! Myra swallowed her protest under Kady's arch look.

" 'Tis fine." Aidan slipped to her side, whispering, "Kady can know of your gift in this house. You know what to do, Myra?"

Myra gulped, nervous under Kady's penetrating and puzzled glare.

"Here," Myra beckoned them both, cringing as she felt her power mingle with theirs. Pride surged within her. *James, I'm doing it!*

And with that, the warm lights of Grafford House winked into existence around them.

They had arrived in the library.

Laurel and James blinked into sight a moment later.

"Good job," James' warm praise chased the chill that was beginning to grow about Myra's heart. She blushed, casting her eyes downward as Kady and Aidan moved off towards the fireplace, leaving her to stand with James and Laurel. The evening rushed back at her, newly colored by that which she had learned in the brief space of time in which she had connected her power to Aidan and Kady's.

Kady. The Kinetic. The remaining member of Aidan's American team. And something much more.

Oh no, oh no, oh no . . . Myra let the tears fall on the inside. They mingled with the noisome crashing of her dreams.

Be happy, a part of her screamed.

Why? the other part wailed.

She knew. And yet nothing had been said.

She heard. But no sign had been given.

Kady and Aidan. Aidan and Kady. They fit together in ways Myra, with her tender years and lack of experience, could only guess at.

He didn't have to feather his hair; she needn't blush and stammer. The two were together in each other's met gaze, making up for lost days and empty nights in the space of two heartbeats.

And Myra was glad. She was. She hadn't realized how dead Aidan had been, how shattered.

The tears made good their escape at last, dotting Myra's cheeks. She did not care. Aidan, at least, would know them for what they were. He was the only one that mattered, anyhow.

"Thank you, Myra."

She jumped. When had Stephen arrived? And thank her? Why? It was she who had gotten them—

"You saved him, you know," Stephen broke into Myra's thoughts, his eyes on Aidan and a slow smile spreading across his face. He turned to her. "Would you believe me if I told you that I felt you—the touch of your powers—as my own faded from my broken and despairing soul?"

Myra sucked in her breath. What was she to do with that?

Stephen, too, seemed to sense that he had over-whelmed her and returned his attention to Aidan. And Kady. "We talked about it, she and I. Kady was—Kady was less accepting of the idea that another mage had assumed her gift—"

"I'm sorry," Myra darted in.

"Whyever is that?" Stephen was clearly taken aback.

"Because if I hadn't assumed, Kady could have gotten clear of the warehouse with you and you could have—"

"Gotten out alive?" Stephen chuckled, acknowl-edging that Myra had still been speaking of him as a dead man. "No, for how it ended up playing out, things actually went better than most of my carefully laid plans. Save for the loss of Walter, of course."

Stephen's eyes grew hard at the last, a reminder that not all their lost had returned.

Myra let Stephen have his silence for a while. She had nothing to fill it with anyhow.

Robert rescued them. "All's well that ends well, then. The cat will mew and dog will have his day, and we go home the victors."

"Victors." Stephen spat the word, eyes hard as he stared into the fire.

Aidan rejoined their group, Kady in tow.

"Kady Moore, Robert Grafford, Myra Wetherby." Aidan paused, arching his neck to look to James and Laurel. It afforded Myra further opportunity to gauge the distance between them. More alive than ever, the truth-teller could not have been further away. Guarded. And Kady could sense it. Or, perhaps, it was simply paranoia on Myra's part.

"The Empathic." Kady reached out a calloused, capable hand to Myra. "Steve, you were right."

"Should've wagered."

Stephen's utterance elicited a round of laughter as James and Laurel joined them, the latter having apparently roused Benjamin from wherever he had hid himself. Aidan finished the hasty introductions. Kady's smile reached her eyes at last. Myra had the uncomfortable feeling she would not be able to help but like the American Kinetic.

James, however . . . His jaw set and his eyes bright, he strode directly to Stephen, foregoing every other nicety. They met, and not embracing, not exchanging even one word, they kissed. Happy, sweet tears and unchecked passion shone within each of their faces. And now the words did come. Whispered murmurings, some were scolding, some apologetic, but most of the quiet sentiments sounded simply happy.

Such love. And from James of all people! Myra understood at last what had been missing in M.I.'s leader, the depth of the loss that he had bravely, silently, faced. But Stephen? Myra could not feel him with her Empathy in spite of the evidence before her eyes. His gift had truly been extinguished by Addair's men. The light and dark of Empathy and emptiness swirled together in an unbalanced whirlwind that threatened to knock her out of herself. The room spun.

"Deep breaths, Myra. I've got you," Ben's reassuring murmur sounded in her ears. Through his gentle touch upon Myra's elbow, he forced his own emotions upon her Empathy. Released from the maelstrom of James' emotion, Myra caught sight of Aidan worrying for her. Not altogether distant, then, in spite of Kady's presence. Sour jealousy—all her own—rose in Myra's chest.

"Stephen."

"Ben."

The two mages eyed the other with a strange sort of distrust.

"You're not dead, then."

"Sorry to disappoint."

Benjamin grunted his response, moving to take up a position by the mantle. In his hands flashed the ward that helped him master his own gift, a sign to Myra that he was still far more disturbed than he let on. It had her fishing for her own wardstone. With the look on his face, it would not do to fall into whatever memories were haunting him at present. Not after the day they had just had. He scowled, prompting at last, "So the Order of the Holy Flame had taken on some new acolytes?"

James gave a rapid rundown of the events of the evening. Stated in terse terms, he bled all color from the shocking discoveries of, first, Addair's direct involvement in the Flameists' ceremony, as well as Stephen and Kady's return to the land of the living. Had Myra not herself been there to bear witness, she would have believed the mission as devoid of emotion as M.I.'s leader painted it.

The debriefing ended on Kady's explosive covering of their tracks, drawing a dark look from Ben. He said, "That's not how we've done things in the past. The style is more Addair's."

Kady snorted her derision. "Maybe it's enough for

your department to take the threat of Silas Addair seriously, then."

More serious than an attempt on the Queen's life? Doubtful. Myra kept her thoughts to herself.

Benjamin roused himself, coming back to stand by Myra. He inclined his head towards Kady and voiced one last question for James, "And this one knows about—?"

"Myra, yes." James shot a quick look to Stephen, who shook his head ever so slightly. Knowledge of Ben's powers were to be kept from Kady. Interesting. Myra wondered if Aidan were capable of keeping such a secret.

"So, how'd you do it? Escape, I mean," Myra blushed through her question as she found herself the subject of surprised scrutiny. "I saw . . . felt . . ."

She took a deep breath. "It was my powers that interfered with Kady's."

There. She had owned to it in front of they who had suffered most for her interference. Hanging her head, Myra waited.

Deep, throaty laughter sounded from across the room. Kady. Head back, hands on her hips, she gave in fully to the roar of her humor, an incredible example of non-feminine expression. Wiping the tears from her eyes, she gave an equally coarse grin to Myra, saying, "Goodness, girl. It was your power that helped us bounce out of that flaming hell on earth!"

Impossible. Myra's guilt refused to leave her. Her shoulders, her soul, too used to its burden.

"It's true," Stephen corroborated. "My gift fully, irrevocably extinguished, it was your Empathic gift connecting with Kady's that gave her the safe path she needed to allow both her and I to escape."

His face darkened. "We had, in fact, been under the impression that the forceful flinging of us to safety had left Aidan bereft of rescue."

They thought Aidan dead alongside Walter? One look at Kady confirmed it. *Oh, my!*

New heartache hit Myra, leaving her gasping in spite of the wardstone in her hand. For all that she was loud, boisterous, and brave, Kady was taking hard the confirmation that her brother had perished in the flames of the warehouse.

James had sunk into a nearby chair, his face rife with horror.

"I'm sorry." Stephen moved to comfort him. His jaw worked as he tried to find the words, "I took a fair amount of Addair's elixir in hopes that it was . . . I'm sorry, Jamie."

"Poison." Robert looked from Myra to Stephen, recalling the explanation that had previously been given of events in the warehouse.

"An injection." Stephen nodded. "It would seem that Addair has been finding alternate uses for his studies."

"But why not simply kill you outright?" Laurel breathed the question. "He kept you separated from the rest."

James shuddered, looking away into the flames of the fire, distancing himself, escaping Stephen's explanation as best he could.

"I don't think Addair's agents were all that certain that the injection would, for one, destroy my gift as fully as it did, and two, not actually kill me," Stephen's quiet answer arced through the room, unavoidable as a flash of lightning. "It was, I believe, an experiment."

James gave vent to a strangled sob, before quickly mastering himself. His voice was husky when he at last spoke. "What you are saying is, not counting Myra here, I'm to be the last?"

"There's a finite and small supply of Addair's compound, Kady," Aidan translated James' despair. "Already Benjamin and then Laurel have elected to stop taking it, should we get to that point."

"Our secret hopes that Stephen might arrange to bring back some of your compound for our use were dashed when we heard what had happened at the warehouse," Robert volunteered further, edging forward in his chair so as to better insert himself in the conversation. "You see, we've—the analyst for DMI, that is— tried and tried to replicate the formula. But it would appear that Silas had kept some key information to himself. Something we hadn't realized until after we could no longer claim the scientist amongst our numbers. The inability to safeguard the magic of our lesser mages is partly what prompted Director Brackenbury to make the decision to cut us from the department altogether."

"It all comes back to Silas Addair again. And Myra?" Kady asked.

"Doesn't need it, for whatever unknown reason," Aidan said.

Myra could not hold against Kady the sour look which crossed her face. *Believe you me, if I could do anything about this gift other than learn to use it, I would likely take that way out.* "Okay then." Kady looked to the team. "Then we must make the most of what time we have. Information, please?"

Caught up as she was in the goings on in Grafford House and exhausted by the harrowing events of the day, Myra was given leave to rest in her room, to recover as best she might, given the circumstances. That she had been all but swaying on her feet, fully spent, by the time James had noticed her enough to free her from the conversation, brooked no protest from Myra. She had gone to her rest without argument.

But now Aidan stood in the doorway to Myra's room, an unreadable expression on his face.

He's here to apologize? Why? Myra soundly cursed her magely powers as she hurried to put aside book and wand, distractions taken up in an effort to contribute more fully to the reunited yet diminishing team.

"Kady . . ." he began, stopping himself clumsily, pointedly. Whatever Aidan had been about to say—to admit—was not to find actual vocalization.

"Kady," Myra prompted, not caring that she made the truth-teller wince as she turned the Kinetic's name into a makeshift weapon. He had come to her. It was Myra's right to speak plainly.

"I wasn't sure if you wanted to . . ." He cleared his throat, trying again, "She's offered to train with you."

"Great." Myra surprised herself with honesty.

"Myra, it'll—" Aidan hunted for the words, stopping himself from ruffling his hair. "It could be dangerous."

While she knew he couldn't lie to her, Myra raised

her eyebrows in disbelief, incensed by his kind concern. *Dangerous. To whom, Aidan?*

It seemed to Myra that he understood. Aidan the Protector, returned to her. He distanced himself from the role, focusing on the wand that Myra had only recently laid aside, "Kinesis is a very volatile magic."

"More than Ways-walking? More than Necromancy? Truth telling?" Myra challenged Aidan, folding her arms in an outward demonstration of her ire. She was a member of the team. Her gift made it essential that she learn all she could from her fellow mages. *James and I. Soon we'll be all that's left.*

It was duty. Honor.

Never mind that I like it, this perilous fire. Myra scowled, a mirror to Aidan's own. She would hurt him, if only to get him to go away. Go away and stop this hot-cold protection and regard. She needed to learn, unfettered by the limits Aidan might otherwise impose. Aidan who, for all this truth telling, had somehow still managed to lie to her in the end.

"It's what I have chosen to do with my life." She turned away, not quite able to stand boldly alongside the force of her words. Did Aidan remember saying as much to her early on in their friendship? She was one of them. James believed so. Had confirmed it time and again, stating it clearly but hours before.

Glancing back to the doorway, Myra saw that Aidan had gone.

Chapter Thirty-One

The training room was strewn with various weaponry and implements of combat. And in the midst of this bedlam, Kady floated through the now-familiar motions of *t'ai-chi*. It would seem that Aidan's slovenly habits extended to his team.

"So. You're an Empathic." Kady's pronouncement was more challenge than introduction as she turned to note Myra waiting hesitantly in the doorway.

Myra shrugged. "That's what they tell me."

She regretted the words in an instant. She hadn't meant to, herself, sound insolent.

Kady smiled, unfolding her arms. "Come on then, Empath. Let's teach you what real combat is. Should be interesting with your particular skill set."

Bending, Kady picked up two staves. Disorderly like Aidan; graceful like Benjamin. Myra both hated and loved her already.

Busy as they had been upon their first meeting, Myra had only absently noted the markedly different clothing worn by Kady. All over black—*like James*—and formfitting, the clothing fit her as though it were a glove made for her entire body. No skirts. No corset. No puffy sleeves. She dressed like a man. The garment moved smoothly with the Kinetic as she reached for the two training weapons. It flouted every convention, countermanded every modesty.

It looked comfortable.

Infatuation turned to envy.

Trousers . . . Myra let the daydream slip away as a stave flew straight at her face. She caught it and gave it a quick inverted turn, as she had seen Benjamin do. Ready for anything. Crying out, as her arm painfully wrenched in its socket, Myra felt Kady's hot breath on her ear, "Nice stance . . . Thales."

Kady let go, the only lasting pain that of the insult she had just given Myra.

Benjamin had told her? Thales was their secret!

Angry—mostly at Benjamin—Myra lashed out, whipping around to catch the mage a blow. Kady wasn't there. Instead she danced a few feet off, back 'round the other way. Rapping her cane upon Myra's toe, she gave one of her breathy wide grins. "Not bad, Thales."

This time Myra waited. Kady vanished and reappeared again. And Myra connected. Her stave caught Kady full on the stomach. The Kinetic's breath went out of her with a whoosh and she fell to the ground. Eyes bulging, for one long moment she did not move save to cough ineffectively.

The bloodlust cleared from Myra's eyes, and she knelt at Kady's side. "Sorry. I'm so sorry."

Kady waved her off, still unable to catch a breath. At length she wheezed, "Don't lie in front of the Maester of Triewes, Myra."

Myra followed the line of Kady's weak grin to the doorway where Aidan lounged. Simply watching. She felt new color enter her cheeks—warmth not triggered by exertion.

"You did what an agent does, what we're training to do, Myra." Kady sat up, clutching her ribs. "Put aside your pride, your personal need for revenge, and act intelligently. With foresight."

"Which, with Kady's gift, is a rare thing to be able to achieve, Moira." Aidan entered the room, complicating things.

Kady nodded, wincing. "I'm not used to having anyone predict my next move."

"Save for me." Aidan sat cross-legged, joining the party. They all laughed at his hurt tone. How could they not? Myra rose, suddenly fearful that she was intruding on a private moment. And in her own lesson with Kady, too. *How dare he.*

Aidan seemed to realize he was in the way, standing as well. He offered his hand to Kady. She ignored it, using her stave to help her to her feet. He persisted, "Ye hurt?"

Scowling, Kady shook off the concern. "Winded. Likely bruised in about twenty minutes' time."

She turned to Myra. "Which gives us just that. On guard? Aidan, move. You're in the way."

Myra remembered to be ready. Still she was caught off guard as Kady did not immediately go on the attack, flickering from sight only to appear behind Aidan. Feminine hands ruffled the wizard's hair and then disappeared in an instant. Myra didn't even bother to turn, whipping up her staff to block Kady's shot from behind. She missed.

The blow came hard, harder than she had any right to expect. Myra fell like a stone, glancing her chin on the hard wooden floor. Pain exploded, drawing tears to her eyes.

Stop it. Stop it, I say, she commanded her tears. If they heard, they did not listen, pouring down her cheeks to mingle with the blood now flowing freely from her chin.

Aidan was at her side in an instant—quicker than even Kady, it seemed to Myra, though that would have been impossible considering the latter's gift.

"Lesson is over," he declared.

"Nuh 'snot," Myra managed, thanking her lucky stars that she hadn't bitten her tongue when she had gone down.

"Before one of you kills the other," Aidan continued, stern. "She's new to this, Kat."

"I know that. But she also landed one on me so I assumed . . ." With Aidan there, there was no real need to elaborate further. He knew. Kady stopped her explanation, opting instead for apology. "I'm so sorry, Myra. I didn't mean to . . ."

"Don lye eebunt a e Aesser Truus." Myra was still trying not to move her jaw overmuch while simultaneously attempting to smile.

"Oh, you poor dear." Kady dissolved into helpless laughter. "Aidan, you idiot. Run and get her a compress." Gently lifting Myra's chin so that she could better assess the damage, she added, "And James. He'll fix this right up, I'm sure."

In the end, it was Benjamin who fixed the cut on Myra's chin. And not with magic but with good old-fashioned doctoring.

Myra found that she was in too much pain to enjoy

the gentle nearness of M.I.'s ever-distant walking, talking encyclopedia. She had been missing that. It was over altogether too quickly. Benjamin was skilled. Where he learned to sew sutures was not really a question, though. Probably in some book, some time.

Myra felt like a sideshow spectacle. *Come one, come all. See the girl with the amazing swollen jaw! Admission only sixpence!* Each of the M.I. agents had their turn with her, eyeing the angry wound, crooning their condolences. And generally giving Kady all manner of chastising glances.

While she longed to defend Kady—and, in fact, at first tried—the pain of talking defeated Myra at last. She sat in sore silence, feeling idiotic and having little available to alleviate it.

Myra's injury had given the team an excuse to call a holiday. After the tumult of tears and high-spirited catching up after weeks apart, it seemed that everyone's jaws were tired. The afternoon was spent in reading and quiet contemplation.

By the time tea was served, Myra discovered that Benjamin's poultices, though a bother to keep upon one's chin, had done a tidy job at reducing both swelling and pain. She could talk again. And, after hours of near silence, she was ready to, having come to a startling realization during that time.

"That machine. I'd seen one before." Myra unfocused her eyes, intent on a past of which she could remember but a fraction.

"The one from the Flameists' ceremony?"

"H-sssh . . ." Myra waved Ben off. "Yes." She frowned, trying to block him out. The memory—not even complete—flitted just out of reach. A dark room.

Big. Cavernous in spite of being filled with crates. And just visible, glinting in the uneasy orange illumination, crouched the now-familiar mass of gears, wire, brass, tubes, and knobs. Twin to that used in the Order's ceremony not even twenty-four hours prior. *Or, perhaps, the same machine.*

But where? Where had she seen such?

Julius? His offices had been filled with similar bric-a-brac, carried much the same aesthetic as the half-remembered thought that so plagued Myra, if brighter and more modern. Practical. Her hand strayed to the pendant at her neck.

No. While the style was most certainly his, the very idea that Julius could be the architect of such an instrument was absurd.

But I've been so few places . . . Also not true. While not well-traveled, she had had her fair share of adventures even before joining up with M.I.

So, the memory was old. It would explain why the recollection was so dim, time-blurred. As though seen through an imperfect lens or glimpsed from the corner of her eye—

"The warehouse," Aidan supplied the answer. "I remember seeing it through the double bars of the cage. In the chaos that followed, I'd all but forgot. Tucked away behind a shipment of munitions, I remember thinking 'That's not one of ours,' and wondering its purpose. I figured it was what powered the outer cage that was holding us there."

"I wonder if it's the same one," Myra and Aidan said in unison.

Myra blushed as the memory came into greater focus, aided in part by Aidan's confirmation. Yes, she had been in his memories. A glimpse and nothing more. Or, rather, it was more like blown through on the way to Stephen's experiences . . .

Kady sat upright, red-faced and clearly upset. "I brought it to headquarters."

"You what?" Seven astonished faces confronted the Kinetic. Stephen hung his head in embarrassment.

"Well, we can get it back, right? I mean . . . After all, it's not my fault! I didn't know they'd ousted you." Kady scowled, defensive. "And it's not exactly like they hate us."

"Just don't trust us is all," James snorted, rising to his feet to pace the room uneasily.

"You hadn't told her? All that time?" Laurel looked to Steve. Myra figured the wizard likely had no idea she was adding to Stephen's pain with her ill-timed compassion.

"I had not. I thought that maybe after what had happened in America, that they'd reopen the lines of communication. Out of decency. I didn't know it had gotten so bad as that. When I heard we were living here, all of us . . ." Steve shook his head.

"Does explain the look I was given by the man in the room when I dropped it off . . ." Kady's clear bitterness made her resultant laugh sour.

"Someone saw you?" James stopped his pacing, face agog.

Kady went back on the defensive. "Well, of course. There was a guard there. His jaw dropped so, I thought he'd dislocated it in astonishment. It wasn't even half a second, James! Look, I'll just nip back in and—"

"Fast. It has to be fast," James practically leapt upon the Kinetic in furor. "They'll be armed, they might know you're coming back for the evidence you so generously deposited on their doorstep."

James' tirade had helped Kady regain her poise. She gave one of her trademark crooked smiles. "Fast? Really."

She blinked out of—and then immediately back into —sight.

Kady swayed, stumbling into a seated position and looking around her dazedly. She appeared undamaged but looked ill. Utterly spent, the Kinetic swore, even that verbiage managing to come out haggard and mangled. Alarm renewed itself in the occupants of Grafford House; Aidan was at Kady's side in an instant.

"All around 'lectric," Kady gasped, managing coherent language at last. "Blocked—blocked us . . ."

All began talking at once, each fruitlessly shouting above the other in an effort to be heard. Myra's eyes stayed on Kady. Kady in Aidan's arms. The normally strong mage seemed small. Indomitability had been bested.

Myra wanted to soothe the woman, give her strength. But her Empathic magic just couldn't quite reach her. That in itself was frightening.

"I'll go," Stephen cut through the din at last.

"Go where?" James rounded on him. Myra tore her eyes from Aidan and Kady with difficulty, focusing on the new drama building within the team. Stephen did not answer. He didn't have to. They all knew where. Myra sucked in her breath.

James sputtered through his rapid turning of emotions. Myra wasn't even certain who he was mad at, Stephen or the now hostile DMI. "What? How? They'll—"

"They'll what?" Stephen threw wide his arms, laughing manically. "I've no powers, and I've already died once. Surely they cannot think they can outright do anything to me."

"What makes you so sure of that? What makes you think your past service protects you?" Aidan, for once was on James' side. It did Myra's heart glad to have him add to the conversation. While still pale, Kady was stirring, gaining a bit of her fire back.

"Why, they've let us live," Steve said, nonplussed. "Knowing what we do, our service clearly has to count for something."

He had a point.

Clandestine or not, someone had to know the M.I. agents held out in Grafford House. And they had not been harassed. At times, they had been helped. Narrowing her eyes, Myra glared at the new thought that rose in her mind. *Where is Julius in all of this? Is he truly that angry with James?*

"I'll take Myra with, if that puts you at ease." Stephen's offer shocked Myra out of her private reflection.

What, me? Myra looked about her for escape, objection from Aidan, James, even Benjamin. None came.

"She is unaffected by the Dampening, is she not?" Stephen turned his eyes on Myra. "You can shadow me, invisible. There to get me out of trouble should the need arise. In light of current circumstances, I do believe you're the only one of us who can do it."

The bright flame of excitement birthed in Myra's chest, fueling her bravery and coloring her cheeks. She nodded. She would do it.

Chapter Thirty-Two

Spilling out onto Wilton Road from Chatham Station, a crowd of hurried travelers threatened to separate Myra from her spell of invisibility. Worse, it endeavored to tear her from he whose elbow she clutched.

"Don't be nervous," Stephen muttered under his breath. "Almost there, love."

Myra considered reminding him of her cursory familiarity with DMI's headquarters but saved her breath. Such memories came from a time when the team had thought Steve dead. Best not bring that up.

Myra shivered in anticipation, invisible to all and therefore subject to pummeling by wayward umbrella tips and tripped up by carelessly swung canes. She checked her spells again, raising a transparent arm in front of her eyes and looking down to espy, well, nothing of herself. The sickly mid-morning sunshine shone right through her, none the wiser. Myra's magic held.

Grumbling to herself over having been forced to walk for the entirety of the not inconsiderable journey, Myra tried to remember which of the identical buildings on the long block was the illustrious office of the Department of Intelligence Formerly Magical. None stood out. In fact, given the leisure to examine them, the entirety of the tenements reminded Myra of a group of schoolchildren each pressing his friends forward to take the blame for some ill deed or another, reluctant and eager to keep the discerning eye of authority turned from them.

Part of its charm, I suppose. Myra marveled once more at the clandestine operation's ability to blend into the background.

Stephen slowed. Myra loosed her grip on his arm slightly as the mage-turned-ord sniffed and hunted about in his pocket for a handkerchief. Nervous, she startled as Stephen removed them from the press of traffic so that he could tend to his nose, positioning them safely in the wake of a light post.

After a snuffling and short cough, Stephen moved to replace his cloth in his pocket only to miss, dropping the small square of linen and juggling to catch it before it met an unfortunate end upon the pavement. His movements were so fast, so fluid, that Myra nearly missed the sign.

"That's better." Stephen's words were a signal to Myra that she cling to his arm once more as he stepped out into the street. Her curious eyes were thus torn away before she could look more closely at the chalk markings adorning the ornamental base of the lamp. Call and response. Unremarkable yet impenetrable as Benjamin's egg cipher.

Myra thrilled as she and Stephen skipped up the steps and in through the front door into one austere and ordinary tenement amongst many, her memory still refusing to recollect the details from her last visit therein. Though it seemed unlikely considering the circumstances, a part of her wondered if there was magic at work there. Something to keep the memory permanently befuddled.

"May I help you?" Clad in the trappings of a modern gentleman but carrying all the haughtiness of an old-fashioned keeper-of-the-gate in a castle, a mutton-chopped and spectacled fellow greeted DMI's unannounced visitor from behind the massive desk that all but blocked the flow of traffic in and out of the front hallway.

Myra frowned. Now that they were inside, the rest was all beginning to look familiar. Granted, the desk had since been emptied of its impressive clutter and now gleamed vacantly in the lamplight, a vast smooth ocean of brown. And the lighting itself seemed a touch brighter. Her mind ticked off each detail, signaling approval and recollection. Save for this fellow. And he gave her the shivers.

Where was Mr. Black?

Sitting with one hand hidden beneath the vastly underutilized piece of furniture, the man glared at Stephen through bright eyes made small by both his glasses and the over-large nose that would have dominated his face but for his bushy wealth of whiskers. Said off-proportioned face turned pale a second later, drained of its blood-flow by pure shock.

"Seems you've a bit of a ways to go there, Mick," Stephen laughed, holding up his hands for inspection. "Your face just now . . . Best beware with that postiche that you keep your mouth from gaping so, else a family of birds might take up residence there."

Still stunned, the man continued to stare, now bringing up his other hand to rest upon the desktop. With a clatter, the pistol that had held a hidden threat toward unwanted visitors to the department dropped to the table, silent as its owner.

"Stephen Tomlinson." A second of DMI's employees entered to join his co-worker, his voice demonstrating that he, too, was perhaps as shocked as the first but better disciplined. He, too, was a stranger to Myra. "You were dead."

Stephen turned to the newcomer, giving a wry grin and slight shrug. "Not the first time, as you know, Lee."

That both men recognized Stephen—and he them—reassured Myra. There had not been as complete a rearrangement of staffing as she feared. She darted her eyes up the stairs, thinking of Julius Griggs.

"Uh, uh," Lee chided, stepping back. Hand straying to his own weapon, he prompted, "Protocols, Agent Mickey."

A rosy hue underscored Mickey's paleness, embarrassment as he fumbled for the surrendered pistol under his cohort's reproving glance. He trained it back on Stephen once more.

Hands still up, Stephen's face grew hard. "I have no wand, Lee. I'm—"

Choking on the word, the former mage fought a standoff more perilous than that of two trained agents of the Crown leveling pistols at his heart. Defeated, he finally acknowledged, "I have lost my gift."

The two agents mentally picked through Stephen's confession, Mickey registering its meaning quicker than Lee. Or perhaps he had greater grievance with the former wizard. A smile spread through his face—far better concealed than his shock but still marked. Long-standing jealousy peeked out and then quickly hid itself.

Behind Stephen, Myra shivered. *They really don't like Stephen and our ilk. Is that why they've been switched out with Mr. Black?*

"And so you came skulking for a job?"

"What business have you here?"

Both men spoke at once, attacking Stephen with words rather than physical force. Again, Stephen rolled his shoulders, effrontery at the intimation. And a signal to Myra.

Loathe to separate from Stephen in the face of such naked animosity—for his sake as much as hers—Myra pondered the consequences of disobedience. And rejected such.

"I came because I needed to see for myself whether the events of my mission in America changed anything, anything at all." Stephen pretended nonchalance, observing his surroundings with a detached professional interest. "Nice lighting, by the by. Bright. Very . . . electric. Newly installed?"

"Mission," Lee snorted and put up his weapon. It gave Myra the opportunity needed to slip past. "Calling your actions such are a perfect example of why your kind have no place in our business. You with your undisciplined, slapdash way of spying. An embarrassment, sir. To the department, to the Crown. More lucky than accomplished. You and your hocus-pocus, your mumbo jumbo—"

"I did not come here for your bigotry." Stephen lowered his hands, prompting Myra to hold her breath. But he merely crossed his arms. The pistol concealed within his vest remained hidden, un-hinted-at.

"No, you'd rather dole it out if you could," Mickey sneered, rising to his feet. "You haven't been ord long enough for us to be comrades."

"Sit down. I'm not here at your behest," Stephen thundered. "I'm here to speak to Brackenbury. Surely you cannot deny me that courtesy."

DMI's director. The agreed upon word. Myra slipped away into the depths of the building, confident that Stephen could keep the two agents talking. And if he didn't, there was always kinetics.

The door that Lee had come through led to another empty hallway. Short, with locked doors on either side, it came to an abrupt turn at its end. There a flight of stairs reached up into another well-lit floor. More electricity. More defense against mages. Again, Myra considered Julius and his prototype machine, the one that had so alarmed James. Perhaps their ord ally had been on to something after all. She would soon find out.

Myra quickly ascended, ascertaining that the second story was also empty before dropping her invisibility so that she could check her connection to Kady. Aidan she could feel. And if he was in the nearby safe house and lacking in panic, Kady, too, must be there with her powers intact. Exhaling her fear in one noisome gush, Myra found the steadiness required to pick up her invisibility once again.

The second floor. Familiar ground. But from the northwest this time. Myra moved to the other end of the hallway. *Best to be correct about such things.*

She counted the doors on the right-hand side, steeling herself for the next stage of her investigation as she hunted in her pocket for the set of lock-picks loaned to her by James. If Julius was in his office . . .

The door yielded to Myra's gentle touch. Odd.

No light emanated from within the room. Bravely, Myra pushed. The door swung open on silent hinges.

Empty. Of Julius Griggs, of his work, of . . . everything. Myra stared into the blank space, her heart dropping in her chest uncomfortably and her limbs going atremble on her. How? How was it empty?

Myra backed out of the room on legs slow to obey.

No, the room was the correct one.

Completely thrown by the turn of events, Myra instinctively reached for Kady, for the kinetics that could take her to safety. But, no, there was Stephen to think of and work to be done. Listening hard, Myra crossed swiftly and silently to the room wherein she knew DMI's director held court. Kneeling, Myra set to work with her lock picks. Brackenbury had the answers they sought.

Footsteps sounded on the stairs. Two pairs.

Sucking in her breath, Myra slid sideways so that she crouched, her back to the wall. Invisible in the bright hallway, she waited as the two men—both unknown to her—passed by unawares. She followed them, thinking fast.

Hard faces accented by short, almost unfashionably cut dark hair, the two could have been twins but for the fact that one was short and stocky, the other tall and lank. The marked difference set Myra to wryly wondering if MI2 advertised for men of varying heights. Perhaps they needed such to fill a need for all manner of disguises and situations, bereft of magic as they were.

"Hold on." One of the mismatched twins—the shorter of the two—turned abruptly. Myra ducked, slipping to the side. She missed colliding with the agent by a hairsbreadth.

"Blasted, drafty building," he complained, walking off to shut the door to Griggs' empty office. "Damp in the summer, dank in the winter—"

"Maybe it's the mage what done it," the other man suggested. The words rang loudly in Myra's ear, startling her. The grip on her spells was now tenuous at best, and she prayed that they would just leave before her strength gave out. Slowly she backed away towards the stairs, eyes on the two agents and ready to run.

"What? Steve? Bah, he's ord as the rest of us now." Shorty fumbled with a set of keys, not bothering to look up.

"He was down there asking for Julius just now." Agent Lanky shrugged.

"Didn't see 'im. What'd Mickey say?"

"Told him he'd pass the word on and that Griggs was indisposed."

"Hmph." Shorty straightened and walked back to join his companion, chuckling. "Didn't tell him he'd been transferred though, right?"

"No, no word of Broadmoor."

Myra resisted the urge to kick Agent Shorty as his laughter turned cruel. "Ironic, that."

Nodding along, Agent Lanky unlocked the door to the office at Myra's side. "Mickey thinks he won't be back. Nasty business, magic. Untrustworthy. Should have stamped it out years back."

"Agreed." The agents' laughing banter followed them into the room, leaving Myra the opportunity to drop her invisibility and grab hold of Kady's kinetics.

Broadmoor. What's that?

Chapter Thirty-Three

Kady and Aidan both caught Myra as she stumbled in the darkness of the safe house. Still unused to traveling via kinetics—leastways by herself—it took a moment for the room to stop its wobble.

"I'm all right," Myra assured her friends as she waved off their assistance. She looked about, noting hazy motes of dust suspended in shafts of light that crisscrossed the upper-story room. She had not yet been to this haven. She could happily have lived without ever having been.

The windows were haphazardly shuttered from the inside with a slap-dash method similar to that of the boards which had gated the door to the other safe house. But that building had been in a suspect end of town. Myra had been under the impression that this was the respectable sanctuary, something of Laurel's that she still kept for sentimental reasons.

Must be a long ago sentiment. Myra sniffed, shuffling her feet on the dusty exposed boards. *And not a stick of furni-*

ture. The plan to wait here until the chime of the next hour looked bleaker by the second.

"It's the attic, Myra." Aidan turned his eyes to beams that converged into a lofted ceiling. "Old servants' quarters long unused."

Oh. Myra tried to ignore Kady's smirk and failed. Somewhere a diminutive squeaking indicated the passing of a mouse. Hopefully it lived in the walls, but with a space like this one could never be sure. Again, Myra eyed the floor, praying for the bell that would signal Stephen's arrival below.

The promised sign came, and the three mages dashed down the stairs, quietly but quickly. It seemed that Myra was not the only one loathe to linger in the long-unused space. And she had had to wait the least amount of time.

Aidan opened the door to Stephen, ushering him in but standing so as to remain largely out of sight from any passersby. The ord entered, lugging with him a curious contraption. From the way his shoulders hunched, it looked heavy, whatever it was. Myra opened her mouth to ask and received a small shake of the head from Aidan. The instructions had been to remain mostly silent while in the main floor. Laurel's safe house apparently had nosy neighbors that she could not shake.

Not that Myra and Stephen felt the need to regale Kady and Aidan with the details of their time at DMI. There would be an opportunity for everyone to hear the news over dinner. Myra was curious to hear what he had learned. And where he had gotten that odd metal box. It looked like a cross between a sewing machine and a safe. And heavy enough to be either.

At length Stephen satisfied Myra's curiosity, leaning forward to whisper, "Typewriter."

No more explanation was offered, and Myra nodded sagely, though she hadn't the faintest idea what he was talking about. Small smiles passed through the group, a ripple that quickly died.

Taking care not to leave telling creases on the sheeted furniture, the foursome sat and waited. Myra found it rather funny. And kind. Kady could easily travel back to Grafford House with both Myra and Aidan. It was Stephen who must travel by carriage, not them—by foot was presumably out of the question now that he was hauling such hardware. Hopefully he had managed such an arrangement.

But it was nice to sit and do nothing for once. Myra, of course, relived her discoveries, pondering again Julius Griggs' absence, her eyes on the typewriter that called to mind all too easily the man's inventions. Perhaps it was something of his! A delighted shiver broke over Myra's skin at this thought.

Six o'clock. Aidan and Kady winked from sight. Myra was slower to follow suit, first meeting Stephen's eyes. He turned, bending to laboriously hoist the type-writer into his arms. Myra revised her comparison once again. The thing looked like an anvil. But it did make for the perfect excuse for Stephen to be slow with the doors, slow to enter the carriage. She and her invisible companions made their way with ease.

They alighted in the mews out back of Grafford House. Kady was the first to drop her invisibility, imme-diately turning to offer Stephen help with his typewriter. Aidan and Myra got the door to the house.

Never before had the warm lamplights of the grand

old home seemed so welcoming. They burned away the shadows that had begun to gather 'round Myra's heart. Imagining secret messages from Julius hidden within, she eyed Stephen's typewriter. But first, refreshment. Her stomach rumbled in agreement, annoyed to have been forgotten for so long a time. To think that they had missed tea!

Luckily, of late dinner had become less a utilitarian affair and now came marked by resplendent feasting. With the larger table, it only seemed fitting that they might gather for greater length and in as high of spirits as they might achieve. Multiple courses and expensive ingredients pleased both plate and palate. Stephen, Myra found, had refined tastes and a skill at cookery which surpassed his companions. He also could afford such.

"Any why not invest so in the entertaining of one's diet?" Stephen had exclaimed heartily at one point, laughing in the face of James' protestations. "We live not long in this line of work, and I have no progeny. I've tasted death and found it bitter, and my tongue cries out for succor!"

"He said that even before we thought him dead," Robert had explained. "Never could abide my austerity of living, could that one."

Myra had scoffed. This from a man with a private club and waistline that indicated excess. But if Stephen chose to spend his largesse thus, who was she to judge? Since Stephen's return to M.I., he had taken it upon himself to act as sole proprietor of the Grafford House kitchen—including clean up! Myra considered it a small blessing that she no longer need take her turn at preparing a meal and thus expose her friends to her still-shocking lack of skill and judgment therein. She could imagine that Stephen's reaction to anything she might dare serve was likely to be five times worse than any tongue-lashing from James.

But today Stephen had been out and a feast had still been managed. Sitting down to table, Myra wondered who had orchestrated such. Her eyes fell to James. He looked altogether too pleased with himself to be a mere partaker in the repast.

It was Stephen who spoke first, his mission at DMI having been the plainer one. In the contrast between his discoveries and Myra's they hoped to realize something akin to the actual truth.

Stephen's report was simple. He had not been allowed to advance past that first corridor. Mr. Black had made appearance after all, coming along once Myra had left to snoop upstairs. Apparently he had taken custodianship of Stephen's typewriter and was loathe to give it up. And apparently Stephen had been blunt with his questions, receiving blunt answers for his honesty.

All evidence of Addair's machine: gone without a trace. The very records of who had been present for the Flameists' slaughter: expunged—along with those detailing the tenancy of the lost party and surrounding. The entire block—those not decimated by the explosion —had been turned out and relocated. They who had suffered loss of property and worse in the gas detonation simply disappeared, and with such folks having much on their minds, they were not particularly missed in the confused rebuilding and resettling of the street.

"So he's a traitor then. Shoulda known from the first," James passed judgment. Heads bent to dinner plates. Robert passed the salt to Kady. Myra was not certain as to how such a blatant cover-up of violence and treachery whetted one's appetite. But there they were.

By "he," James meant Griggs, no doubt. After all, he had gone silent, and then DMI had grown chillier than ever to the former agents. Julius' necklace lay heavy against Myra's skin, the metal hot with her guilt. She waited for her turn to speak, wondering if her discoveries in the first story of the Department offices damned the ord further still.

Myra noted Benjamin looking at her, his eyes on the pendant she hadn't realized she fingered with an idle hand. Silent protest. Benjamin understood the import. He had helped fan that flame, written those silly letters.

Benjamin. Compassionate, curious Benjamin who sat at Myra's side—both figuratively and literally—in these trying times. He was an enigma to her still, as impenetrable as Aidan and Kady were transparent. They huddled together, a team within the larger team of M.I. Disgusting. Sweet. And altogether enviable.

James and Stephen, too. And yet, to Myra's gift, a rift stood between them, some quarrel she could not name nor even properly see. Blinding bright, Steve and James danced upon the fringe of each other's regard, a careful safe distance balanced against terrible passion. Not even extraordinary measures in the kitchen on James' part could do much against such.

Perhaps it had something to do with Steve's lost gift? If so, how dare James be so callous. Robert, Laurel, Aidan, they'd all had trouble adjusting to the new reality within which Stephen operated, sometimes with melancholy, oftentimes with humor and grace. The absence remained, an un-being that lived as a ghost in their midst. Perhaps, like Robert's infirmity, they would come to terms. But how quickly and at what cost? Stephen and James' careful maneuvering—after experiencing what their kiss had done to her gift, it pained Myra to see it. And that with her barely understanding such.

Laurel was absent again. It reduced their company by one and forced Myra nearer to Kady by merit of their being the only two women present.

It was unsurprising. Laurie had been doing it a lot of late, said disappearing. And not to her rooms, either. Myra checked.

"Following a lead" was often the simple explanation given. Recalling the truth of Laurel's condition, learned upon her first trip to the DMI offices, Myra did not believe it. And yet, it was truth. Sometimes, at least. For Aidan had confirmed it on the occasions where Kady went with her.

Ways-walking. Jealousy smarted for Myra. She, too, had the talent to walk the OtherLands. Why not take her as well? Was she an agent or no?

"Good of you to join us."

As though conjured by Myra's thoughts, Laurel entered the dining room. The mage glared her disapproval at James' cool greeting and made to sit between him and Stephen. Each obliged by shifting to make room.

"Thank you," Laurel bestowed her graceful response and turned to beckon a chair with her magic.

Nothing happened.

She tried again, swaying ever so slightly and clutching the table with hard fingers. Stephen was on his feet in an instant, offering his chair and grasping Laurie's elbow to steady her.

Laurel waved off the assistance. "I'm fine. Just tired. Thank you."

"You look fine," James' response was carefully callous but his face carried the evidence of having feared —and feared deeply—for Laurel's safety.

Laurel's eyes flashed angrily. "Don't you start—!"

"Such a martyr." James pushed back from the table. He wiped his mouth viciously and threw down his napkin. "But don't—not for one second—think that I care what happens. That I'll go looking after you when something befalls you. When. Not if."

He rose, addressing the table, "We've few enough of us as it is. I'm not about to go sparing one of you so that —" Jaw working, James fixed his eyes back on his napkin and then, gently folding it, he laid it back over the plate and gave a small bow. "If you'll excuse me."

He exited the dining room, leaving seven astonished faces in his wake.

Laurel was first to recover, turning to follow and crying, "James—"

"Leave him." Steve's hand resumed its grasp on Laurel's elbow. He deftly steered her into James' abandoned chair. "You must eat. Aidan?"

At this last, five pairs of curious eyes turned to the Maester of Triewes. Aidan did not respond, taking the opportunity to fill his fork and shove its contents into his mouth.

"Eat," he instructed through the mouthful, ignoring Stephen's question.

Or had he? Myra felt Aidan's anger from where she

sat in shock. He had pondered Stephen's query and found answer . . . even if he kept it for himself.

James had meant it. Had meant every word. The bastard.

Suppressing a shiver, Myra turned her eyes to her own plate, a temporary escape. The news from the Department that she was to impart now seemed of little importance. They had to see to themselves first.

Another screech of a chair on the floor drew everyone's attention once more. Stephen rose to his feet, throwing down his napkin. "Excuse me." He left without further explanation. Laurel followed a half a moment later.

Without James, Stephen, or Laurel present, there was no point in Myra's telling the team what had transpired in her clandestine snooping in the DMI offices. They agreed, instead, to meet in the library in half an hour's time. And while Myra was, herself, shaken by the very public argument between Laurel and James—and, to some extent, Stephen—no one else seemed to share her sentiments. Perhaps her Empathy was overplaying things. In any event, such would never have been tolerated at her house.

She sought out the three absent mages upon dinner's conclusion. The dishes could wash themselves. Oh wait, they did.

Myra's ill-humor melted into curiosity as she neared the library. A strange, metallic chunk-chunk came from within the room. Stephen sat before a roaring fire, tapping at his typewriter. He did not look up as she entered.

Myra crept forward, fearful of disturbing him at work. A large desk held the machine, and its lid had been opened to reveal four rows of keys. A sheet of paper stuck out of the top, wrapped around a large black roll positioned to hold it in place against the levers that stamped the letters onto the page.

"It's beautiful," Myra said.

"It ought to be. 'Tis a Sholes." Still Stephen did not look up. The fury he had carried with him from the dining table translated into the force with which he struck the keys.

Myra sat in a nearby armchair, content to watch and wishing she could use her gift to soothe him. She supposed that the mechanical hammering at his piece of paper could be therapy enough.

"You want to ease my black mood." Stephen chuckled, pushing back from the typewriter to hold his arms behind his head and stare up at the ceiling. "Harder on my lot, isn't it?"

Nonplussed, Myra silently acknowledged the difference. What she wanted to talk about was Laurel and James. Which reminded her . . .

"So, they were saying that you had a theory about me. About my powers, really," Myra amended.

"Not a theory. A hunch," Stephen corrected. He settled further into his chair and raised his hands as if to steeple his fingers. He stopped short, looking puzzled as though he, too, believed the gesture would look out of place on him. Again, Myra's natural empathy rose within her. He was incredibly ill-at-ease with teaching. "A theory is more developed, has breadth and design. I merely postulated that, considering the rest of the Major magics, there ought be the possibility of a lesser mage exhibiting the powers of empathy."

"Major magics?"

"Retrocognition. Thymesis. Apportation. Prescience. Ways-walking . . . to name a few. Major magics. The gifts." At Myra's blank stare, he continued, "As opposed to the Minor magics. You don't know what I'm talking about, do you?"

Stephen slapped his hand to his forehead, groaning dramatically, "What are they teaching you in this house? Basics. You need the basics."

Myra rushed to defend James and the rest, "The first day I was here, I asked. There was talk of lesser mages having one gift amongst the many. So it was not ignored."

Stephen snorted, flat rejection of Myra's clumsy defense. "You know, then, the shape of magic; what makes something a Major or a Minor Arcana; what constitutes a gift. No?"

Myra shook her head, both dumbfounded and excited. It was theory, to be sure. The dullest part of learning, and yet she was drawn to it. It was active in a way some of her other lessons had not been.

Stephen leaned forward, eyes alight. "The magic within a mage. It has shape, it is a thing as tangible as heart or liver, yet no being has ever seen it. It is like that which makes our lungs continue to draw and expel air, like the thought that allows us to walk, to talk, to move." He lifted an arm in illustration, staring at it contemplatively for an instant before letting it drop. "It is muscle, bone, sinew, and spirit."

"And only mages have it."

"Only mages have it, yes, Myra." Stephen nodded. "The why and the how, much like the mystery of the extent of magic's form, is unsolved. Currently, the main belief is that the trait—much like mismatched eyes or a malformed organ—is inherited."

Myra had a thought, dismissed it roughly. *Alice.*

No, there was no chance any of her family was magic in some way, not with how they had treated her gift. Myra remembered Agent Black's questions to James with regards to Laurel. "Mages make mages . . ."

Stephen blanched at her words. "Yes, Myra. That is true. True also is how, with the Dampening, no more full wizards are being born. And that is how we get an alignment of one Major Arcana per lesser mage. A full magus has the freedom to learn and develop the skill to perform higher magics of all sorts—generally choosing a specialty or two to focus on. Like building up a muscle, channeling and shaping their magic to the exclusion of other Major magics but without the limit of permanence. Such a wizard can choose to change themselves later on, pick a different Major Arcana, remake their art and gift.

"Whereas a lesser mage has the direction of their Arcana, their gift, picked for them. Stuck. Permanent. And permanently 'turned on' . . . Like a full mage, they can work to learn and perform other Minor magics, but the Major gifts are a series of locked doors. The shape of their magic is fixed."

"Like that malformed liver—"

"—or mismatched eyes. Yes, Myra."

"And all—full or lesser—are subject to Violectric Dampening." Myra lowered her gaze, remembering Stephen's current state.

He nodded. "Addair suspected that there was something in the human body, specifically, that acted as conduit to the magic within, a weakness built into ourselves which electricity resonates with in a detrimental fashion. But that's all something for another time, perhaps."

Muffled voices could be heard through the open door of the library. James and Laurel's argument, exposed by the silence in the wake of Stephen's having ceased his typing. Myra could now understand why he had chosen that activity in particular upon exiting the dining room.

Stephen seemed to sense Myra's dismay and met it head on. "We were talking about Laurel, Myra, yes?"

Myra blushed, striking boldly, "Laurel. And James. What's their deal?"

"Deal?" It was Stephen's turn to be nonplussed. Or, perhaps, he was simply amused. "That's just how those two are. How their friendship works."

"What do you mean? Doesn't he—?" Myra looked from Stephen to the argument-amplifying doorway. "He's the father of her child, right? Doesn't that mean he loves her?"

Again, pain crossed Stephen's face. "After a fashion, sure. But not the usual way. I mean, it's hard to develop that sort of thing when you have limited options before you. You feel trapped."

Limited options. Myra could tell Stephen wanted to say more but wasn't sure he ought.

Reluctant and politely mandatory pause complete, he continued, "Wizardry, as you might have guessed, is not exactly the most genteel of callings. And neither is spy-craft. Which makes for limited options in courting if you wish to be even remotely honest about yourself."

Again, a pause, this one hard. Personal. Myra remembered the kiss between Stephen and James upon the night of his return to the team. She'd seen and experienced that love—albeit secondhand through her gift. But then why had James and Laurel conceived? Laurie was far enough along that such would have happened before they believed Stephen dead.

"A shared past, mutual dangers faced, can provide a closeness that might otherwise be absent between friends. That, my dear Empathic, is the base of their regard for one another. Which makes their duty more palatable." Stephen found a way out of his discomfort enough for him to give a wry smile.

"Duty."

The question must have been writ on Myra's face where words fell short, for Stephen chuckled and elaborated, "As you yourself have said, the gift of magic is— to some extent—hereditary. James therefore believed it his obligation to combine his and Laurel's bloodlines in hopes of providing M.I. with its next generation."

Oh! There was no hiding the shock that crossed Myra's face. And in any event, she wasn't sure she would have wanted to. To so casually talk of such things crossed so many lines of propriety. She actually hoped that her judgment showed. As well as her prudish surprise.

But Stephen was not to be judged so easily. He waved off Myra's puritanical pout with a broad smile. "Come, we cannot all afford—"

"Good to have it back then, Stephen? I had told James he needed to go collect it." Laurel's presence robbed Stephen of what he had been about to say. Turning first white then red with embarrassment, he closed the lid on his typewriter, covering the keys with a metallic clang. Apparently such lapses in propriety were not something that happened around just anyone in the house.

Laurel approached the table, and Myra wondered if she looked as guilty as Stephen. James and Laurel? Lovers out of duty alone? Stephen and James—their romantic entanglement put aside for duty to crown and country. That explained a lot about dour and impassioned James James.

Stephen seemed eager to make his escape, muttering something about "going to check on James" before disappearing through the still-open door. Myra hadn't time to process the new dynamic before Aidan, Robert, and the rest all filed into the room. It was time for her to give report.

She began, telling how she had slipped upstairs unnoticed, intent on Brackenbury's offices at Stephen's signal. Myra confessed how, rather than going straight there, she instead made for Griggs' office, finding it empty—

"What the devil is he up to now?" Robert strode straight past Myra, eyes drawn to the abandoned typewriter with its white sheet of paper covered in neat print. She watched as Robert's gaze swept back and forth, rapidly taking in the contents of Stephen's abandoned rant. His brow grew dark, eyes graying with the oncoming storm of his anger.

"Robert—" Laurel half-rose, as if to intervene.

But it was too late. For Robert had torn the half-finished article from the machine. Crumpling the page, he waved it about. "Look at this! Accusations. Insurgent commentary not fit for print! 'S not like him. Not like him at all. Why would James let Steve write such incendiary garbage?"

He fed it to the eager fire, growling, "He's not careful he'll end up in Broadmoor like Maclean."

"Broadmoor!" Myra hadn't meant to shout the word but there it was. Five curious pairs of eyes turned her way. For a long moment nobody moved. *Well, at least I finally got everyone's attention.*

It was Ben who broke the spell. "What was that?"

"Broadmoor," Myra breathed, seeking Aidan's face. Blank unrecognition. Kady stood at his side, equally puzzled. Something to do with the British agents, then, she concluded, turning back to Benjamin for answer.

He was still looking at Myra as though she had grown two heads. "You've— Have you been?"

"I'm sorry. What?" Myra revised her initial impression. He wasn't looking at her with stunned surprise so much as fear. She gave him the barest shake of her head. Benjamin's wand was out. Not threatening. But . . . insurance.

Guilt hit her from the side, an attack on her Empathy that rang almost physical. Myra again darted her eyes to Aidan. He, too, had his wand out.

It was pointed at her.

Chapter Thirty-Four

"Aidan." Fear rippled through Myra, ice-water in her veins that brought back painful memories of the North Atlantic Apex. *I've misread him. We all have.*

She gasped, clutching her chest, her fingers tearing at her bodice in a frantic, automatic attempt to get at her wand. Robert and Laurel were on their feet, each shouting in an attempt to keep the peace. Even Kady had risen to her aid, throwing a restraining arm to Aidan, her eyes begging explanation.

Myra felt a tickle on the back on her neck and knew that Ben had leveled his wand at her as well. What is going on? What had any of this to do with her having gone to DMI with Stephen?

"I'm so, so sorry Myra." Aidan's words cut. He spoke truth. His wand was pointed at Myra's heart, and he had intent to hurt her if need be. And yet he was sorry for whatever he was about to do. It was tearing him apart.

He loved her. This, too, had bearing. Somehow.

"Aidan. Don't." Myra forgot the wand, instead

opting to hold her hands out in front of her. Empty. Surrender. How had she missed it? He was a Maester of Triewes. He could not lie.

"He told me, Myra," Benjamin supplied the rest. "Told me what you entrusted to no one else in this house."

"Told you what?" Myra whipped around, flinching as Benjamin's wand jerked in response. A hastily checked action. A warning.

Fine. Hit me then. Live with that memory, Benjamin Egrett.

"Where he found you. Why he found you." Benjamin's voice trembled, as did his wand. He was going to do it. He would use his powers on her. Murder lived in his eyes—perhaps, always had.

Myra met it head on. "Told you what?"

Anger snuck in, catching Myra unawares. It might have been Benjamin's. Not that it mattered. Her voice rose, cracked under the strain, "I told you all. The night that I arrived. The night you made him question me."

"The doctors, Myra. The asylum." Aidan had her attention once more. There. There was the source of his guilt. Myra cringed, a kicked and cornered animal, a frightened child. "The reason you had run away."

This time there was no mistaking it. The anger that swelled in her chest was absolutely her own. Myra did not bother turning around. She kept her voice even, facing Benjamin as she addressed Aidan and reveling in the crumpling of the former's resolve. She said, "That was something I told you in confidence. Something I told you because I feared—"

"And caused subsequent fear in me, Myra. I let you have your secrets. Even when James had me questioning you right here, in this very room. Yours has always been an incomplete truth, and someone had to know of it. It was too heavy a burden for my gift to bear alone." Aidan's voice pleaded. He wanted her to turn around. Needed her to. Benjamin shifted his stance, using both hands to hold out his wand. As though such would make any difference now that he had seen her pain, experienced it firsthand.

"Burden." Myra spat the word, fighting back with her gift, her Empathy. She felt for Aidan, truly. But she would not satisfy him.

Benjamin could not face her. She could see that now. And Aidan? He would have to strike her in the back.

"You know that he had to tell me, Myra," Benjamin reasoned. "He knew the truth of your heart. Surely your gift grants you that knowledge. But Broadmoor . . ."

He shook his head.

"What is this Broadmoor?" Myra shrieked, patience snapping.

Benjamin's eyes darted over her shoulder. Whatever he had seen in Aidan's reflecting surprise stunned him into dropping his arm. A saving truth.

"That's what began all of this, Myra," Laurel's quiet voice cut through the dying animosity, cool water to quench the fire. "That's where we had to send Addair's firstborn mage for attacking the Queen eight years ago. His power had rendered him . . . mad."

Laurel's simple statement shook her more than had the dual threat of both Aidan and Benjamin. The words had Myra sinking to her knees. Surrender and grief washed over her in waves. Theories and half-wild hopes chased each other through her mind.

It was Robert who helped Myra to her feet, his angry brow shooting figurative lightning bolts at Aidan and Ben—neither of whom dared approach just yet. "Come, my dear. 'Twas an honest misunderstanding. We don't shoot rashly. Leastways with one of our own."

Myra wished she could turn grateful eyes to the wizard. She wished she could find the source of what turned her knees to jelly and burn it out with the power of all the world's magic. Most of all, she wished that such were all that was wrong with her.

Madness. Her longstanding fear come back to haunt her. And with evidence damning and impossible to run from this time. Aidan had been right to warn Benjamin. Myra could well have used such a warning about herself.

Echoing in her ears: the laughing words of the MI2 agents, unaware of the spy in their midst. The memory was dulled, indistinct under Myra's shock. Only the two men's disdain for wizards remained. And the fact that Griggs had been transferred to Broadmoor. The empty office swam in her vision, a life raft towards which she eagerly swam.

Transferred to Broadmoor. And though they had not since heard from Julius, perhaps there was some good to come of it. Likely he was in charge of those of Addair's men that had been apprehended. It was not beyond reason to think that such tied into his work.

Relief won out. Myra said as much, repeating what she had overheard in DMI's offices, "Julius Griggs was transferred to Broadmoor."

"Is that where you heard the name?"

"How did you hear such?"

"When? From whom?"

All three questions came at Myra simultaneously. It was near impossible to tease out which came from whom. She covered her ears in protest, cringing as

M.I.'s mages, noisy crows flapping about, crowded 'round her.

"DMI. When I went there with Stephen," she said.

"You told us you found his offices empty," Aidan pressed, kneeling to peer at her, an unavoidable confrontation.

Myra nodded, truth spilling from her, "That I did. But I also overheard two agents mentioning Broadmoor. They . . . laughed. I assumed it was just a bad office to have to work out of and didn't think any more of it. Nobody asked, you see. Nobody else really seemed to care that he was gone."

Again, it was Laurel with answers. "It's a hospital—"

"—an institution," Benjamin corrected. "The full title of the place being Broadmoor Criminal Lunatic Asylum. And Maclean was not the only of Addair's affiliates to end up in that place."

He still had not approached Myra. She addressed him next, hurt that he was still distancing himself so. Hurt at the none-too-subtle implication. "What would Julius be doing there?"

"What indeed." Benjamin folded his arms. His wand stuck out, still grasped as it was between his fingers. That he had not yet secured it away was telling. He smirked. "Perhaps he's played us all."

"Now see here," Robert half-rose to defend the honor of one of their own, ord though Griggs was.

"No. You see here," Benjamin shouted, for once abandoning his lackadaisical demeanor. "Informant; even to the point of compromising his position within DMI—deny it if you will, Robert! He does things, knows things, that no ord ought to know. Julius Griggs is slippery."

At this incendiary statement the battle was joined. Shouting erupted all around, and Myra lowered her gaze, escaping it into yet a new flavor of pain, that of heartache.

She wanted to blush. Stammer and deny it all. Benjamin had, himself, called Myra's correspondence with the agent a game. But all too quickly that game had become real. First when she had found Julius gone without a trace. And now at the real possibility that Griggs might have been a traitor all along.

The ache of betrayal hurt so that Myra almost wished Ben and Aidan had hexed her and been done with it. Then she might have been saved this pain. Tears blurred her eyes, and she closed them to their sting.

For there was no mistaking it. Memories laid waste to Myra's heart: Julius' attentions to Myra, her being the only member of the team he might not otherwise account for. The doomed reconnaissance of the Flameists' ceremony and the happy accident that not even Griggs might have predicted. That of Stephen's and Kady's indiscriminate massacre, an act that had most likely saved Myra and James and Aidan's lives. The glaring fact that it had been Griggs who had been their inside man at DMI; his providing of the corpse whose information they had acted on with regards to the Order. Lastly, James' anger at Julius himself over Griggs' device ostensibly meant to siphon electricity from the air, but could easily be turned to harness and direct such power against mages.

Distantly, Myra noted that even Aidan and Benjamin had joined the fray. Which was nice, she supposed. But nothing compared to Julius' squashed face and crooked smile, his kind eyes. His kind, deceitful, infinitely cruel eyes.

Myra found the thread of her anger again and grabbed at it, holding on for dear life. A lifeline, pulling her back out of herself and into the land of the living, she let fury take her from the mire of her broken heart.

Perhaps it was time for M.I. to go to Addair, put his men in danger and force him to make the next move. Myra would relish the confrontation with Griggs. She had words she would like to give him . . . along with a pendant she no longer wanted.

Chapter Thirty-Five

Myra glanced around the library, thinking. *Someone ought to get James.*

"Does Stephen know this?" Aidan's piercing eyes tunneled into Myra's own, forcing her to look away. He might read the truth of things but amends were still to be made.

Someone ought to get James. Myra's thought repeated itself more urgently. She searched the room for someone who might do just that.

"I doubt they would have spoken so if they thought Steve could overhear them." Laurel rose to her feet. Robert slipped to her side, shaking his head. She was not to interrupt James and Stephen at this time. It would be someone not tied to their troubles who fetched them.

Benjamin volunteered.

His leaving gave Myra the peace of heart she had not known she needed. Still, she understood. In light of what Aidan had told him, how was he to know she was not an enemy? Julius had played them for fools. Luckily the Department had, apparently, caught on to his deceptions and sent him to Broadmoor like the rest of his sorry ilk.

But he's not insane. The thought was little comfort to Myra. It was, in many ways, worse. She suppressed a shudder and went to go sit by Kady, who offered her an arm 'round the shoulder.

"Come, dear," Kady whispered. "We're all mad here."

Myra looked up sharply, finding the Kinetic grinning like the Cheshire Cat. And suddenly it made a little bit more sense how they dealt with the path they had chosen. Grief. Danger. Love. All was very much the same to them. There was a fractured wisdom to it, she supposed.

Stephen had returned, bringing James. Benjamin had not come back. The looks on both their faces told Myra that they had been briefed. James spoke, "You lot. Clear out. We need to test a certain theory of Stephen's and require a space uncluttered by people."

A discordant shuffle arose. Myra moved to leave along with the rest.

"Not you." James pointed a quivering finger at her. "You're the one going to be doing the magic."

Myra sat, gulping back her trepidation.

A disappointed cry told them Stephen had discovered his precious typewriter had been tampered with. "My article. For the paper."

He looked wildly about, gaze stopping on the flickering flames of the fireplace.

" 'S all right, Stephen." Robert did not own to the destruction, instead opting to pat Stephen on the back. "Story's not over yet. Gotta keep your chin up and eyes clear."

"Come on. Out, you." James tapped Robert as he passed. He then turned his attention back to Myra. "You're going to find Julius Griggs for us."

"How?" Her powers didn't work that way. Her Empathy was drawn towards a wizard's gift. They all knew that.

Stephen explained, "When you first discovered your powers, how did they work, Myra? You felt only what another mage felt, and only if their emotions were very strong at the time."

"Visions. Yes," Myra said.

"You thought yourself mad."

Myra flinched. Neither of them had been present for the confrontation just then.

Stephen hurried to explain, "That is consistent with the experiences of most wizards when they realize their powers. Ben, he— His was a rough Emergence."

James said, "But Stephen also has postulated that an Empath could connect with anyone, anyone at all, provided the gifted mage had the details necessary to find them. For it would make little sense that your magic is only applicable to other magic. No gift works that way."

"What we're getting at is that you can hone your skills. Just as you've learned to control your gift, keeping it from running away on you and pulling you left and right and everywhere, you can learn to do this," Stephen finished.

"Laurel can see into the dreams of the Queen just as she can feel us through the Ways," Myra ventured.

"Exactly!" Stephen crowed. "James, she is quick. Yes, Myra, Laurie's gift of Ways-walking is one of the mental Arcana. All magic taps into emotion, some more than others. Those gifts which utilize the powers of the mind—and subsequently, heart—are technically in kinship to the pure power of traveling the OtherLands. When you use your gift, Laurel can see your spirit wander the higher planes."

"So to speak," James chimed in.

"So to speak." Stephen nodded. "It is infinitely more complex than that. But it's enough to say that your power should allow you to connect with anyone with whom you have grown close. With time—and we are talking years of practice, patience, and study—you could well unlock a power of the mind that we can only, at present, theorize."

"But for now, you'll settle for me seeing if what I heard about Griggs is actually true," Myra drew it all together with a heavy sigh.

"Yes." The two men spoke in unison, their eyes alight. And for the first time, Myra could see how two individuals, one so completely different from the other, might have grown so close. She took out her wand in preparation.

"No wands, Myra." Stephen gently laid his hand over hers. James moved off into the shadows, watchful and himself once more. "As I have no power, we'll be practicing this on me."

He closed his eyes. "Look for the picture that I paint. Don't try to imagine it. Smell, taste, and hear it. See if you can tell me something about it that I haven't told you. Ready? In the countryside, not all that far from here, is a house. Small, unremarkable really, it sits near the crest of a hilltop."

Myra closed her eyes and felt nothing from the man.

"The house is old without being ancient. Walls

comprised of grey stones prized from the surrounding fields, a slouch roof, and a couple of well-placed windows make up the whole of it. The fence is in need of mending but does not indicate rife disrepair. Altogether, it's a tidy little place. Comfortable and—"

"Ow!" Myra's eyes snapped open, and she looked to her hand, at pain so sharp she expected there to be blood.

Nothing. Her fingers, her palm, all were pink and whole.

James was on his feet, breathing hard. "Myra. What have you done?"

A very good question.

It might have worked, then. Whatever it was they were trying to accomplish. But it didn't feel right. Myra felt weak. And not just from the imagined injury. In addition to her fast-fading pain, she had felt anger— James'—and had, in fact, felt so the whole time. An uncomfortable buzz with which she was well acquainted, it had taken residence in the back of her mind until it had crescendoed to the point where she had thrust it from her.

And lost something of herself in the process.

"Come with me." James walked past her towards the door, his eyes still wild. Stephen seemed as dumbfounded as Myra.

She stood her ground. "No."

James paused, anxious. "No?"

"You can say it here."

This time James' gaze swept to Stephen, but it was to Myra he spoke. "You weren't supposed to be able to do that."

"Do what?" Stephen and Myra spoke their annoyance at once.

At least Steve's on my side. Myra fought to keep her fear in check.

"She pushed her power onto me." James' accusation bit.

Myra shrank from it. "I was trying— It was so hard to feel anything, you understand."

"But your gift. You gave me magic. Atop my own." James seemed to be struggling to breathe, and for a moment, Myra worried that, somehow, her mislaid magic had done him injury. She stepped back from him, as though that might make any difference.

"Wær spells." Stephen's rejoinder blended triumph with strangled dismay. He looked stricken.

Both he and James.

"I'm sorry, Steve." James' compassion rang louder to Myra's gift than did his grief.

"I knew it too late for me a month ago, Jamie," Stephen waved it off. He set his troubled eyes on Myra. "Myra, have you heard the term 'warlock' before?"

Myra shook her head.

"Ah, well." Stephen glanced to James.

"Go on. If she can do it, she should at least know what it is she's doing," James grumbled. He wanted to leave. But he also wanted to stay. Caught in between, he folded his arms and leaned back against the doorway to the library. When Stephen did not continue the explanation, however, he offered, "The term 'warlock' has its root in wær magic. Old spells, such were the everyday ken of a mage. In times long past, power was oft borrowed and given."

"And more freely taken than otherwise." Stephen

gave a wry smile. "Hence magic's stellar reputation amongst true gentlemen."

James winced at the bitter interjection. "We'd have to ask Benjamin to be certain, Myra. But what you were able to accomplish without thought or direction just now, has not been done in at least three hundred years."

Three hundred years? Myra's mind boggled at the thought. She could feel the walls of Grafford House closing in on her. Her gift. Secret. Powerful. Unique. Myra looked to Stephen, himself giftless, hoping he could not read her heart.

Stephen was the first to fall but would not be the last. Already Benjamin's powers were compromised. Could Myra lend even him magic via the wær spells? Kady, Aidan, Laurel. Their gifts would soon fade into nothing lest they did something. Lest Myra do something.

James broke into Myra's newfound resolve. Or escaped it, more like. She looked up to find the door to the library yawning emptily. M.I.'s leader was gone, presumably to ask Benjamin something on the history of wær magic.

Stephen confirmed it with a hearty, "Well then!"

Myra turned back to him, cross. "So we accomplished the wrong thing."

"Did we now?" Surprise colored Stephen's features. He held up a hand, moving on as though nothing had happened. "We'd come back home for a season, and I was helping James out at his family home. There was a plow. My hand slipped on the handle and . . ."

"I felt the cut," Myra gasped, rubbing her fingers over her own palm at the sharp memory.

"I had assumed as much. I figure that the surprise of

your discovery is what freed your gift for James, not your pushing him away. This said as one who has experienced a lifetime of trying to hold that man at bay." Stephen grinned, breaking the last of the tension between them.

With it, Myra saw a way to make amends and pounced on the idea. "The plow, the memory that I felt . . . Maybe you're not actually an ord—"

"Myra."

"—Maybe it's like with Robert—"

"Myra!"

"And just a shred of power remains," Myra completed, defiant.

"Myra! No. I'm an ord. I've no magic. No shred, no whisper. Addair's men made sure of it. They knew what they were about and did their job well." Anger raised each word above the last, leaving Stephen poised on a cliff, wild-eyed and despairing.

Myra feared he would jump, led there by her own forced naiveté. She met his outburst with a silence made uncomfortable by her own sense of being horridly out of her depth. Twice she had hurt him.

At length Stephen spoke.

"I'm sorry. I didn't mean— Why else do you think James was so afraid of speaking of the wær magics in front of me?" His eyes cleared of their madness, brightening with hope. "Could you feel that?"

Myra shook her head, coming down hard on the wistful tone of Stephen's words.

"Not a thing. Well, I cannot be certain. But it didn't seem like anything specifically magic." She frowned, trying to make herself clearer, "I think it's hard with you here because I care as a normally sympathetic person would."

"I know. And that's to your credit, love. I—" Stephen's eyes darkened then brightened, a swiftly passing cloud. "You wait here. I'm going to go talk with Aidan. Stay here. And keep trying. I'm going to . . . going to see if something works."

Talk with Aidan . . . Myra nodded and did not move from her chair as Stephen jumped to his feet and left the room without further explanation. The minutes slipped past and still Stephen did not return. Nor was there any perceivable tug on Myra's Empathic powers. She waited still, wondering how long she ought to wait. Maybe Aidan was unavailable. Maybe Stephen's idea didn't work at all . . . Maybe . . .

Suddenly, Myra felt something—a magic something. Bigger and noticeable, like what she was used to with mages but . . . blurrier.

Stephen was hurting. Badly. And it hurt. It really hurt. And with no magic for her to join with, Myra could only feel herself splitting in two, ripped apart by Stephen's despair. But neither could she leap into him, see the world through his eyes. No visions came. No fits. Just the pain and her gift's indecision of where to put Myra in all of it.

Myra could not wait any longer. Rising, she ran from the room, desperate to console Stephen. What was Aidan doing to him? What on earth could they be—?

At the far end of the hallway, Aidan stood talking quietly with Stephen. Stephen had tears running down his cheeks and was leaning back against the wall. They stopped as Myra approached.

"Myra," Stephen breathed, smiling through his pain. "You felt—?"

"What did you do to him?" Myra turned angry eyes to Aidan. And Stephen. They were both in the wrong here so far as she was concerned. Playing with high emotions, triggering her own pain. Didn't they understand?

Stephen understood.

"Myra, dear. It's all right." Stephen forced a smile, wiping a sleeve over his tears. It was clear to her that he felt foolish and self-conscious, having now seen his own pain reflected back to him. "Meet me back in the library?"

The horrid throbbing in Myra's magic retreated, a fire quickly quenched, but still she didn't budge. The pain was too fresh, too ill-defined to be put away without explanation. And, besides, there was still Aidan to deal with. Impassive as though made of stone. *Talk with Aidan, Stephen? Why would I bother? Aidan's gift is to be unfeeling, as inaccessible to me as a chair or stick of firewood.*

"Really. It's fine. I wanted it to work and knew what it might take." Stephen maneuvered himself to stand between Myra and Aidan. She watched as the two men locked gazes, each making his peace with minimal fuss.

"Aidan."

"Stephen."

With a hard squeeze on Aidan's shoulder, Stephen shuffled away. Myra was surprised that he would give her up so easily. James would not have. He would have hauled her back to the library for another bruising of her psyche. A gesture kindly meant, of course. But she was grateful for the reprieve, the chance to confront

Aidan who had still not spoken to her, had still not looked at her.

"Aidan, what did he . . . ?" Myra pleaded.

"It is not my place to say." Aidan remained carefully closed. "Stephen told me what you two were attempting. He came to me aware that, with my art, I'd know the deeper truths of his soul enough to cause the appropriate level of pain. And if your powers did not bring you to knowledge of what went on between he and I just now, that is for Stephen, himself, to tell. I'm sorry, Myra."

He met her gaze at last, staggering her with the full force of his own emotions, manipulative and goading.

She bit. "But I have to know."

"No, Myra, you really don't."

"Aidan. You have to tell—"

"The truth? Ha. Telling truth does not necessarily mean telling all. I can tell the truth with my mouth closed." Aidan leaned in, intense. "Be grateful for what Stephen is trying to do for you. What he's willing to go through to teach you some simple task. Now go, do what you came to do."

"What I came to . . . ?"

"Console him! Isn't that what your powers are most useful for?" With a withering look that had her wishing she hadn't made eye contact after all, Aidan assessed and then dismissed Myra. He turned on his heel and strode away. It left Myra with a healthy dose of her own guilt and the unspoken command that she return to the library to find Stephen. Was that all this lesson was to be about?

Chapter Thirty-Six

My name is James James, and I do not exist . . .

Myra dreamed that James had again taken up his letter.

The mage sat alone in the library. Once more, the furniture in the room had been re-arranged. The massive oaken desk at which James sat had been drug close to the fireplace, possibly for warmth, possibly for the light it offered. Pen and ink discarded at his elbow, he ruined the silence with the metallic click-clack of a typewriter. The flames on the hearth licked at the pile of logs therein, a quiet observer to the scene.

"A bit melodramatic, don't you think?" Laurel sidled up to read over James' shoulder. "Stephen okay with you using his Sholes?"

"I thought it fitting." James' muttered answer was met with raised eyebrows.

"I thought you hated the thing." Laurie rifled through the discarded papers, drawing an irritated hiss from James.

"Yes, well, the damnable bell's been taken care of."

Laurel interpreted James' complaint with the pursed lips of judgment. "So he's not fine with your using it. You'll fix it when you're done? James?"

A grunt. James resumed his typing, tipping his head to the papers Laurel had shuffled and muttering incoherently.

"You don't have to do this, you know," Laurel tried again, turning to lean back against the table's edge so that she faced James. He looked up at her then. Danger thickened the air of the library. The scene was poignant, two silhouettes backed by the bright shadows of flame. It felt almost like a portent.

"It's just a letter."

"Is it?"

"Yes, Laurie. A formal letter of resignation, long overdue—"

"It's a suicide note." Laurel's normally melodic voice grew sour.

James lowered his gaze. "Well, call it that if it makes you feel better about yourself. You've gotten what you've wanted out of me. Now I must do what I need to do. To protect you—all of you. Steve came back. He came back, Laurie. Doesn't that—" He choked on his emotion. "Doesn't what that means to me mean anything to you?"

"You and Steve. Hotheads, both of you." Laurel shifted, crossing her arms in false petulancy. "You're going to force a move."

"That's the idea of it." Even unable to see his face, Myra could feel James grinning.

"Be careful, James James. Don't do anything rash by these words." She leaned forward to kiss him on the cheek. "And don't stay up too late. Neither of you are superhuman." At this last, Laurel looked straight towards where Myra watched from within her dream.

James waited. The machine grew silent under fingers that hovered impotently over the keys. Laurel shrugged and walked away. For a long moment, James remained frozen, his eyes on the words of the drooping page, his ears trained to the sound of the woman's retreating steps.

Nodding to himself, as though he had arrived at a decision, James continued his moody prodding of the machine's keys. The storm in his soul was ebbing, his energies having bled out onto the paper before him. It was believable after such an expenditure that James James might well no longer exist. Violent as raindrops dashed on a window pane, the final notes of his typing rang out and then ceased.

Myra sat up in bed, called to waking by a low rumble of thunder. It broke over the house, rattling all within.

Including nerves.

Myra flung herself back down upon her pillows, willing her dream to conclusion. But it was no use. A flash of lightning beat against her eyelids and roused her further as thunder like booted feet pounded the hallway outside her room.

Turning over with a groan, Myra stuffed a pillow to her ears. The thunder deepened, drew nearer.

The door to her bedroom burst open. A hooded figure leveled a wand at her heart. Shrieking, Myra reached blindly for her wand, her gaze caught on the intruder. More lightning. And then? A blank, black silence.

Chapter Thirty-Seven

Myra came to in the Grafford House library. Unusually dark and damp, the lack of roaring fire and glowing wall sconces rendered the room hostile. A bookcase was at her back, and its contents poked uncomfortably through Myra's nightshift. Hands and ankles bound, she tried to maneuver her tongue around the dirty rag that had been stuffed into her mouth.

She was not alone.

Robert, Aidan, Benjamin, Kady, Stephen . . . all were similarly trussed and left bolstered up against the furniture, each out of reach of the next. None seemed conscious.

Where was Laurel? Where was James?

Myra attempted to crane her neck and found the motion pained her. From the corner of her eye, she could now see that a black-ish stain marked the shoulder of her nightgown. Blood.

Myra froze, newly terrified and fearful that she might injure herself further, not knowing the extent of the damage. Unmoving, she mentally took stock of her aches and pains. No immediate wound presented itself, no ready explanation for the blood at the base of her skull. She simply felt drained.

Emboldened, Myra tried looking around again, this time espying three hooded men standing huddled in the shadows near the doorway holding hushed conference. They appeared to be arguing.

Myra swept her eyes over the room once more, feeling her brain sharpen into wakefulness. A hulking shadow loomed next to the fireplace, obscuring her view of the ash-choked hearth. Her pulse quickened, recognition even in the dark. A large oaken writing desk. *So it wasn't a dream?* Myra imagined she could see the Sholes atop it gleaming in what faint light there was in the room.

Still doesn't answer where James and Laurel actually are. Okay, Myra, think . . . Shaking grogginess from her mind, Myra tried to call upon her gift to see which of her friends was lucid, which was injured—*please, no*—and who might be counted on.

Behind her Myra heard a sluggish, sliding thump, a low moan. She froze. Someone else was awake. The sound roused their captors into motion. Lightning flashed, sharply illuminating the library for one, brief instant. Stephen's eyes met hers.

The three hooded men darted into the room, heads swiveling in jerky, tight movements. Another lightning flash showed Myra that each held a wand.

Mages, all of them.

" 'Nough of that, Quimby," one of the men spoke. "Adlay says we've enough power to hold 'em here for long as it takes."

Quimby laughed, white teeth glinting in the flash of

another bolt from the heavens. "I'll do what pleases me. Besides, Silas has wanted to know exactly how strong a field Griggs' harvesting devices can achieve. That right, Garrison?"

Garrison raised his hands, begging to be left out of it. He earned his escape from the argument by applying a nasty kick towards Stephen. " 'Ere now. This'ns awake."

He jerked his head, complaining, "Eaton, ye've erred in yer hex here." Garrison raised his wand and flashed a wicked grin that even his wide hood could not conceal.

Eaton gave Garrison a rough shove, forcing him away and swiftly crouching at the side of his victim, his wand raised in the familiar illumination spell. "He's ord, Garrison. Saw no need to damage him like the rest. Dampening won't even affect him, so's he's good."

Stephen lifted his eyes to the hooded man at his side, animosity straining at his bonds. Recognition.

"Tha's right. You remember me from yer adventures in America, don't you? Survived to fight another day, did we?" Eaton crooned, reaching out to loosen the gag around Stephen's mouth, pulling it down around the ord's neck. "There now, in't that better? No worries about you casting anything on us."

The same hand struck, a viper grasping Stephen's chin and giving it a cruel twist. The pale light from the mage's wand painted Stephen as a madman. Eyes wild with hatred, skin bone white and crossed with the angry marks where the gag had bitten, M.I.'s mage-turned-ord worked his mouth, maneuvering around his instincts, seeking an answer that reached beyond mere recognition or threat. The thin line of Stephen's lips parted, emitting nothing but an impotent hiss.

"Thought so." Eaton gave Stephen's face a quick, condescending slap before retreating. "This'n is James' boy. Didn't give us what we wanted back at the Heartland Apex."

Quimby snorted. "And killed off three of ours to one of theirs. Not exactly a rousing victr'y, Eaton. You'd best remember things accurate like if'n you're gonna go around flapping yer yap about it."

"And then there's this'n."

Myra flinched. Garrison had discovered her. He said, "Don't remember her."

And she them. Those who had gathered in the cellars for the Flameists' ceremony had been monied, cultured, and connected. In contrast, these men were rough as their accents. They were men who worked for a living. She could see it in the way they moved their bodies. Hard men.

A woman's scream made Myra's heart stop.

Laurel!

Myra jolted upright, hissing through her gag as her as-yet-unknown injury added to her subconscious a scream of its own.

"Lookat, she's stirring. Yer hexes ain't worth a damn," Quimby nudged Eaton. The two came to join Garrison in his scrutiny. "Whatya suppose her gift is?"

"Young'n. And pretty. I bet if'n we ask her nicely, she'll show you, Q," Eaton nudged back, his mirth not reaching his eyes.

Through narrowed eyes Myra glared at her jailers. Another of Laurel's screams, wild and sorrowful, cut in. It drowned the rain, the darkness, the evil that these men had brought into Robert's home. Cleansing even as it bled, Laurie's agony provided M.I.'s captives with a shield.

"Gah. Can't the Nomanguere shut her up? She'll wake the rest of 'em like that." Eaton glared up at the dark ceiling. "Between that and the AethCaster's lightning, it's getting on my nerves."

"A thousand apologies to your delicate nerves, Eaton," Garrison growled. "Didn't know what you were signing up for with this line o' work? It's Adlay's job to do what 'e's doin' up there. What, you want I should get you next in line for his services?"

"Still—"

"Adlay ain't gonna touch her lest he risk Silas' wrath."

"Not physically, anyhow. Can't speak to her mind." The three men chuckled and turned away, distracted by the wailing from the floor above, unsettled by Laurel's pain. Garrison readied himself for another kick, this in Myra's direction but stopped short, waving his hands half-heartedly at her as he stomped away to go build up the fire with a quick hex.

Myra latched on to Laurel's wailing, wandering spirit and found her Mind Speech. She and Stephen locked gazes. *Are there weapons in this room that you can use?*

Stephen nodded. Curt and cautious. Distracted as they were by the clamor from elsewhere in the house, the enemy mages did not appear to note the communication passing between their prisoners. Myra worked fast, her connection to Laurie's gift pulling her into the woman's pain. *If I can free us, can you move in our defense? Are you injured?*

Myra needed no Voice from Stephen to read his wide-eyed response: *Are you?*

Never mind me, Steve. Myra kept her reassurance clipped, feeling Aidan's magic buzz its doubts into the back of her brain. She agreed with Quimby: Eaton's hexes weren't worth a damn. **Hullo, Aidan. I presume you can hear me as well. We have to help Laurie. If you can rouse Kady, I can use her Kinetics to shut down whatever is causing the Dampening for you. They said something about Julius' harvesting devices. My guess is that they somehow have set up several to create a field around the house, using the AethCaster's weather working to charge them. Be ready for my move.**

Myra waited. She waited as Laurel's cries dimmed to a whimper and ceased their pulling at Myra's Empathy. Waited as the storm outside again made itself known and their captors settled into moody silence around James' fireside table. Waited as the roving ghost of Laurel's tortured spirit ceased its haunting, coalescing into a Voice in all her friends' heads: **Hold. They do not wish me harm . . . yet. I am too valuable due to my most precious gift. And, Myra, I do believe you will not find Kady's Kinetics available to you due the electric field set 'round our perimeter by Griggs' devices. I maintain my magic as I was quick to flee into the OtherLands.**

Laurel's Mind Speech echoed in Myra's chest, loud as a thunderclap and reassuring with its strength. **James, if you can hear me, I'm sending her to you.**

Her? Myra looked sharply to Stephen. But she never met his gaze.

Chapter Thirty-Eight

"Myra."

Myra startled at the sound of her name, blinking off a sudden daze of blinding-bright. The hazy light retreated, and she returned to herself.

"Myra." Repeated with much greater urgency, James' summons shook Myra from herself once more. The Grafford House library faded into memory. The sticky wet of her injury died into nothingness. Myra joined her gift to James, saw through him.

"Good girl," James muttered under his breath. "Laurel needed you to be eyes for the rest of the team, Myra. Just in case."

In case of what? Having never been specifically "sent" before, the sensation of Myra's vision was not as seamless as on previous occasions. She was disoriented, bewildered. And annoyed.

How dare he. How dare Laurel. She was needed back in the library. She was the only one in Grafford House with power. *Not true, Myra, Laurel sent you to James, remember?*

But to where? Where, exactly, was James? Head-quarters? The Underground? Somewhere else equally implausible and inexplicable? Did James know what was happening in Grafford House right at that very moment?

"Yes, Myra, I am well aware. Laurel explained it to me," James murmured, checking his surroundings again for Myra's benefit. Stone walls—plastered over in a dull white—pressed in from the sides. Wood flooring creaked beneath his feet. A long hallway punctuated with closed doors, it seemed to go on forever. The effect would have been ominous had it not, more importantly, come across as cheap.

Hospital.

"Broadmoor." James let the menacing word soak in before creeping forward. "I need to know where I might find our wayward Mr. Griggs. We have business, he and I."

A thrill shot through Myra—*his or mine?* Her mind again caught on the differences in sensation that came from having been sent into one of her visions rather than come of her own volition. *Since when have I come of my own volition?*

And then Myra was gone. Gone but present.

She was him and he was her. James marveled at it, wondering how he might actively communicate with the Empath now that she was too close to be felt.

'James, I'm sending her to save you.' Laurel's warning—not even a plea, considering its tone—echoed in the back of James' mind. The one-sided conversation had proven to him that the wizard had entered the Ways, communicating to him effortlessly with her Voice

though her body lay more than 30 miles east. Power like he had not seen from her in over a decade.

And fear. Fear that had echoed in Myra's psyche when she had joined with him but a moment later. Grafford House was under attack. The team neutralized, if not worse.

And there James was. Ten leagues away. In Broadmoor Criminal Lunatic Asylum.

Why had he come alone? Whatever had possessed him to be so rash? That Laurel had not scolded him for such was telling. They were past such niceties and hadn't the luxury to stand and argue. James pulled his wand and ducked into a recessed doorway. The air was rife with power, not all of it magic. He wondered how long his gift would hold, how long he could last unaided in such a place.

Warmth blossomed in James' chest, a summoning of power that left him staggering within his small hiding space. *No. Not a summoning . . . a lending.* Myra. Her gift pulsed within his own veins, fighting the Dampening on his behalf.

Yes, I'm helping. And then I'm going straight back.

Mind Speech. Fascinating. James wondered if Myra could hear his own thoughts.

Yes. That's right I can hear you, Myra scolded, adding, **How dare you come here alone!**

James smiled, letting her pummel him with guilt, his tag-along conscience, picked up along the way. Laurel had seen to it that Myra would save him. Knowing her, she had also predicted that Myra would apply the proper dressing-down in her absence.

You must promise me you won't go after him alone.

That surprised him. Quirking an eyebrow, James mused. *We are negotiating now? That's not happening.*

Silence. And a retreating of strength. The Dampening pressed into James. Myra's gift was unavailable to him.

James found his anger, cousin to the blur of emotion that had driven him from Grafford House in the middle of the night. The same sparking drive that had saved him from being present for the team's capture would serve him in Broadmoor. He would tear the asylum apart, brick by sorry brick, until he located the traitor. He would make Julius release his friends. He would make him tell where Addair was hid. And then Griggs would die. Slowly. An ord's death.

A new tremor shook James. He presumed that Julius was still an ord. After all, he was weaponizing the Dampening to fight magic; relied upon his usual tricks and ticky-tacky methodology that had so enthralled the Department. The Department that James and Stephen and Robert had built with their blood, their tears.

And Silas Addair. Myra's cruel rejoinder knifed back into James' consciousness.

And with it, James became aware of knowledge he had not before possessed and the other the reason that Laurel had sent Myra to him: Julius Griggs' whereabouts. He could feel the ord through Myra's intrusion into his own gift.

She was still directing him, and that was all that mattered for the moment. And besides, she had earned the right to complain. He'd done a stupid thing, running off on his own like that.

James' newfound awareness of Griggs' nearness wavered and failed. Inwardly he swore. Stuck halfway down yet another of Broadmoor's labyrinthine hallways, the girl's powers did not extend as far as hoped. Not on ords, anyway.

"But he's still an ord, thank the gods."

Just you wait, James James. Just you wait until the others get there . . .

Others?

James stopped short, his heart pounding. No, she had not told them yet.

But she wanted to. And would upon her return to the library, per Laurel's wishes. *And good common sense.*

With thoughts of Laurel came thoughts of his frantic attempts at completing his missive. He had had no intent to post it. Rather he had hoped to bleed out . . . whatever it was that had gotten into him. Again, he still wasn't sure why he had been so impulsive. It was as though someone had gotten into his head, stirred his emotions and roused him to action. It renewed James' sympathies for Myra's plight with her own powers.

Griggs' location sounded itself in James' mind, strong as ever. Myra had mastered the part of her gift that allowed her to travel within James' psyche and could now work as fully as she might within her own mind. Fascinating. Terrifying that she could be so strong.

Damn it, Myra.

You cannot act alone, James. I've got to help the team. And then we're coming back. Just . . . Just learn what you need to and no more. Promise me, James James.

Laurel's words in Myra's mouth. Laurie's empathy thrown in James' face like a slap. Angry, he tried to banish Myra from his mind, finding that she only gripped the harder the angrier he got.

That's right you half-cocked, stubborn, trigger-prone mage of a man, Myra crowed. ***And when we—***

The scolding stopped short as James espied his quarry: Julius Griggs, stretched out on the covers of an old mattress, reading. Secured behind a barred and padlocked door. And with a heavy chain fixing his left ankle to the frame of the bed.

Bait.

James had time enough for the thought to register before the world exploded in color and light. As the ground rushed up to greet him, he was dimly aware of soothing words spoken at his side.

"Ah, there you are. Black informed me that you would be arriving soon. You've my thanks for being so obliging, Mr. James."

Gasping, Myra tore herself away from Broadmoor, returning to her own present. In the short minutes she had been gone, little had changed save she could now guess that Kady had gained lucidity. That is, if the tiny twitching in the back of her Empathy was to be believed.

I'm sorry, Laurel. But I'm needed here if James is to have any chance at all. Myra made her quick apologies, wondering, with a sudden trill of fear, if any of the enemy mages could hear her Mind Speech. None had, so far, reacted as though they had. Curious.

Kady first. She can help the rest. Even without her gift, she's the quickest. Myra arced her neck, finding that she could not meet the Kinetic's gaze but that her own wound pained her less with each passing moment.

Myra feigned that she had again lapsed into unconsciousness. Watching through slitted eyes, she tried to still her rising anxiety. Her training took over. The spells that would free her could not be worked unless she had found calm concentration.

The question was: should Myra free herself with a bang or a whimper? With Kady her goal, how much time might she reasonably count upon between throwing off her restraining ropes and helping the Kinetic before the enemy neutralized Myra?

As if in answer, one of the men returned. Quimby. Leaving his two companions by the fireside, he approached and knelt at Myra's side, his wand out. He said nothing. It made his presence all the more menacing, all the harder for Myra to read.

Thinking of James, of Laurel who had counted upon Myra to act as intercessor—had Laurie known where James had actually gone when she sent Myra to him?—she found the strength to act.

With a flash and a bang, Myra leapt forward. Ignoring the protesting of her wound, she cut down Quimby and flew to Kady's side. Outside the storm continued to scream and thunder, steadying the flow of energy to the machines which Dampened the skills of the mages within. Wandless, Myra simply allowed her fingers, and the magic that flowed within, to free Kady. Pure intent. Pure rage.

For a new pain lanced across Myra's shoulders and green fire lit the library. Rounding, she left Kady to the freeing of the rest and shot back fire of her own towards Garrison and Eaton. *This for Laurel. This for ruining the sanctity of Grafford House.* She refused to think of James; refused to think what the forced conclusion of her Empathic vision might mean.

Lightning and fire, twin furies loosed from Myra's hands. It forced Addair's men onto the defensive. Ducking behind bookshelves, each tried to shoot their spells at her from the relative cover of the furniture in the room. Robert's quiet library had become a battle field.

Deafened by the wild sparks of magic, blinded by their roar and crackle, Myra whipped and whirled, using every ounce of her training, not sparing a glance to see if she was alone. The sharp report of a pistol soon indicated that the fight now included some of her own. Quimby rose to his knees only to fall, cut down invisibly by a bullet.

Myra now risked a quick glance to the side and was surprised to see Benjamin coming straight towards her. His mouth was moving, one frantic syllable.

What?

The answer came in the form of Robert leaping in front of her.

With shock, Myra watched the M.I. agent hit the ground hard, purple and blue lightning arcing over his exposed hands and face. Robert's eyes were open. They looked . . . empty.

"Duck, dammit," Benjamin's voice caught him up, and he knelt by Robert's side, his pistol at the ready. But no second strike came. Aidan stood over Garrison's body, gun smoking in his hand. The other two enemy mages had already fallen to the deadly combination of Myra's magic and the less mystical fire-power of the team.

"Take care of the barrier." Stephen was at Myra's side, breathing hard as he took charge of the team. Kady nodded and left with Aidan. But not without first passing sympathetic glances toward Ben, still crouched by Robert's body. Hard-faced, Stephen prompted, "Go!"

Robert is dead. Myra did not need anyone to tell her this. It was obvious in and of itself. She moved to follow Aidan and Kady, eager to be of help and knowing she was the only one with her gift available to her until the barrier was removed.

Stephen put out a hand. "Not you. You need to tend to yourself first."

Myra moved to force her way past him. She had work yet to do. Pistols and knives were all fine and good, but she was the only one with functioning magic as of yet.

"Myra, you're injured." Steve's simple words seemed a spell that made them true. Myra swayed, her various hurts jostling with each other to make themselves heard. Sitting, she allowed the room to stop spinning, listening hard for any sign that she was needed, any sign that Addair's men had been more than the three who had taken them prisoner plus the Adlay fellow who stood guard over Laurel.

Benjamin sat with head bowed at Robert's side. Too exhausted to feel his pain with her Empathy, Myra tried to look away from the grief which gripped the young mage. His shoulders quivered with poorly-contained sobs.

Not Robert. Please. He was the kindest of us. Myra wasn't sure with whom she silently pled. She felt one large tear break free from its bounds to wreak destruction down her cheek. Empathy, true Empathy, followed in its wake.

And then, a miracle.

At first, Myra thought it a trick of her eyes, the fire-light giving birth to unreasonable hopes, or her injuries making her see things not real. Robert's chest rose and fell. A breath.

"Steve . . ." Myra breathed.

"Shh." Benjamin had moved to sit on his knees. He bent over Robert, his hands on the wizard's still form. Stephen now attuned to the scene, his own excitement tangible enough that Myra could feel it through her tired gift.

But it was true. Robert stirred, shifting under Benjamin's watchful attentions.

"Oh, thank the gods." Stephen rushed forward to help Robert into a seated position. Without thinking, he turned and buried Benjamin in a tight embrace. M.I.'s Necromancer received the outburst with embarrassed reluctance, and Myra found herself wondering what had happened in the past to make those two such adversaries.

Aidan and Kady burst back through the doors of the library.

Both gave the news at once, "They've taken Laurel."

Chapter Thirty-Nine

Myra could see James.

He lay upon the floor of his prison, arms and legs splayed, his fingers, his back, contorting at irregular intervals. To her it seemed she floated above him, an unusual vantage point. It was strangely sickening.

And then, everything went blessedly black.

"Oh, thank goodness," Benjamin exclaimed.

Ben's worried face hovered mere inches from Myra's own. She glanced about, noting how kindly M.I.'s Necromancer had attended to her needs. She lay in state, Benjamin kneeling at her side and stroking her hand, his coat a pillow beneath her head. Someone had fetched her some clothing, it waited next to her, a patient dark bundle. Aidan and Kady sat nearby. Robert and Stephen had moved to the hearth.

Around her, the library flashed with the light of extinguishing magefire, much of it Myra's. The room would never be the same after this. As if in agreement with her thoughts, the dying thunderstorm outside gave a rumble that shook the house.

"James. And Julius. I've got to go back," Myra relayed her message with shaking voice. She tried to sit up and found that the wound in her shoulder had reasserted itself. Wincing as the room performed a warning spin, she breathed, "They're in Broadmoor."

"Myra . . ."

"Just trust me, okay? Get the team, get us there . . . Please, Benjamin."

"Myra." This from Aidan. "The Dampening. Even having killed the AethCaster and even having shut down the field that surrounded the house, there is a time required for recovery if we hope to have any magic at all!"

Kady rose.

"I can fight. I can do some Minor Arcana but my Kinetic gift?" She shook her head. "I cannot take myself anywhere further than a dozen odd feet at present. Never mind a handful of mages also struggling to regain their own powers and Robert recovering from his near-death experience. It would be throwing our lives away needlessly, useless to James and Laurel. We must think beyond the safety of our team and consider how to stop Addair. If Silas has exposed himself, if Julius is there—"

"Then I have to go back," Myra insisted. "Julius. He's bait. Trapped and waiting for rescue. James, I think he was, himself, captured. Stephen—"

"I agree." Stephen rose to his feet, casually moving off toward one of the hidden caches of weapons still concealed within the library. His face was hard, that of a doomed man stolidly facing execution. "But neither can we, as Kady says, fly to anyone's rescue at present. And there's Laurel to consider."

"They'll keep Laurel safe," Aidan cut in, also now rising to arm himself. "I don't need a gift of truth telling to see that they meant no real harm to her. The future of their own plans, it would seem, is tied to her fate. No, they will not risk hurting her. And so I would recommend we see to James first."

"And to Julius, who was not a traitor after all," Robert agreed. He was slower to rise but gained his feet nonetheless. "That sort of loyalty deserves our own."

"Which means, Myra," Benjamin said, "you ride with me. And burn that power of yours to keep an eye on James. Let that stubborn idiot of a mage know we're coming."

"Robert? Horses?"

"We've the four available for our use, yes. Stephen and Aidan will ride separate, and I, Kady my dear, am still feeling a mite shaky and would ride with you. I'll not risk the carriage—too slow, too easily accosted should Addair have left any men between here and Broadmoor."

"I'll see to it that they are ready at the door. Arm yourselves. Kady?" Together Stephen and Kady dashed from the room.

Benjamin helped Myra to her feet. "I can go fetch your wand if you'll allow me."

She nodded, as much confirmation as testing her shoulder. For all that it still throbbed, she had full range of motion. The gash was a surface wound, nothing more. *A surface wound and nothing more? Truly, Myra, you have become an agent.*

She ducked into the next room over to change, feeling her strength return.

Hurrying back to where Benjamin, Aidan, and Robert waited for her, Myra swallowed her fears and reached out with her gift towards Broadmoor and towards the waiting James and Julius.

STAY AWAY.

Myra skidded to a halt, throwing a hand to Aidan in the dark hallway. "James."

"Where?" His voice, though quiet, was so tense as to be cutting, and Myra flinched.

"Hang on. I'm finding out." She screwed shut her eyes and leaned upon the wall, a shiver floating through her as she felt Aidan's sensitive fingers brush against her temples.

"He wants us to stay away," she warned. Obviously there was little chance of that.

Frantic, she sought the plane of magic that connected her to all mages. James was doing his best to elude her. Thin as spiders' silk, but just as strong, she could feel a thread of his magic and little more.

I'M WARNING YOU. GO!

James' anger shot through Myra like lightning. Searing light blazed within her psyche, the shock of the assault stealing her breath. Startled out of the connection, she swayed and went limp, gasping as Aidan neatly caught her in his arms.

"He's not letting me in." Myra blinked back tears.

"Like hell he's not. Robert, can you manage?" Aidan scooped Myra up into his arms, whispering, "You're strong, Moira, don't let him keep you out."

Chapter Forty

'My name is James James, and I do not exist . . .'

The hallway outside the Grafford House library dissolved into a fog of sound and light. Aidan's strong arms, the pain of Myra's injury, even the thrum of her own racing heart retreated behind the veil as, through James' need—though he did not know it himself—M.I.'s Empath lost control of her gift and, all too easily, fell directly into his pain.

James was empty. Empty of all save for blistering, searing agony. He no longer felt pain; he was pain. It was the beginning and the end of him. It was no wonder Myra would not leave him be. He wondered, absently, if she even could, if she was as much a prisoner as he.

Let her see, then.

He was dying. And far from experiencing his life in flashes, the pain that was James' entire being had replaced each memory, each experience, one by one. And he could feel its loss. He mourned it.

Thoughts of Laurel, marred by anguish to the point of un-recognition. Her face a blur, unfindable in the inferno of his shattered nerves and scattered brain. Robert, dependable rock of a man even in the waning hours of his gift's life. And Stephen. Steve whom nobody could kill. Stephen who held his heart in safe keeping far from this hellish place.

Love, wiped away like mist on glass.

And now that glass was broken. James imagined he could see pieces of himself shattered upon the cold tile floor, refuse to be swept up and discarded. And yet, looking at his shaking hands, he could see that he was whole. His fingers and wrists had not a mark on them. His arms—

A small puncture wound in the hollow of his right elbow pulsed with dull pain. Tiny and hardly bleeding, it seemed inconsequential in comparison to the rest of his agony. Certainly it could not be responsible for such.

Staggering forward—*I was in a war. This body has seen and experienced hardship unfathomable!*—James cursed his weakness. He shouted hoarsely, addressing the ugly door to his ugly room, "You've no right to keep me here. No right!"

What was out there? Where was he? That James could not remember was more frustrating than terrifying. Angrily, he grasped the bars that crossed the high, tiny window . . .

Rainbows and blinding sparks of light warred for dominance in James' vision, and then the world went black on him. Every nerve screamed in a discordant jangle, and he felt searing-yet-icy fingers—the touch of

Death himself—snake their way up his quivering arms to squeeze his heart. James' breath was snatched cruelly from lungs that boiled. His lips crackled. And his hands, they would not obey.

His vision returned to him, James watched in horror as his fingers—his perfect, wholesome fingers, hands, and wrists—seemed to shimmer, grasping the window bars as though their existence depended upon it.

Absently, James realized that he could see a grassy hill. Far off in the dark it stood, a lone tree atop its crest, James' childhood home not fifty yards off. A smattering of rain spattered down, dampening his forehead, and James watched as the sky lit up and the heavens roared their fury, God Himself throwing a blinding bolt down into the heart of the lonely tree.

Electrocution. James' mind slurred, trying out the new-fangled word for himself, all the while screaming at his hands to let go the prison bars. The tortured cacophony coming from his scorched throat vied for the honor of drowning out the sickening sizzle of his flesh, the sound somehow covering even the acrid smell of hot metal and burned tissue.

And then he was freed, James stumbling backwards into his cell on legs that collapsed but an instant later. He lay in a tangled heap, unmoving save for the uneven hammering of his heart. Able to breathe at last, James focused on drawing air in and out of his tortured lungs.

Nobody came.

And his pulse refused to settle, instead reaching a fever pitch of frantic leaps and jolts. And still James lay, not daring to move. Minutes passed, short and stuttering under the irregular beat of a heart that refused to calm. At length he could hear footsteps in the hall outside.

"Help," James gasped, rolling over so that he faced the door. But why even hope? He had waved his rescue away and had no expectation that it would be—

He couldn't recall their names! Hell, he didn't know his own! Faces, half-remembered, sifted down through the smoldering wreckage of his mind. But nobody, no matter how inhumane, could refuse treatment to a man in his condition. He needed to go to hospital.

I'm in hospital. The thought came lightning-fast, offering little illumination and vanishing from his mind as quickly as it had come.

James lay on the smooth, cool tile with his heart pounding. He was distantly—clinically—curious as to how he had gotten there. The air smelled funny, and he hurt all over. What was he doing here? Blackness threatened. It sounded like peace.

"He's still alive, sir. He—"

"I did not ask if he was still alive. If he were not, you'd be in much the same shape as he. What I asked was whether our mage was conscious."

Two voices. One smooth, aristocratic, and crisp; the other uncultured and carrying a hint of whine—*The weaker party*, James assessed, wondering who they were and why they did not rush to his aid.

Mage. James' parched brain soaked in the foreign word. Were they referring to him? Was that the name of his particular malady? Sluggishly, his brain chugged into motion, reordering itself and trying to delve out more words from his life, more lost memories.

Mage. Magic. Recollection flashed back into fractured focus, and James instinctively looked inside of himself for the bright threads of power that led to his magic. More details of his life slid into place. More memories. He did not like what he saw.

Two silhouetted heads had appeared in the barred window to James' room. Enemies. *Why do I know that?* No matter. He knew, just as a part of him had remembered what magic, what power, was.

Hatred sprang. James followed the emotion like a lifeline.

"He's awake all right. See his eyes?" One of the silhouettes cocked his head to the side, watching.

"How much current did he get when he touched the door? He looks damaged."

"Help." In spite of his hatred, James tried again.

"No more 'n the last two times, doctor. But I think he's starting to lose it up here." The answer came punctuated by an ill-mannered guffaw, the speaker tapping his head in illustration. Still, James managed a momentary lifting of hopes as the second man—said "doctor"—chided his companion for his callousness.

"James James—"

That's me! James struggled to lift his head.

"—Have you any left in you for another go around? Or will I be forced to end the experiment here and give the bout to my—"

The doctor's speech abruptly cut off, and James could see the two heads come together for an urgent, whispered conference.

"He what? Damn you, Tacke, I—"

"He was doing magic to the very end! But the machine, it overwhelmed him. Same as it might any man. Their basic mortality is not altered by your—gah!"

The air filled with sizzling brilliance, and the doctor's assistant found himself thrust face-first into the bars of James' cell door. The odor of burnt flesh and worse wafted into the tiny room, an added horror atop the man's death screams.

Remembrance jerked hard on the reins of James' heart, and he forced himself up upon elbows and knees. His brain tried to put his fractured memories into some sort of useful order. Another mage . . . A man who had had great power and no small skill . . . A man who James had loved.

Bits floated up to the surface of James' mind, thought bubbles bursting and releasing names. Places. Events. Steve. Stephen.

Stephen's torturers had used poison to drain him of his magic.

The rest they had held within a cage with walls you could not touch. Much like the walls of this very cell.

Julius Griggs. Myra broke through James' pain at last, aiding him with power of her own. He welcomed the gift—of both magic and memory—wondering if somehow she had been subject to his punishment alongside him. More likely, he had simply been too close to death for her to do little more than observe. But, Julius Griggs . . .

Details came flooding back, daylight through a cracked window, fractured yet tangible.

M.I.'s informant within the new Department, brought here as bait. That they had known how James would react, how to set him up for the fall and remove him from his own team. Incredible. And who were the "they"? How deep did the corruption go?

By all the heavens above, Brackenbury was right. Our time is over. Undone by technology. DMI is cracked. We're sending the enemy his own men when we put them into prison. Trembling, as much with the tremendous effort of movement as with the enormity of his discovery, James worked to clear his head.

Another name returned to James. Memories burned like uncontrolled fire through the dry tinder of his brain. Doctor Silas Addair. The silhouette in the window. James' captor. The man who clearly had the new MI2 ord-based intelligence unit of the British government under his thumb.

A man who had now, himself, entered James' cell. No, it was not Silas. James did not know this man.

"The Department will not miss you, James James. Look at you. Undone by a little bit of power." Dropping to a crouch, the man cocked his head so that his brilliant blue eyes stared into James' own. "You've felt the future. Felt its burn."

With a small sigh, the man in James' cell affected a Mien-casting. Mop of sandy hair shrinking and then disappearing altogether, cheekbones softening and nose growing sharper, the man before him became Doctor Silas Addair.

With a roar, James leapt forward. Only to be cut down, felled in a whirlwind of electrical fire. Shaking, he lay with his head against the smooth tiles, his eyes on the wand in Silas' hand. More device than wizard's wand, it too seemed a perversion of magecraft.

Addair leaned forward, whispering, "Thou art to appear weak when strong. Strong when weak. That is the path to assured victory."

James coughed and tasted blood. The quivering of his limbs continued, involuntary jerks and quakes that threatened to tear him apart. He spat, "You were always jealous. Jealous of our kind."

"Jealous is not the word I would use, my dear old friend." Addair remained crouched, still intent on meeting James eye to eye. "Curious. Clinically stirred with horror, perhaps, like most so-called ords. You know how many days I spent, sitting in the shadow cast by your brilliant light, using my gifts in the service of your gifts."

He lowered himself to sit, having deemed James not a threat. He fingered the wand in his hand, insurance. "And then your kind wanted something of me that I could not give. My son. My son, James. Do you know what that's like?"

James groaned, inched his fingers forward along the floor. He would go down fighting.

"You will soon learn. The plan is to take your child. It's only fair, you see." Silas let a slow smile overtake his face. "What, you're surprised that I knew? Not every doctor practices the discretion that your agents hold to, James James. And, as you know, I have found ways of being . . . persuasive."

He flicked his wand, dancing electricity over James once more.

Crying out as his body spasmed and his head cracked against the unyielding floor, despair gripped James. Despair laced with anger. *I'm to die here. In a hole. Amongst the criminals and evil men that we so diligently fought.*

"Not yet, James. Not yet." Silas knelt close, cradling James' head within his hands. "You must survive inoculation. You must survive. The baby's got to have a father, yes?"

James moved his lips, wishing for sound. He settled for blazing hatred from his eyes.

"Come, James. Strike me. I want you—no, I need

you—to do so. Prove me right. James!" Silas shifted James' head onto his lap, gripping his shoulder and shaking him. "No. You are not allowed to die, coward. Show me you have your magic. Show me that I've succeeded."

"Why?" James gritted his teeth, a grim smile. He must expose Addair. He must not let the man—the mage—slip quietly into the night with his followers, smoke upon the wind, free to work their poison unseen and unstoppable. The doctor's experiments at Broadmoor must not be allowed to continue. Duty first. Myra was listening.

"The Carrington Event. September the first, 1859. Laurel's birthday. And, if I'm right, the date of your own conception. Something happened, James. Something happened in those two days to they who would be mages. The child that Laurel carries—your child—will be immune to the Dampening. I need that child, James. Just as I need you to survive, else everything that we have worked for is wrong."

"Then you lose," James croaked and summoned his gift. He had learned the deep magics, something this pretender with his tricks and lies could never hope to know. He dipped into his very life force, hoping, praying, that Myra was still listening for him, that she might bear witness to his final moments and know it for what it was. Feeling the power swell within, knowing then what it felt like to die, James watched, unhearing, as Silas screamed frustration at his victim.

James closed his eyes. *Myra. I leave him to you. Please accept my gift into yours. Save Laurie. All my love to Stephen and the rest.*

Chapter Forty-One

A cruel wind tore at Myra's hair and the inky black of night pressed into her eyes. It was like staring into Death's own face. Aidan's hand closed over her mouth before she could scream.

The world shifted and whinnied beneath Myra, pulling Aidan's hand away. The horse, one of Grafford House's patient steeds, gave the man the lead he required and slowed to a gentle walk. The whisper of grass gave way to the crunch of gravel. Winking lights gleamed warmly out over the driveway, welcome and warning from those within the hulking red brick and gray stone building that rose from its modest surrounding curtain of trees.

They had arrived at Broadmoor.

And they were too late.

Myra now caught sight of the others, faces tense with worry. Robert came up alongside to see what was the matter.

Everything. Everything was the matter.

And then Myra locked eyes with Stephen, found

pain she could not deny. Dismounting, she ran straight into his arms as cold waves of understanding broke over her. She began to sob, "He's dead. James. I watched him . . . I experienced . . . He's dead."

Myra didn't shut herself out of Stephen's grief. She wasn't sure if she could have, so closely it lived to her own.

James dead. Impossible.

Myra felt more than saw her friends turn their eyes to Aidan, seeking relief, dreading confirmation.

"It's true." Aidan choked on the forced truth and turned from them. The echo of his agony was burned into Myra's soul. Guilt set her to freeing Stephen from her desperate and thoughtless embrace.

She had known a way to rescue James. She would have had to. That's what the others were thinking, surely. Bleak faces surrounded her, anxious and crossed with the tracks of tears, lash marks left by the cruel master of grief.

Those same bruises were raised upon Myra's conscience. James was dead, and she alone amongst them could have raised the alarm. The wizard's death would forever lie heavy upon her.

Or was it merely grief that she felt? Crushing, suffocating sadness—magnified threefold by the openings to her psyche left by her magic. Doors to pain that she could not bring herself to close.

"Had they meant to kill him?" Stephen's voice cut through the roar of rushing sorrow, a whisper in a gale. It took Myra a moment to register that the man had actually spoken aloud, that the words hadn't merely been present in her mind. It was an interesting question, and she clung to it with desperation.

"Does it matter?" Robert was the first to respond, his objection heavy as a rock and just as hard and jagged. Despondency made its way around the little group.

"Are we enemies or merely expendable laboratory rats? Would James have lain down for anything less than the former?" Myra continued the line of thought. Surprise brought a blushing heat into her cheeks, and she lowered her eyes, embarrassed to have been so presumptive as to speak aloud to these people. People she had let down.

You could have saved him. The added burden of James' gift, freely given her in his last moments, lay heavy against her soul. What had he meant for her do to with it? *Would James have lain down for anything less?*

Bright resolve swept through Myra, searing wildfire that dried her tears with its hot wind. She had seen James' death—felt, herself, what he had gone through and been as trapped as he by her powers. There had been no hope for him. Far more than the Dampening, his body had been broken beyond reclamation by the torture he had sustained.

James had given Myra knowledge of the deep magics through his link to her. Freed her with the same. And left her with the charge to stop Silas Addair.

Myra had not even realized she had turned away, wand in hand, ready to march straight into the hospital until a hand on her arm recalled her to herself.

"Myra, stop. Think of James."

"I am."

"Magic doesn't make you invincible."

"I know." Myra hardly recognized her own voice. Cool as water, she turned her gaze back on the team. "Confronting them is to fight for my life. That fact alone gives me power that they don't have. Also, I did not expect I should be alone."

Robert was the first to stand by her side, a slow smile darkening his face. "One of us you are, my dear."

Cloaked in nighttime, the team rushed the hospital. Fortified by the last of James' magic, Myra was able to lend some semblance of power to her companions in turn. Kady let them in the doors, unlocking them from the inside with a quick flicker of Kinetics. Stephen and Robert secured their path with the more ordinary weaponry of pistols and knives. Few stood hard in their way. All were cut down, lest Addair be amongst them with false face.

Here Benjamin was finally able to put his gift to proper use, and so it was he who Myra aided the most. Unable to fight—or perhaps unwilling—he patiently fell behind the team, checking on each victim and willing them back into life with his own strange power. A Necromancer knows the shape of a soul. None there was Addair's. No innocent that fell before the wrath of the M.I. agents was left to perish.

The initial skirmish spent, most of the hospital staff retreated with screams and panicked mayhem. Relying upon her broken memories and steeling herself for the emotional strain the asylum put on her Empathic gift, Myra guided the team further into Broadmoor. She wondered if they oughtn't see to Julius before all else. It would save her from going deeper into Empathic danger herself.

No. Addair. You must stop him before he adopts a new disguise and flees into the night with the rest. Closing her eyes, Myra sought the peace that would give her control of her Empathy. Addair she did not know, having only experienced the ghost of his emotional landscape. But the snap and buzz of electricity that emanated from the farmost wing of the building felt like anger.

"This way," she beckoned, dashing off. Aidan and Kady stayed close at her heels. The hospital, being designed for care if not comfort, was logical in its lay. They arrived at the hallway outside James' prison within moments.

Slowing, Myra waved her companions to silence, creeping forward at the sound of Addair's voice, her wand at the ready. Echoing through the empty hallway, the doctor's words reached the unintended audience, "First born. I'm not losing my first born. Not again. Do you hear me, James? You cannot leave this business. My men—me—my men are why the department did not burn you. I let you—I wanted you to live."

A pause, a shuddering sob. And then a chuckle that rent the silence and set the hairs on Myra's arms standing on end.

"Yes, James. Yes. I can now see, see through the accident of my own powers what it is you meant all along when you called the rest 'ordinary.'

"It's my fault, would you know it? My fault that many—that most—of my men are here in Broadmoor. Ah, but the process, the process to make a mage, is a tricky one. You saw that, I believe, when you visited the Order of the Holy Flame. Yes, I knew you were there. I knew all. All, James.

"Would you believe me when I tell you that I see the faces every day of the men whose lives are ruined, and it haunts me. Haunts me surely as you see the faces of the men that you've killed in your line of work. We're very alike, after all, old friend."

Another pause, this one long enough that Myra slowed her breath, focusing on James' gift within her own in anticipation of the confrontation sure to come. Silas' voice again echoed through the open door. This time it had edge, the fresh bite of anger, as though Addair truly believed James carried the other side of the conversation and had just hit home with a point. "Guilt. Heroics. Honor, and bravery, and loyalty, and service. Do you honestly think I do not know what these are? What they mean, James? I was there. I was at your side. If you ask me about sacrifice, I believe you have your answer. Now it's your turn; show me I was right, that I solved the riddle. Show me!

"You cannot die on me! James! We're brothers now. Don't you see? I'm one of you."

"I understand." Myra shot magefire from her wand, aimed at Silas Addair's heart.

And she did, for she could not lie in front of the Maester of Triewes.

Chapter Forty-Two

Myra's magic exploded across Silas Addair's chest, illuminating his stunned face and throwing him backwards
from James' body. Slumped sideways over the room's
low mattress, the doctor did not move. His legs were
bent at an odd angle, one arm splayed up and over his
head. None seemed broken, but then again, Addair was
beyond pain at that moment.

Emboldened, Myra stepped into the room, holding
aloft her wand for light as the power to the building
quivered and then died. Somewhere, Stephen and
Robert had gotten eager hands on whatever controlled
the electrical supply to the asylum.

It was in that moment that Doctor Silas Addair
stirred.

Lightning glanced through the room, the familiar
hiss and sizzle of an electric arc bounding towards Myra
across the narrow space. Addair had his weapon in
hand, and it was pointed towards her. And towards the
door. And towards—

"Aidan!" Turning, Myra slammed shut the door in

Aidan and Kady's astonished faces. The heat of the doctor's attack crackled over her back and up her arms, stopping to dance menacingly upon the doorway.

Lost to the agony, Myra felt James' memories melt into her own, flickering through her psyche in kaleidoscopic fashion. Myra forced her way through, holding on to herself, her memories.

The door. The door was locked. No, the door was unlocked. Myra remembered the key, recalled seeing it as she and her companions had approached the room in cautious silence. Something of its dark promise had stuck in her mind as she had listened to Addair's ramblings to James' corpse.

"Lock it! For the love of all that is good, lock the door!" she screamed.

Myra felt more than heard the click of the bolt. She saw the truth of it in Aidan's pale face. She did not need Mind Speech to warn him and Kady back. She simply set her gaze and listened for Addair to take his next shot at her. When he did not, she slowly turned 'round to meet him. Meet the man who she hated above all else. The false mage who'd killed James.

"And who are we? Someone who has power when they oughtn't. Grit on the lens. A fly in the ointment. Or, if you're me——" Addair grinned and allowed his features to flicker through a series of different aspects. Race, age, and sex—clay for an expert potter. "If you're me, you're a prize. One who elected to be locked in here with me."

Myra inclined her head, silently standing her ground.

"Don't they love you enough to want you back? To rescue you from the likes of terrible me? Isn't that how your team works?"

A shadow of a memory prodded her, and Myra's eyes flicked to Addair's hand. "How did you get that scar?"

Surprise colored Addair's features, and he made a show of covering the thready red scar burned into his wrist. With the motion, it put him at a disadvantage, and Myra leapt forward to disarm the Mien-caster. Like his countenance, the move was a feint. Myra found herself with two unforgiving hands wrapped 'round her neck. They squeezed, prompting the room to flash light then dark to her fear-stricken eyes.

"Who are you?"

"I'm—" Myra croaked and struggled futilely, giving him her weakness.

He released her, pushing Myra away and leveling his weapon at her once more.

"I'm Myra Wetherby. Agent of Magical Intelligence." Myra stepped to the side, quick as Kady and deft as James. Without looking, she grabbed for the electrified wand and thrust down hard with her elbows, catching Addair across the wrists. Something snapped. She whirled, breaking another of the doctor's bones with a sideways blow to a knee.

And, as she had hoped and prayed, Kady's gift was available for Myra's use.

Materializing into the hallway an instant later, Myra whirled breathless and triumphant upon the prison of Doctor Silas Addair. Turning, she thrust his electrified wand into the handle of the metal door, jamming it so that the power flowed without ceasing.

Aidan and Kady both caught Myra as she stepped backwards, stumbling in her shock and terror. "James."

She hadn't thought of James. Of the body and of the honor due M.I.'s fallen agent.

Sparks, blue and white and blinding, glared against the bars of the tiny window and peered through the cracks at the door jamb. Addair's wand crackled and spit, a most unforgiving jailor. And through it all, the wails of M.I.'s one-time natural philosopher screamed his last breaths.

"Leave him. There's none of James within that body now." Aidan gave Myra's shoulder a gentle pull, turning her away from the horror of Silas' death sentence.

"We see to the living first," Kady added in her own hard logic. "We've Julius to think of, and you're the fastest route to him."

Not wanting to look away, not wanting to seem as though she was running from what she had both started and finished with respect to Silas Addair, Myra simply closed her eyes and tried to find her Empathy so as to locate Griggs. What she saw within herself startled her.

James' magic, mingled with Myra's own, was darker than she would have ever thought it when viewed from the outside. There was light. But there was, too, an antilight. And it was not lesser. Not nearly. It distracted Myra from her own gift, and she opened her eyes, shaking her head. "I cannot feel anything."

"Come. Let's away from . . . this."

Myra nodded, unwilling to explain to her friends that Addair's screams and the crackle of his power would follow her everywhere from then on. Horror like that was not easily set aside or walked away from.

But then, the Empathy came easily after all. In fact, it seemed as though Julius' own voice could be heard echoing through the quiet, dark corridors of Broadmoor. Myra looked up to see patches of brightness lighting the walls from somewhere around the corner.

Three wands were raised in unison. Myra, Aidan, and Kady skidded to a halt as Stephen and Robert came round the corner, supporting Julius Griggs between them and carrying ord lanterns. With a cry, Myra felt her dead heart leap within her. She ran to the trio, noting with quick eyes both what was wrong and not wrong with M.I.'s informant. A mangled ankle, wrinkled and stained shirt, and a clotting of blood further darkening his mop of hair seemed to be the worst of it.

"They tell me you're not what you seem to be, Myra." Julius' voice worked, if only in breathy bursts. Myra revised her assessment of his health downward, adding in the probability of cracked ribs . . . or worse. He was quick to reassure her. His idiotic smile was no worse for wear, and this he fixed upon Myra with generosity. "I like that in a gal."

She rolled her eyes. "You do know that it was Benjamin with whom you've been corresponding, yes?"

Stephen's eyes were upon Myra. "Addair?"

"Dead," Kady volunteered with almost too much eagerness.

Julius looked to the Kinetic. "And his men?"

"Scattered."

"The ones here," Aidan was equally quick to remind them.

"Laurel." Julius' statement was not even a question. That he likely knew something of Addair's plans for the Ways-walker was evident in the pain which lanced across his face.

Accordingly, Aidan was pointed in his answer, "Next on our list. We figured her safe enough after she was abducted from Grafford House and proceeded here first."

Julius nodded. "The rest of you he wanted dead. But her . . . she was key to his plans. A new generation of wizards with immunity to Violectric Dampening. Mages like he was trying—unsuccessfully—to create through his experiments. Mages without madness in them; ones he could control." He paused, darting nervous eyes around the team. He was clearly fearful of voicing his next question, and this he gave to Myra herself: "James?"

"Silas got what he wanted there." Myra set her jaw to the tears that threatened and found they retreated at her command.

Stephen still had questions of his own, and these he voiced as they walked back towards the entryway. "Laurel. What was he planning to do with her?"

"Develop another elixir, I believe. One based on the same principles used for his first cure for Violectric Dampening. A new formula to replace that which he had developed from Florence's—"

"Gift. Using blood magic, yes." Robert stepped in and forced a redirection of Julius' explanation. "We don't need a history lesson."

Stephen nodded, pressing further, "Were they taking her here?"

"I believe this was not the sole place Addair felt comfortable. He had an estate just southwest of here—a pledge of loyalty from of one of his Children. Close. I believe it was there he was to take her, near but not so much as to raise suspicion. He did, as you gather, presume total victory and did not anticipate Myra being one of your kind." Again, Julius flashed his quirked smile to Myra, this time adding the benefit of a raised eyebrow.

"Yeah, well," Myra brushed past the uncomfortable compliment, "you're welcome."

Taking off at a run, Myra hurried to Benjamin who was still administering to those injured in M.I.'s first incursion into Broadmoor. He smiled at her as she approached, but his heart was out of it. He seemed heavy, more grounded than usual. He turned back to his work, murmuring, "In a minute, Thales. Then we can go. We must undo what we can."

"Myra, can you seek her with your Empathy?" Robert had caught her up. The rest were close at his heels.

Myra turned to him. She had already considered that difficulty. "Yes and no. It's as though Laurel is both everywhere and nowhere."

"She's in the Ways."

"I can feel her in here"—Myra lifted a hand to her chest. Laurel was in the Empath's heart; in her magic —"but she's not close; I can no longer use her gift."

"But if we were to get close? Close enough for your Empathy to sense her corporeal self?" Benjamin joined the conversation. White-faced, the hospital orderly to whom he had been tending stared at the group of people standing over him. No one bothered to explain, nor did they bother to hide what it was they were up to. Wands were produced, sparks igniting on tips.

"It's very likely our only chance for now," Myra agreed to the wisdom of the plan.

"You'll have greater spread if you fly upon the Ways that fuel the TurnKey." Sometime during the exchange, Aidan had found a cleaning cupboard. He held out a broom to Myra. "The rest of us can ride below on Robert's horses."

"I'd . . . I'd rather not chance it alone," Myra admitted weakness at long last. "I can only share my gift with one, spent as I am. Who of you wants to fly with me?"

Chapter Forty-Three

The trick of flying, Myra found, was in not thinking at all of what one was doing while they did it. And with Aidan beside her and the press of Laurel's distress somewhere in the dark below, Myra found distraction enough to find the first edge of the Ways that lived in the air far above the ground and ride it upon little more than a broom meant to sweep a hospital floor.

The Ways. Onion skins upon the aether. Layered worlds.

And within which layer does Laurel wait? Myra wondered, seeking Laurel's nearness with her gift.

Perhaps none at all. The darkness of James' magic echoed in Myra's chest, a weight that threatened to send her crashing from the sky. She meditated upon the loss, trapped in it.

In the end it had been as simple as the snuffing of a candle. He was simply gone, had been there one moment and was now empty and still. All that noise and fuss, followed by absolute silence. An unmaking.

And for what? It wasn't sacrifice. It wasn't even

murder. It was . . . a waste. A complete and utter waste. A life of service, cut down without ceremony or care. In his final moments, James had broken. Fractured. Is that how M.I.'s adversaries had felt? Had he ever done to others what had been done to him? Even having ridden within his soul, Myra was unsure of this last. James had been hard. Unbreakable.

A lie.

The warm buzz of Aidan's Triewes settled around Myra like a mantle of sweet comfort. Come, fly with me, it said. Do not lose yourself to this soul-wearying grief, this loss of self. It is a fear that destroys a mind. An unraveling, an antithesis of self. James lives on in the truth of the world.

Pulling herself at last from her dark ponderings, Myra fixed her eyes on the handle of her broom, finding that, at last, the sight of the ground far below her did not make her sick or dizzy.

Aidan has more skill traveling in the Ways of the TurnKey than he owns to. I wonder if he realizes that such modesty is perilously akin to a lie. She sent out her compliments along the thread of power that connected the two of them and marveled at how vast tracts of land were made small as she and Aidan flew over the countryside.

It made sense now, where maps came from. But it had Myra wondering how such were made without the aid of magic. Her education spoke up, answering for her. Magic had been used thusly. DMI's origins were the Department of Topography and Statistics, after all. To hear James tell it, all they had done in the early stages of the second Afghan war had been to redraw the maps, mile by painstaking mile. Myra's heart faltered.

James. How could he be dead?

Tears gathered on Myra's cheeks, slipping over and down her chin. Rain for the fields below.

They slowed, Aidan came close alongside, reaching out and signaling to Myra with a squeeze of his hand that they had reached the furthest point where Laurel's captors might have come. The blur of magic lessened, grew transparent, more akin to frosted glass in the wintertime than the rushing of a waterfall. Myra gasped, fearful that they might tumble to the ground, luckless angels.

Vengeful angels. Myra realized that her Voice was available to her, should she need it. Which meant they had located Laurel after all. Looking downward into the darkness, she cursed the fact that they had had to attempt such a rescue on a moonless night. Granted, with the enemy AethCaster's cloud cover still holding sway, such assistance as moonlight would have been rendered useless.

Squinting, Myra could see next to nothing in the black on black of the life-sized map below. Patience won out as her sharp eyes parted the veil of magic surrounding her and Aidan. Here and there a late-night illumination still held comfort for the traveler, tiny points of yellow light, dulled by distance. It reminded Myra of how far up they were, and she fought the urge to scream. She swallowed the impulse with difficulty, grateful when Aidan again squeezed her hand, reassuring and solid. He would not let go. He would not let her fall.

Using the guide lights of sparse civilization, she could almost make out the thin ribbon of road winding through the forests and fields.

"We have to get closer." Or at least that's what Myra

presumed Aidan said. To her eyes it seemed he merely mouthed the instruction, his words cruelly snatched away by the whirling wind and magic around them.

Together, they shimmied low as they dared. Too far and they would fall below the magic which held them aloft. Myra crinkled her brow in concentration, seeing nothing but a world of darkness made darker by their terrible urgency and the horrors they had left behind but minutes prior.

Laurel was down there. And close by. Myra was certain of it. She tried her Voice again, able to reach the others now that she and Aidan were nearer the ground. ***Everyone, I can use Laurie's gift from here.***

Beneath her, the riders converged, called by Myra, an arrow pointing towards victory. She and Aidan followed the diminutive clouds of dust with eager eyes.

There. On the road far ahead rumbled a carriage.

Aidan pulled close to Myra, this time making sure he was heard. "Go."

Together, they shot through the heavens, speed blurring the magic. Myra's eyes watered with their efforts, and her skin tingled. It was as though invisible ghosts tugged at anything left exposed and twisted any loose article of clothing.

They neared the carriage. Myra breathed deep, quelling a memory from what seemed like ages ago. A hearse, driven into an alleyway under cover of night. A driver, foppish and endearing in his dishevelment. A corpse, victim of James' magic.

But Laurel was alive. She had to be.

A spark of light blossomed from the end of Myra's wand. A beacon to call the team. ***Laurie, we're coming.***

Something heavy slammed into Myra and sent her spinning out into the black sky. "Aid—!"

Luck more than presence of mind allowed Myra to keep her wand as she tumbled end over end towards the growing ground. Grasping hands clutched fruitlessly for a broom no longer there, and bereft of its stable presence and Aidan's guidance, Myra could not right herself before dark trees rose up to meet her.

With a shriek, Myra burned frantic magic in one last gasp of effort to save herself from a broken neck. A shield of protection, fractured and yielding, blossomed around her. The oak tree into which she had fallen took much of the damage otherwise meant for her. Leaves and branches passed in a slowing blur. Ducking, Myra tucked her head into her chest and braced for contact with the hard dirt.

Every part of her body screamed at once. Pain. Never-ending pain engulfed Myra, and her lungs and heart spasmed in heroic effort to continue pumping. But, jumbled as she was, nothing seemed to be working right.

Panic rose within Myra, confusing lungs that already were refusing to draw air. Closing her eyes, Myra prayed for a quick death and found steadiness in the gentle whirl of sparks against her closed eyelids.

The pain receded, became separate aches and throbs vying for attention.

The impact with the earth had robbed her of breath. It was just as it had been for Kady when Myra had taken the Kinetic by surprise during combat training. She concentrated on breathing shallowly. Air in; air out. Better.

She moved to sit up and found that she could. Nothing was broken. Maybe.

Myra looked about her, seeing little more than trees and an old, narrow path. The half-buried stones of the road gleamed eerily in the light of her still-illuminated wand, ancient witness to her tumble from grace.

She was alone.

"Myra Moore. Or was it Wetherby? I never could get your story straight."

Scrambling to her feet, Myra hissed as she discovered that certain parts of her were quite a bit more injured than first thought. Her left ankle refused to support her fully, and several ribs screamed fractured protestation as she prepared to meet he who had spoken such haunting words. "Who are you?"

Where are you? The latter question was more pressing, but Myra dared not voice that ignorance. Not into the face of such menace as she felt from the unknown assailant. She pointed her wand in what she believed was the correct direction, its bright spell wavering in her shaking hands.

A hooded and cloaked figure stepped out onto the road. The man had a wand of his own. With an ominous crackle, the mage's weapon sparked to life and shot its broken lightning straight at Myra.

With a spryness that surprised even her, Myra spun to the side, lifting her own wand in battle. Lightning answered lightning. The hooded figure was forced to give ground.

Both put up their wands, the enemy mage out of mocking admiration and Myra from exhaustion that she prayed he did not see. The hood was moved back, revealing dark hair, swarthy skin, and a nose that looked like it had been broken more than once in its lifetime. White teeth—distinctly even and bright—flashed as he broke into a mad chuckle at Myra's expense. His eyes, however, held no mirth. Myra could see as much, even at the distance of the twenty-odd paces at which they stood apart.

How had he gone undiscovered so long within DMI's employ? One look at the man now, one word from him, gave Myra the shivers. She lifted her wand again, testing Black's fortitude.

The smiling mouth turned downward, growing sour. "You never answered my question, girl."

"And why would I answer to the likes of you?" Myra challenged. "Seems you know more than enough as it is. If your nasty, underhanded betrayal of your associates did not give you this last bit of information, I'd rather the victory of leaving you unsatisfied."

Taking great pains not to limp, Myra met Agent Black on the road. Equals. Or something like it. For all that she refused to give him her name, it bothered her that she did not know more than his surname.

The breath that had earlier eluded her tugged at her chest, new panic that she must quell, else her enemy believe Myra as vulnerable as she felt. She waited to see if DMI's mole had more to say to her. He put up his wand but did not throw more words between them.

Myra took her shot.

A whirlwind of magic lit the night. The blast from Myra's power threw her assailant to the ground. She advanced, wand at the ready. She would end it here. Black groaned, and shifted. Too slow to rise, taken utterly by surprise at Myra's boldness, Addair's man had lost his wand and now reached vainly for it.

Myra slowed, putting up her wand.

Get him! He's right there! Internally, Myra screamed at

her reluctant arms and legs. A deeper part still, argued in contrast. She could not strike an unarmed man. She would not commit cold-blooded murder.

He attacked you. It's not the same. That same conscience hammered at her. The pressure of the impulse banged at the back of her eyes. *This man is responsible for James' death, Julius' imprisonment, Laurel's capture, and Stephen's torture. He betrayed everything you and your friends have—*

Black rolled over onto his back, collapsing with a moan. He met her gaze, eyes glinting. "Do it."

Myra raised her wand. She hesitated.

"Do it," Mr. Black cackled, coughing blood. "Give in and become a murderer. Then you'll be like us. Like Maclean and Hutchinson and Roberts and anyone else who has taken the mantle of power without understanding the cost. Mad with magic. Nobody is on the side of right, you know. Not you. Not your friends. Not even the government which they served. Do it."

Myra waited. The war within her conscience waged, paralyzing her. Her wand wavered, its bright point quivering as her eyes dimmed with tears, with pain. He was right. Oh, he was right about her, about her desires and needs and moral ambiguity.

Myra found her heart calling the darkness. She felt within her the strange and wild desire to pull the stars from the heavens and grind them to dust. With such terrible futility came a desire to kill, to maim, to unmake the world, or in the absence of such an option, to wreak as much damage as she could with her small, mortal hands. It was the bleeding out of love from the heart. An emptying and a filling up of fear, of the suspicion that there was a terrible rightness to the wrong.

Past and present converged. Questions and fears

bubbled up from the mire of Myra's rotten core. Sluggish, the brown miasma stirred, causing her to gag upon the memories of lives she had ruined, choices made for reasons that served her pride rather than prudence. Mother. Father. Sister. Allies and enemies alike. The wreckage stretched in a line, long and straight as the Roman road upon which she stood.

"Stop it." Tears squeezed past Myra's defenses, eroding the foundation. Her hand brought her wand higher. She could see its bright point raising up before her eyes, arcing around as she brought the tip of the weapon to her temple.

"Yes. The world is better off this way. Better off without you mages mucking it up. Causing trouble and going against the nature of how things ought to be." Black's words echoed the thoughts in Myra's head.

He's right. Oh, he's right.

"Better off without me. Yes." Myra shut her eyes to the searing pain of her Empathy and summoned her power one last time.

Aidan.

He stood within a space ill-defined but somehow inexplicably full of light.

It's like the Ways. Myra's brain ponderously called the knowledge to her.

Aidan was sad. Infinitely sorrowful. Why?

She moved to meet him, herself saddened. Empath. She smiled at the realization of her powers. Perhaps she could comfort him.

Aidan, she called.

He turned to her, honest love in his eyes. Overwhelming caring and regard.

Myra stumbled, overcome. The hand that held her wand wavered. The horrid realization that, in the real world, she was about to take her own life with magic, hit her like the icy waters of the North Atlantic Apex.

The Maester of Triewes opened his mouth to speak. "The enemy lies, Myra."

The loud rush of magic called Myra back from the Ways, and she screamed, throwing her wand to the ground. But it wasn't her casting that had called her away from the doorway to the OtherLands.

Mr. Black lay broken upon the ground, blasted unrecognizable by his own magic.

Myra's legs buckled, and she sobbed knowing that, through Aidan, she had seen the truth, seen through the enemy's black lies. And it had been her own Empathic power that had turned Black's magic against him so that, in the end, he killed himself. It was done.

Oh, what terrible, terrible power, what a horrid gift to have had. She glanced again to the ruined husk of the black-robed man and retched. *That could have been—should have been me. Were it not for . . .*

Aidan! He was close by. Had to be, else his truth telling would not have affected Myra so. She rose, grimacing at the pain of her ankle. Sharp and real, the agony of the injury called her back to the urgency of the situation. If she was this hurt from her fall, perhaps Aidan, too, was—

"No." Myra shut to her mind to the thought. They

had already lost one of their own today. The world was not so cruel as to take a second of the M.I. mages from her. She abandoned the broken road, hobbling to the tree line so that she might fashion a crutch for herself. How she would be useful to anyone when they found Laurie was beyond her.

One step in front of the other. Myra reached for her resiliency, found it mostly intact.

"Myra!" A familiar voice rang out. Kady's.

Heart leaping, Myra forgot her search for a walking aid and turned to the sweet sound of rescue. "Here."

Running along the road, Kady held aloft her lighted wand. Burning power best left conserved, she looked wildly about until Myra had left the deeper shadows of the surrounding woods once more.

"Oh, thank the gods." Kady was at Myra's side in an instant, offering support. "Aidan?"

"Nearby. I think." Myra leaned gratefully into the Kinetic. "I used his powers."

"The rest are coming. When you were blown out of the sky . . ." Kady shook her head. "Robert and Stephen are catching me up. The carriage—it was empty."

"Bait. To separate you from myself and Aidan." Myra nodded, gesturing to the corpse that had recently been Mr. Black. She quickly caught Kady up—stumbling as she approached the point of her own near-defeat at Black's hands.

"Hush, dear." Kady hugged Myra close, not needing to be told more. Together they trudged onwards, Myra leaning on Kady and leading them as best she could through her connection to Aidan's magic.

They had not gone far when Myra caught a second

power. She whispered excitedly, "It's Laurie. Aidan and Laurel. They're together somewhere nearby."

The barest glimmer winked at them through the trees ahead. A light, small and white. Kady drew her wand, and Myra fumbled with her own, unable to let go of the Kinetic lest her ankle truly give.

A hulking rectangle of black sat amongst the dark tree trunks. A coach.

Only one man stood guard. He was cut down before he could defend his prize.

Gesturing that Kady go on without her, Myra rested against a tree, sighing in relief as, a moment later, the Kinetic signaled success. They'd found M.I.'s Ways-walker.

"She's here," Kady called out, turning to Myra. She froze, leveling her wand at the surrounding forest. Her next words rang broken, "Oh, Aidan!"

Chapter Forty-Four

Myra tried to follow Kady as the Kinetic broke into a run. But, stepping away from the tree that held her upright, Myra's ankle crumpled at last. Sticks and rocks bit into her hands as she fell. Her various hurts twinged again, causing stars to dance in her vision.

Kady's mournful wail echoed eerily through the wood, and for a moment, Myra was grateful she was unable to be present at whatever her friend had discovered. Her heart, practiced in grief from the events of the day, prepared itself for its next loss.

She glanced up to see Kady return, Aidan on her arm. He limped, and blood darkened his face so that he was near indistinguishable from the surrounding. But he was alive. She could feel it through her gift. Myra choked on her joy and scrambled forward, dragging her useless foot and not caring one bit.

"Moira." The sound of Aidan marring her name with scratched throat was heaven itself. Myra responded with a noise that had no direct translation. The heart of it was love, gratefulness, and exultation.

Kady brought them together then left to go see to Laurel once more. None of their petty jealousies and romances and attachments mattered. Equally, they mattered all the more, if only for the honesty of it all.

Aidan and Myra embraced, each burying themselves in the familiar warmth of the other, drowning out the noise of their pain with simplistic, unthinking joy. A moment later, more familiar voices colored their newfound peace. Ben, Stephen, Robert, and Julius had caught them up.

Myra allowed herself to be extricated from Aidan. She looked to Kady and could tell, even without using her Empathy, that something wasn't right. Something in the way the Kinetic stood, a tightness and a fear. A help-lessness as she stood looking into the back of the aban-doned carriage.

But Laurie is alive. I felt her; could use her gift. Myra repeated the mantra in her head like a prayer. James was dead. Addair was dead. Mr. Black was dead. Laurel could not be. Could not be.

Laurel lay within the dark coach. She did not move nor did she rouse at their attempts to wake her.

Silence fell over the group.

"My gift can still feel her," Myra whispered reassur-ance. "She's in there. I can tell."

"We know, dear," Kady said. "And yet—"

"She's in the Ways, Laurie is. There'll be— There'll be no telling her what happened to James." Stephen broke down, not to be consoled by anyone, including Myra. His sobs echoed amongst the trees. Myra imag-ined that the leaves themselves might be shaken to the ground by the force of his grief. Each turned away, trying to find solace in one another's presence, escape

from Stephen's agony. All save for Robert, solid dependable Robert, who embraced his friend and let their tears
mingle. Only Myra's own pain and utter exhaustion
kept her from falling fully into either Robert or
Stephen's emotional turmoil, so strong was the pull of
the ord's heartache.

At some point, someone—Myra wasn't certain who
—decided that the team appropriate their enemy's
decoy coach in order to better facilitate their return to
the relative safety of London. Stephen, inconsolable and
immovable, waited amongst the injured, leaving Robert
and Kady the task of riding for the other carriage.

To Myra it felt as though the earth's rotation had
taken a dizzy turn. Nothing made sense. James. Magic.
Professor Silas Addair. Broadmoor seemed but a bad
dream. Her injuries, a horrible illusion. She watched,
listless, as Robert and Kady returned, and Laurel was
gently moved into the larger carriage. The Ways-walker
looked like a corpse awaiting burial. It was all too
horrible.

Safe within the other conveyance, Myra leaned back
against the seat, surprised at the comfort it afforded. She
hadn't expected to be comfortable. Ever again.

She woke from a dreamless sleep to find London
growing around them. Julius sat at her side, his face taut
with worry. Robert dozed on the opposite bench.

Noticing Myra's eyes open, Julius jumped and
quickly pasted a reassuring smile onto his squashed face.
The idiot. Myra loved him for it, absently wondering
how many people she could love in one day. But that
was all right, the world needed more love just then.

"She'll be all right. Almost there, Myra."

Myra blinked wordlessly. He did not press her for

more, growing into the space she left him. It felt good to hear him simply talk. "I'll likely be able to recreate Addai— *The* elixir," he swiftly corrected himself.

Julius patted his breast pocket, taking pains not to move too quickly. It reminded Myra: he had his own hurts with which to deal. "Part of his plans for me made me privy to quite a lot of information. Apparently Silas did not anticipate losing this fight."

And just like that, Myra wanted to know more. All of it, in fact. But Julius Griggs said no more about his time spent in Broadmoor under the care of Doctor Silas Addair. And that, in itself, was telling. She turned to the window to spare Julius her mistimed empathy and counted the street corners until they returned home.

It was Stephen who brought Myra out of the carriage and in through the doors of Grafford House. Struggling to avoid jostling her various injuries—all rather terrible, now that she could see herself more clearly—he managed to give her a small, tight squeeze akin to a hug as he deposited her in one of the library chairs. A thank you? An apology? Myra couldn't understand him at all.

Through eyes growing dim with exhaustion and pain, Myra watched as Aidan was brought in under similar care—Benjamin ferrying his one-time rival with a gentleness that brought new tears to her eyes. Laurel she did not see again. She assumed she was being cared for under more urgent ministrations.

The last thing Myra witnessed before sleep took her was a hushed argument amongst Robert, Benjamin, and Stephen. In the end, it was decided that Julius and Robert would brief DMI's director on the day's events. Griggs' report of his ordeal would serve as warning enough for Brackenbury to see to the security of his own house in the wake of Black's treachery. Aidan's services would, of course, be offered in sorting friendly from traitor.

That's nice of them. Myra yawned her approval, noting distantly the splitting headache that the gesture gave her. Then all was black.

Myra woke to the jangling of the Grafford House front bell. With a start, she realized that, while no longer in the armchair that Stephen had left her, she was still in the library, though the hour was far later. Morning sunlight streamed in through the library windows. Myra's wounds had been bound and set. Benjamin was by her side though his head was lowered in sleep.

As were both Aidan and Kady, the former awake and looking at Ben and his protective stance over Myra with stern, unreadable eyes. Myra looked away, uncomfortable and unable to deal with Aidan's mercurial temperament just then. In looking about the room, she saw that Stephen was nowhere to be seen. To her knowledge, Julius and Robert had not checked back in. But then she could well have slept through any comings and goings if she slept through the tending of her injuries.

The bell at the door continued to clang, setting already-frayed nerves to tingling and waking both Kady and Benjamin. A small commotion in the front hall signaled that someone had gone at last to answer the summons.

Looking harried, Julius and Robert entered the library, a very nervous looking Director Brackenbury on their heels. The DMI director's eyes alighted on Benjamin, and he quailed.

"I didn't know," Henry Brackenbury worked quickly, and simply, to establish his innocence in the whole affair. Though, that he did not know of the undermining of his own department was black enough mark. From his corner, Aidan watched the director's apologies with unsympathetic eyes. But he did not move to call the man a liar. Which was enough to confirm that Brackenbury was truly terribly sorry for everything that had happened.

As well as grateful beyond measure for the rash and loyal actions for they who his department had tossed aside.

Impassive, Robert and Benjamin absorbed the director's apologies and expressions of sympathy over James' death. Her own heart numb to the words, Myra wondered if she would ever feel again. Perhaps she had found a cure for her Empathy.

At length, Benjamin rose to speak with Julius in hushed tones while Robert took Brackenbury over to the fireplace for their own tête-à-tête. Myra tried, unsuccessfully, to eavesdrop on both conversations and ended up, instead, with a mess of both which she could not understand. Coming to some sort of conclusion at last, Julius nodded at Benjamin's hushed request and moved towards the door.

Catching Myra's eye, Benjamin inclined his head to beg leave. The polite formality of the gesture, contrasted with the wrecked appearance of the library after the battle that had been waged there but yesterday somehow sparked a strange humor in Myra, and she found herself choking back a manic giggle.

Aidan gave Myra a quizzical look as he strode past on his way to taking up his usual post, lounging by the mantle to eavesdrop on Brackenbury's rather useless apologies. Her head awhirl, still full of the horrors of the past day, Myra only half-heartedly used her Empathy to snatch at the words between the three men who stood by the hearth. Her heart was equally full. Or, rather, empty. She would sort it all later.

Weak demands were raised. Robert protesting, "Addair's men . . . not all are accounted for . . ."

Brackenbury bricked up, growing bureaucratic in an instant. "Apology and thankfulness on our behalf does not necessarily mean direct reinstatement or even involvement. If what you have told me is true—and we'll have to investigate this ourselves, you know—then the threat from Professor Silas Addair is over. The conflict involving wizards is through. Agent Griggs will, of course, come back immediately as is prudent . . . we have to be careful with such things, after all. Appearances, you know. Too many moves at once would make too much noise.

"That said, your service to the country is not something we are inclined to overlook," he continued. "Past acts, James' heroic sacrifice, are to be fully considered."

Myra was grateful that Stephen was not present for Brackenbury's restated sympathies. She watched as the starch went out of MI2's director, rendering him as ordinary, as human, as any other. She knew the tear in her eye was present in every other person in the room and just as authentic. But Stephen's grief over the loss of James—none of them could handle his grief just yet.

Brackenbury recovered himself. Aidan and Robert

accepted the obligatory gentlemanly handshake. The former moved to escort him out.

Julius returned a moment later, Stephen and Benjamin in tow.

"Laurel?" Myra's heart had somehow relocated to her throat. She managed to squeeze the name past and rather wished she hadn't. She didn't want to know. Not yet.

Stephen shook his head. "Gone."

Myra nodded, mouth suddenly dry, heart moving southward, past where it belonged and dropping down towards the bottom of her stomach. She rasped, "How?"

"The appropriate question would be to ask 'where?' " They all turned at the sound of Griggs' voice. He faced their assembled shock with raised eyebrows. "What, you think I don't pay attention at all to what goes on here?"

"And the baby?" Robert's rumbling rejoinder came rolling through the group, a wrecking ball that scattered them again.

"That'd be more your area than mine, unfortunately. I don't know enough about the OtherLands to know if it is possible for Laurel to have brought the wee one safely over with her." Julius looked to Benjamin. "It would, at this stage, likely be something that your gift could determine."

"So the baby is dead." Benjamin sat heavily, horrified that Julius would even ask such of him.

Griggs shook his head. "Indeterminate. Condition is the same as the mother, for all that I can tell. But . . . heartbeat or not, I cannot tell where the soul resides."

"He's suggesting you look for James, Ben, for then

we might find Laurel and call her back," Aidan joined in.

"I know what he's asking," Ben snapped. But the heart was out of it.

Robert roused himself at last, and it was glorious. Zeus himself stood in their midst, all lightning, smoke, and fire. He fairly bristled with power as he shouted—quite possibly the first time Myra had heard such. She hadn't known he had it in him. "Laurel went to look for James. And that is that. Woman wants to go wandering off like that, it's not on us to go after her. Not our responsibility. Not in my house. Irresponsible. Idiotic. Like that James, running off half-cocked with no real plan . . . And with the future of wizardry in her care. Idiotic." Lapsing into repetition, he stopped and blinked, staggering slightly under the shock of having realized his outburst. "I, er . . . Well, like I said. That's that. And we're not about to waste anyone else going off on some fool's errand. She wants to be dead like him, let her."

He turned on his heel and stormed out, as though thoroughly disgusted with the lot of them. The ringing of the front bell—*what now?*—gave his escape purpose. Myra assumed he needed such at this time. They all did.

"She's stable. For the moment," Julius ventured into the heavy silence. "I . . . I can keep her such for a while, so long as her condition does not deteriorate. And the baby, too." He added the last with a darting look to Aidan and Stephen, daring them to come up against his plan to stall, to give them all time to think and recover.

Myra believed it the best course at present. They all needed time. And Julius was giving it to them. Freely, and without question. She could kiss that man. Though she, obviously, would never.

"Well, then. Welcome to the team, such as it is." Stephen offered his hand, an olive branch. Myra wondered if such a pact held. Was he the leader in James' absence—correction, now that James was gone?

Robert returned, eyebrows frowning his fury though his face was blank with resignation. All eyes turned to him, ready for the apology that was sure to come from M.I.'s gentle giant. He held a letter in his hand, seeming to question its contents.

"From Victoria?" Benjamin peeked at the remains of the royal seal clinging to the bottom edge of the crisp paper.

Robert nodded wordlessly and fell heavily into Stephen's newly vacated chair. He tossed the letter onto the tea table so that they might read it for themselves.

"Well. It's official at long last. We're fired."

"And by fired you mean . . . ?"

"We can't stay here, no," Robert rumbled and closed his eyes. "We're enemies of the state now. Perils of the job."

And so concludes Volume I, *M.I.*

Acknowledgments:

Publish a book, I said. It'd be fun, I said.

Many thanks to J. D. Spero and Theresa Elsey Skov, who stepped in to read an unpolished manuscript and help me see things clearer. I tip my hat to artist Egle Zioma, taking the vaguest of vague visual ideas from me and turning them into something dynamic and exciting. <Strives to say something clever in Latin. Fails> Additionally, I offer my appreciation and thanks to Alexander (Sasha) Volokh, stepping in here and there to verify—or, more often, correct—the Latin in my manuscript. And from the bottom of my comma-misplacing heart, I sincerely thank Tanya Gold and MeriLyn Oblad, editors extraordinaire who have taken in stride my eccentricities of voice and style and have worked to help me give you, dear reader, the book you have in hand today.

Let me also express so, so much thanks for the never ending support which I find at home. ♥

. . . Publish a book, I said. It'd be fun, I said.
To the folks who *made* it fun: I thank you.

About the Author

M. K. Wiseman has degrees in Interarts & Technology and Library Science – both from the University of Wisconsin-Madison. (Books and animation have long been passions for M.K.) Her office, therefore, is a clutter of storyboards and reference materials. When she's not mucking about with stories, she's off playing brač or lying in a hammock in the backyard of her Cedarburg home that she shares with her endlessly patient husband.

Also by M. K. Wiseman

The Bookminder (Book 1, *Bookminder* series)

The Kithseeker (Book 2, *Bookminder* series)

Forthcoming:

The Fatewreaker (Book 3, *Bookminder* series)

Sherlock Holmes and the Ripper of Whitechapel

CPSIA information can be obtained
at www.ICGtesting.com
Printed in the USA
FSHW020100100520
69794FS